*My name is Lucy Winter*
*I'm 23 years old*
*I have many skills...*

No! That sounds too stupid, I've just found my perfect job on the internet and I'm having a hard time trying to apply for it, *why can't I string a normal sentence together?* Let's try again. More formal this time.

*Dear Sir,*

No. What if it's a woman?
*Oh my god.*

*Dear Sir/Madam,*

*Please find attached to this email, a copy of my C.V, for your kind consideration. I feel I would be an excellent candidate for your vacancy, as it closely matches my skills and experience. I look forward to hearing from you.*

*Yours sincerely,*

*Lucy Winter*

As I get off my breakfast barstool with a smug look in my face, I catch a glimpse of the clock that says fifteen after five. *SHIT!* I have to meet Jack in fifteen minutes. I run into my bedroom, change into a deep blue dress that comes just above my knee and clings to all my curves in all the right ways, and then to the bathroom to pull my hair band out of my hair to make sure I look presentable. My long brown hair falls just below my shoulders and it has a nice curly thing going on from where I've had it up. I wipe away my smudged mascara from under my eyes with a make-up wipe and re-apply; I use a small amount of eye liner on the top of my eyes so it makes my blue eyes piercing. As I'm running to grab my bag, I hop trying to put my shoe boots on, grab my bag, my keys, my phone, and slam the door behind me. As I run down the steps from my apartment I look out the window and see the bus is reaching the bus stop, I pick up my pace, but my attention is grabbed by my phone ringing in my bag. Running down the stairs, panicked and rifling around my bag, I grab it.

'Hello?'

'Hi, its Jack.' I instantly halt on the stairs, and try to steady my breathing,

'Hi Jack, you okay?' I whisper.

'Yeah I'm okay. I'm running ten minutes late Luc, is that okay?' I let out a sigh of relief and answer.

'Yeah Jack that's fine I'll see you soon'. Then the call is over and I slowly step down the stairs, not minding that the bus has just gone past my stop. I finally get to the bottom of the 6 flights of stairs, catch my breath and then sigh in annoyance, wondering why I didn't just use the elevator. I step out of the lobby and breath in the cold sharp winter air of New York; I walk over to the bus stop and check the time of the next bus.

'TWENTY MINUTES?!' I shout without realizing how loudly I just exclaimed. It's only five blocks away, I think I can walk there and probably get there at the same as Jack. As I start strolling along the sidewalk swinging my purse back and forth, I stumble a bit in my heels and decide to shout for a taxi. I wave my hand out and yell for one, but they all just glide past me like I'm not even there. I shout 'TAXI' again, and again they ignore me. I get a little angry and shout.

'AM I INVISBLE TO YOU PEOPLE?!' Just then a deep, soothing voice bellows 'TAXI' behind me and a young guy steps out and hauls a cab. As I stare at him in disbelief he holds the door open.

'Hi, I'm Drake', and then, after I stand there, too shocked to reply or move, he says:

'After you Miss.' and points to the cab door. I clamber in and sit far more upright that I normally would because I feel a bit uncomfortable and awkward. Then he breaks the silence and says with such a smooth voice:

'Ae you okay Miss?' I mumble in reply,

'Hi yes I'm fine, I'm Lucy' and when I hold my hand out to shake his, he shakes mine back. I then lean forward and say to the driver.

'I'm going to west sixty-ninth street.'

'Oh, me too' Drake chirps up, making me jump. I look at him, give an awkward smile and look out of the window. As we pull up outside the bar I hear my cell ringing. I quickly try and find it, regretting that I made Aqua's Barbie Girl my ring tone. I feel myself turning crimson as I see him, from the

3

corner of my eye, smiling at me.

'Hello…. Mom? Are you okay?' She shouts down her cell because she doesn't think people can hear her clearly.

'Mom please don't shout I can hear you.' I answer, while pulling the phone away from my now damaged eardrum.

'Mom, yes you and dad can stay with me, can I phone you tomorrow? I'm busy right now… Love you too, Mom'.

I look round at Drake who is now red in the face, desperately trying not to laugh at me, while I blush.

'Sorry.' I say tersely, storing the urge to hit him for giggling at me away.

'No worries.' He replies. I then start to study his face. He has jet black hair that looks like bed hair style, big green eyes, perfect looking lips with the most gorgeous smile I've seen in a long time…

'West sixty-ninth street.' grumbles the cab driver, interrupting my thoughts.

'Oh, thanks how much?' I ask.

'Sixteen dollars.' The cab driver mumbles, but then Drake then sits forward and hands the driver a twenty, flashing a smile at me.

'I've got this'.

I let out a giggle like a schoolgirl and instantly regret it as he looks at me confused, with his right eyebrow arching upwards. I try to climb out of the cab gracefully, and then Drake comes to my side and to shake my hand.

'Until next time Lucy.' He flashes me a smile and then vanishes around a corner. As I stare down the road like a lost puppy I hear someone shout my name.

'LUCY?'

I turn around to see Jack running towards me, he picks me up by my waist and spins me round with a smile on his face,

'Ready babe?'

'Yep,' I reply trying to get my balance back. Jack grabs my hand and pulls me into the bar behind him, we stop at a table and he turns to me with both his for fingers and thumbs like guns.

'What are you drinking?'

'Vodka and coke, please.'

'Oh, cut loose, have a cocktail or a shot!'

'Nah, I'm fine just that to start with.' Jack spins on his heels towards the bar, and I stare at him wondering why I'm not attracted to him because it baffles me. He's definitely handsome, longish black hair, which is styled, blue eyes, and very white teeth; he could easily be mistaken for a model, he's that perfect looking. At six-foot tall, he's about a head and a bit taller than me, with a muscular body, even though he actually works as an I.T consultant in a very big company, and he loves it. We've been friends since high school, he was the grade above me and his brother Dean. We lived just down the road from each other and we were in separable. He has liked me since then and he often tells me, but I find him more of a brother than a lover. We still have a very good relationship but having different lives, it's difficult to hang out like we used to. Just as I start to reminisce, Jack comes bundling back over with our drinks and disturbs my thinking.

'So, what's new Luc?' Jack asks. I shrug my shoulders,

'Nothing much, you?' Jacks lifts one eyebrow and copies me like a parrot.

'Nothing much?' I look up while slurping from my drink and nod my head. Jack keeps up his questioning.

'Not found a job yet?'

'No not yet, I found my dream job online today and I emailed my resume just before I came to meet you.'

'Oh, that's great!' Jack shouts as he gets up to hug me.

'I only applied I didn't get it yet', I answer in defense.

'Yeah I know', Jack mumbles, 'but it's good you have found something to apply to.'

'Oh, and my parents are coming up on Friday!' I say trying to change the subject.

'We should all go out for a meal, when they're here, I'd love to see them. 'Jack says excitedly. They grew up in my house with my younger sister Gemma and I, until Jack went to college. After high school, Dean found life very difficult to deal with and often bunked college and got in a lot of fights. My dad took him under his wing and taught him carpentry and now Dean and my dad have a very successful Carpenter's company. Dad has since retired but helps out over the phone if needed. Which has reminded me, so I turn to look at Jack.

'Is Dean still coming?' Jack smiles.

'Yes, he is, he's running late, as usual…' We both giggle. Dean likes to look at himself in the mirror, and does at every given chance he gets. We always catch him looking at himself or correcting his hair. Jack jumps up out of his chair when we hear someone shout 'GUYS!' We both sharply look in the direction of the noise, to see Dean walking over to us. I jump up from my chair and run to him, to I hug him tightly because I haven't seen him in about six months. Dean has been away traveling around Europe, four months of it in London.

'Dean did you have a good time away?'

'Yeah I loved it, especially London, I really want to go back.' Dean answers with a massive grin on his face.

'Where did you go in London?' I ask, really intrigued about his holiday.

'Trafalgar square, London Eye, the Queen's Palace, River Thames, Nelson's Colum, Piccadilly circus, Covent Garden,

M & M world, Madam Tussauds, I met a girl and I visited this little village you would have loved it Luc.' Dean lists over-excitedly, while catching his breath back.

'Dean what do you want to drink?' Jack interrupts.

'Vodka and coke please.' Dean quickly looks at Jack and turns back to me, eager to finish my questions.

'What's the Queen's Palace like?' I ask eagerly, 'and tell me about this girl!' I quickly add like I wasn't listening properly and slowly processed the information he just threw at me. Dean claps his hands together and gasps loudly, and shifts to the edge of his seat,

'Well Luc, it's massive, they had those guards with the red coats and tall black fluffy hats, and there were loads of people trying to make them laugh and yes you will meet her tomorrow.' he says, really happy with himself. I nod along to his answers,

'Wow Dean that sounds amazing!'

'Here you go.' Jack puts his vodka and coke in front of him,

'Enough of my stories, let's get drunk and have a good night?' Dean picks up his drink and downs it. I look at him in surprise, nod my head and down the rest of my drink, Jack then follows, and Dean then looks at us in turn to ask,

'Whose round is it?' Dean flashes his gorgeous smile at me, so I reluctantly get up and collect orders.
'Jack?' I ask as if I'm a waitress.

'I'll have a shot of apple sours and a vodka and coke.' He smiles at me.

'Dean?'

'I'll have the same as Jack.' He winks at me.

'Okay I'll be back in a minute.' I slowly walk to the bar, while trying to find my purse, I lean on my elbows on the bar to get the bartenders attention, he quickly walked over to me.

'What can I get you?' He asks, while looking me up and down and smirking.

'I'll have three apple sours, three vodka and cokes and three JD and cokes please.' I say trying to square off my shoulders.

'Drinking on your own, are you?' He asks jokingly.

'Ha-ha no I never drink alone.' I say with a bitchy tone to it.

'You're a bit aggressive, aren't you?' He states while winking at me.

'Well I do get that way when my drinks take so long.' I wink back.

'Oh, and very feisty, I like it.' He laughs while placing all my drinks on a tray,

'The JD's have the straws in,' he quickly adds in, 'and this is my number so you can call me, my name is Jarvis.' He winks at me again turning to the till to tot up my drinks. I look at him up and down. He's so confident the way he stands, the way he winked at me, he obviously knows he's attractive in his tight black jeans, and tight white top. My attention is quickly grabbed by the half-naked girl screeching the bartender's name.

'JARVIS!'

He also quickly turns to the noise, in fact, all the men then turn and wolf-whistle at her. She loves it, twisting and twirling for them, with her long bleached blonde hair, heavy make-up, her belt she obviously calls a skirt, her boob tube and her knee-high boots. I smile to myself, as I note the resemblance to Pretty Woman, when Julia Roberts was the hooker. Jarvis turns to me and says,

'Forty-seven dollars please.' I hand him the notes I'm already holding in my hand, but before he gives me my change, he leans over the bar so we're face to face and asks.

'So, what's your name?'

'You'll have to try harder.' I wink at him and lean out of his face.

'I'm detaining your change till you tell me.' He says not breaking eye contact and closing his hand on my change.

'Fine, keep it.'

'I'm keeping it as a tip, see you later on sweetheart!' Jarvis answers smirking and moving to the next customer. As I struggle to balance the tray to pick it up,

'Here, let me', says a voice I don't recognize. I quickly look up at the stranger and I'm startled to see its Drake, from the cab.

'Oh, thanks.' I stutter, shocked to see him.

'Where are you sitting?' He asks over his shoulder. I point to the table just as Dean waves in my direction, and follow Drake through the crowd trying to push my way through after him, as it's getting busy now. Drake places the tray on the table.

'Hey guys!' Drake nods at Dean and Jack, turns to me winks and walks off, I blush and melt a little inside. Dean looks at me with a smile and before he says anything, I hold my index finger up in the air, Dean smiles and uses an imaginary zip to zip his mouth shut. I notice Jack scowling after Drake. I slap Jack on the shoulder and mouth 'cut it out', Jack childishly rolls his eyes and downs his shot.

'Hey,' Dean shouts to Jack, 'we were supposed to do them together!' He gives him a look.

'To your trip!' I say clinking my shot glass to his, he nods and we down them together. The music in the bar starts to get a bit louder as it gets later, and everyone has started finishing work. A couple of rounds later, I'm feeling a little light headed, so I sit back down on the chair to catch my breath.

'Jack's getting another round, what do you want?' Dean shouts in my ear.

'No thanks, I have to go home, I have loads of things to do,' I lie to him so they don't think I'm a lightweight. Dean taps Jack on the shoulder and shouts in his ear; Jack nods and comes over to me.

'You going?' Jack shouts at me.

'Yes, I am, I'll call you tomorrow? Yeah?' Jack nods, strokes my hair and kisses my forehead, Dean gives me a big hug, as pull away I huff to myself as I have to try get through the crowd, after a couple of pushes and sweating people I step onto the street, I shiver, I didn't even bring a coat. *Stupid.* I stumble along the pavement to try find a taxi, as I'm not steady enough to walk. As I spot one, I try to pick up my pace; but I've downed a few too many and gravity is working double time tonight. My feet lose the floor, and I am well and truly lying on my front doing the actions for a backwards snow angel on the very cold pavement. I scramble off the floor and back onto my feet, extremely embarrassed about what has just happened. I kick my heels off and sit on the curb, a few people come over to me to see if I was okay. As they all reach me they gasp at me, I touched my face and felt a warm liquid coming from my nose. *Great.*

'Can I call someone for you?' A girl looks at me worryingly.

'Yeah actually, my friend Jack.' I get my cell out my pocket, she unlocks my iPhone; she takes my hand in hers and shows me my cell.

'Jack Base or Jack Fenton?'

'Oh, erm… Base' I answer quickly, her male friend tells me to sit down on the cold floor, and checks me over for any other injuries, I can hear that girl with my cell talking quietly into it. I can't hear what she's saying as her friend is asking me questions. She knelt down next to me and held my hand,

'Your friend is just coming now' she looks at me sympathetically. A couple of minutes later Jack and Dean come running towards me and stopped suddenly at my feet, they both gasp in horror like my face had melted off.

'Luc, you okay?' Jack grabs my face in his hands.

'Yeah I'm fine, I just wanted to see the pavement closer' trying to make a joke of this, the girl touches Jacks shoulder.

'Shall I call an ambulance?' Jack looks at me for an answer.

'No, no I'm fine, I just want to go home' I answer kind of rudely, which makes me instantly feel bad as they're only trying to help me, Jack looks up at Dean.

'Do you have anywhere to be or do tomorrow?'

'No nothing' Dean replies. Jack then looks me in the eyes with my face still in his hands.

'We will both come to yours and stay the night' I start shaking my head, while Jack just nods his back to me.

'Just in case' he adds. Dean also is nodding at me; I slump on the spot and reluctantly accept.

'Can we go though; my ass is numb from the cold floor?'
Jack smiles at me and helps me up, Dean grabs my cell off
the ground, shakes the guys hand and thanks the girl for
coming to my rescue. We start slowly walking down the road,
with Dean on my left and Jack on my right. I'm draped over
Jack as I feel light headed from standing up, and Dean
carrying my shoes and phone.
Dean hauled a cab and we all climb in, with me in the middle
using them both to sit up right.

'Fifth Avenue' Jack says to the driver.

# CHAPTER TWO

I'm jolted awake suddenly as I fall where Dean was sitting.

'Come on Luc, we're home.' I climb out and fall into Dean.

'Drink a bit too much did we Luc?' Dean laughs at me while helping me to the lobby of my building, Jack quickly jabbing the elevator button.

'It won't make it come any quicker dufus,' I add a little slurred.

'Listen to the drunk chick.' After a long two minutes the elevator arrives and we climb in. Jack fishes in my bag for my keys, he rattles them as he pulls them out and laughs at my key rings with a picture of me, Dean and Jack on Santa Monica beach. As the elevator pings on the sixth floor, I slowly push myself off of the wall of the lift and walk to my apartment, I slump on the sofa; I can hear someone in the kitchen running water and someone rummaging through my DVD collection next to my bedroom. Dean strolled in front of me holding a
bowl of warm water with kitchen wipes, dragged one of my dining room
chairs in front of me and handed me the bowl.

'Hold this Luc.' I just nod and do as I'm told, whilst Jack walks to the TV with a smile on his face holding a DVD. I stare at it with squinted eyes but can't make out the title.

'What is it?' I ask, confused.

'It's Shrek' he smiles at me, 'your favorite, if I'm not mistaken.' Jack puts the DVD on, while Dean is cleaning my nose of all the blood.

'You're going to get a bruise on that tomorrow babe' he says looking all worried, I just nod my head, as Dean walks away with the bowl of water, I suddenly get taken down by my duvet that Jack just threw at my head, they both sit beside me and enjoy my favorite film.

I wake up with a sudden pain as I hit my nose while I'm sleeping. I look around and see that Jack and Dean are both asleep, and the TV has the black and white static flickering on the screen. I climb out from between them and clamber to my room, grabbing a blanket out of the cupboard; I climb into bed and fall instantly into a deep sleep.

I slowly open my eyes, and immediately close them as I'm blinded by the sunlight coming in my window; the sun is pleasantly warm on my face. I cup my eyes and sit up; I can hear talking very quietly, but I can't make out if it's the TV or someone talking.

'Oh, I wonder if they are still here?' I whisper to myself. I jump out of bed and into the living room, I see feet poking out the end of my sofa as someone is lying on it, I peer over and scare Dean 'AHHH' he shouts as he falls of the sofa.

'Lucy, what the hell?!' he says while looking up at me, I

giggle and walk off to the kitchen and turn the kettle on.

'WANT A COFFEE BUTTHEAD?' I shout to Dean.

'Yes please' he mumbles back from the floor, as I set to make the coffee, Dean comes stalking in the kitchen. I look around him.

'Where is Jack?' He looks surprised by my question.

'At work, he left at 7:30 this morning.'

'Oh, okay' I whisper back, actually feeling a bit let down.

'Why, do you love him so much you miss him?' Dean laughs at me.

'No!' I immediately answer back.

'Alright Luc, calm down, I was only joking!' he replies, putting his hands up in surrender.

'I know, I'm just a bit tired, sorry.' I lie; *maybe I do have feelings for Jack*. Dean starts belting out 'Sweet Child of Mine', which brings me back to the present.
'Can I use your laptop, Luc, to log into work?'

'Yeah yeah, sure.' I reply, but I'm miles away, staring out the kitchen window whilst I stir the coffee. Dean's shout grabs my attention.

'Luc, you have an email!' I frown thinking who it could be from, and then it suddenly hits me like a bus. I throw the spoon and run towards Dean, and right there on the screen it says what I hoped it might: 'TEELYS INTERNATIONAL'. I squeal –

'OPEN IT, OPEN IT!' I shout, rather excited to see this reply.


*From: Beth Ryan*
*Subject: Resume*
*To: Lucy Winter*
*12/11/10 09:37*

*Dear Miss Winter,*
*I have carefully looked over your resume and the job title and am very pleased to announce that Mr. Teely would like you to attend an interview at TEELY'S INTERNTIONAL, on the corner of ninth on the 18th floor, Wednesday 17th November at 0900.*

*Yours sincerely,*
*Beth Ryan*

*P.A. to Drake Teely*

'OH MY GOD!' I squeak, Dean immediately jumps up and hugs me and cheers with me. The phone rings in the background, Dean drops me as I run over to answer it.

'Hello?'

'JACK,' I shout, 'I GOT OFFERED AN INTERVIEW FOR TEELY'S INTERNATIONAL! Yeah, Wednesday nine in the morning, on the eighteenth floor!' Then I let out a heart-stopping screech. Dean takes my phone off me and starts talking to Jack. I'm buzzing with excitement, totally forgetting that it's the morning and I probably just woke up all my neighbors.

'Email Gemma and text Sarah.' Dean orders.

'Oh yeah' I answer, and starting typing an email to Gemma my sister at Harvard.

*From: Lucy Winter*
*Subject: My Life*
*To: Gemma Winter*
*11/13/10 09:10*

*Hey Gem, I have an interview at Teely's international on Wednesday, I just thought I'd let you know, when are you back in the York?*

*Love you lots*
*Luc xx*

I also text Sarah.

*Sarah its Luc I'VE GOT SOME BIG NEWSS! I'll pop in, Luc x*

Sarah is my best friend in the whole world. We met in the second grade and have been friends ever since. We went through every stage together: the Spice Girls stage, the Britney stage, riding bikes everywhere stage, so I class her as much as family as everyone else. As I press send, I think of my parents, so I grab my phone and dial their number. It rings and rings.

'My parents are never out!' I whisper in disbelief, before I leave a message.

'Hello this is the Winters, we're not in at the moment, so leave us a message and we will call you back.'

'Hey Mom and Dad, its Luc. I was just phoning to say I got an interview on Wednesday at Teely's international, you can congratulate me later byeeee!' I hang up the phone. I swing round to Dean, who has once again found the sofa and Jerry Springer

'Want to come shopping with me?'

'Yeah sure, I still didn't get my coffee' he answers.

'Give me a minute while I get ready.'

'No prob-lay-mo' he answers, while turning the TV over to watch baseball.
I check myself out in the mirror; my nose is looking purple around the edges with some dry blood still on my nostrils. I wince in pain as I wipe it off. I haven't got the energy to have a shower, so I pull on some jeans, knee high boots, a loose top, tie my hair back, put a woolly hat on and slip my coat on. I smile at myself in the mirror as I remind myself of a young child all wrapped for winter. I walk out in the living room and tell Dean I'm ready by shouting 'TA DA' over the TV volume, which has crept up to stupidly loud. I grab my bag and phone. We walk to the lift and reach the bottom floor in no time; Dean looks over his shoulder at me as we leave

the lobby.

'Where are we going shopping?' he asks. I let out a little girly laugh as we both know we're going to the one shop everyone goes to, and my best friend works in so I also get discount, *YAY!*

As we arrive outside Bloomingdales, I hear a girl screech. I look in the shop and Sarah is running towards me, waving her hands in the air. She hugs Dean and me, standing in the middle of us, links our arms and drags us in the shop.

'What's the big occasion?' she eyes us up and down.

'I have an interview at Teely's International' I smile at her. Dean and I cup our ears as she squeals again, making us frown. She hugs me again, grabs my hand and starts dragging me further into the shop. I grab Dean's hand quickly and we're a 3 people chain walking through the shop. She halts at a sleek professional looking dress, holds it against me, throws it at me and pulls me along again. She keeps handing me dresses as we follow her, and then she points at the dressing room.

'In.' Sarah points with a raised eye brow. I stalk off, holding about 5 dresses, while Sarah and Dean wait outside. I try the first black one she picked up. It fits perfectly, stops just before my knees, it's a nice little shift dress. As I'm looking in the mirror admiring the dress, something hits me in the back of the foot; Sarah had thrown some shoes under the door of the changing room for me to wear with this dress. They are shiny and black with what looks like 10-inch high heels and a recognizable red sole. I crinkle my brow and snort.

'There's no way can I walk in these Sar'.

'I'll teach you how to walk in them Luc, don't worry, now come out and show us the dress' she orders. I slip my feet into the shoes and breathe in, square my shoulders and open the door; Sarah and Dean's mouths drop open, and they stare at me. I instantly feel self-conscious.

'What?' I say sharply.

'You look...so stunning Luc...' Dean mumbles, not taking his eyes off me. Sarah can't even find any words, which is not normal for her.

'I look okay then, yeah?' I question, watching their responses, they quickly answer me together.

'Yes.'

'One more thing...' Sarah jumps off the couch and disappears and then reappears with the most beautiful bag I have ever seen!
'This would go perfectly!'

'Marc Jacobs?'

'The very same, young lady, a nice blue color to break the black up. She explains confidently, not mentioning the hefty commission I know she will receive. As I change out of this outfit feeling pretty good about myself, I decided to buy the lot and the other outfits, trusting Sarah's knowledge in her job. As Sarah bagged up my items, she gives me her staff discount, and I pass my card to her not wanting to know the total. She slips my receipt in the bag and smiles at me.

'See you tonight, yeah?' she asks me as I walk off. I put my thumb up in the air to signal a yes and walk out the shop with Dean. As we're stood outside Bloomingdales, I get to checking my phone. I see in the corner of my eye Dean eyeing up someone's corn dog.

'Are you hungry, by any chance?' I smirk.

'How did you work that out Luc?' he laughs at me. As the rain starts, he grabs my hand and pulls me along the pavement so fast I have to jog to keep up with him, and pulls me into our café. We walk over to our always-reserved table orders us coffee. A couple of minutes later, the waitress brings us our coffees.

'What do you want to eat?' Dean says passing me the menu.

'I'll give you kids a couple of minutes' the waitress says and walks off, wiping the coffee spill on her hands onto the pink pinafore uniform, and pulling the pencil out of her hair to write down someone's order. Dean takes my attention away.

'Do you mind if my friend comes to meet us?' asking me while staring at his phone.

'No not at all' I answer still staring at the waitress, the little bell hanging above the door rings as people walk in and out. A girl who walks in jolts my brain back to life, she seems to walk in slow motion. Her long brown hair blowing like she's walking with a fan, her green eyes and a beautiful smile as

23

she sees Dean, spreads across her face; in black skinny jeans, brown knee-high boots with a white floaty top and a black leather jacket. She reaches our table and Dean gets up to hug her. She holds her hand out:

'Hi, my name is Belle!' She says in a slick English accent. I lift my hand to meet hers and reply.

'Hi, I'm Lucy', I give Dean a look of *what the hell?*

'I met Belle in London, she lives just outside the city, she showed me around and I stayed with her for a bit too.'

'Uh huh.' I answer looking at the pictures of food on the menu.

'She lives in a lovely village called Peter-something.' Belle pipes up –

'Petersfield.' – and lets out a little giggle. I instantly frown at her.

'That's the one' Dean agrees, 'it's so peaceful, there was a big pond.'

'Heath' Belle adds. My head is rolling between them like I'm watching tennis.

'Yeah, we went on boats, Luc' Dean adds in, but I start to fade out of this conversation, Belle being so happy and beautiful makes me depressed. I look for my phone in my bag, to find something to do while they talk about London. I see a message from Jack.

*Hey Luc, I'm on lunch in a bit, where you eating? How's your nose? J x*

I smile instantly, and text Jack back.

*Hey Jack, were in Betty's, my nose is fine I have a nice outfit for Wednesday, when's your lunch? L x*

I sit and phase in and out of Dean and Belle's conversation, awaiting Jacks reply. I sit slurping my coffee as it's starting to get cold, and I feel quite hungry just then my phone beeps again.

*I'm about five minutes away from Betty's; I can't wait to see your outfit ;) J X*

I smile.

'What you smiling at?' Dean says bringing me back to the present.

'Jack will be here in five minutes' I try and say with a steady voice, the bell on the café dings and we all look at the door. Jack strides in, spotting us and making his way over to us, Belle stands and smiles at Jack, holds her hand out and as she did to me.

'Hi I'm Belle'. Jack quickly shakes her hand and walks around her to come talk to me, I feel a little relieved and maybe a little jealous. *What the hell as come over me, am I starting to get feelings for Jack?!*

25

'What can I get for you kids?' the waitress makes us all jump. She looks at Jack, he smiles at her and she blushes. He has that power over women.

'Do you want to know the specials' the waitress quickly adds.

'Oh, yes please' Jack says politely.

'Chicken salad, tomato soup, BLT' she lists, but Jack interrupts.

'Oh, I'll have a BLT please' Jack smiles, the waitress looks at Dean.

'And for you?'

'I'll have a BLT as well thanks.' Belle orders the same and then the three of them stare at me. I lose my voice as I'm put on the spot and whisper.

'I'll have a BLT as well thanks'. As she goes to walk off, she turns on her heels to ask for our drinks. Together Jack and I both say 'coffee', then smile at each other, Belle asks for tea *because she's English maybe* and Dean has a Coke. Dean introduces Belle to Jack, just as he did to me, explaining her hometown as 'Peter-something' again. Both Belle and I correct him, saying 'Petersfield' in unison. Dean and Jack both look at me.

'How did you remember that?' Dean questions.

'I remember things easily' I quickly answer. Jack shrugs off Dean's story and grabs my hand.

'How is your nose?'

'Its fine, hurts a bit but that will teach me for having a fight with the pavement.' *What a bad joke* I think. Jack smiles at me, probably to humor me. The waitress then appears with our drinks, and conversation dies as everyone takes a sip.

'What time do you have to be back at work Jack?' I ask trying to break the silence.

'One-thirty.' Jack replies, eyeing up his lunch being carried by the waitress, and once again we all sit in silence while we eat our lunch. I excuse myself so I can go to the bathroom; to my surprise Belle follows me. When we enter the bathroom, Belle taps me on the shoulder.

'Lucy? Are you okay with me being here?'

'Yeah course, why wouldn't I be?' I answer. She looks at her shoes.

'Because you didn't seem to look impressed when I turned up.'

'Oh, I'm just distracted it's not you' I lie. She's up her own ass and there is something about her I dislike, but I don't want to piss her off if she's friends with Dean, so I smile at her and offer my arms in a hug, she hugs me back and then smiles.

'Can I talk to you about Dean then?' she asks.

'Oh okay,' I look at her wondering what she wants to share.

'I really like him and I came to New York just to see him, but I don't want to come across really desperate or needy?' she asks looking at her shoes the whole time, my brain having a private joke about her accent. I stroke her arm.

'Of course, you should tell him,' I smile and lie, 'I must go pee, meet you at the table?' I mutter, she nods and walks out, and I stare at my face in the mirror. I look ghostly.

'Oh god I need some make-up.' I say in disgust, then ten minutes later Belle comes into the bathroom.

'We're going Luc' and runs back out – since when did Miss English Belle start calling me Luc? I take one last look and stalk out the bathroom. Jack, Belle and Dean are all standing near the door for me, I take my stuff from Jack and we walk outside in the cold air once again. The rain is coming down heavily now and Jack puts his coat and arm over my shoulder and hugs me close and kisses my head, Dean grabs Belle's hand and we all run to my apartment to get out of the rain. My phone starts to ring, I try feel for it as we get into the lobby – it's Sarah.

'Hey Sarah,' I instantly smile, 'erm about seven, we can pre-drink and then get a cab out yeah?' I answer.

'Hang on let me ask the others –' I hold the phone to my shoulder – 'do you three want to come out tonight?'

'Err sure.' Jack answers. Dean looks at Belle, and they both nod, so I go back to my conversation with Sarah.

'Yeah the three of them will come out' I whisper. She can tell something is wrong, but I tell her I'll explain later when she asks. We say goodbye and I end the call. I get my keys out and open the door for us to enter my apartment, taking my Bloomingdales bag to my room. Jack follows me and shuts my door behind me.

'Luc' he whispers, making me jump.

'Yeah?'

'What you getting Dean for a birthday present? *SHIT!* I totally forgot!

'I can't think what to get him as a present' I lie.

'I've got him something, want to go halves with me?'

'Oh yes please, you're a life-saver, how much do I owe you?' I look up at him and look in his dreamy eyes.

'Ten dollars babe.' He slaps my ass and walks out my room. I sit on the edge of my bed and think about my confusing feelings I've had for Jack today. I try kick the thoughts because I want to out-shine Sarah tonight. She is always the centre of attention, her mid-length blonde hair, which has a slight wave to it, her skinny frame, I'd say she was about a size eight, long legs that annoyingly go all the way up to her bum. I always feel short and fat next to her, but no, I'm not letting myself feel like that tonight. I grab some towels and stalk of to the bathroom, as I quickly walk to the bathroom without stopping I shout,

'I'm getting in the shower, if you need to pee, then tough!' After my shower on the way back to my room, I can hear them talking about my Mom and Dad. I slip on a plunge bra, matching panties and some clear stockings. As I'm bent over drying my hair; I look between my legs and see a pair of men's feet.

'Jack, stop being a pervert and get out!' I shout, and then I see the feet disappear. I stand up flatten my hair and put the one of my black floaty dresses I brought today on. I spray my dress with perfume, and start to apply my make-up. I put my new Louboutin's heels on, open my bedroom door, hands on my hips. Belle and Jack stare at me with their mouths open, but before they can say anything I ask demandingly,

'Who came in my room?' Jack blushes and answers.

I did, I wanted to ask you something but all I saw was your ass.' I wink at him and then tell the others to close their mouths because I don't want dribble on my rug. Dean claps his hands and laughs rather loudly and makes me smirk, I sit on the couch near Jack. The downstairs buzzer goes and makes me jump. I kick my shoes off and run over to the box on my wall to press the button.

'Hey it's Sarah.' An out of breath voice came through. I press the button to unlock the main door. I hold my apartment door open awaiting Sarah, the lift dings and she walks out in her red mini-dress that is fitted, with her hair up in an up do and high Louboutin's heeled black shoes with a clutch bag, she smells amazing. She hugs me tightly and walks into my apartment past me, wafting some more of her perfume. Instantly, I feel not-done-up-enough next to Sarah. Jack walks over and pulls me out of the way and shuts the front door.

'DRINKS' Sarah squeals, Dean walks back in the sitting room from the kitchenette with 5 glasses and Sarah pulls a bottle of vodka out of her bag.

'You got Coke babes?' they all look at me; I shrug my shoulders and stalk off to the kitchen, as Belle comes running in after me. *Again.*

'Lucy?'

'Yes?' I take a step back, because she doesn't understand personal space.

'All I have is what I'm wearing, do you have anything I can borrow? What size are you?'

'I'm size ten take your pick from my wardrobe' and I signal towards my bedroom. I walk back in the sitting room and share the Coke.

'When are we leaving?' I ask while slumping on the sofa, Dean hugs me

'You smell nice' he explains, and I let out a small smile.

'What's up chick?' Sarah comes over and hugs me.

'You look like a sexier version of Kate Moss and I look like Shrek and Donkey's love child' I moan. Jack tries to hold in his laugh, so I grab a pillow and launch it at his head.

'You look gorgeous,' Sarah strokes my hair like she's petting a dog, 'doesn't she Jack?'

'Yeah you do, honest!' We all clink our glasses and celebrate well nothing, but who needs an excuse to drink.

We all bundle into the lift, get downstairs and while giggling, stumble out the lobby door. I trip over my own feet but Jack catches me.

'You're my hero Mr. Base' I giggle. He side-smiles at me, with his gorgeous mouth. We haul a taxi and all clamber in.

We arrive outside a club called 'AQUA' with blue and green lights around the sign with a big queue of people outside behind a red velvet rope. *That* dampens my mood immediately, as do the big bouncers at the door. Sarah squares her shoulders and marches up to the bouncers. She nods and fires two names 'Lewis, Steve' and they let all five of us walk straight in, while all the people in the queue groan loudly.

The club is dark, with a few blinking pink and orange disco lights. The DJ is straight in front of us at the front of the dance floor, fist pumping with his headphones around his neck. The bar on the left has bartenders in waistcoats, flinging bottles up making cocktails. Sarah grabs my hand and pulls me on to the dance floor, Dean, Jack and Belle follow us in a chain, and we all start dancing. The exact moment mine and Sarah's favorite song plays over the DJ's system, we both squeal.

# CHAPTER THREE

I wake up because I hear my front door slamming shut. I'm lying on my front, but when I flick my hair over my shoulder and lay on my side, I look down and to my surprise I'm wearing last night's dress. As I look over my shoulder I see someone's feet in my bed, I double take and spin to get onto my knees to see Jack sleeping on his front on the other side of the bed, in just his boxers.

*Oh no did something happen?*

I pull my dress off and put on my dressing gown and make my way into the sitting room. Belle is asleep on my sofa and Dean is sprawled on the floor, so it must have been Sarah that left. I turn the kettle on and yawn, getting 4 mugs out the cupboard ready to make everyone coffee. I look at the clock – *blurgh too early.* I leave everyone alone for a moment while I focus on making coffee. Grabbing two mugs I walk over to Belle and Dean. I kick Dean in the side to make him jump, he sits up suddenly, yawns and takes the coffee while nodding at me with his eyes still half shut. I place Belle's coffee on the little table near the sofa and I shake her gently until she wakes up and sits up slowly, I smile at them both, swing open the blinds and whack some windows open. I grab the other mug of coffee and go to my bedroom and place it on the bedside table next to Jack's head, and shake him awake like I did to Belle, he smiles at me. As I walk back to the kitchen I slip some bread in the toaster, and my cell rings, I run frantically trying to find it.

*Sorry I left in a rush, what happened between you and Jack? X*

I rack my brains before I text back.

*No worries, nothing I woke up with him next to me X*

Sarah texts back instantly.

*What did you wake up in?*

Oh god, twenty question time.

*This sounds like we're sexting! I was wearing my dress ;) but no panties :(*

I laugh to myself about my joke.

*No panties oooooh :) sexy time!! Lucy and Jack babies.... first client here byeeee Xxxxxxxxxxxxxxx*

As I tut to myself at the baby thought, I carry my coffee to the breakfast bar, and start up my laptop, sipping my coffee, Dean and Belle are slowly waking up, but I haven't heard any more movement from Jack.

'Where is Jack?' Dean asks while looking at me like a meercat over the chair.

'In my bed' I answer. Belle and Dean both spin their heads to look at me with raised eyebrow.

'Bloody hell,' comes a very English voice, 'the first day I get here…'

'Nothing happened,' I roll my eyes as if I've been asked a hundred times. As I get my emails up I see my sister Gemma had emailed me back.

*From: Gemma Winter*
*Subject: your life*
*To: Lucy Winter*
*11/14/10 07:45*

*Dear Luc*
*That's fantastic, I'm happy you have found a job to apply for, I'll be visiting the York near Christmas time at the end of my semester, have you heard from Sam?*

Sam? What Sam? I set to email her back.

*From: Lucy Winter*
*Subject: Sam…..?*
*To: Gemma Winter*
*11/15/10 08:15*

*Gem,*
*Sam? As in Sam Lewis? What did she want?*
*I can't wait to see you*
*Love you*

To my surprise, my email tings back, whoa Gemma must be bored.

*From: Gemma Winter*
*Subject: you heard*
*To: Lucy Winter*
*11/15/10 08:20*

*Yeah Sam Lewis our cousin, she's been kicked out of Auntie Pauline's and wants somewhere to stay.........what else would she want?!?!?!?*
*I can't wait to see you either, I brought your Xmas pressie today*
*Love you back*

Awwwww...

*From: Lucy Winter*
*Subject: oh god*
*To: Gemma Winter*
*11/15/10 08:25*

*Oh no again? Did you give her my number?*
*I'm picking up yours Monday; I got it ordered in specially*

My email doesn't ting back immediately so I'm guessing she started a class. As I finish my coffee, I smell my toast burning, so run to the kitchen put my mug in the sink and pop my toast up.

'Oh, it's burnt' I say really disappointed. Dean walks in the kitchen behind me with two empty mugs and senses my sadness.

'I'll eat it!' Dean has a smile on his face, I pass it to him over my shoulder, and walk out the kitchen.

'Chuck some more bread in the toaster doll!' I shout.

'Yeah' Dean replies.

And I see Gemma emailed me back.

*From: Gemma Winter*
*Subject: YAY!!!!*
*To: Lucy Winter*
*11/15/10 08.35*

*No, I didn't because I wanted to ask you first... shall I give it to her??*
*Ohhhh I'm sooooo excited!*
*What you getting for mom and dad?*
*What are you getting the boys??*

*From: Lucy Winter*
*Subject: YAY!!!!*
*To: Gemma Winter*
*11/15/10 08:37*

*Yeah that's fine, you can hand it over, and I want to know why Auntie Pauline kicked her out......*
*I was thinking of getting Mum and Dad a weekend away to see Auntie Pauline.*

And to my amusement Gemma emails back quickly again, Jack entered the room and half naked, while Dean and Belle are watching re-runs of Jerry Springer, laughing and cheering.

*From: Gemma Winter*
*Subject: YAY!!!!*
*To: Lucy Winter*
*11/15/10 08:41*

*Yeah me too, let me know what she says….*
*That's is a good idea actually Lucy I'll go in with you, just let me know how much.*

*From: Lucy Winter*
*Subject: sorted!*
*To: Gemma Winter*
*11/15/10 08:45*

*Are you bored by any chance you're emailing back quite quickly?*
*I will speak to you soon*
*Love you xxxxxx*

*From: Gemma Winter*
*Subject: sorted!*
*To: Lucy Winter*
*11/15/10 08:50*

*Yes, I'm bored ha-ha*
*Love you toooo Xxxxxxxxxxxxx*

That's the most I have spoken to Gemma in one day, so now I know I can organize Mum and Dad's Christmas present.

'Guys? Still want to go in with me and Gemma to get Mum and Dad a weekend away to see Auntie Pauline?' I ask.

'Yeah sure' they both agree together, while nodding and looking at each other for approval. I search on Google for cheap trips to Tennessee, but then my phone beeps with a text alert.

*Hey Lucy, Gemma gave me your number, hope you don't mind. Can I ask you a favor? I need somewhere to stay can I come stay with you for a bit? Sam xx*

Oh well, I was expecting this text, I slump on the breakfast bar stool and text her back.

*Hey Sam what happened? Yeah you can stay for a bit, Gem will be staying in a couple of weeks when she finishes school for Xmas L x*

I put my phone on the side as I go to sit on the sofa with the others; I look at Jack.

'Did you not have work today?'

'Yeah but I phoned in sick.' Jack replies without even looking away from the TV.

'Oh okay.' I whisper. I hear my phone beep again on the counter but I choose to ignore it, but then Gemma wanted to know what she said, so I get up and read my phone.

*We just had an argument so we just need some space, that's fine we should have made up by then, can I have your*

39

*address? I'll be with you soon Sam x*

I open my laptop again and reply to Gemma's last email.

*From: Lucy Winter*
*Subject: Sam*
*To: Gemma Winter*
*11/15/10 10.35*

*Gem*
*Sam just texted me, all she said was that they had an*
*argument but ill find out more when she's here, I've told*
*her that you are coming to stay here in a few weeks.*

I turn my laptop off and I don't text Sam back, I just need to
do nothing.

'Luc, want to go for breakfast?' Jack asks staring at me.

'Oh, yeah sure.' I reply.

'Go get dressed then, babes' Jack adds.

'I did put bread in the toaster for you.' Dean says.

'Yeah but I forgot I'd prefer fat on a plate.' I smile.

'Betty's?' Jack asks us all in turn. Jack runs into my bedroom
after me and puts his clothes on from last night; I walk out my
room in slob clothes smile at everyone. I grab my bag and
text Sarah as we leave my apartment.

*Sarah, I'm off for breakfast with Dean, Jack and Belle, if you want you can come meet us at Betty's?*

Sarah texts back immediately.

*Babes, you can read my mind from across town, be there in 10 S x*

I smile as I read it.

## CHAPTER FOUR

As I slump on the sofa watching trash T.V., I suddenly remember I didn't text Sam back with my address, so I pick up my phone.

*Hey Sam sorry my address is the blue building on Fifth Avenue, floor 6 apartment 18. Xxx*

I turn my laptop on as well, but Gemma hasn't emailed me

back so I turn it straight off. My main door buzzer goes off and startles me.

'Hello?'

'Hey, it's Sarah!' I buzz her up, and then quickly look around my apartment for my panties from last night. I find them behind the sofa, I crinkle my nose *WTF?* I pick them up and put it in the laundry basket, just as Sarah comes running in my front door.

'Hey, you alright?' I ask in surprise. Sarah tries to get her breath back.

'Ye...ah, I wanted to help you get ready for tomorrow.' She breathes.

'Oh, okay, I just found my panties behind the sofa.' She makes the same face I did.

'Yeah I know.' I joke. Sarah sits on the sofa and signals with her hand that she wants a drink, so I give her a bow and say 'yes ma'am'. As I walk into the kitchen, Sarah shouts after me.

'Are you curling your hair for tomorrow?'

'No, I don't think I will, I want to look like I haven't tried.' I explain.

'Make-up?' Sarah lists of her fingers.

'Minimal.'

'Fair enough you fitty.' Sarah says whilst I walk back into the living room.

'I'm sorted for tomorrow by the way.' I say. Suddenly Ricky Martin's 'She Bangs' starts blasting out – we both jump and then Sarah does a little dance before picking up her phone and answering 'hello?' with a massive smile across her face.

'Hey Jacob.' All I hear from the conversation is her giggling and agreeing to whatever he was saying.

'Okay let me say bye to Luc then.' She makes a kiss noise and hangs up.

'Sorry Luc I have to go meet Jacob.' She says like it's common knowledge.

'Jacob?' I question her.

'I'll explain tomorrow.' She hugs me and walks out.

**********

I awake with my alarm ringing. I reluctantly sit up on the edge of my bed, yawn, and stretch; walk off to the kitchen to turn the kettle on. I open all the blinds just trying to wake myself up. When I hear the kettle whistling I run into the kitchenette and pour myself a coffee, go to my room and start getting ready. Stockings, my plunge bra, my black shift dress, half straightened hair, Louboutin's and apply a small amount of make-up just to make myself look awake. My beautiful new bag in hand, I carry my shoes and coffee into the other room, sit up at the breakfast bar and turn my laptop on. My phone buzzes next to me.

*Hey good luck for today, love Sarah xxxxx*

Bless her. Still no emails from Gemma and no texts from Sam, but oh well, I have to be in a good mood for my interview because I really want this. It's already eight, so I grab my stuff and leave the apartment. I haul a taxi, as Teely's International is on the other side of town. As I try to keep my calm, I pay the cab man and stand outside Teely's International. When I look up, I feel dizzy because the building is so tall, but I take a deep breath and walk in the main doors. I walk up to the main reception and see a young man, brown hair with crew cut, in a smart suit with a pink tie, pacing behind the reception desk talking on a headset. Next to him is a young blonde woman in a grey trouser suit, also on a headset. I stand there with my hands perched on the desk like a meercat until one of them has finished their conversation, I peer over my shoulder at the black marble floors and see potted plants everywhere.

'Can I help you?' The young girl smiles at me.

'Err, yes I'm here for an interview with Mr. Teely at 09:00.' I state.

'Oh, okay you're a bit early, I'll let him know you're here, if you can please take a seat and I'll call you over when he's ready for you.' She says not making eye contact with me. I slowly walk over to the seating area and perch on a soft leather seat. As I'm staring around, I look at the main door and I double take when I see Drake walk through the door. I stare at him whilst he walks to the front desk.

'Is Miss Winter here?' The young girl points in my direction, Drake smiles at me and walks over, holds his hand out to me.

'Hi, I had a feeling it might be you,' he says, 'shall we?' He asks after I shake his hand, whilst pointing towards the lift. As we wait, he looks me up and down.

'You look nice.' He says. I look him up and down and reply.

'You too, Mr. Teely, but I'm sensing this conversation is a tad too personal for our first meeting.' I say trying not to smirk. The lift tings and opens.

'After you Miss Winter, and I'd like to point out it's our third meeting.' He quips back. I walk into the lift with a smirk. We stand in silence until we reach the eighteenth floor, he walks out in front of me and jogs over to a woman behind a desk and I stand there awkwardly.

'Follow me Lucy!' He shouts across the room, so I try keep up with him, the receptionist smiling at me.

'Hi I'm Beth.'

'Hi Beth.' I answer with a smile as I step in his office.

'Please sit here Lucy.' Drake says and points to a chair in front of his desk.
I mutter okay then sit and wait for him, he finally comes over

and sits on the other side of the desk, grabs a pad and a pen and stares at me with his green eyes. He has a bit of a tan and his hair looks sexy as ever, with his smart dark blue suit. He clears his throat.

'Name?' I look confused. He raises his eyebrows. I quickly reply.

'Lucy Winter.'

'Your age?' He fires just as quickly.

'Twenty-three, you?' I add, not curbing my interest. He looks at my face, then at his paper and back to me, he then whispers.

'Thirty-three.'

'WHAT?!' I reply without restraining my volume. He stops and stares at me.

'Is there a problem?'

'No sorry, I was shocked that you have your own company and you're so
Young.' I reply, attempting to explain my behaviour.

'Well, it's my Granddad's company, he passed it on to my dad and my dad hired me. Anything else you want to know?' He says trying to hide his smile.

'No, sorry, carry on.' I look at my shoes.

'Right, now I have the floor, I've done some research on you, and I've read through your resume. I'm very pleased with what I have found out about you, but I'm not so happy with you accepting lifts with strangers. You're lucky it was me and not someone more dangerous.' He looks at me and smiles.

'That I am Mr. Teely.' I say.

'Miss Winter, please call me Drake, Mr. Teely is so formal and is also my father.' He states.

'Then just call me Lucy.'

'Okay Lucy, we're done here.'

'That's it? When do I find out if I got the job or not?'

'Right now. I can confirm you have the job.'

'Oh my god, thank you!' I jump up out of my chair and go to hug him, he stiffly hugs me back.

'You're most welcome; you start Monday morning at nine.'

'Oh, thank you so much!' I repeat.

'Shall I show you out?' He asks.

'No, no, it's fine thanks, see you Monday... Oh! I need two days off in two weeks' time.' I add.

'You haven't even started and you're asking for time off?' He raises his eyebrows with a smirk.

'Yeah, it's my cousin's wedding.'

'Okay Lucy, what are the dates?' I grab my diary out of my bag.

'Third of December and the sixth.'

'Okay, see you Monday.' He says, dismissing me. I make my way out of the building and take a sigh of relief as I lean against the wall outside. Since I'm in this part of town, I think about going to see Jack and tell him my good news. I stroll along the path until I reach Jack's building; I walk up to the reception.

'Hi,' the receptionist beams at me 'can I help you?'

'Yes, actually can you please get hold of Jack Base and tell him Lucy Winter is down here, thanks.' I smile, turn around and sit in the seating area. I hear the woman talking to someone down the phone and then the call ends. A couple of minutes later Jack comes from behind a corner with a concerned look on his face.

'You okay, Luc?' He hugs me with his hands round my waist.

'Yeah I'm fine I just wanted to let you know I got the job!'

'What? Are you serious?' He asks.

'Yes,' I beam up at him, 'well I'll let you get back to work; I just wanted you to be the first to know.'

'Well thanks, I'm very happy for you. Want to go out to celebrate tonight?' He looks at me.

'Yeah sure why not?'

'I'll see you later.' He turns and then disappears again; I spin and walk out the building. As I walk out, a huge smile on my face, swinging my bag back and forth, I remember I need to tell Sarah. Whilst I text her, I think of all the people I need to tell. I decide to just stroll home and let everyone come to me, but at that moment my phones beeps.

*Hey its Sam, I'll be with you at approx 5pm.*

Oh, well that's dampened my mood, that means she has to come out tonight with us. I shrug my shoulders and as I finally get to my lobby. I reach my apartment, kick my shoes off, throw my bag on the couch and go straight to the breakfast bar to turn my laptop on and let it load, flip the kettle on and put some bread in the toaster. My phone beeps again.

*Hello Lucy, its Drake here just wanted to congratulate you on getting the job! Drink tonight? D x*

I instantly smile, and there's a reply from Gemma. I feel lucky.

*From: Gemma Winter*
*Subject: Sam*
*To: Lucy Winter*
*11/16/10 09:05*

49

*Oh, you can find out more when she reaches you.*
*How was the interview?*

I hit reply without even thinking.

*From: Lucy Winter*
*Subject: My life*
*To: Gemma Winter*
*11/16/10 09:50*

*I'll quiz her!*

*I GOT THE JOB!!!!!!!!!!!!!!!!!!!!!!!!!!!!!!!!! I START*
*MONDAY*

I set back to texting back Drake, when my phone beeps twice,
a message from Sarah and Dean.

*Drake thanks for offering me the job, I can't make tonight*
*as I'm celebrating with my friends but tomorrow night?*
*How did you get my number?*

I turn my laptop off and as I hear the kettle and toaster both
ping at the same time, I jump up like an excited schoolgirl. I
make coffee and butter my toast and slump on the sofa ready
to relax, but then my phone rings.

'OH MY GOD' I sigh before answering.

'Hello dear, its Mom.'

'Oh, hey Mum.'

'How did the interview go sweetheart?' She asks.

'Good! I got the job and I start on Monday!'

'OH, THAT'S GREAT! DAVE, LUC GOT THE JOB.' I hear my Dad shout congratulations in the background.

'THANKS DAD!' I shout back.

'Have you told Gem?' Mom asks.

'Yeah I emailed her just a minute ago.'

'Okay, is it still okay for Dad and I to stay on Friday?' My Mom asks, and I suddenly remember Sam.

'Yeah it's fine you can stay in the spare room, but Sam is coming to stay because she fell out with Aunty Pauline again.' I add.

'Oh no, again? That poor girl.' Mom says sounding sad.

'I'll find out what happened, but she will be here tonight. Sam can stay on the sofa Mom.' I quickly add in.

'That's fine Luc, I best go your father needs me.' I can hear my father swearing in the background.

'Okay Mom, bye, love you both!'

'Love you too, bye Lucy!' She hangs up. I put the TV on trying to make the day go faster as I have to wait for everyone to finish work, I suddenly remember the texts on my phone, and I grab it.

*Hey how was the interview? Sarah x*

I text back.

*I GOT THE JOBBBBBBB!!!!!!!!!!! L X*

I can't be bothered to write anything else, next is Dean's text.

*Luc how'd it go? D x*

I text Dean the exact same message I sent to Sarah, nothing back yet, they both must be busy. I notice the massive pile of dirty laundry staring at me from my bedroom, I put as much as I can in a bin bag and stalk off to the lift for the laundry room. The laundry room is empty which I'm happy about, I split my washing and turn the machines on; as I go to walk out I spot a big sign on the wall, which reads:

*PLEASE DO NOT LEAVE LAUNDRY UNATTENDED!*

I now have to sit in this tiny room that is always so hot from the dryers. I sigh in annoyance, realising I didn't bring my phone or a book, so I cross my arms and slump against the wall. I've been here for 10 minutes and no-one has come in, so I channel my inner ninja and tip-toe along the floor, slowly open the door and look around. I can't hear or see anyone so I leg it to the lift, up to my apartment and grab my phone and my book out my bag, and leg it back down; as I slowly open the laundry door I sigh in relief when no-one is in the laundry room. As I sit down feeling proud of myself, Harold walks in the laundry room. Harold is the maintenance man, he's about

50, stumpy with a beer belly, a grey comb over and dressed in blue overalls. He looks at me and raises his eyebrows.

'Lucy, that sign is there for a reason.' He points at the sign saying not to leave. I shy smile and apologize, he tuts at me and walks out, I look at my phone. I start reading my book, check my phone nothing. It's already one, GEEZ! Where did the day go? I start reading my book.

\*\*\*\*\*\*\*\*\*\*

I'm startled awake by the beeping noise from the washing machine, letting me know it's finished. *How long was I asleep for?!* I get up and put my laundry in the dryer, I wipe my eyes and yawn, Sarah comes bursting in the laundry room, holding the door open with her right arm and panting out of breath, she glares at me.

'What the hell?' I ask surprised by her bursting in.

'Why haven't you been answering your phone?' She's still glaring.

'I was asleep, I feel asleep in the chair and just woke up.' I say scared to move or look away.

'I've been worried about you, I rang the buzzer, no answer, I rang your land line, no answer, I rang and texted your mobile, you scared the shit out of me!' She finally looks away and slumps in the chair, I glance at my phone, five missed calls and three text messages. Ooppss! As Sarah sits in the chair with both her index fingers on her temples with her eyes closed and slowly breathing, I tip-toe around the laundry room, finish putting my wet laundry in the dryer and going to sit next to her.

'Sorry.' I mumble.

'It's okay, I just panicked.' She says without even moving. I try change the subject.

'Sam's coming to stay with me.' I tell her. She sharply turns her head and glares at me one more time.

'Why?'

'She had a fight with Aunty Pauline and needs somewhere to stay.'

'Make sure she doesn't take advantage like before Luc, or she'll have me answer to.' She says, then looks away. She sighs loudly, sits up straight and looks at me with a smile.

'You look so bored, good job you start work on Monday.' I smile at her and sigh. We both laugh when Harold walks in the laundry room and puts his index finger to his lips, shushing us. We both try hold in our laughs, Sarah's phone rings and startles us both.

'Hello... yes... no... can you cover me... it's only half an hour... yeah... thanks... bye.'

'What was that?' I ask, confused.

'I've got the rest of the day off, so we can hang out.'

'Oh okay, my laundry is nearly done, and I'm not allowed to leave it.' I point to the sign.

'Harold told me off for leaving it for five seconds while I snuck up stairs.' I say sarcastically. We both laugh again.

## CHAPTER FIVE

We both carry my massive load of laundry up the stairs, laughing and joking about stuff. Sarah chucks her arm full of laundry on my bed and jumps after it, and lays there.

'I'll fold it and put it away then.' I tease, she doesn't move but I can see her smile, she kicks her shoes off and gets under my duvet.

'HEY!' I tease and throw socks at her. As I'm hanging my laundry, I hear a knock at the door, so I walk over and open the door and there is Harold, holding a pair of my panties in his index finger and thumb like they're a nuclear weapon at arm's length. I blush and thank him, but he just rolls his eyes and walks off. I run back into my bedroom laughing trying to explain to Sarah why I'm laughing, when I hear another knock at the door.

'Harold is back for more.' I joke, as I swing the door open and Sam is standing at my front door. As she stands there I look her up and down, she looks a lot more grown up since when I last saw her, her mid length auburn hair, big brown eyes, wearing a summer dress with black pumps.

'How did you get in the building?' She looks shocked and blushes.

'Sorry a man let me in'.

'It's okay.' I hold the door open for her to walk in. Sarah walks around the corner and laughs.

'Was it Harold with your pants again?' She suddenly stops mid-walk and looks Sam up and down.

'Hey Sam' she finally says.

'Do you two want a coffee?' I ask, trying to ignore the tension. They both nod.

'Sam, follow me' I say. She follows me into the spare room.

'This will be your room for a bit, but I need a favour.' Sam nods.

'My parents are staying on Friday night, so do you mind if they stay in here and you sleep on the sofa?'

'No, I don't mind' Sam whispers.

'Are you okay?'

'Yeah sorry just a bit nervous' she mutters.

'Okay, well I'll leave you to unpack' and I walk out, making a face at Sarah. Sarah stands close behind and whispers in my ear.

'What's wrong with her?' I shrug my shoulders.

'She's never quiet', Sarah agrees. *Weird.* The kettle finishes boiling and I make three coffees. As I put them on the coffee table, Sam walks out her room.

'I like your apartment' Sam says. I love my apartment. Gemma and I inherited it from our Nanna who died three years ago from cancer.

'What you making for dinner?' Sarah asks me.

'I was thinking of making spaghetti Bolognese, but I have to go shopping if I want to make that' I frown.

'I need to go to a shop so I'll go' Sam chirps up. I look at Sarah, Sarah nods towards Sam as if to say 'yes get her to do it'.

'That's really helpful thanks, let me write you a list' I run off to the kitchen grabbing my pen and pad of paper.


*Shopping list*

*1. 5 big mushrooms*
*2. Tomatoes*
*3. Cheese*
*4. Sweet corn (loose)*
*5. Bottle of white and red wine*

I pass the list to Sam, and hand her forty dollars.

'Thanks Sam that's really helpful of you' I say with a smile. She takes the money and list.

'I'll be back shortly' she replies and shuts the door behind her.

'Whoa' Sarah says.
'I know it's strange. I'm going to email Gem.' Sarah nods at me and turns the TV on; I turn my laptop on and see I have a reply from Gemma.

*From: Gemma Winter*
*Subject: Sam*
*To: Lucy Winter*
*11/16/10 14:37*

*WOW IM SO HAPPY FOR YOU…. I now have a big-shot sister.*

I smile at the reply I have. Gemma always makes me smile. We're close in age, she's only two years younger than me but we have always got on and hardly ever argue. We act like we're best friends when we meet up, and I really can't wait to see her at Christmas. I've got her the coolest present, she's been after this dress in Bloomingdales for months but they have never had one in her size, so I asked Sarah extremely nicely if she could get one. Of course, Sarah held up her end of the bargain and got it for me. Sarah laughs rather loud that makes me jump.

'Have you spoken to Jack or Dean? I ask.

'No, I haven't, want me to ring them?' She looks at me.

'Yeah tell them to be here for six-thirty, to bring a bottle each and warn them Sam is going to be here.'

'Oh, right yeah, two secs and I'll phone them, do you think Belle will come?'

'I haven't told her or invited her' Sarah turns quickly and looks at me.

'Are you jealous?'

'No' I say too quickly.

'Yeah right Luc, you give Jack mixed messages.'

'Whoa, where did that come from?' I snap at Sarah.

'Well you say you don't like him, then you're all over him the other night at the club, then you sleep with him and never mention it.'

'WHAT?!' I yell, getting angry.

'You...slept.... with...him.' She says like I'm stupid and

didn't understand what she said.

'No, I didn't.'

'Yes, you did Luc!'

'How do you know?' I snap back.

'I could hear you, you kept me awake.' She says looking back at the T.V.

'OH MY GOD!' I put my head in my hands. Sarah gets up and comes over to me.

'Did you really not remember?' She asks.

'No, I didn't!' I don't know if I should cry or not.

'You two would make a perfect couple, give him a chance Luc.' She looks down at me and hugs me.

'I've been thinking about him the last couple of days.'

'Oh, have you? Do you like him?' Sarah questions.

'I don't know, I think I do' I shudder at the thought of that night again, I suddenly think.

'Does Jack remember sleeping with me?' I ask coyly.

'I spoke to him about that night and he doesn't seem to remember either, Dean and Belle were both asleep, so I don't think they know, so it's our little secret.'

I'm still worried.

'Don't worry Luc,' she says and pats my arm, 'now go have a shower and look stunning for Jack.' Sam comes walking in the door with couple of bags of shopping, Sarah pushes me to my room, saying 'GO' forcefully. She helps Sam unpack the bag and puts the wine in the fridge, I can hear them talking but can't make out what they're saying. I poke my head around my bedroom door and shout.

'SARAH, RING THE BOYS!'

'Oh shit!' I hear Sarah run across the living room for her phone, I shut the door and get ready for a shower, my phone starts ringing.

I jump in the shower singing 'Toxic' by Britney Spears. I spend longer than I have to, making sure I've shaved. I feel all girly and pampered, and half an hour later I step out the shower in a very good mood. As I walk out the bathroom I look at Sarah and double take as I see Drake sitting with her and there talking, I clear my throat and they both look at me, Sarah with a massive grin on her face.

'Afternoon Lucy.' Drake says.

'Hi, what are you doing here?' I say sharply.

'Well I phoned you and I had no answer and I got worried so came over to check you were okay?' He says with his big eyes making my insides melt.

'How do you know where I live?' I ask warily.

'It was on your C.V. that I read this morning.' He says. *Damn it.* Sarah butts in.

'I have told you you're a very stressful person to get hold of...' She teases.

'Okay, okay, I'm getting dressed.' I stalk off to my room. I check my phone – four missed calls, damn it. Why do I never hear my phone? Sarah is behind me like a shot.

'Who is that? He's so dreamy!'

'That's my new boss at Teely's International, his name is Drake Teely.' Her mouth drops open and she stares at me.

'He's hot...'

'Yes, I know.' I turn and walk into my wardrobe, to my surprise Sarah follows me in.

'Can you please wait in my room while I change?' I look at her with an eyebrow raised.

'Yeah sure.' She says daydreaming, I quickly change into a summery dress, and throw my towels in the wash basket. I automatically think of my Mum, she would have told me off for putting wet towels in the basket, I smile at the memory and Sarah pops her head around the corner again.

'Ready yet?'

As I'm looking in the mirror sorting my hair, Sarah is still blabbering about Drake.

'SARAH!' I say sharply which stops her talking, and she looks at me.

'If you like him, then go for it.'

'I might just try things with Jack.' She squeals kisses my cheek and runs out the room, I hear the buzzer go and someone talking. I wipe my big panda eyes and walk out my room, I'm met by a hoard of people; Jack, Nick, Jack's good friend, Belle, Dean, Sam, Sarah and rake, they all have drinks and are talking amongst themselves. I walk to the kitchen and to my surprise the spaghetti is boiling in a saucepan and so is the Bolognese sauce. I turn and Sam is smiling at me from the other side of the room. 'Cheers' I mouth to her. I carry plates to the table and set out eight places on my six people table, and put knives and forks out. I clink a glass and get everyone's attention and shout 'SIT'. Everyone looks at me and heads for the table all taking the glasses; I put the bottles of wine in the middle of the table with a bowl of grated cheese, and start serving dinner out. Everyone holds their wine glasses up and shouts 'CHEERS', I blush a little.

The conversation between everyone flows naturally, with lots of laughing and joking. The bottles of wine empty quickly and Dean and Drake go out for more. While they're gone, I leave the table, putting the dishes in the sink. *Gives me something to do tomorrow,* I think. *How sad.* We sprawl over the sofas and chairs, awaiting the arrival of the extra wine. The boys come back and we drink for a couple more hours. It reaches eleven-thirty, Nick helps pick up Jack from the floor and leaves, Dean and Belle follow, Sam goes to her room, and Sarah and Drake are going to share a cab home. I say night, kiss Sarah on the cheek, lock the door and retire to bed. I don't even have the energy to get undressed, I just get comfortable in my dress under the duvet. As I'm drifting off to sleep I hear a weak male voice shout 'I LOVE YOU LUCY!' I know instantly its Jack. That makes me smile.

**********

I wake up to a knocking on my door. I sleepily tell them to come in. It's Sam; she walks in with a mug.

'Thought you might need a coffee.' She says placing it down and walks out.

'Thanks.' I say through a yawn. I stretch and get out of bed, grab my dressing gown, and stumble to the living room to dump myself on the couch.

'Is that it?' I groan. I look at Sam.

'Have anything to do today?' I ask her.

'No not really, I'm going to look for a temp job, to help with bills and stuff.' She replies.

'Oh…' I'm shocked, I wasn't expecting that. I smile at her and give her a little nod, I dose off on the sofa and wake up suddenly to a warm liquid spilling on my lap. Sam can't help but laugh, which I don't blame her for, I now have a brown dressing gown. I stalk to my room and throw it in the laundry basket, again thinking of my Mum. I put on my other dressing gown and grab my phone to text Sarah.

*Hey Sar did you have fun with Drake ;) L x*

I immediately get a response back.

*Hey Luc, he dropped me home in the cab and went home* ☹
☹ ☹

Oh, she must feel heartbroken. I text Jack, teasing him about his lovely shouting last night.

*Jack, I know you love me but do you have to shout it at 23:45 ;) L x*

I can imagine Jack is at work slumped over his desk with a big hangover, he doesn't take drinking lightly. I always make fun of him. I decide to surprise him, and I call his office and to make sure he's at work today. The very cheery receptionist confirms he's clocked in; I quickly get dressed and haul a taxi outside my building. As I get out outside his building, I notice the conveniently located coffee shack, I grab two lattes and head inside. The woman recognizes me and shouts 'fourth floor' I smile and nod at her and I run to the lift before it shuts. As I arrive on fourth floor, I see Jack doing exactly what I thought he would, slumping over his desk holding his head.

'Surprise stranger.' I whisper. He jumps up and looks at me with a frown.

'Hey.' He manages to say, then his head goes back in his hands.

'I brought you some coffee.' I hand it to him, smiling.

'Sorry I shouted I loved you last night.' He groans.

'It's okay, it made me laugh.' I reassure him.

'Good, I like your smile.' He grabs the coffee and takes a swig.

'Have you had breakfast?' I ask.

'No, I got up late.'

'Come on let's get a bagel.' He reluctantly gets up and follows me to the lift, he leans against me as if I'm keeping him up.

'I need to go to the bathroom quickly.' He says, as we reach the bottom floor he runs off and I wait in the lobby. After about five minutes he returns from the bathroom with a grin on his face.

'You okay?' I ask.

'I just threw up.'

'Eurgh.' That automatically make me feel queasy.

'I feel a lot better now,' he smiles at me, 'but now I'm hungry.'

'Betty's?' I look up at him, he smiles and nods, GEEZ! He's handsome today, his grey suit pants, which hang off his hips, a white shirt tucked in and a black tie. He puts his arm round my shoulder and he pulls me close.

'Are you cold?' He asks me. Now I feel his body heat on me, I feel cold, I wrap my arms around his waist and we walk arm in arm until we reach Betty's. We walk over to the table we always sit on; the waitress comes straight over.

'Here again?' She smiles.

'Can I have a bagel with scrambled egg, pancakes with bacon and the biggest coffee you can get me?' Jack orders and smiles at the waitress then at me.

'Oh, I'll have pancakes with bacon and a coffee please.' She writes it down quickly smiles and walks off, I look at Jack. 'Sounds like you haven't eaten in about a week.' I smile. My phone beeps, I groan.

'It never stops...' I sigh, before reading it. It's from Dean.

*Hey can I pop over? Dean x*

I quickly peek at Jack then back at my phone and text him back.

*I'm at Betty's with your brother come join us X*

Jack's phone then beeps, he smiles at the screen and puts it straight down, I then feel really jealous to who made him smile. I curiously ask him:

'Anyone good?'

'Just someone from the office.' He smiles.

'Dean just texted me, so I invited him here.' I add.

'Okay that's cool; did he say if he was hungry?'

'I didn't ask.' I feeling myself blush.

'I'll text him.' He says, then fiddles with his phone for five minutes. While I'm sat there awkwardly, I stare out the window, thinking about my new job and how excited I am to start. The waitress brings our drinks over and says our food will be here in five. We both nod, Dean comes in the café door, smacks Jack on the back and kisses my head.

'You two alright?' Dean asks. Jack just nods but doesn't look away from his phone.

'Rude.' Dean says which makes Jack look up.

'Sorry, I was reading an email from Gemma.' I sigh in relief.

'Jack threw up.' I quickly say, then I frown. *Why did I just say that?* Jack and Dean both look at me, as confused as I am.

'Well anyway, last night was fun wasn't it?' Dean adds.

'Yeah, it was good, where's Belle?' I suddenly realize she didn't follow him in.

'She's packing, because she's leaving tonight.' He frowns.

'Oh, I didn't think it was so soon.' I sense his sadness.

'Yeah she has to go back, to her job and her life.'

'Whoosh her off her feet and ask her to stay, she obviously makes you happy!' I suggest.

'Shall I?'

'Yes,' I say eagerly, 'call her now.' I pass him my phone. Dean disappears outside and I can see him talking and smiling. Jack looks at me and says,

'That was a really nice thing you just did.'

'Well when you have the chance, you must seize the day.' I smile at wink at Jack, just as our food arrives. He looks at me stunned. I tuck into my breakfast as Dean walks back in.

'She wants to stay but she wants to talk to her family first,' he says, 'she wants me to go with her.' He adds.

'Go with her then.' I offer.

'I don't want to go on my own.' He says. Jack pipes up with his mouth full and spits.

'She doesn't start work till Monday, take her to England.' He says, pointing his knife at me.

'Me?!' I say in shock.

'Will you come with me Luc?'

'Err, sure how much will it be? I ask.

'I'll pay for you, we can leave tonight and be back in time for Monday.' He says grabs my phone and runs outside again. Jack looks at me and says:

'Well, when you have the chance you must seize the day…'
He smiles his sexy smile again it makes me melt.
'Don't you have work to do?' I say quickly, secretly loving the England idea. He looks at his watch and shakes his head.

'The boss is in a meeting till twelve-ish I have loads of time.'
Dean comes bounding in the café.

'The flights are booked, take off is at seven, so meet me at the bottom of your building at four, yeah?' he kisses my hair gives me my phone back and disappears. I finish eating my breakfast and drink my coffee. I best start packing then and I have to tell Sarah so she can keep an eye on Sam, what about my mum and dad tonight? *OH SHIT*. I hadn't worked this out. I ring Sarah but no answer, I text her.

*Sarah ring me ASAP Lucy xxx*

'Is everything okay?' Jack looks at me and asks.

'No.' I answer sharply.

'What's wrong?'

'My parents are coming to stay with me tonight but I won't be there because you shipped me off to England!' I whine.

70

'Oh shit,' he answers, 'I totally forgot about your parents, I can keep them occupied.' He answers. At the moment my phone beeps.

*I can't phone I'm with a client, what's up? S x*

I stand up from the table.

'Where are you going?' Jack asks.

'To pack my things and to speak to Sarah.' I say and walk off; I set to text Sarah back.

*I'll be at your shop in two secs, I'll be your next client it's important x*

I ran as quickly as I can in my UGG boots. I reach Bloomingdales, I run in and up to the customer service desk.

'Hi can you please call Sarah Wildon, it's an emergency.' I say out of breath.

'Of course.' She walks to the microphone and speaks elegantly over the speakers.

*'THIS IS A STAFF ANNOUNCEMENT CAN SARAH WILDON PLEASE REPORT TO THE CUSTOMER SERVICE DESK NOW, I REPEAT THIS IS A STAFF ANNOUNCEMENT CAN SARAH WILDON PLEASE REPORT TO THE CUSTOMER SERVICE DESK NOW, THANK YOU.'*

I smile and mutter my thanks as I still try to catch my breath, Sarah comes running around the corner and hugs me.

'Is everything okay?' She looks at the woman on reception.

'Can you get Shelley to cover my client and if anyone asks for me say I'm taking personal time' and we walk into the back room.

'Lucy what the fuck is going on?' She glares at me.

'It's not that important, I just had to talk to you before four.' I add in.

'Why? What's happened?'

'Nothing, calm down, and sit down, I've got a long story.' Sarah sits down and stares at me.

'Dean has fallen in love with Belle, but she's going home today, I said to ask Belle to stay, but she has to go home and speak to her family, and Jack told him I'd go with him as I don't start my new job till Monday, then he booked and paid for my ticket and I leave at four, my parents are coming to stay with me tonight and Sam will be alone in my apartment.' I stop for breath.

'Breathe for God's sake Luc.' Sarah finally says with a worried face, I go to speak again and Sarah holds her finger up to my mouth.

'You did a good thing about Belle and Dean, have a good time away, I'll get Jack to deal with your parents, and I'll deal with Sam, now go home and get ready because you have to leave in a couple of hours.' She hugs me and sends me on my way. I make my way back to the apartment and I start to get excited.

'I'm going to London!' I say to myself. I get to the apartment and I explain the situation to Sam, and tell her my parents can stay in my room. I quickly turn my laptop on and email Gemma.

*From: Lucy Winter*
*Subject: England*
*To: Gemma Winter*
*11/18/10 15:30*

*Hey Gem I'm going to England for a day... Yes, a day*
*Don't panic, Mum is here if you need her, I'll email you*
*when I'm back*
*Love you Luc xx*

I start packing and put my iPod on my dock and blast out Kesha's 'Tik Tok'. Time catches up with me and it's suddenly it's time to go. I grab my passport, my phone, my credit card, and say bye to Sam. About ten minutes later, Dean is pulling up in a taxi, he jumps out and puts my case in the trunk Jack gets out the other side, he stands about an inch in front of me, puts his left arm on the bottom of my back and the other behind my head. For a moment I freeze, thinking he is going to kiss me, but he just hugs me. As I pull away, his hand on my back pulls me against his body and pins me there, and he leans his head down to mine and kisses me right on the lips. I take a second to kiss back as I'm frozen to the spot; he pulls away and as he does I open my eyes and he flashes me

73

his perfect smile. He leans to my ear and whispers,

'I'll see you when you get back.' He slaps my ass as he enters my building. I squeal not expecting the slap, Dean just laughs and gets back in the taxi.

'Sorry I sprung this on you.' He says looking out the window.

'It's okay, I'm quite looking forward to it actually.' I answer with a smile, one that Jack put on my face.

'Belle is already at the airport, she was getting an earlier flight and they had no seats left. We have quite a trip ahead of us, thanks for coming.' Dean says while grabbing my hand.

'It's seriously okay,' I squeeze his hand back, 'but why do we have a long trip?' I ask curiously.

'Well, we have our flight to London Gatwick airport, then we have to get a cab to a train station called Waterloo, then on a train for an hour to Petersfield.' Dean lists.

'Oh, I see.' It makes me tired thinking of it. I feel sorry for Belle having to do this on her own, I think I would cry, sit cuddling my knees and rock back and forth, like a little child. At the airport, I grab a magazine at JFK for our train ride to Petersfield, but when I sit back down next to Dean in duty free, I only read half the contents pages before I feel sick, sitting up straight.

'Is there a toilet in this airport?' I ask. Dean just points to the far side and looks up at the screen, watching for our gate number. As I am trying to get to the toilet as quickly as I can,

I stumble over something. Dean shouts to me,

'BE CAREFUL FOR GOD'S SAKE WE DON'T HAVE
TIME FOR A HOSPITAL!'

I get up and walk back and sit down looking embarrassed, I
pick up my magazine and start reading.

# CHAPTER SIX

Finally, we're on the train to Petersfield. It was quite an easy trip actually, and now I get to sleep for an hour. I get nudged by the train guard asking for my ticket, I sleepily look at him and point to Dean and mumble 'he has it' so that I can go back to sleep. After what feels like a minute later, I get woken up again.

'We're here!' He says to me with a massive grin on his face.

'Really, that was quick?' I sleepily get up and grab my case, I see Belle standing on the platform waiting for us. I give a little wave and smile, we walk out to the front of the station and climb into a cab waiting outside. Belle is talking to the cab driver and it's interesting listening to the way they speak to each other. He starts driving on the wrong side of the road, it's strange, and Petersfield is deserted.

'What time is it here?' I ask.

'Eleven in the morning.' The cab driver barks back. Whilst we ride in the cab, I look out the window, watching the streets as we go. After a couple of minutes, we arrive outside a house. Belle deals with the cab cost and says goodbye as we all grab our suitcases and scramble out. I stand on the sidewalk with Dean like a lost sheep waiting for Belle to finish talking another language with the driver. She looks at us both before beckoning us to follow. We both kick our cases onto the wheels and pull along the sidewalk. We follow her into the house and I can hear the loveliest sound; the family are talking amongst themselves and laughing. It reminds me of the house Gemma, Jack, Dean and I grew up in and I smile. Belle introduces us to her family whilst they all hug and say hello to Dean.

'This is my mother Angie.' Belle says and I shake her hand.

'This is my father Michael.' I shake his hand.

'This is my younger brother Reece.'

'Your house is lovely.' I mumble, feeling a bit awkward.

'Thank you very much,' Angie answers, 'anyone want some tea or coffee?'

'Oh yes please, black coffee, thanks.' I reply. I need the caffeine. Everyone in the room sits in silence, instantly I feel awkward again. I look out the window, and to my surprise, I see chickens.

'I love this house.' I whisper to myself.

Angie walks in with our teas and coffees and they all ask about our trip, mostly talking to Belle and Dean. I study the room, it's a light green with brown leather sofas, pictures everywhere of the family, with plants and flowers. I feel at ease in this house the more I look around. While I try and seemed involved in the conversation I finish my coffee and clutch the cup.

'Want to go for a walk around the heath?' Dean looks at me.

'Sure,' I answer, 'I need some air before I fall asleep.'

'Jet-lag will do that to ya.' Michael adds, as I thank Angie. As we walk along the streets almost everyone stops to speak to Belle, like a story you read in a book about a princess. A while after, we reach the heath and it's breathtaking. There's a kid's playground on my left, with big willow trees, ducks and swans floating on the pond, the kids running around in, what I'm told are called, wellie boots and big coats giggling with glee. We see people walking their dogs, it's wonderful to take a slow and peaceful walk around the big heath. As we reach where we started Belle leads up some steps and slowly strolls down a long road with big beautiful trees each side, it's extremely calm here. We reach a small town with some shops, and Belle walks us towards a café. Dean turns to me,

'Go find somewhere to sit Luc, I'll be five minutes.' I go inside and find a nice seat. I shudder, not realising how cold I was until I walked into the heat. Dean comes in and sits opposite me.

'Belle is going home to speak to her family.' He sighs.

'So, we're hanging out here till she's done?' I ask.

'Pretty much Luc.' He looks really sad and twiddles his thumbs and looks at them. I've never seen him like this before, and I really feel for him.

'So, what are we going to do?' I say making Dean jump.

'Sit here.' He answers.

'Is there nothing else to do around here?'

'Yeah probably, but I don't know.'

'Want a drink?' Dean shakes his head; I get up and go over to the worker behind the bar.

'Is there anything to do around here?' I ask.

'Depends what you like.'

'We're up for anything, we have to kill three hours.' I respond.

'Well, the best way to occupy your time is to go the arcades down on the seafront, south sea' he says. I raise my eyebrows and look around at Dean, he's still sadly looking at his hands. The worker picks up a napkin and a pen and starts writing something down. He then hands it to me, I read it, realize its instructions on how to get to this south sea, so I jog over to Dean grab his arm and pull him up to his feet.

'What you doing?' He looks at me.

'We're going to some arcades and a seafront.' I add, grabbing my stuff.

'You don't know where you're going.' He sounds angry. I hold up the piece of napkin and flap it in the air.

'I do actually!' I pull him out the shop. We walk back up to the train station after asking about seven people for directions, I read the napkin and crinkle my brow.

*At Petersfield station get on a train heading to Portsmouth harbour, the fast one not the slow one (ask the train man). Stay on until it says Portsmouth harbour (the last stop). Get off, down the steps and walk around the barriers and walk to the taxi rank and ask for a taxi to south parade pier or a bus and get the bus or passengers to tell you when to get off.*

I can't handle that in a place I don't know so I run up to a taxi and ask him to take us to South Parade Pier. The cab driver looks at me.

'Yeah okay love, it's going to be pricey.' I shrug, wave Dean over and we climb in the cab.

'Do you know where you're going?' I ask the cab driver.

'Yes love, it's my job.' He retorts. I spot the sea on in front of us, almost leaning over the cab driver to see it. There're joggers, people walking dogs, people flying kites, and lights flashing, and a cheery tune playing inviting us to the arcade. I'm so amazed how picture perfect this place looks. We exit the cab and I run across the road dragging Dean with me. We enter the arcades, full of blinking machines. I walk over to the person sitting in what looks like a cage with CHANGE COUNTER above them.

'What money do I need?' I throw my dollars from my pocket on the counter. The man scoops up my money in his hand and grabs a blue pot, he puts some big brown coins in the pot and hands it all back.

'The money in the pot is for the two penny machines.' He points at my hand.

'Okay, two pennies.' I add with a smile on my face. Dean has instantly cheered up. For the next couple of minutes, we play on the machines until I run out of money.

'Want to walk on the beach?' Dean asks while grabbing my hand.

'Sure.' I answer. As we walk outside the wind hits us in the face and my hair stands on end, we both giggle and stroll along the beach.

'I thought beaches had sand.' I ask confused.

'Yeah me too, Luc.' Dean looks at me with a crinkled brow. He reluctantly gets his ringing cell out his pocket and answers it.

'Hey Belle,' he raises his eyes at me, 'yeah… we're at south sea… cab… yeah… yeah, she's here… okay… yeah now… okay bye.' I look at him waiting to hear what she had to say.

'She's finished.' Dean says.

'Okay we can go find a cab back then,' I say, 'did she say how it went?' I ask, wary. Dean just shakes his head. I grab my bag and Dean follows me as we find a cab.

********

We arrive in Petersfield outside Belle's house. We walk up the drive and the door swings open before we even reach it. Belle has a massive smile on her face that makes both our shoulders relax, and she nods and hugs Dean.
I wait awkwardly behind them until they break from the embrace they had.
We all make our way into the house and all our cases are sat in the sitting room.

'I'll give you a lift back to Gatwick, shall I?' Michael says making me jump. I quickly turn and he's in the doorway holding car keys. I kick the bottom of my case to set it on its wheels and say my goodbyes to everyone on the way out the door. Belle and her family hug and her mom cries, which makes my eyes water. I look away and wait outside before I become a blubbering mess. A couple of minutes later Dean and Belle emerge from the house, Michael loads our cases and we wave goodbye once more.

*********

I wake suddenly by smacking my head on the window as my hand slips from my chin.

82

'Are you okay?' Belle asks.

'Yeah I'm fine are we here?' I look around half asleep.

'Nearly, about another ten minutes.' Michael says from the front seat.

'I've slept more in England than I think I ever have in the York.' I say.

'True that.' Dean nods, he looks like him old self again, happy-go-lucky.

'Is there an internet café in the airport,' I ask suddenly remembering I haven't emailed Gemma since I left, or spoken to Jack, 'can I phone the York in the airport?' I add, fidgeting in my seat.

'I'm not sure Luc, I'll ask someone.' Dean says and we come to a stop in the car, Michael gets out so we all follow.

'Bye Bells.' Michael says, as he is wrapping his arms around her.

'I'll see you at Christmas, won't I?' She sniffs. *Oh no please don't start crying again, I'm so tired I don't need a reason to cry.*

'You will see us at Christmas, Bells.' he answers.

'Good, I look forward to it.' They hug once more. Michael shakes Dean's hand and says sternly:
'Look after my little girl.'

'I fully intend to, sir.' He replies. Michael hugs me to my surprise.

'Thanks.' I whisper.

'See you kids very soon!' He waves to us and gets back in the car. As we stroll through the airport I see a set of pay phones.

'Dean!' I exclaim and run off. I scurry off to the phones and read a list next to the phone which has different countries written on it with numbers, I skim down the list until I find New York, I drop my cases and reach in my pocket for my change, as I fill the machine up, I quickly dial 002 and then type in my home number.

'Hello?' A voice on the other end of the phone answers.

'Hi, it's Lucy who's this?' A screech comes through the phone.

'It's Mom!'

'Mom.' I sigh, so glad to hear her voice that I instantly relax.

'How are you mom?'

'I'm fine dear, so is your dad, Jack has been looking after us very well'

'Good, were at the airport now, we have to wait another two hours for our flight' I add.

'What time is it there dear?' Mom asks. I glance around for a clock before answering.

'Six, I'll be in the York at about eleven, is Jack there?'

'Okay, we can stay and wait for you.'

'Yes, Mom, please. Can I speak to Jack?' I ask.

'Of course, honey.' The phone ruffles around for a bit and I hear whispering in the background.

'I'M PAYING A FORTUNE FOR THIS CALL!' I shout down the phone, and then someone quickly comes on the line.

'Hello?' The voice says, I recognize it instantly and I melt inside.

'Jack' I say.

'Yeah, what's up?' He says, not very happy to hear from me at all.

'Can you get us from the airport at eight-ish tonight your time?'

'If I have to' he says. I crinkle my brow.

'If you don't want to Jack, just say no.'

'Lucy I'll be there okay?' he says sounding angry. Belle and Dean both watching me, frowning listening to my side of the conversation.

'Okay, thank you, JFK yeah?'

'Yes, at eight, I heard you' he says.

'I'm bored of your attitude, Jack, put my mom back on.' The
phone then rustles again and I hear a faint beep beep beep.
And the line is dead. SHIT.

'What happened?' Dean says looking confused.

'Jack sounded angry, but he's picking us up at eight-ish.'
Dean senses from my tone not to ask any more questions,
Belle opens her mouth to say something, and then Dean cuts
in.

'Drinks?' He asks, then gives Belle a look and shakes his
head.

*I smile to myself; I'm really looking forward to seeing mom
and dad, oh and Sarah.*

'Is Sam still at yours?' Dean asks bringing me to life from my
thoughts.

*SHIT. I totally forgot…*

'I don't know.' I sit and wonder if she is.

'You don't think she ticked off Jack, do you?' Dean says, not
making eye contact with me
'Oh god…' I never thought of that.

'What?' Belle asks not understanding what we're talking about.

'Nothing' Dean adds and we don't say anything else on the matter. We pretty much sit in silence for the rest of the wait.

'What are you reading?' I ask Belle. She ignores me until Dean elbows her and puts her book down and looks at Dean, he points at me with his chin, Belle then looks at me.

'Sorry Lucy?'

'What you reading?' I ask again.

'Breaking Dawn' she answers. I look confused and then mumble in reply:

'What's Breaking Dawn?' She stares at me in disbelief, and I get the feeling I'm going to instantly regret asking this.

'It's from the Twilight Saga' she states.

'What's Twilight? She slaps her book on her legs.

'Have you never heard of it?'

'No' I whisper feeling embarrassed. Dean suddenly stands so we both look at him.

'They're calling us, let's go!'

\*\*\*\*\*\*\*\*\*\*

I sit on the plane, uncomfortable in my seat, not ready for a five-hour flight back to the York. I put my head on the head rest and sigh, the flight attendant at the front of the plane waving her arms around and smiling, I stare out the window. I feel a tap on my shoulder I look around and see another flight attendant standing there smiling.

'Would you like a drink?' She asks me.

'Oh yes please, something alcoholic.' I look away, she returns about five minutes later with a small bottle and a glass, and I smile.

**************

*I get to the bottom of my building and a taxi pulls up. Dean and Jack get out, Dean grabs my case and Jack stands in front of me.*

Wait – WHAT?

*This has happened before. Jack stands about an inch in front of me, puts his left arm on the bottom of my back and the other behind my head, for a moment I freeze thinking he is going to kiss me, but he just hugs me. As I pull away his hand on my back pulls me against his body and pins me there, and he leans his head down to mine and kisses me right on the lips. I take a second to kiss back as I'm frozen to the spot, he pulls away and as he does I open my eyes and he flashes me his perfect smile. He leans down and whispers*

*'I'll see you when you get back' and slaps my ass as he enters my building. I squeal not expecting the slap.*

I jolt and wake up on the plane.

'Oh god it was a dream…' I whisper wiping the sweat from my forehead. I sit there, confused about why I dreamt of the moment I left Jack before I went to England.

**********

We touchdown in NYC, collect our suit cases, and I already feel settled knowing I'm back home. We all fight our way through the crowds and wait out the front looking for Jack, but he is nowhere to be seen.

'Where is he then?' Dean pipes up. I shrug my shoulders.

'I told him we would be here at eight.' At that moment we all jump as we hear a car horn, we look to our left and a cab pulls up, Jack jumps out.

'If you weren't driving we could have got a cab on our own.' I say, walking straight past him to put my case in the trunk. We all climb in the cab and sit in awkward silence until we reach my building. I get out and Jack follows me, I grab my case, hug Dean and Belle and say good night.

'I'll buzz you tomorrow Dean, bye Belle.' They both wave at me and the cab carries on.
'Why did you get out?' I snap at Jack.

'Whoa Luc what's eating you?'

'What?! I exclaim, but Jack just stares at me.

'You were so rude to me on the phone, I don't want to be around you at the moment, I'm so tired, and I'll see you tomorrow.' Jack just stares at me as I walk in the building, I call the lift, walk in and slump against the wall. It dings on the sixth floor, I reach my apartment, swing the door open, and walk in. Sam is on the sofa with the TV on.

'Hi Sam!' I shout over the TV.

'Oh hi.' She turns the TV off and gets up.

'Did you have a good time?' She asks eagerly.

'Yes, thanks. Where are my parents?' I look around.

'In my room asleep.'

*Oh, shit I slammed the door open.*

'I'm going to bed Sam, I'm exhausted.' I say while yawning.

'Okay night.'

\*\*\*\*\*\*\*\*\*\*

I wake up from the sun shining in my bedroom window and can hear some birds; I sit up, wondering what the noise in the kitchen is. I open my bedroom door still in my clothes from last night; my mom is in the kitchen singing 'Slow Dancing in a Burning Room'.

'I like that song.' I say through a yawn.

'Me too,' Mom answers, 'it's mine and your dad's first dance song from when we renewed our wedding vows.' I coo at her, but I can see she didn't appreciate that.

'What are you doing today? I quickly ask her.

'Spending the day with you kids.' She says smiling.

'Oh, that's nice.' I smile back.

'They will be here soon, I'm making breakfast for you all, so you don't need to eat at that greasy café...' She says looking me up and down. I instantly feel self-conscious, so I leap off the worktop and stalk out the kitchen. I sit on the breakfast bar the other side, and turn my laptop on, and see I have an email from Gemma.

*From: Gemma Winter*
*Subject: ENGLAND!!!*
*To: Lucy Winter*
*11/18/10 17:57*

*ENGLAND!! For heaven's sake why?*
*Be safe I know what you're like.........*
*Gemma xx*

I hit reply.

*From: Lucy Winter*
*Subject: homeward bound*
*To: Gemma Winter*

*11/19/10 09:47*

***I'M HOME…***
***I had a fun time actually***
***I fell over in the airport but other than that it's all gravy***
***baby***
***Luc x***

The apartment door knocks, and 'the gang' *as my dad calls us* stride in. Jack doesn't make eye contact with me, but they both hug Mom and Dad. Belle walks up to my parents.

'Hi, I'm Belle.'

'Oh, you're Dean's girlfriend from England.' Mom squeals.

'Yes, I am!' Belle lets out a little giggle. Everyone sits around the table, I grab plates and cutlery, and hand out drinks. We all eat our breakfast in silence with just Mom asking questions and receiving short answers.

'What the hell is going on?!' Dad suddenly shouts, dropping his cutlery. Everyone looks at him in shock, and then Jack and I look away.

'What is going on between you two?' He asks just staring at us. I go red and get up from the table.

'David, you've upset her.' Mom slaps his shoulder.

'What's up, darling?' She gets up and pulls me by the arm to my room. I tear up before confessing.

'Jack kissed me before I went to England, and was rude to me on the phone.'

'So, you're upset about Jack?' I nod.

'I think I have jet-lag.'

'That won't do, will it my sweet?' Mom says as she wipes the tears from my face and straightens out my hair where it's still rumpled from sleep. I shake my head and steady my breathing. She gets up, opens my bedroom door and shouts for Jack. I hear chair legs squeak across the floor and Jack walking towards my door.

'You two need to talk.' Mom pushes him in my room and shuts the door behind him. Jack sits on my bed looking awkward.

'What's wrong?'

'Don't start that Jack.' I sniff. He moves closer and hugs me, kisses my head and we sit like this for a couple of minutes. Jack then speaks into my hair.

'I like you Luc, you know that, I'm just waiting for you to let me know when you feel the same way back.'

'I know,' I sniff, 'I do.' He lets me go and holds me at arm's length.

'You do?' I nod my head and wipe my nose with my sleeve in the least lady like way.

'How long have you felt the same?' He asks, pulling me closer.

'For the last couple of weeks, and when you kissed me I was surprised but happy you did.' He smiles.
'I didn't know you felt the same way, that's why I was snappy on the phone.'

'Oh.' Is all I can think of to say back to that. There is a tiny knock at the bedroom door.

'Come in.' I say trying to stop crying. Mom walks in and see's us hugging; she smiles.

'You kid's going to finish your breakfast?' We both get off the end of my bed and follow her out. As we start eating again there is no awkward silence everyone is talking trying to be heard over each other, laughing and having a good family moment. I help mom clear the table and wash up, while the guys all go to the sofa and turn on the football.

'You two made up then?' She smiles.

'Yeah sort of.' I smile back.

'Do you mind if me and your Dad stay again.' She asks.

'No, I love you being here, all of us being together, it reminds me of when we were all younger.' I look at the mug I'm drying up.

'We like that too, we love being here.' She smiles and hugs me.

'Do you mind if I go and see Sarah for a bit?' I ask.

'No of course not dear, go see your friend.' I walk out the kitchen, grab my bath towel and head to the bathroom, have a lovely warm long shower, I'm in there longer then I normally am. As I walk out Jack looks at me like he caught me doing something I shouldn't be, I frown and close my bedroom door, slump on the end of my bed and pick up my phone from the bed side table.

*Hey Sarah what you doinggg? Want to get drunk? x*

I put my phone on my bed as I dig out some warm clothes. My phone beeps and I jump with joy, it's Sarah.

*Hey babes I'm doing nothing YES I would like to get drunk on a Sunday afternoon where we going? S x*

I punch the air with excitement; I walk out my room with black skinny jeans on, beige UGG boots, a white floaty top, with a red scarf on.
'You look nice.' Mom says.

'Thanks.'

'I don't want to sound Mom-ish but are you drying your hair? You'll get ill otherwise.' She shows a small smile.

'Of course, Mom.' I turn on my heels and march back in my room and blow-dry my hair. I walk back out and my Mom smiles at me.

'Going anywhere nice?'

'Not sure yet, I'm going to meet Sarah and it will properly be the first bar we see.' I see the frown Mom makes, so I change the subject.

'You and Dad can sleep in my bed tonight, I'll sleep on the sofa.' I grab my coat, do it up, grab my bag and shout goodbye. I get off the bus at Sarah's place and ring on her buzzer. A crackled voice comes through the speaker.

'I'll be right down!'

'You better.' I answer. Sarah comes running out the door, we walk arm in arm down the road, until we see a bar and walk in, take the comfy seats and order cocktails, and we giggle and chat until my phone starts ringing.

'It's Jack.' I frown.

'Hello?'

'Lucy, what time you back?' Jack demands.

'I don't know, why?'

'Let me know when you're on your way home.' He hangs up.

'What's up?' She asks. I shrug.

'I have no idea.' We talk about Sam, my Mom and Dad, Gemma, Belle, my trip to England whilst downing pitcher after pitcher of cocktails. Sarah looks at her watch.

'We have to be up early, we should go.' We both down the rest of our drinks and slam the glasses on the table, then smile at each other. We once again walk arm in arm, and I get my phone out and text Jack just as I was asked to do.

*Butthead I'm en-route to my apartment*

That will tell him, I laugh to myself, actually quite happy with my text. I say my goodbyes to Sarah and I grab a cab, not in the mood to walk. I reach my building and see no sign of Jack. I pay the fair and fall into the lift. When I reach my apartment, I fumble with the keys in the lock, but finally I get it open and I freeze. There are candles everywhere, and 'Slow Dancing in a Burning Room' is playing quietly on the stereo system. I drop my bag. I'm speechless, looking around the room like I've never seen it before. The door behind me closes, I swing round and there's Jack, hands in his pockets. Tears stream down my face and I fall to my knees. Jack rushes over falls to his knees and hugs me.

'What's wrong?' He soothes. I say nothing, look into his eyes and kiss him, he kisses me back. We lie in the middle of the sitting room floor, his arm under my head and I'm lying looking at him.

'What's this for?' I finally say. The candles are randomly going out as they have reached the bottom of their wicks.

'I wanted a simple way to say I love you Luc.' Tears appear in my eyes again.

'Please don't cry,' he strokes my hair, he places his right

palm on my cheek, his fingers in my hair and his thumb brushing against my face, 'I missed you so much.' He adds.

'Then why did you ship me off to England?' I say with a tone.

'I thought you might like England and you wouldn't have offered.' He says.

'I did have a good time actually.' I can feel his smile against my face. I sit up suddenly –

'Where are my parents?'

'Out to dinner, then to the movies.' He says.

'Where's Sam?' I ask.

'At work.'

'AT WORK?' I say louder then I should have.
'Yeah she got a job at Betty's.'

'Oh, I'm happy for her.' My voice doesn't sound convincing. Jack sits up and stands up; switching the stereo off helps me up and slowly blows the candles out and pulls me into my bedroom.

\*\*\*\*\*\*\*\*\*

My alarm wakes me up, but I groan and press snooze. I sit up suddenly when I smell toast and hear the kettle whistling. I look around my room, Jack isn't in my bed, but his underwear is on the floor with his t-shirt and trousers. I smile at the memory of last night. I put on his t-shirt and walk out my room to find him butt naked in my kitchen buttering toast. I stand and stare, watching him from the doorway of my room. He walks round the breakfast bar whistling, until he sees me, flashes me a gorgeous smile, which makes me melt. I slowly walk over to him; he looks me up and down.

'That t-shirt suits you.'

'Thank you.' I reply, curtseying. He points at the chair for me to sit, so I do, switching on my laptop at the same time. Jack walks to my room and comes back out with his boxers on, so I pout.

'What are you pouting for?'

'I liked the show before.' I say, not being able to stop the smile spreading across my face.

'I have to go home soon.' Jack says, that wipes the smile off my face.

'Why?'

'We both have work and I have to get changed, I can't go to the office in jeans babe.'

'I suppose, why don't you bring some work clothes with you here and leave them, just case this situation happens again.' I say.

'Oh, so this is situation will happen again?' Jack teases with a boyish grin.

'Only if you want it to.'

'It's your choice Luc.'
*Mine? That's weird.*

'Eat up; you have to get ready for your first day.'

'Oh, yeah.' I'm excited about my first day but I'd rather stay in bed with Jack all day. Oh, I've got two emails from Gemma.

*From: Gemma Winter*
*Subject: homeward bound*
*To: Lucy Winter*
*11/21/10 14:26*

*Glad you're home safe… did you have a good time??*
*How is everyone??*
*I'm home soon YAY YAY!*

I open the second email.

*From: Gemma Winter*
*Subject: your first day*
*To: Lucy Winter*
*11/21/10 23:45*

*Hey good luck on your first day, call me after to tell me all about it*
*Love you lots*

*Gemma xxxxx*

I smile to myself. As I finish my coffee and toast, I sniff myself and head to the bathroom to jump in the shower. To my surprise, the bathroom door open. I peer round the curtain and Jack is taking his boxers off.

'What are you doing?' I ask.

'Having a shower.' He replies with a smirk.

'Oh, I see.' I answer shyly. He stands about an inch away from me, with his left hand on my lower back and his other in my hair and kisses me, just like he did before and just like in my dream. I walk backwards until we're both under the water, I pull away and see him frown.

'I have to be quick.' I say. He smiles and starts washing his hair. After we finish showering I jump out and grab my bath towel, Jack whips it from me.

'HEY!' I shout. He puts it over his shoulders.

'I need a towel for my wet hair.' He smiles and strides out of the bathroom.
I have to get another towel to wrap my hair in. Then I look in my wardrobe for something to wear on my first day, and pull out the dress that I wore for my interview. Jack snatches it out of my hand, so I look round at him in surprise.

'No, this dress makes you look too sexy and I can't have other men staring at you.' I frown, but as I turn around I smile. I find a grey pencil skirt, and white blouse instead.

101

Perfect. I put on bra and panties and slip on some stockings. I bend over to dry my hair, I don't want my mom telling me off again, slip on my skirt and blouse and wear the shoes I got for my interview. I also put on some mascara and lip-gloss.

'Are you ready to go?' I ask while walking out my room.

'Yes.' Jack answers and I feel his eyes on me. I look up and he's staring at me with his mouth open.

'Catching flies again?' I ask feeling pleased with my joke.

'You look a...a... amazing.' He stutters.

'Can you take a photo of me?' I smile handing him my phone, I stand in my doorway, with my left hand on my hip and arch my back while pouting.
I laugh to myself, thinking that Sarah will find this hilarious. I walk back over to my open laptop and email Gemma back quickly.

*From: Lucy Winter*
*Subject: my first day*
*To: Gemma Winter*
*11/22/10 07:35*

*Attachment .jpeg*

*Everyone is good, I'm having breakfast with a naked Jack.........I have a lot to tell you. Can't wait till you're home, I miss my sister time!*
*Thanks for the good luck; I'm very nervous I've attached a picture of me in my first day clothes.*

102

Turning my laptop off, I grab my coat and my bag and we head out the door.

'What time is it?' I look at Jack.

'Eight.' He puts his watch in my face, so close I can't even read it. I smack his hand away tutting; he grasps my arm and squeezes it.

'Are you going straight to work or are you coming up?' Jack asks.

'I'll come up for a bit, I have fifteen minutes till I have to be at my desk' I smile. We stop at his building, enter the lobby and file into the lift. He presses the button for floor twenty-one, I grab his hand, and GEEZ. I forgot how far up he lives. I haven't been to Jack's apartment in months. We finally reach his place, he fumbles with the key, opens the door, and I stare around as I walk in.

'You changed it?' I say surprised.

'Yeah, it looks bigger, doesn't it?' he says clearly happy. His apartment used to be extremely dark, with one red-brick wall and the others a deep blue. Complete with the dark blinds, it used to look like the perfect place for bats. Well, for men with Xbox's I guess. Now, it still has the red brick, but crisp white walls. I feel very comfortable in this new apartment. He disappears to his bedroom.

'Wow, nice table.' I spot it in the dining area.

103

'Thanks, Dean made it, apparently it wasn't good enough to sell and was going to throw it, so I grabbed it.'

'Good save.' I smile as I hold my hand in the air, we high five each other. Random. Whoa he looks handsome, black suit pants, white shirt. He's styled his hair as well, and I breath catches in my throat.

'Ready?' he asks while holding his hand out for me to hold.

'Yep!' I answer, closing the door behind me.

************

I arrive at the front desk of Teely's international.

'Can I help you, Miss?' The blonde-haired receptionist asks.

'Yes, it's my first day here and I have no idea what I'm doing.' I answer honestly.

'Right.' She says.

'I know I have to see Drake Teely.' I offer.

'Oh, that helps, thanks. One second.' She picks up the phone.

'Hello Mr. Teely, I have a...' she stops and looks at me, 'yes, that's right, Lucy Winter here for you sir.' She puts the phone down.

'He will be right with you, if you would like to take a seat.' She points to her left. I smile at her, saying thank you. As I sit on the chair in the waiting area, I get a horrible feeling in my stomach. Nerves, maybe? The receptionist looks at me.

'Miss Winter, you can go up to Mr. Teely's office, on floor eighteen.'

'Thanks.' I get up and walk the way I had on Wednesday. I reach floor eighteen and Drake is waiting for me, but he's on the phone. He ushers me over, and points to a room off his office. I walk into it and he follows. There's a wooden desk, it looks familiar, with an office chair, an iMac and the main wall full floor to ceiling with books.

'I love it!' I turn to look at Drake, who has just finished his phone call.

'Good,' he replies with a smile, 'I'll leave you to it, if you need me I'm in the next room or extension thirty-eight.'

'Okay thanks.'

'I've left some manuscripts on your desk, to start you off slowly.' Then he's gone. I sit at my desk and turn my computer on, log onto my emails. There's already two, to my disbelief, one from Sarah Wildon and one from Drake Teely.

*From: Sarah Wildon*
*Subject: your first day*
*To: Lucy Winter*
*11/22/10 09:00*

*Hey I'm emailing you while I'm at work, do you feel posh now?*

*S x*

*Personal shopper, Bloomingdales*

And Drake Teely's.

*From: Drake Teely*
*Subject: first day*
*To: Lucy Winter*
*11/12/10 08:45*

*Hope you have a good first day; remember I'm in the next room if you need anything.*

*Drake Teely*
*Editor at Teely's International*

How did Sarah get my email address? I've never known Sarah to email anyone.

*From: Lucy Winter*
*Subject: my first day*
*To: Sarah Wildon*
*11/22/10 09:25*

*How did you get my brand-new email for the job I started for the first time 25 mins ago?*
*And how are you emailing me at work?*
*This is a new experience for me with you*
*Luc x*

*P.A. to Drake Teely at Teely's International*

106

As I shrink the page to my emails it tings. JACK?!? How does everyone have my email address?

*From: Jack Base*
*Subject: your first day*
*To: Lucy Winter*
*11/22/10 09:27*

*Hey Luc how's your first day going? Is this freaking you out yet?*
*Jack xx*

*I.T manager of Freshman's LTD*

*Has it freaked me out yet? They all planned this; this plan stinks of Sarah. My email tings again. I'm going to kill her.*

*From: Sarah Wildon*
*Subject: new experience*
*To: Lucy Winter*
*11/22/10*

*We arranged this the other night, when Drake was there he gave it to us to freak you out, is it working?*
*And I'm emailing off my blackberry, I told you it would come in handy when you and Dean were telling me to turn to the iPhone revolution.*
*Love ya S x*

DRAKE! Hhmm I don't answer those emails. To be honest that did freak me out. I email Drake though.

*From: Lucy Winter*

*Subject: giving my personal details out.........*
*To: Drake Teely*
*11/22/10 09:37*

*Hello Mr. Teely,*
*I regret to inform you that I haven't started my working day*
*as of yet, because someone gave out my work email address*
*to my friends, and I've been harassed by them, I do not*
*appreciate this type of behavior and I plan on giving no*
*mercy to the person responsible.*

*Yours Sincerely*
*Lucy Winter*

*P.A. to Drake Teely of Teely's International*

I press send, and grin to myself. I pick up the pile of
manuscripts on the desk and find a small envelope, with Lucy
Winter written on it, so I open it. It has a big black and white
flower drawn across it and with a thick black pen.

*Dear Lucy,*

*I made this Desk for you as a present for your first day,*
*hope you love it.*

*Dean Xx*

I start to feel tears in my eyes. I pick up my phone and
immediately text Dean.

*Dean, this desk is the most beautiful thing I have ever seen,*
*thank you so much Lucy xxxxx*

I slip the note in my bag with a loving smile on my face.

## CHAPTER SEVEN

'Hello Drake Teely's office, Lucy speaking?'

'Hello Lucy, it's Mom.'

'Hi Mom, how did you get this number?'

'Drake gave it to me.'

'Drake again.' I whisper, somewhat annoyed.

'I was calling to ask if you had a good night with Jack.' I blush.

'Yeah mum it was nice. Did you have a good night out?'

'Your Dad and I helped set up your sitting room, and yes we did.' My eyes start to tear again.

'You did?'

'Yeah, I put on my favorite song and got to work.' I suddenly remember "Slow Dancing in a Burning Room".

'Your first dance song.' I whisper.

'Yes, well I'll let you get back to work, I'll see you when you get back. Your Dad and I are leaving tonight.'

'Oh, okay Mom, we can go for dinner yeah?' I ask.

'Yes, that would be lovely sweetie.'

'Meet me at the restaurant on fifth, Elliot's, okay Mom?'

'Okay dear, at six?'

'Yeah Mom. See you there, bye.'

'Bye Lucy!' I hang up and pick my phone and send a group text, to Jack, Sarah, Dean and Sam.

*Hey guys meet me at Elliot's tonight at 17:45 dress up smart thanks L xx*

I check my emails again and there is a reply from Drake.

*From: Drake Teely*
*Subject: oh no*
*To: Lucy Winter*
*11/22/10 09:45*

*Dear Miss Winter,*
*I am angered someone would give out your personal email*

110

*address from your place of work; I will not give mercy to the person responsible either. However, I do find it humorous that all your friends emailed you at the same time. Subtle!*
**Yours Sincerely**
**Drake Teely**

**Editor at Teely's International**

I pick up the manuscripts and read the title of the top one, Devil's Island. Seems dark. Don't judge a book by its cover; I tell myself. I start reading when the girl from the reception outside pops her head round the door of my office.

'Lucy?'

'Yep?' I look up at her.

'Want a coffee?'

'Oh, you're my new favorite person, yes please.' She grins and shuts the door. As I pick the manuscript up to continue reading, my phone beeps three times.

*Babe I'll be there Jack x*

*Me and Belle will be there D x*

Oh yeah, I forgot about Belle. The phone beeps again.

*I'll try get couple of hours off Sam x*

*Babe count me in, EMAIL ME BACK, I'm enjoying this business feeling Sarah xx*

111

I find the number for Elliot Read and ring him.

'Hello?'

'Hi, it's Lucy Winter.' I say hoping he recognizes my name.

'Ahh Lu-cy, how are you?' I let out a sigh of relief.

'I'm good thanks, you?'

'I'm good, what can I do for you?' He asks warily.

'Would I be able to book a table for eight people tonight?'

'Of course it's okay, what time?'

'Five-forty-five, please.'

'No worries Lucy, I'll see you then, bye!'
'Bye' I reply, hanging up. Elliot is an old friend from my old job when we were seventeen. We both waited tables to afford college, he's also extremely gay and has fancied Jack since he set eyes on him. Elliot has light brown hair with blonde spikes, blue eyes, he always has a sparkling shirt on. I suddenly think that I could invite Drake – but no he's my boss, I think that might be a bit awkward. My emails rings with a notification.

*From: Drake Winter*
*Subject: Tonight?*
*To: Lucy Winter*
*11/22/10 10:47*

*Sarah just informed me about tonight, thanks for the invite, want to travel together?*
*Drake*

*Editor at Teely's International*

Oh, thanks Sarah, at least I didn't have to ask. I text Elliot quickly.

*Please make that nine places on a table, Lucy Winter xx*

Elliot texts me back straight away.

*No worries sugar. E xx*

The receptionist comes back in and sits on the chair the other side of my desk, puts my coffee down and puts her hand out to me, introducing herself.

'Hi I'm Beth Ryder, I just man the reception outside.'

'Hi I'm Lucy Winter, I'm the P.A. to Drake Teely and I man this desk.' I smile and she smiles back. She leans on the desk with her elbows and tells me the names of all the people I need to know.

'The guy and girl on front desk, his name is Jamie, and her name is Hilda.'

'Hilda? That's an unusual name.'

'Yeah, she's Polish.'

113

'Okay cool.' I sip my coffee.

'There's me, Beth,' she smiles 'and Jenny who work on the desk outside, she's a part timer.'

'Thanks.' I smile.

'I really wanted this job.' She says to me, looking at her shoes.

'Oh really, you like books?'

'Yeah I love to read.' I hand her two manuscripts.

'Be my guest!' She smiles and grabs them from me.

'Oh my god, really?! I get so bored on the desk.' We hear a phone ringing, then she runs out my office.

'Bye Beth…' I say after her. I get back to reading Devil's Island. The next time I look at my computer, it's four-thirty. WHOA, where did the time go? I check my emails I have an email from Drake. Oh, I didn't email him back.

*From: Drake Winter*
*Subject: have I killed you already?*
*To: Lucy Winter*
*11/22/10 16:14*

*Lucy, have I over worked you on your first day or are you enjoying it too much and ignoring me? I hope it's the second reason (crosses fingers)*

*Do you want to share a ride with me?*
*Drake*

**Editor at Teely's International**

Ooopss, I'm glad he has a good sense of humor. I put the manuscript down and email him back.

*From: Lucy Winter*
*Subject: have you killed me?*
*To: Drake Winter*
*11/22/10 16:50*

*Drake, you have not killed me or over worked me, I was reading a manuscript, and liked it too much and I'm now on chapter seventeen, please publish this book!*

*Yes, I would like to share a lift.*

*Lucy*

**P.A. to Drake Teely at Teely's International**

I smile to myself as I pick up my phone, no message or missed calls. I'm surprised – it's normally beeping all day. I pick up the landline and phone Beth outside. I hear her through the wall.

'Hi, Drake Teely's office, Beth speaking.'

'Hi, its Lucy will you come here?' She hangs up and comes running into my office.

'Hi Lucy!'

'Hi, what happened earlier?'

'Drake phoned through and told me to stop gossiping and get back to work.'

'Whoa bossy, did you read that manuscript?' I ask. Beth's face lights up.

'I read them both.' My mouth hangs open.

'Whoa, you're quick at reading.' I say gob-smacked.

'I told you, I love it.'

'What's your opinion?' I ask.

'Well…' She pulls a bit of paper from her lap and hands it to me.

'You wrote reports on them as well?' I look at her, stunned.

'Yep' she smiles and stands up from the chair.

'Where are you going?'

'It's gone five, I want to go home bye Lucy.' She smiles and walks out.

'Bye Beth.' Drake comes into my office through that little door, joining our offices together.

'Ready Lucy?' He asks.

'Erm, not yet but give me a minute.'

'Okay I'll be in my office but come in when you're ready' he says and walks out. I check my email one more time, there's nothing, so I log out and turn the computer off. I put the other three manuscripts in my bag and put the two from Beth with her reports in my drawer for tomorrow, grab my things and walk out my office turning the light off as I go. When we get outside, Drake whistles for a taxi, we climb in and shortly after we arrive at Elliot's. His name is lit up in a blue neon light written in calligraphy, and there's a massive line of people outside. I didn't know it was this popular.

'I've booked a table under winter for nine people for dinner' I say, as I approach the bouncer, who nods and lets us through the red velvet rope. We walk in and it's quite dark, only lit by candle light, with big booths full of people and a jazz band playing in the far-left corner. A waiter comes running up to us.
'Have you booked a table ma'am?'

'Yes, I have, nine people under Winter.'

'Oh, follow me please.' We follow him to a big booth, with a rope with a V.I.P sign hanging off it.

*Hey guys when you get to Elliot's tell the bouncer you're on the table book for Winter, and Sarah please can you wait for mom and dad and come in with them L xx*

My phone makes a constant noise again while 4 messages

117

come through.

*I'm outside see you in a sec, J x*

*We'll be 5 mins D xx*

*I'm going to be late I'm finishing at 6 so ill be with you at 18:15*
*Sam xx*

*Yes babe course I will, see you soon S xx*

I stand up, looking out for Jack. I see him, and wave as he walks towards us. He looks casual: blue jeans and a white shirt, in dress shoes. He reaches us, puts his right hand on the bottom of my back and kisses my right cheek. I smile and blush, as I'm fully aware Drake is looking at us. Dean and Belle then turn up, Belle in a light pink evening dress and Dean in his suit pants and white shirt. We all sit down and order drinks.

'What's the occasion? Dean asks while Jack protectively puts his arm over my shoulder to show Drake I'm his.

'It's my parents last night and I want to have everyone here to give them a nice good bye.'

Everyone cocks their heads at me and coos. We all suddenly turn our heads when we hear Sarah squeal with my Mom, Dad and Sam in tow. Mom and Dad hug everyone in turn, and order some bottles of wine. We all start talking amongst ourselves, when Drake stands up with his drink, and tings it with this knife.

'To Lucy, and her new job.' He winks at me, which makes me wince as Jack tightens his grip. In chorus everyone repeats:
'TO LUCY AND HER NEW JOB!'

As everyone finishes their meal and drinks Mom gets up and walks away from the table. Everyone smiles at me, so I look around self-consciously, wondering why everyone is looking at me. I turn to look at Jack and whisper to him:

'What's going on?' I ask, but he just raises his eyebrows and nods in the direction of my Mom, and to my surprise...

'GEMMA?!?' I scream.

'LUCY?!?' she screams back, I scramble out my seat and run towards my sister, we both start to cry.

'We'll give you a minute' Mom says while patting me on the back. When Gemma and I let go of each other, I hold her hand and pull her to the table, to introduce her to Drake.

'What's with everyone going behind my back at the moment? I ask dryly, while start to form in my eyes again.

'We all thought it was time we all gave back to you, after what you always do for us, you deserve it sweetheart' Mom says as she holds her glass up. Everyone follows her, and we all clink glasses.

'What else have they done behind your back?' Gemma asks.

'Well,' I shift in my seat to look at Gemma, 'Drake here gave them my work email address before I had even started, so when I logged into my work email, I had an email from Jack and Sarah' they both smile.

'Then, I find a note from Dean on my desk, he had made my desk specially for my office' I continue.

'Oh, Dean that's lovely' Gemma says. All Dean can do is smile at her.

'And Drake had given Mom my number and extension, so she phoned me.' Everyone bursts into laughs.

'Were you mad?' Mom asks.

'No, of course not, it was nice. I still have my friends and family with me on my first day at work'
'It's getting late' Drake says as he gets up.

'I'll see you tomorrow' I say while waving at him, Sarah running after him.
Mom and Dad get up and say their good-byes; Dean and Belle follow, leaving just me, Jack, Gemma and Sam left.

'Mine?' I suggest. We all get up to leave, but Elliot comes running over to me.

'Are you going Lucy?' he says, hugging me so tight that Jack has to let go.

'Yeah, we're off home now, thanks for an excellent night Elliot.'

'No worries, but before you go, I want you to quickly meet my boyfriend' he turns around and stood there is a man, with black hair like Justin Bieber, with an extremely tight top and baggy jeans. He smiles at me and shakes my hand.

'Hi, I am Henry' he says in a Spanish accent.

'Hi, I'm Lucy.' I turn and point at everyone as I say their names.

'This is Jack, Gemma and Sam.' They all shake hands and we stand at look at each other a bit awkwardly.

'Thanks again for tonight Elliot, I'll see you soon.'

'Bye Lucy.' We get outside the club and are hit by a massive crowd of people trying to get in and the cold air. I shiver. We get a cab and get out the cab at my building.

'You staying here tonight Jack?'

'Yes please' he says trying to keep his eyelids open. When we get upstairs, Jack disappears into my bedroom, Sam stalks off to the spare room, so Gemma and I are left. We smile at each other.

'What question do I ask first?'

'I'll start from the beginning' I say, and start talking.

**********

After what seems like minutes, I yawn and stretch, looking at the clock. It says its half-eleven.

'Whoa Gem, we've been talking for three hours.' My bedroom door creaks open: it's Jack in his boxers.

'Babe. you coming to bed? You have work tomorrow.'

'Yeah I'll be there in a sec.'

'Can I have a blanket Luc?' I walk over to the cupboard and launch a blanket at her head.

'Night Gem.'

'Night Luc' she replies sleepily. I crawl into bed next to Jack, who's half asleep.

'I've been waiting for you' he says, pulling me close so I'm facing him and I cuddle against him. We fall asleep together.

********

I wake up before my alarm. I flick the switch off so it doesn't wake Jack, and I slowly crawl out of bed like a ninja, trying not to disturb him. I go to the sitting room, where Gemma is already awake on her laptop. I put the kettle on and put some bread in the toaster, and sit next to Gemma.

'I normally check my laptop now, but as you're here I won't. You're disturbing my morning routine' I smile at her.

'I'll be leaving soon, I have to be back at Harvard by twelve.' She explains.

'Okay want a coffee?' She nods.

'Breakfast?' She nods again. I walk off to the kitchen. Jack comes out my bedroom with just his boxers on. He yawns while stretching and walks to the bathroom, without looking at me or Gemma. We both giggle. I sit next to Gemma on the sofa once again, but this time with food and drink.

'Want to come see my office?' I say to Gemma.

'Oh yeah, sure!' Jack walks back through.

'I'm going to jump in the shower.' he explains.

'Oh Luc, I loved that picture of your first day, not loving the pose' Gemma quips, looking at the photo Jack took yesterday. I decide to get ready, putting on my interview dress and walk back out to Gemma like I'm walking on a catwalk without making eye contact, she laughs and spits her coffee everywhere.

'You look nice, babes.' Jack says, which pulls me back to reality.

'Super sexy.' Gemma says. I frown.

'That's weird coming from my sister.'

'Ready to go?' Jack asks.

'Why are you always in charge?' I say, thinking out loud. Gemma and Jack look at me and frown.

'What?' Jack stares.

'You're always the one who is in charge, deciding when we go, eat etc.' I explain.

'Fine, you be in charge.' He kisses my cheek and sits down.

'Did I just witness your first fight?' Gemma asks.

'No, ready?' I smile at them both. They both get up and grab their stuff; we get to the lobby and haul a taxi. We stop at Jack's place and let him out.

'Bye babe.' I blow him a kiss.

'Bye babe, I'll see you tonight.' He says, catching my kiss and placing it on his heart while shutting the cab door.

'You two are so cute.' Gemma says. We reach my building, getting a latte on the way in and make our way up to the eighteenth floor.

'Morning Lucy!' Beth shouts across the big lobby.

'Morning Beth, this is my sister Gemma.'

'Hi Gemma!'

'Hi Beth!'

'Is Drake in yet?' I ask Beth.

'Not yet, it's too early for him, he normally strolls in gone nine.' Beth smiles at me. Gemma and I walk into my office and I put my bag on my desk.

'Whoa, is the desk Dean made?' She asks, as she sits down on the visitor's side.

'Yep, want a coffee?'

'No, I'm okay.' She replies, so I walk out my office leaving Gemma on her own.

'Want a coffee Beth?' I offer.

'No thank you.' As I walk back in my office, Gemma is nowhere to be seen. I shrug thinking she's gone to the bathroom, turn my computer on and log into my emails, but then I hear a big giggle. I knock on the joining door to Drake's office and see Gemma and Drake playing chess.

'Chess?' I question. They both stop mid-game and look up at me.

'Drake is taking me back to Harvard.'

'Really?'

'Yeah, he's doing a speech – that's what I had to be back for actually. I didn't know you were such good friends with Mr. Teely himself.'

'Oh okay, how long are you going to be out for?' I ask Drake, Gemma goes red and looks awkward.

'About two-three hours.'

'Okay. I need to talk to you about Beth and about my weekend off, when you have a spare few minutes.' Drake nods and goes back to playing chess with Gemma. I walk back in my office and see I have two new emails. One from Elizabeth.

*From: Elizabeth Brown*
*Subject: Afternoon meeting*
*To: Lucy Winter*
*11/23/10 08:45*

*Hello Lucy,*
*Congratulations on getting the job. Can you please remind Drake at 3:30 he has a meeting with Mr Teely (his father) and myself in the meeting room.*

*Yours sincerely,*
*Elizabeth*

And one from Jack.

*From: Jack Base*
*Subject: your choice*
*To: Lucy Winter*
*11/23/10 09:15*

*I love waking up with you, it puts me in a good mood and my staff love me in a good mood.*
*Can I bring some work clothes round yours tonight?*

*From Cracker Jack*

*I.T Manager at Freshman's LTD*

Oh Jack, he always knows how to make me smile. I email him back.

*From: Lucy Winter*
*Subject: Mine??*
*To: Jack Base*
*11/23/10 09:25*

*Morning, I love waking up with you as well and me being in charge.*
*Yeah, you can bring some clothes round, are you staying tonight again?*
*From Lucy xx*

*P.A. to Drake Teely at Teely's International*

And I email Drake about Elizabeth.

*From: Lucy Winter*
*Subject: Elizabeth Brown*
*To: Drake Teely*
*11//23/10 09:28*

*Dear Drake,*
*May I please ask you who Elizabeth Brown is and why she is emailing me requests to remind you of meetings you have written in the diary on your desk?*
*Or do you choose to ignore them and expect people like me*

*and Beth to remind you?*

*Woman in next room.*

*P.A. to Drake Teely at Teely's International*

As I press send I feel a bit ashamed of that email. It was a bit uncalled for, after all I am his PA and that is part of my job description. My email pings.

*From: Drake Teely*
*Subject: Elizabeth Brown*
*To: Lucy Winter*
*11/23/10 09:35*

*Attachment jpeg.*

*Dear woman in the next room,*

*Elizabeth Brown is my mother.*
*I can't read my awful hand writing so I do count on you or Beth to remind me as that is in your job description, which I have attached.*

*P.S. when you don't have sex you're grouchy*

*Your boss (as explains in my foot notes)*

*Editor at Teely's International*

SHIT! I'm not grouchy; I cross my arms and pout. I open the attachment on the email Drake just sent me and the picture from my first day springs up on my screen. Oh my god. My

128

email and my phone pings. I have a text from Gemma.

*You okay?*
My email is from Jack.

*From: Jack Base*
*Subject: us <3*
*To: Lucy Winter*
*11/23/10 09:49*

*Babes, if it's okay yeah, I'll meet outside your building at 17:15 yeah?*

*Jack xx*

*I.T manager at freshman's LTD*

Jack is so cute, I email him straight back. I must do some work.

*From: Lucy Winter*
*Subject: us <3*
*To: Jack Base*
*11/23/10 09:56*

*Course it's all right*
*See you at 17:15, Drake just called me grouchy because we didn't have sex by the way.*

*Lucy*

*P.A. to Drake Teely at Teely's International*

I shrink my emails hoping to get some work done, and my phone beeps. Jack? That's strange.

**Don't worry about Drake saying you're grouchy, I love you the way you are and we can sort the sex thing later ;)**

I blush. Then I hear a knock at the door.

'Come in?' I answer. A man walks in with a box, he walks to my desk and slumps it down.

'Hi I'm Jeremy. Drake told me to bring you these manuscripts.'

'Oh, err thanks.' I mutter and as he gets to my office door.

'Jeremy, can you tell Beth on reception to come in please?'

'Sure thing, Miss.' Beth comes bounding into my office just as my phone rings.

'Hello?'

'It's Mom.'

'Oh, are you home?' I ask.

'Yeah, we did get home last night but didn't want to wake you.'

'It's okay, I stayed up late talking with Gemma.'

'Oh, did you have a good talk? When is she heading back?'

Mom asks.

'Yeah, we did. She's getting a lift with Drake.'

'Oh, that's nice of him. I'll let you go, bye love.'

'Bye Mom!' I put the phone down and look up at Beth.

'Hey Lucy, what's up?' Beth says eyeing up the box on my desk.

'This is a box on manuscripts, if you want you can take some and work your magic.' I offer. She has a massive smile on her face.

'Are you sure Lucy?'

'Of course, I'm sure!' I smile at her, she sits on the chair the other side of my desk and starts looking through the box.

'Lucy?' The door opens.

'Yes?' I look up and Gemma is in the doorway.

'Hey Gemma you alright?'

'Yeah are you mad at me?'

'No, why do you both think I'm mad?' I ask warily.

'You just seemed pissed off when you came in Drake's office.'
'No, I'm not mad; I'm just mega busy today already.'

'Okay.' Gemma leaves, shutting the door behind her.

'How many can I take?' Beth asks.

'As many as you want, as long as you leave me some.' I smile.

'I have five that caught my eye.'

'That's cool, I'm talking to Drake later. I'll mention this.'

'Oh, please don't, he will tell me off!'

'Oh no Beth, I won't get you in trouble. I want you to have my job, and it's what you love.'

'I don't want you to go, though.'

'I'll talk him into hiring us both and we can share an office.' I wink at her. Beth smiles then runs out my office clutching the manuscripts.

At three-thirty Drake strides back into the office from Harvard. I run quickly into his office.

'DRAKE. MEETING. PARENTS. NOW!' I remind him.

*******

When the clock hits five I let out a sign of relief. I get to see Jack. Oh, I need to email Drake. He hasn't come back from his meeting and I need to remind him of my four-day weekend.

*From: Lucy Winter*
*Subject: My four-day weekend*
*To: Drake Teely*
*11/23/10 17:05*

*Drake please remember I have a four-day weekend next week, please put Beth in my place, she is wonderful at this job, night x*

**P.A. to Drake Teely at Teely's International**

I make my way down to the lobby.

'Hi!' The guy from the main reception jumps in front of me.

'Hi Jamie.' I step back.

'How are you enjoying the job?'

'It's good, thanks.'

'Don't you think Drake is fit?' He asks me eagerly.

'Erm, well yeah, but I have a boyfriend.' I point to Jack standing outside staring at us. The guy looks at Jack and turns back to me with his mouth wide open.

'Whoa, you go girl!' He hugs me and walks off. Jack gives me a what-the-hell-was-that look. I shrug and run up to him and hug him tightly.

'Missed me babe?' He hugs me back.

'Yep!' We walk arm in arm all the way across town to my apartment.

'Do you want to stay in tonight? We can order in or I can cook?' Jack asks.

'I think we should order in, I've tasted your cooking before' I giggle, teasing him. He starts to tickle me in retaliation.

'PLEASE...DON'T...I...NEED....TO...PEE' I manage to get out.

## CHAPTER EIGHT

Bruno Mars singing 'Just the Way You Are' wakes me up; I sit up on the edge of my bed and go to turn off my alarm.

'Wait a minute…' I turn my head to look at the alarm clock. My alarm clock doesn't sing, where is that song coming from? I get up and follow the noise. I get into the living room and Sam is holding my phone in the air. Jack keeps phoning.

'He's called six times.' Sam says. The song starts up again.

'Make that seven.' She adds, chucking my phone at me.

'Hello?' I answer the call.

'Lucy? Why aren't you up yet?' Jack asks.

'I just got up, when did you change my ring tone?'

'Last night, before I left.' He answers.

'Oh okay, what do you want?'

'We're leaving in twenty minutes, have you packed?' He asks.

'What?!' Oh my god, I haven't.

'I'll be down stairs in twenty.' I say then hang up. We're driving to Tennessee for cousin Jenny's wedding. I'm not looking forward to the sixteen-hour drive but we are stopping in a scary motel. I've seen too many scary films, so I'm not letting go of Jack.

'Sam, are you ready to go?' I ask running around.

'Yeah, just about.'

'Why didn't you wake me?' I ask.

'I was asleep on the sofa, until your phone woke me up, then you came in.'

'Okay, have you got your bridesmaid's dress?'
'Yep, I have yours too'.' She answers.

'Let's get downstairs before the boys beat us there.' I kick my suitcase onto its wheels and run to the lift, while Sam follows. We reach the bottom and look around. There's no sign of them and we both sigh. Jack pulls up in a car that isn't his usual style. Sam and I look at it in disgust.

'What is that?' I say in horror.

'It's a people carrier babe, like it?'

'Not really, it's hideous!'

'Ahh babe, don't be mean to Marie!'

'What now? You named it?' I say, still horrified.

'Yeah, alright, come on, put your stuff in. We need to get going.' Jack says while smacking the driver door with his palm. I reluctantly put my case in the back, trying not to touch it like it's an explosive. We start off, Dean reading out the states we will be going through,

'Aim for Philly, then were going through Maryland, West Virginia.' He explains. Sam and I burst out singing –

'WEST VIRGINIAAAAA!'

'THEN KENTUCKY!' He shouts over us.

'CAN YOU TWO CUT IT OUT?' Jack shouts at us.

'Right Dean, what were the last ones you said?' We stop singing.

'Kentucky and then we get near Tennessee. It's easy from there. Dean replies.

'Are we still leaving you at the wedding Sam?' Jack asks while staring at her in the rear-view mirror.

'Yes please, I can go home with my Mom then.' She smiles.

'Did you make up with her?' I ask.

'Yeah we did, she apologized and I apologized, it's all gravy.'
'That's good. I'm going to try sleep because car journeys make me barf, and this vehicle choice is not helping.' I explain, before getting comfy and shutting my eyes.

*********

I get woken up by Dean gently shaking me.

'Luc...Luc!'

'Yeah?' I open one eye and look at him.

'We're having a break. Want to get something to eat or drink?'

'Where are we?' I ask still half asleep.

'Just outside West Virginia.' He answers. I smile and sit up.

'Oh, my neck.' I exhale, moving my head around.

'Come on, moaner.' He grabs my arm and lifts me out the car.

'You alright babe?' Jack asks.

'My neck hurts, I must have slept funny.'

'You looked like you had a broken neck.' We all look at Sam.

'What?' I mumble.

'I didn't want to wake you up so I didn't touch you.' She explains. Jack grabs my hand and gives a gentle pull so I stop frowning at Sam. We walk into a diner, which has red booths, white and red checked flooring with old guitars on the walls. It looks like the 1950's.

'Right, let's sit here.' Jack points at a booth, Dean and Sam sit on one side, and Jack and I on the other. The waitress comes straight over.

'What can I get for you?' She asks.

'I'll have pancakes with bacon and coffee please.' Jack says first.

'Chili dog with a coffee please.' Sam asks.
'I'll have waffles with sausage and bacon and coffee please.'
Dean says.

'Um, the biggest cheese burger you can get me and a coca
cola please.' I ask.
The waitress writes down our mixed order. Jack looks at me,
eyebrows raised.

'Hungry?' He asks, kissing my temple.

'I'm starving, is a girl not allowed to indulge in a fatty burger
every so often?'

'Well, considering you eat at Betty's every day, a fatty meal
isn't every so often.' Dean says smiling at me.

'You're so picky!' I giggle, my phone starts ringing in my
pocket. jack doesn't let go, so I try get it out really awkwardly
with his grip around my waist not budging.

'Hi Mom!'

'Hello dear, where-abouts are you?'

'I have no idea, I've slept since we have left. We're at a diner,
I'll put Jack on to explain where we are.' I pass the phone to
him.

'Hi Mom' He says, which makes me smile.

'We're just outside West Virginia, where are you? Oh okay,

140

how late did you leave?' As the one-sided call bores me, I look around the diner. The waitress then brings up our drinks. my ears prick up when I hear Jack say:

'You're near us then do you want a break?... Okay bye!' He hangs up my phone.

'Mom and Dad are just down the road, they will be with us shortly.'

\*\*\*\*\*\*\*\*\*\*

After the meal, we say a quick goodbye to Mom and Dad and get back into our car. We set off, this time with them following us. I try to stay awake and get involved in a conversation with Sam, but we don't have anything to talk about so I slump in my chair and look out the window. After a couple of hours, I start fidgeting in my seat.

'What's wrong?' Jack ask me, through the rear-view mirror. 'I need to pee.'

'Okay, I'll get gas while we're here.' Jack pulls into a rest stop, and I run off. I reach the toilet and wince at the state of them. I hover over the toilet as there is no way in hell I am touching them. I walk back around the corner and walk into the shop where Dad is buying drinks and Dean is standing paying for the gas. I grab some bags of sweets and some drinks, pay and run after Dean to the car. They've all swapped seats, Sam in the front, Dean driving and Jack in the back with me. He wraps his arm around my shoulders as I get back in the car and pulls me over so I'm lying on his chest. I listen to his heart thumping and it starts to relax me. I pass the sweets and drinks around as Dean turns the radio up a bit, to keep us all awake. After a couple of dull songs, Shania Twain's 'I Feel Like a Woman' comes on. Sam and I smirk at each other and start singing the words. After singing out some classics on the radio we pull onto a dark road, and Mom and Dad follow. I grab Jack's hand, he looks down at me and kisses my hair.

'Where are we going?' Sam looks worryingly at Jack and me.

'I thought I'd get rid of you all.' Dean says laughing.

'What? Sam replies shocked, obviously not understanding his sense of humor.

'This is where the motel is.' Dean looks at Sam. We pull up to a building that looks like a house, not a motel. It's all dark with big trees towering over it. Suddenly a light over the main door flicks on. Dean parks and we all reluctantly get out the car. Jack pulls me close to him, as we open the main door. There's a bell above the door, as it rings it scares all of us. A cozy room with burgundy walls greets us with off white leather sofas, and lamps everywhere.

'Hello there!' A short lady appears behind the desk, she has off-blonde hair in a French plait, with a wrap dress on and no shoes.

'Hi, we booked a room for four people.' Jack says while stepping forward.

'Oh yes, the Base crew.' The lady says while letting out a cackle.

'And we booked a room under Winter.' Dad adds.

'I'm Linda, but please call me Lyn.' She holds her hand out and we all shake her hand in turn.

'Are you staying for breakfast?' Jack looks around at us all, turns back to Lyn and answers.

'Yes please.'

'Okay, breakfast is from six-thirty 'till ten.' She turns away from us, grabs a key and begins to walk off.

'Follow me please.' She says from the dark room she walked into. We all jog to catch up with her. She flips a switch and all the lights in the hallway light up. We walk past a couple of doors. There was a pattern of color, the doors went pink, purple, green, yellow, pink, purple, green, yellow. *That's strange.* We reach our room; with I notice has a blue door.

'Why is this the only blue door?' I ask curiously.

'It's our only four-bed room.' She smirks at me. She opens the door and we follow. The room is quite big considering the size of the house, the walls are painted light blue with a border around the top of the room. There are two double beds made up with very floral bed covers, and a brown sofa. I look at it in disgust as I try work out if it was made brown or if it is a dirty brown. She hands Jack the key, smiles at us all and strides out.

'Follow me.' She repeats to Mom and Dad, we all kiss and

hug goodnight, and they leave with Lyn out of the room.

'Have a good night.' Lyn whispers. Dean runs after her, locking the door.

'This place gives me the creeps.' Sam pipes up.

'Me too.' I say, Jack wraps his arm around me once more and pulls me close into a hug.

'Don't worry, nothing is going to happen.'

'I hope you're right.' Sam adds.

'Which bed is which then?' I ask trying not to change the subject.

'Jack and I in one, and you two in the other or both girls in one and both boys in the other?' I suggest. Jack interrupts the last of what I was saying, by throwing his case on the bed.

'This is our bed, Luc, you guys are in that one.' Sam goes in her case, pulls some clothes out and stalks off to the bathroom. I jump into one of the beds, where Jake strips down to his briefs, and gets in next to me. He puts his arm under my head and I roll on to my side so I'm facing him, he kisses me gently on the lips and closes his eyes, Sam gets out the bathroom and gets into the other bed, while Dean is stripping next to the bed.

\*\*\*\*\*\*\*\*\*\*

Jack shakes me awake.

144

'Come on sleepy head, we have to get on the road again to make it in time.' I roll over to my side and put the cover over my head, a second later the duvet gets pulled off me.

'Get up!' Jack gets on the bed and jumps around.

'Okay, okay, I'm up.' I say as I jump off the edge of the bed.

'Where are Dean and Sam?' I ask.

'Having breakfast, waiting for you.' Jack raises his eyebrows at me.

'What?' I ask.

'Nothing.' He smirks, he puts my case on the bed.

'What you wearing?'

'Probably what I wore yesterday.'

'Okay cool. He throws my clothes at me and closes my suit case. He stands in front of me with his arms folded.

'Get dressed or we're going to be late.'

'Okay you're so bossy this morning, I don't like it!'

'Well, do as I say when I say it.' He winks at me.

'It's like being at school or in the army!' I put my hand to my forehead to salute him. I quickly get dressed and brush my hair. We walk — well no — Jack drags me to the dining room. 'You look rough.' Dean looks at me.

'Oh thanks, you know how to make a girl feel good in the morning. I haven't brushed my teeth yet, if you carry on with the insults I'll breathe on you.' My threat works.

'Eurgh, get away from my breakfast!' Dean laughs picking up his plate. I sit and look around the dining room. It's a bright sunny yellow, with all wooden furniture and a whole wall of French doors. It doesn't look scary at all. Lyn strolls into the room with a big smile on her face.

'I have some more toast; does anyone want anything else before I turn everything off?' In chorus we all answer 'no thanks'. I giggle and we all break out in to conversation. When we're all done, a young girl comes in the dining room and clears the table.

'Lyn is waiting at reception when you're ready.' She says and rushes out. We grab our cases, walk around the outside of the house to the car, put all our cases in the trunk. Sam and Dean climb in, as Jack wanders off to thank Linda and pay. I walk over and sit in the back of Mom and Dad's new red mini cooper.

'Are you coming with us dear?' Mom asks.

'No, just wanted to see if you were okay with driving? I can take over if you're tired?' I offer.

'No, its fine dear, I'm used to it.' Dad replies.

146

'Okay, I'll see you in Tennessee.' I smile and wave and climb into the people carrier.

********** 

When we reach Tennessee, I sigh with relief. We stop outside Aunty Pauline's house, her massive pale blue farm house in the middle of nowhere, with their pale blue VW camper van. I jump out and walk around to stretch my legs. It feels like I'm ten years old again. Auntie Pauline comes running out the house with Jenny and Rose. Rose is Sam and Jenny's other sister. She has long auburn hair with brown eyes like Sam. We all hug and say hello. Auntie Pauline leads us in to their house, Uncle William comes into the kitchen and sits with us while we have tea and coffee. Uncle William looks very thin and fragile. He has just recovered from testicular cancer. He looks gaunt but he plasters a smile on his face anyway.

'Dave, want to come see the new engine?' William asks my Dad, who jumps up like an over excited school kid.

'Boys and their toys, hey!' Auntie Pauline says as they wander out. Jack and Dean get up from the table, muttering something about Xbox.

'It's just us girls now.' Jenny says.

'So, what's new with sex? Rose asks and everyone looks at me. I spit out my coffee and dribble it down my chin and jumper.

'Well, judging by the looks I got from everyone, you all know.' I say taking another mouthful of coffee.

'Well, yeah, but we want to hear it from you.' Rose adds.

'I'd rather not, Jack doesn't like me talking about him like that.' I lie. They all exchange glances, Auntie Pauline then pipes up.

'Did you remember your bridesmaid dress Sam?'

'Yeah, we made sure we had them before we left, they're hanging in the car.'

'Good good…' Pauline adds and we all sit awkwardly.

'How is the wedding coming along?' Mom asks.

'It's all done, we've just got to help it all goes well tomorrow.' Jenny states.

'Of course, who's doing your hair and make-up?' Sam asks.

'Well I was hoping that Lucy would do it.' I look up, shocked.

'Me? Why me?'

'For one, I can't afford a professional, and second, you're quite good at natural flawless make-up' Jenny says shrugging her shoulders. As I stare at everyone, shocked that I was even thought about to do make-up, Jack walks in.

'Shall we all go out for dinner tonight? I really want to go to Edwards's diner. I haven't been since we last came in

148

February' Jack asks with his eyes wide, waiting for us all to answer.

\*\*\*\*\*\*\*\*\*\*

My alarm clock wakes me at eight. Jack is still fast asleep next to me. I slowly and carefully untangle myself from him and slip on my dressing gown. As I open the bedroom door I can hear Mom and Auntie Pauline having a chat. I try sneak past to the bathroom.

'Morning dear.' Mom says. I turn to look at her, she's holding a mug of coffee towards me.

'Ahh, thanks Mom.' I sip my coffee. Mom and I jump when a chilling scream fills the house.

'What the fuck was that?' I ask.

'I don't know, it's properly Jenny having a bad hair day.' Auntie Pauline adds, not evening flitching at the noise.

'And she has to scream like that? That's the noise you make when you see a spider, or you know, when you are about to be murdered...' I reply.

'MMMMMOOOOOOOOOOMMMMMMMMM!' Comes another scream. Auntie Pauline tuts and gets up. Mom and I reluctantly get up and follow.

'Knock knock...' Auntie Pauline says knocking at the door.

'Mom, my curlers won't stay in, my tan is uneven, my dress is crinkled and no-one is helping me!' Jenny whines.

'Breathe honey, stop panicking or you will break out into spots, isn't that right Lucy?' Auntie Pauline says, looking at me in Jenny's dressing table mirror.

'Err, yes that's true.' I say raising one eyebrow. Auntie Pauline throws me a look.

'I'm going to get ready?' I lie to get out of this room full of tension. I run into the bedroom Jack and I share. He's lying on his back with his hands behind him head, and his eyes closed, so I decide to do the one thing that anyone would do, jump on the bed.

'Whoa, Luc, I thought there was an earthquake!' He shouts.

'I'm not that fat!'

'Well, I did just hear the bed creak.' Jack says smirking at me.

'Rude. I'm having a shower.' I add while skipping out the room.

'Hurry up in the shower or you're going to make us late to the wedding.' Jack shouts into the en-suite in our room.

'Okay, okay, I'm just getting out, don't pull your hair out.' I laugh as I reply.

'We have two hours before it starts and if I'm correct from previous experience, you take about four hours getting ready for any occasion.' Jack adds.

'Oh, stop overreacting.' We kiss briefly as he runs past me into the bathroom.
As I'm bending over, drying my hair ready to get it curled into ringlets by Sam. I see feet appear behind me as I'm looking through my legs.

'We could have showered together you know?' Jack says. I stand up to speak to him and freeze. Jack is leaning against the door frame with just a white towel around his waist, dripping wet, like he jumped in the shower, thought that thought and jumped out to tell me. Strange boy.

'Erm…I…erm…'

'Luc, you okay?' He says laughing.

'Erm yeah.' I quickly turn around. I finish drying my hair and tell my brain to cut it out. I slip on some sweat pants, a boob tube and slipper boots with frizzy hair looking like a lion's mane, mascara stains down my face.

'You're so beautiful.' Jack teases.

'Hey!' I answer punching him in the arm.

'Owwww…' Jack rubs his arm and pouts at me. I stride into the living room with Sam just finishing off Jenny's hair.

'I'll be five minutes Luc.' Sam says.

'I'll do your make-up shall I, Jen?' I ask warily knowing what mood she is in today.

'Oh, yes please Luc!' I drag a stool in front of Jenny and pull a table close, which has all her make-up on, and start applying moisturizer to her skin.

'Let that just dry.' I say.

'Will my hair be in the way?' Jenny looks at me worriedly.

'No, it's fine, if it does I can just clip it back and get Sam to re-curl it.' I say more confidently than I'm feeling right now. I'm sat within arm's reach of bridezilla and I'm definitely seeing my life flash before me.

'Dry.' Jenny says with a massive smile.

'Okay, let's make you breath-taking!' Jenny makes a face in my direction.

'I mean, even more breath-taking.' I add, which Jenny smiles at. I sigh with relief. I slowly apply the liquid foundation with a brush, cover that with power foundation and blow on her face to get the excess power off. I pull her blusher out of her make-up bag and apply this to her cheekbones.

'I'm not good on touching people's eyes, so if I tell you what to do will you do it?' I ask Jenny.

'Yeah, course.' I hand Jenny the eyeliner.

'Please just draw under your bottom lashes.' I fetch her false eyelashes, and put a coat of glue on them while Jenny adds mascara to her lashes. Then I slowly and carefully attach her fake eyelashes. While we wait for them to dry, Mom walks in with some champagne.

'Thanks Mom! Okay, Jenny, I'm going to draw a line on your eyelid with this liquid eyeliner okay?' I ask. Jenny looks like she's in a trance with her eyes closed, but she nods. As I pull Jenny's hair around her face, I stand and stare at the face I just created.

'Whoa Jenny, you look gorgeous.' I say. Mom and Auntie Pauline walk into the living room and freeze on the spot and at the same time they both say:

'Jenny!'

'Mom don't cry!' Jenny says running over to Auntie Pauline. I sit in her seat to have my hair done.

'It's okay, I'm just so happy for you. Don't touch me, you'll ruin your hair and make-up.'

'Okay Mom.' They both air-kiss each other.

\*\*\*\*\*\*\*\*\*\*\*\*

Rose, Sam, Jack, Dean and I stand outside the chapel, as Auntie Pauline's old VW camper van drives up to us. Rose runs over to help Jenny out the car.
Auntie Pauline comes running out the church.

'You're late, let's get going.' She pants.

As I slowly walk down the aisle with my arm linked around Dean's we smile nicely at all the people looking us up and down and cooing. The chapel has white lilies everywhere… and I mean everywhere. Very minimalist but perfect. 'She Will Be Loved' plays throughout the room, everyone turns to the back in the room to see Jenny enter. As she makes her way through the chapel, the guests gasp.

'Her dress is stunning.' I breathe. Jenny meets Eric at the altar, where he stands, waiting with the Minister. They hold hands and smile at each other.

**********

The after-party is well under way, the DJ blasting music and his disco lights flashing. There's a queue of people for the buffet and the rest of the guests are dancing on the dance floor, their moves clearly affected by how much they've had to drink. Dean and Jack are doing the robot while Dad spins Mom around.

'Right, everybody, the bride and groom need to have a first dance!' The best-man announces. The dance floor empties and everyone cheers as Jenny and Eric make their way to the floor. The DJ puts on 'Truly Madly Deeply' and they slowly dance together. Then, the music suddenly cuts out and everyone looks up at the DJ, but he just shrugs his shoulders. and fiddles with his controls. Suddenly, Beyoncé's 'Crazy in Love' comes on. Jenny and Eric break out in to a dance routine, as everyone stares, mesmerized. I look at Jack and mouth *'what the fuck?'* but Jack just shrugs at me. I look up at the DJ and he has the biggest smile on his face so he was obviously in on this show they're putting on. When the dance finishes, everyone claps and gives them hugs.

The later it gets, the fewer people on the dance floor. Eric was passed out on a table near the buffet, with his friends chucking water in his face, Jenny had changed into a small black dress and dances with her friends. Jack and Dean are at the buffet table trying to make the biggest sandwich. I smile at how normal my family is.

\*\*\*\*\*\*\*\*\*\*

I wake up the next morning to the nice warm sunshine coming in through the windows and the birds chirping. I reach to where Jack should be next to me, but no one is there. I sit up and look and his side hasn't been slept in. I put my slipper boots and my dressing gown on, and walk to the kitchen to where everyone is squeezed around the table eating pancakes.

'Where is Jack?' I ask. Dean and Dad point to the front door. I walk over and see Jack lying on his back on the porch, with no trousers on and his shirt undone. The cat is curled up on his chest. I walk back into the kitchen, find a seat and enjoy breakfast.

'I didn't know Jack got drunk last night?' I ask.

'He didn't drink that much at the party, but Willy gave him some home-brewed beer from the shed. He took one sip and was gone.' Auntie Pauline adds scowling at Uncle Will.

'Oh.' I say smiling at Uncle Will.

'It's not my fault he's a lightweight.' He laughs.

'We're going to Hamilton place, want to come?' Rose asks me.

'What's Hamilton place?'

'The big shopping mall.'

'Oh, okay that sounds good.' I agree, actually excited by the prospect of shopping.

'How can we wake Jack up? No one can go out with him in this way?' Mom asks.

'Do you have a bucket Auntie Pauline?' I ask, getting up from the table. She points to under the sink. I grab the bucket from there and fill it with freezing cold water, walk out the front door to where Jack is sleeping and tip it on him.

'JESUS!' Jack shouts, as he moves faster than I've ever seen him move.

'We need you to move.' I smirk and walk off.

'You could have just woken me LIKE A NORMAL PERSON?! Shit! My head is killing.' Jack shouts after me.

'Jack's up.' Dean laughs.

'Yep, I'm going to get ready.' I walk out the kitchen and into my room. I pull a summer dress out my suitcase, as Jack walks in stares at me.

'Let the game begin…' He mutters before heading straight to the bathroom.

'What?' I ask. Jack doesn't reply, but I hear the shower turn on. Jack comes back in to get a towel and again I ask:

'What?' Jack just glares at me as a response.

'You will regret what you did.' He says eventually, and he shuts the door. As I giggle to myself at how personal he's taking the bucket of water, I cringe thinking about what he's going to do to me as revenge.

'Lucy, are you ready?' Rose asks, knocking on the door.

'Yeah give me five minutes and I'll be out.' I walk over to the bathroom to say bye to Jack, but the doorknob won't turn.

'Jack, you've locked the door? For heaven's sake, I'm going out, I'll be back later.' I wait for a reply but nothing comes, so I stalk out the bedroom and slam the door behind me.

********

On the drive home, I'm exhausted. I slump in seat with all the shopping bags around me. As we pull onto the drive, we see Uncle William and Dad are playing with a flying helicopter. I smile at how boyish and care-free they seem. I climb out and barely hear a small shout of warning, but when I look around I can't see anything. I turn to get the bags and something hits me in the back. I touch my back and there's something gooey on my hand, I pull it round to see it then something hits me in the head.

'Egg??' I whisper and I hear a laugh.

'JACK?' I shout as an egg narrowly misses my face. I grab my bags and run inside. Rose screams as an egg nearly hits her, I manage to dump my bags.

'Where is Jack?' I demand.

'What is that in your hair?' Mom asks reaching out to touch it, but I duck my head and walk around the house shouting Jack's name.

'He's on the roof.' Dean looks up from his book.

'How do I get up there?' I ask.

'The ladder he has against the house.' Dean says smirking and goes back to reading his book. I walk out into the garden and look up at Jack, laying on his front.

'Jack? What the hell?'

'I told you I would get you back.'

'Yeah and it's now a game. I'm taking your ladder, bye...' I stand under the ladder and push it so it lands lying down on the garden.

'Lucy, you can't leave me up here!'

'Well, you shouldn't have thrown eggs at me.'

'Lucy, don't you dare walk away from me.' He warns. I hide under the canopy, and Jack starts to panic.

'Dean, where is she?' Jack shouts. I look through the door at Dean and put my finger to my mouth and raise my eyebrows. He just smiles, and goes back to reading his book. Then, we hear plastic cracking and see Jack's feet hanging off the side of the house.

'Someone help me?'

'Shit I'll get the ladder Jack, hold on.' I run to the ladder and quickly put it back on the house where it had been before. Jack climbs down, Dean quickly jumps up and runs out so Jack doesn't know he ignored him. I stand there stuck to the spot. Jack gets off the ladder and walks past me slamming his shoulder into mine. I grab my shoulder and fall to my knees.

'Oh my god.' I exhale, winded by pain and trying not to cry.

'Whatever Luc.' Jack ignores me. Rose walks in to the garden to see me on my knees.

'Oh my god Luc, are you okay?'

'No, I hurt my shoulder, I think it's popped out the socket!'

'MMOOOMMMM!' Rose shouts, and Auntie Pauline and Mom come running out. Auntie Pauline lies me on my back as I cradle my shoulder. As I look up, everyone is crowded around me, including Jack, with a worried look on his face.

Mom pulls my cardigan off my arms and everyone gasps.

'What?' I ask worriedly, not able to see my own shoulder.

'Can you call Bernie, Will?' Auntie Pauline says.

'I'm so sorry, Luc.' Jack says, pushing through everyone to sit next to my head and hold my hand. I pull my hand out of his and he bows his head in shame.

'Step aside.' Bernie says, as he runs over to me. He pushes Jack out the way and sits near my head to get access to my shoulder.

'Lucy, I have two choices for you.' He looks at Auntie Pauline.

'Okay?' I ask. Bernie looks me in the eye.

'I can pop your shoulder back into place with pain-killers and gas and air, or I can call an ambulance and they can do it at hospital.'

'Drug me and pop it now.' I say as I squeeze my eyes shut.

'Glass of water, Pauline, a comfy seat and I need you boys to pick her up.'
Jack and Dean come running over to me and awkwardly pick me up and place me on the seat Dad has put there. As Jack turns to walk away, I grab him with my good arm.

'Please stay and hold my hand' I whisper.

'Of course, I will.' He kisses my head with a little smile. Bernie passes me a glass of water and two big tablets, my eyes widen.

'Will I be able to swallow these or will I choke?'

'No, swallow them or it will be painful.' Bernie laughs. After five minutes the pain starts to disappear, Jack holds my hand and crouches next to me while Bernie checks I'm okay and hands me a nozzle for a gas and air cylinder.

'On five.' He says, and then begins counting and holds my shoulder.

'One, two, three –' He pulls and shoves my joint, there's a loud click and everyone winces. I suck on the nozzle for a couple of minutes after, just so I don't faint from the pain.

'Lucy, are you feeling okay? You've gone a bit white' Bernie asks.

'You said on five! Oh god, I feel like I'm going to barf!' I reply. Auntie Pauline hands me a bowl just in case. I smile weakly as I take it. Bernie pulls Auntie Pauline by the elbow to speak in quiet and Mom runs after them. Jack hands me my glass of water to sip and asks if I'm okay.

'I'm fine.' I lie.

'Do you want to go for a lie down, dear?' Auntie Pauline asks me while rubbing my good shoulder.

'Can I eat something?' I look up at everyone.

'Yes.' Bernie says over everyone. Mom throws a packet of chips at Jack: he opens them and tries to feed me.

'Please can everyone step back, I feel very crowed and I need some air, thank you.' I spit.

'Bad moods are usual for the tablets she just took.' Bernie adds in, as everyone looks horrified at my demand. Everyone takes a step back and Mom opens the door to the garden.

'Can someone turn the light on, it's getting dark?' I ask.

'Lucy do you feel light headed?' Mom asks. I nod.

'CATCH HER!' I hear Bernie shout. I can hear people talking around but I don't recognize the voices. My eyelids are so heavy I can't even open them to see who the voices are. I fade back into a sleep, but it only seems to last for seconds, before I open my eyelids. The sun is beaming in through the window onto my face, and it's warm – wait, am I in a hospital?

I look around the room and it's empty. I feel a pinch of sadness when I realize no one was in my room when I woke up. I hear some people talking in the hallway outside the door, now those voices I recognize. A smile spreads across my face, I try move and sit up but my arms ache, *oh yeah, I dislocated my shoulder duh*. I wince in pain and push the 'call the nurse' buzzer. About a minute later a crowd of people run into my room, all talking at once.

'Please one at a time, she's just woken up.' The nurse shushes everyone.

'Hi.' I whisper and try clear my throat.

'Water?' Mom passes me a cup of water.

'Thanks.' I mutter into the cup.

'Sorry it's just me, Dad, Jack and Dean. Everyone else is at the café.' Mom says, not making eye contact.

'It's okay, how long have I been in here?'

'About a day, it happened yesterday afternoon, but don't worry I've phoned Drake and told him what happened.' Jack adds.

'Okay, thanks.'

'How's your head feeling?' The nurse asks me.

'I have a headache, but only a small one.' I answer still sipping my water.

'Okay, it seems to healing well.' the nurse reassures me and walks out.

'What happened?'

'After he popped your shoulder back in, you fainted, and hit your head. Bernie should have kept you on the floor.' Dad comments, grabbing my hand in his.

'Oh okay.' I say, remembering yesterday.

'I'm starving, can I eat?' I ask as my stomach makes rumbling noises.

'I'll ask the nurses.' Mom says while running out the room.

'I don't blame you Jack, you know that?' I say to break the tension. Dad shifts his eyes to Jack and then back to me with a confused look on his face.

'You don't?' Jack replies stunned.

'No, it was both our faults. Okay, you smacked me a bit too hard but I left you on the roof. I tested your patience. I would have been mad as well.' I smile at him.

'That makes sense,' Dean adds, teasing us, 'but I'd carry this on if I were you.' Mom comes running back in my room with a piece of paper.

'Here, love.' Mom thrusts the paper in my face.

'What's this? Ah, the menu.' I say, miming reading it like I'm in a restaurant.

'I'll have a tuna salad, chocolate cake for dessert and some orange juice.' I smile at Mom handing back the menu. She goes to leave but I stop her.

'Mom?'

'Yes dear?' Mom stops on the spot.

'Can you ask when I'm allowed home please?'

'Sure thing'

# CHAPTER NINE

*A week later…*

'Wake up, gorgeous.'

'Hhmm?'

'Luc, you're going to be late for work.'

'Oh, Jack don't spoil my nice dream.' I move my arm to stretch and accidentally hit Jack's face.

'Owwww!'

'Sorry babe.' I kiss his face better.

'Don't start that or we will both be late for work.' Jack jumps out of bed in his boxers. I lift my head to look at the time. *Seven-am.*

'Jack it's only seven, I've got ages before I have to be at work.' I get up, reluctantly, and walk towards the kitchen. Jack is singing whilst cooking pancakes – since being at Auntie Pauline's he doesn't eat anything but pancakes for breakfast.

'Luc?'

'Yep?' I turn to look at Jack, who is making puppy dog eyes at me.

'This may be forward, please tell me if it is, but do you mind if I move in?' I catch my breath, then spend the next few minutes debating in my head. I love Jack being here but I like my own space, but then Jack is paying for an apartment that he's not living in, and he can cook...

'Luc?'

'Sorry, I was weighing it up and its three against one...'

'Is it three good points or three bad points?' Jack looks worried.

'Three good points.'

'And they are?' he asks, flipping a pancake in the air.

'Well, one, I love you being here, two you're paying for an apartment that you're not living in and you could spend your money on me instead.' I smile sweetly at him; his expression doesn't change.

'And the third?'

'You can cook.' He laughs loudly at that.

'Well yes, obviously.'

'You're not that good, you're always having to use the Jamie Oliver cookbook I got you from England.'

'No one has to know that though, just say I made it with no help,' he smiles at me, 'Anyway, Luc, going back to what we were talking about. I was going to phone some realtors to see if they could sell my place, and we could keep the money, go on holiday, and buy a new place?'

*Record scratch.*

'Buy a new place? I love this place!' I answer.

'I wasn't saying we had to, just that we could if we wanted to.'

'Oh okay. Why don't you just rent it out? You still get money but monthly and it's there just in case we need it, plus your place is bigger than mine.' I suggest.

'Okay, that's a good idea, in case we had two kids' Jack adds with a smile. I freeze.

'Whoa, ease up!'

'Only thinking of our future Luc, normally it's the men that freak out when kids are involved.' Jack shrugs his shoulders and flips another pancake.

**********

At work, I sit in a daze all day, thinking what it would be like living with Jack and our future together. The phone rings sometime in the afternoon, bursting my bubble.

'Hello Drake Teely's office, Lucy speaking.'

'Luc, when are you finishing?' It's Jack.

'At five, why? I add.

'Well, it's half-five, and I'm waiting outside for you.'

'Oh, I didn't even realize the time, I'll be right down!' I put the phone down, turn the computer off straight at the wall and run to the lift.

'Night Lucy, you alright?' Beth shouts after me.

'Yeah, thanks, why?'

'You just look a bit pale and you're really distracted this week' Beth answers.

'Oh no I'm fine, I'll see you tomorrow.'

'You won't Lucy, it's Saturday tomorrow' Beth raises one eyebrow.

'Oh yeah, silly me' and I jump in the lift and wave as the doors shut. What the hell is wrong with me? I reach Jack outside, where he grabs my shoulders and looks at me.

'What's wrong?' he asks.

'Nothing, why?' I answer.

'You're so pale, have you eaten today?' Jack asks.

'Erm…' I try and think but I really can't remember lunch.

'Can't remember.' I answer; Jack raises his eyebrow and hugs me.

'We're ordering pizza tonight, and I have good and bad news.'

'Hit me.' I reply. Jack playfully slaps my arm.

'What was that for?' I answer, confused.

'You said hit me.' He beams at me.

'Oh ha-ha, what's the news?'

'I found someone to rent my apartment to, but it's lower than what I said.' I rack my brains for what he said but I can't remember.

'Who you renting it to?'

'Dean and Belle.'

'Dean and Belle?' I frown as I realize I just repeated what he said.

'Yeah Dean's lease is up in two weeks and he was looking for a new place. His isn't big enough for both of them, so they're renting mine.' Jack explains and it does actually sound like a good idea.

'Okay that's cool!' We walk hand in hand down the road and Jack stops outside a cupcake shop.

'What are we doing?' I say while being pulled in the shop.

'Hello there, welcome to Baby Cakes, what can I get for you?' the girl behind the desk chirps from across the shop.

'Can I have a red velvet, blueberry, vanilla and what do you want?' Jack looks at me as I stare into the cabinet of a million cupcakes to find the one I want.

'That one, please.' I press my finger onto the glass covering them.

'Strawberry swirls, good choice!' The girl presses some buttons on the till and puts the four cupcakes in a pink box with Baby Cakes written on each side.

'That's eight dollars please.' Jack hands over the money grabs the box of cakes and says bye to the girl. We arrive at my, no, our apartment – *that's going to take a while to get used to* I think. When we enter the apartment, Jack runs off to the kitchen and puts the cakes in the fridge.

'You're like a dog hiding its bone.'

'Ha-ha, they're so worth it and they're even better colder. Shall we order? I'm starving.'

'Yeah, me too.' Seeing the cakes has made me hungry. Maybe I did skip lunch today.
'I'm ordering from Charlie's; do you want the usual?' Jack stares at me.

'Yes please, order extra sauce though, I always run out.'

'Okay, hello can I order delivery please…yeah that's us on fifth…can I have a large pepperoni with extra cheese and pot of Charlie's sauce…a large chicken surprise… yes please…a bottle of coke? … cool… thanks…okay… okay…bye.'

'It will be thirty minutes, Luc.' Jack shouts at me.

'Okay.' I answer while lying on the bed. I kick my shoes off and climb under the cover. Jack walks in and jumps on the bed next to me.

'What's wrong with you lately?'

'I don't know, I'm always tired. I didn't have an appetite but now I feel I could eat everything in New York and don't get me started on me going to the toilet every second.' I sigh.

'Oh, maybe you're coming down with the flu?' Jack then gets up and changes clothes. We lounge for a bit until the buzzer rings, and he jumps to answer it.

'Luc, pizzzzzaaaa!' I get out of my bed but drag the bed cover with me and slouch on the couch, where Jack has lined the pizzas up on the coffee table.

'Switch the TV on, babes.' While we're watching TV and eating our delicious hot pizza, the buzzer goes and makes us both jump.

'I'll get it.' I climb out my duvet and stalk over to the door.

'Hello?' I answer.

'It's Sarah.' I buzz her straight up with no questions, run to the sofa snuggle in my duvet and start on yet another piece of pizza. Sarah comes falling in the door. We both spring our heads to look at her.

'Jeez, Sarah, are you okay?' Jack ask getting up and helping her over to the sofa. She starts sobbing, mascara running down her face. I notice her shirt is ripped.

'Sarah? What happened to your shirt?'

'I…was… attacked!' She answers in between sobs.

'OH MY GOD!' I shout and stand up, I grab the house line to phone 911.

'No, please don't!' Sarah stops me.

'Why the fuck not?' Jack questions.

'It…was… Jacob.' She sobs again.

'Who's Jacob?' Jack and I say together.

'That…guy… I was seeing… I ditched you for him one night.' She manages to say between sobs, sounding guilty at the end.

'Oh…'

'And why can't you report him?' Jack asks with raised eyebrows.

'Because it's my boss's son.' Sarah looks at the floor.

'Where does he live?' Jack says getting a pad of paper and pen from the table.

'Why?' I say putting my hands on my hips.

'So that I can go talk to him.' Jack is staring at Sarah waiting for his address. Sarah looks at Jack and I, before she decides to give him his address.

'Okay, okay, he lives on Madison avenue penthouse.' Jack rolls his eyes.

'Of course he does.' He says sarcastically, before picking up his mobile and walking off into my bedroom. I sit on the sofa and open my duvet inviting Sarah in. She nods as her eyes water again.

'Don't worry, Sarah, it will be fine. Want to talk about it?' I hug her; she shakes her head and sobs.

'Want some pizza? I ask pulling the box onto my knee.

'Yes please.' She puts her hand in the box.

'Whoa it's nearly all gone!' Sarah says. She knows I'm the only one who eats pepperoni pizza.
'Yeah I've been feeling strange the last week.'

'Oh, why, what's up? Sarah answers stuffing the pizza in her mouth.

'I'm not sure, I've been peeing loads, I didn't have much of an appetite but as you can see I've got that back and now it's bigger than normal, and I'm tired all the time.' I explain.
Sarah stares at me before her eyes go wide.

'You're not, are you?'

'What?' I ask and then it hits me, 'Oh my… I hadn't thought of that…'

'Do you use, you know, protection?'

'We did sometimes, but now that we're together we don't.'
Sarah is still staring at my face.

'Oh god, do you think I'm pregnant? I ask.

'I don't know, what does Jack think?'

'No. I told him I'm not well, he said it could be flu.' I answer.

'Men!' Sarah answers with a cackle. I shrug my shoulders and start to think. When Jack walks back into the room, Sarah nudges my arm, interrupting my thoughts.

'I'm going out to meet Dean, I'll be back in an hour.' Jack mumbles.

'Hang on a minute.' I go to get up and Jack slams the door after him.

'Sorry.' Sarah looks at me with puppy dog eyes.

'I'm ringing Dean.' I jump up and redial the last number called.

'Hello?' A female voice on the other end says.

'Hi, is that Belle?'

'Yeah, what's up Lucy?'

'Is Dean there?'

'Yeah, hold on.' I hear some fumbling noises and then Dean comes on the line.

'Where are you and Jack going?' I question him.

'For a drink.' Dean answers as if nothing odd is happening.

'I know you're going to Jacob's house.' I spit down the phone.

'And?'

'Can't you stop him? I don't want Jack to get hurt.'

'Well, Jack's mad, so best just leave him to knock this guy out.' Dean reasons.

'So, you can't do anything? I beg Dean.

'Sorry Luc, but no, I'll see you in an hour.' I put the phone down and start to well up.

'Oh yeah and I cry a lot recently too.' I say to Sarah who has a frown on her face.

'I'm sorry, I didn't think he would actually go.' Sarah says to me.

'Its fine, he's only protecting you.' I add.

'Let's just watch Dear John, stare at Channing Tatum, eat his pizza and wait for his return, don't worry Luc.'

\*\*\*\*\*\*\*\*\*\*\*

Jack and Dean come into the apartment laughing and joking with each other, then Dean playfully punches Jack in the arm.

'You're both okay!' I say, as I get up and go over to hug Jack.

'Yeah, we're good.' Dean answers.

'We scared him so much he wet himself, then we went for a drink.' Sarah and I can't help but laugh.

'Any other troubles, Sar, come to me or Jacky-boy.' Dean walks over and hugs Sarah.
'How you feeling?' Jack holds me at arm's length to examine me.

'Much better now I've eaten.' I lay my head on his chest so he can't see the expression on my face.

'Good, have you two eaten my pizza? What's this on TV?' he asks.

'No, we haven't and it's Dear John.' Sarah answers running over to sit on the remote, so that Jack can't turn it off.

'We're dribbling over Channing Tatum, he's so fit.' I add as Sarah and I giggle like schoolgirls.

'Right, I'm ordering more pizza, Dean get Belle here, we're having a little par-tay.' Jack says. Belle arrives about half an hour later; Jack and Dean went to thee shop to get drinks and playing cards. We played drinker snap; which is whoever gets snap has to down their drink and we played the original drinking game, two large pizzas arrived and the party was under way.

'Want another vodka and coke babes?' Jack shouts over to me. Sarah and I exchange looks. We'd been making sure I was only drinking coke, but telling everyone it's alcoholic.

'No, it's fine, you sit down, I'll make them.' I grab Sarah's arm and drag her to the kitchen.

'Don't panic Luc, he's had loads to drink, he's a goner soon.'

'Okay' I let out a big sigh of relief and we carry the drinks in to carry on with the party fun.

**********

The next morning, I wake up freezing cold, cuddled around Sarah on the living room floor. Dean is asleep under the coffee table, Belle is cuddling her knees in the arm chair and Jack is nowhere to be seen. I let go of Sarah and climb over her to make my way to the kitchen.

'Oh my god, this apartment is a state.' I complain to myself. I flip the kettle on and start to load the dishwasher, clean the kitchen sides and sigh in relief once that at least one room is tidy. I leave the kettle and walk towards my bedroom to get my dressing gown. Jack is asleep on the bed with my duvet wrapped around him. I tiptoe over to the alarm clock and set it for 2 minutes time and turn the volume up, and tiptoe run out the room. I open all the blinds in the living room and open the windows to welcome in some very wanted fresh air. I tidy around everyone trying not to wake them up, as the kettle boils I hear the alarm clock and Jack jolt awake.

'What the hell?!' I hear Jack shout. I try hide my smile and snigger while I make five cups of coffee.

'Wow we didn't make a mess last night, we're such tidy drunks.' I hear Dean say.

'Actually no.' I walk in with cups of coffee.

'Oh well, I could have guessed you would have tidied it.' We smile at each other. Jack comes out the room.

'Luc, did you turn the alarm clock on?'

'No, why?'

'It went off and it was on full volume.' He grumbles.

'Oh, I haven't touched it.' I shake my head innocently.

'You did, didn't you?' Sarah asks already knowing the answer.

'Did you not learn your lesson about messing with him last time?' Belle raises an eyebrow. Trust Belle to sound like my mother.

'Yes thanks, but I like a little fun in my life.' I answer.

'Yeah we know, what with you being up the fluff.' Sarah quips, taking a sip of coffee and immediately spitting it back in the cup when she realizes what she just said. Dean and Belle both spin their heads to me.

'What?!' They both exclaim. I glare at Sarah before explaining.

'I don't know if I am.'

'But you were drinking last night?' Belle says.

179

'No just coke, I told everyone it was vodka so no one would guess.'

'Oh smart.' Belle adds.

'Please don't mention it to Jack, I want to be sure before I tell him.' I beg.

'You know he will be over the moon, don't you?' Dean adds.

'Yeah but I don't want to say I am and find out I'm not, that will break his heart.' I mutter looking at my hands.

'Okay, we will do whatever you ask.' Dean gets up to hug me.

'If you need anything let me know.' Belle says hugging me.

'Yeah. What they said Luc.' Sarah adds. I giggle just as Jack comes back in the room.

'What's going on?' He says while jumping over the arm of the sofa. Everyone goes quiet and look at me, mumbling variations of 'nothing'.

'Why is everyone looking shifty?' Jack eyes us all up.

'We were talking about you, then we had to stop because you came in, duh.' Sarah says, while everyone smiles awkwardly.

'Well we should go.' Dean chirps up and pulls on Belle's arm.

'Bye.' We all answer together.

'What we doing today?' Jack looks me up and down.

'I don't know, why are you looking at me like that?'

'Don't know, you just look different.' He answers. My eyes shoot straight to Sarah's whose are also wide and panicked. Just then I get a stomach pain and crouch over and wince.

'Babe, what's wrong?' Jack is instantly at my side.

'I don't know, it's gone now, I just wasn't expecting that.' I answer, very aware of Sarah staring at me.

'Want to go shopping Sar?' I ask, trying to distract him.

'Yeah that's a great idea.' Sarah adds.

'Are you sure? After that?' Jack says.

'Yeah don't worry if I need you, I'll phone you.' I smile and kiss him.

'Best get ready Sar.' We go to my room.

As Sarah and I leave the apartment, we say our goodbyes to Jack, who's laid on the sofa with a bowl of chips watching TV. When we're out of earshot Sarah turns to me.

'We're going to the hospital, right?'

'Yes please.' I answer. We sit in the cab in silence until we reach the hospital. We walk up to reception and explain the situation.

'Okay, please fill this form out and someone will be with you.' The lady behind the counter says. We both smile and take a seat. We look at the form and it's just the usual questions, my full name, my address, in case of emergency, my insurance etc. etc. etc. As I hand the form back in I get that horrible stomach pain again, and crouch over in pain. The woman from behind the counter comes running around while another gets a wheel chair.

'Honey, are you okay?' The woman looks at my face.

'Yeah sorry, that happened earlier.' I reply with gritted teeth.

'Okay, don't worry, I'll get the doctor to see you now.' She runs off and leaves me with the nurse with the wheel chair. Sarah helps me in and follows us to a nearby room.

'The doctor won't be long, is there anything I can get you?' The nurse asks.

'No thanks.' I respond and she leaves us alone.

'I'm scared.' I admit, my eyes welling up.

'Don't be, you're in the right pace. Do you want me to phone Jack?'

'Erm…' I want Jack here but I don't want him to worry.

'It might be best, he needs to know Luc.'

'Okay, yes, please phone him.' Sarah leaves the room and I can't help but sob to myself. Then the doctor walks in.

'Hello there, I'm Doctor Bruce,' the doctor shakes my hand, 'I've been informed of your symptoms and I believe you have an idea yourself?' I nod at her.

'Okay good, can you please lay on this bed and pull your trousers down a bit and your top up just to show your belly?' I do as I'm told, still sobbing, wondering how Jack feels right now. Doctor Bruce pulls a tall machine over on wheels and pulls a bottle from the side of it and says.

'This may be a little cold.' She warns. I just nod. I can't find any words. As she squeezes the contents of the bottle onto my tummy she fires up the machine. She puts her finger on the screen, saying:

'You might want to watch this.' Then there's a knock at the door, and Sarah and Jack walk in. Jack comes straight over to me and holds my hand and Sarah stays near the door. Doctor Bruce then repeats what she said about the screen while tapping her nail on the little screen. She runs an object in her hand over my tummy, it looks like a portable razor for men, and a noise appears that startles me and a tiny beat, and I see Doctor Bruce smile and look at me and Jack in turn.

'What?' I ask worriedly.

'That's a baby, you're pregnant!' She announces. I look at her stunned. Doctor Bruce presses a button and it starts printing a picture. Sarah squeals where she is standing and Jack grips my hand tight. I can't pull my eyes away from the screen. Jack kisses my hair.

'I just need to work out roughly how old so I can give you an expectancy date.' I manage to look at Jack, who is beaming from ear to ear, but I just can't seem to smile.

'Are you okay?' Jack pulls my chin so I'm looking in his eyes; all I can do is frown. No words come out when I open my mouth.

'She's probably in shock.' Doctor Bruce interrupts. Doctor Bruce hands me some leaflets and gives us advice. I don't take in a word she is saying, but just nod every so often. The rest of the ride home seems a blur and I don't remember anything since she said *'that's a baby, you're pregnant'*. It just keeps circling in my head that *I'm pregnant!*

************

'I'm going to lie down.' I croak and stalk off to my bed. I get straight under my covers and cry uncontrollably *I'm going to be a mom! Little old me?!*

After a couple of hours, I hear a knock at the door. I don't even move.

'Babe, how you feeling?' Jack asks lying down next to me on the bed, puts his arm under my head and pulls me close and rests his head on mine.

'It will be okay.' He mutters into my hair.

'Do you have questions?' Jack speaks again after a while.

184

'How old is the baby?' I mumble.

'The baby is fifteen weeks old.' Jack whispers.

'Fifteen weeks?!'

'Yeah I've worked it out it to Sarah's party, back in August.' Jack explains.

'So, it's yours?' I ask, feeling the hurt I just gave him.

'Well, did you sleep with anyone in or around August?' I sit and think for a minute.

'No, I don't think so. I broke up with Chase in July and then you at Sarah's party when we were drunk.' I feel him smile against my head.

'So, it is mine, I'm going to be a dad!' I look up at his face and how happy he is, *so why aren't I happy?*

'We can have a DNA test when its born if you want?' I ask while not making eye contact.

'I trust you, but if it makes you happier, then okay, we will. When can I tell people?'

'Whenever.' I say back, I lift my head up to meet his and kiss him.

'You promise it will be okay?' I ask him.

'I will do everything in my power to look after you and baby.'
Jack kisses me back.

'Get the phone then! I want to tell Mom.' I smile. Jack runs
out the room like a young boy, he's so happy, I can hear him
talking on the phone already.


'Jack who is it?' I ask, but he doesn't answer. I get out of bed
and walk into the living room to find Jack pinned against the
wall by a massive guy. Jack has a bleeding nose. I pick up my
cell phone and dial 911.

'Hello, I need the police and an ambulance, some guy is in
my apartment beating up my boyfriend and I'm pregnant.
He's tall with a long black trench coat, that's all I can see, and
my boyfriend is bleeding, come quick, my address is Fifth
Avenue, blue building, Apartment eighteen.' I blurt down the
phone to the operator. I'm sure I know what's going on, given
that Jack and Dean threatened Elliot recently, so I put the
phone down and walk out the bedroom straight across to the
kitchen, pretending that I haven't seen anything. I fake a
double-take them. Jack is on the floor and the man is smiling
down at him.

'Oh, hello, sorry, I didn't know we had company. Come sit
down I'm making coffee.' I offer, keeping my voice level.

'Oh, no, thank you ma'am' the man answers.

'Please don't make a pregnant woman beg you, have a coffee!
And don't call me ma'am, I'm twenty-three.' The guy
reluctantly walks over to the table and takes a seat, Jack is

186

trying to make faces at me but I'm not looking at him. Jack sits on the other end of the table, both guys looking each other up and down.

'So, what's your name?' I ask the guy.

'Err… Dave, yeah, my name's Dave.' He answers, obviously lying to me.

'Oh, how do you know Jack?' I ask still ignoring Jack's faces and ploys to get my attention.

'I work with him?'

'Really? You're a lion tamer too? I didn't realize there were so many in New York.' I ask Dave, Jack smirks.

'Err, yes ma'am.' His agreement confirms my suspicions. I clear my throat.
'Not a ma'am, remember.'

'Oh, sorry ma'am, I mean lady, I mean nothing.' 'Dave' looks at his fingers.

'Coffee's ready!' I put a mug in front of Dave just as the buzzer goes. Jack gets up from the table to answer it. I swing round to look at Jack and mouth '*sit down*'. He looks horrified but sits back down. I press the door release button without even asking who it was. Dave looks at Jack.

'That must be Elliot, checking I'm good.' He says arrogantly. I swing open the apartment door to two uniformed cops, who storm in and order Dave to get on the floor. Jack looks confused.

'Officers, he threatened and hurt my boyfriend, all for blackmail. His boss attacked my best friend. I turn on my heels and rush over to Jack.

'You okay?' I whisper just as a paramedic comes in. They check his nose and if he's in any more pain. They clean his face, putting strips across his nose. After half an hour of taking statements, the apartment is empty again.

'How did you know?' Jack asks.

'I opened the door to see where you were, heard him talking to you and saw you bleeding, phoned the police on my cell and came out to get him to stay.'

'I don't know what he would have done if you hadn't called them, Luc.' Jack smiles a boyish grin at me and snakes his hands round my waist. I wiggle out of his vice like grip and reply.

'We're not doing that, I'm phoning around about our baby.' I smile, pick up the phone and dial a number.

'Mom? Jack and I have some news for you…no no, good news… very good news…we're having a baby.' I announce. After a beat of silence, I hear her scream down the phone, so I hold it at arm's length.

'Mom, are you okay? Yeah, I'm sure, we worked it out…August at Sarah's party…yeah… I'm going to phone around, will you tell Dad when he gets back and call

Gemma… love you, bye!'

'Mom happy?' Jack jokes. I hand the phone to Jack.

'Tell Dean?'
'Me?' He answers walking towards the bedroom.

'Yeah he's your brother, he would appreciate it more.'

'Okay.' Jack dials the number, but there's no answer. He leaves a voicemail.

'Hey, it's Jack, I have some news for you, good news, don't worry, I just want to tell you. Can you phone us back?' He shrugs like he did something wrong.

'We're growing up Luc?' Jack lays on his back with his hands behind his head and lets out a massive sigh.

'I'm starving.' It's all I can say in response.

'Well, you are feeding two people now.' Jack smiles kissing my forehand and grabs my hand.

'Where we going?' I ask.

'Into the living room, we're ordering in again. We have so much to celebrate!' Sarah comes bursting into the apartment out of breath.

'Jacob just got arrested.' She slumps onto the sofa, breathing heavily.

'How do you know?' I ask warily.

'Just saw them taking him into a police car.'

'Oh' Jack laughs.

'We're celebrating again tonight, want to join us?' I ask Sarah.

'Sure, how much do you want?' She says, slumping even further down the couch.

'A hundred dollars' Jack says. Sarah sits bolt upright.

'Are you serious?' Jack bursts out into a laugh.

'No keep your money, I'm so happy no one can take it away from me. I'm going to be a Dad!' The phone rings in the background.

'Hello? Hi Dean…yeah come over then…bring drinks… bye.' I put the phone down.

'Dean and Belle are just around the corner' I say.

'Oh, did they get my message?' Jack asks.

'Not sure.' The phone rings again.

'Hello…Gemma?' I squeal, 'you heard…yeah I'm 15 weeks…you're going to be Auntie Gem Gem' I slide down the wall so I'm hugging my knees and start to cry. Jack comes over sits next to me and takes the phone.

'Sorry Gem, she's very emotional…yeah we got a picture, I'll get her to email it to you...okay bye.' Jack puts his arm around me.

'I'm sorry, I can't help it' I sob.

'I know' he laughs. Sarah breaks up our little emotional party.

'So… what are we eating?'

\*\*\*\*\*\*\*\*\*\*\*\*\*\*\*\*\*

At eight in the morning, Jack wakes me up.

'I'm so tired, I woke up every hour, on the hour last night.' I complain.

'Oh, so not a good sleep then?'

'No, at least I don't have a hard job,' I smile, 'oh but I'm not allowed coffee!' My smile fades and I groan loudly. I get out of bed and jump in the shower. It makes me feel a hundred times better, and I slip on my interview dress. Looking at myself in the mirror, I pat my tummy.

'Oh baby, I'm not going to fit in this dress for much longer,' I whisper to myself still rubbing my tummy, 'I'm going to call you Beano till we find a more permanent name for you.' I head off to work. As I stand in the lift to the eighteenth floor, I feel slightly sick. *Please don't be sick in the lift* I think to myself. The doors ping and Beth is beaming at me across the hall.

191

'Good morning Lucy?'

'Morning Beth.' I answer.
'Wow, you look good today, coffee?'

'Thanks! I can't drink coffee for a while... I found out I'm pregnant.' I whisper to her. Beth sits at her desk with her bottom jaw almost touching the floor. She runs into my office after me.

'You're pregnant?' Beth repeats.

'Yeah.' I give her a massive smile.

'Oh my god, that's great news.' She hugs me.

'Thanks, I haven't told Drake yet.'

'Haven't told Drake what?' Drake says closing my office door.

'Oh, err that I'm pregnant.' I stare at him, waiting for his expression to change into something positive or negative, but his face doesn't change. Drake takes a couple of steps towards me until he's standing in front of me.

'Congratulations.' He says and pulls me in for an awkward, uncomfortable hug.

'How far gone are you?' Beth interrupts.

'Only fifteen weeks, you're not getting rid of me just yet.' I warn. They both laugh at my comment.

'I best start the day's work or I won't get paid' I smile.

'I'm holding a meeting at two, I need you both there.' Drake says and walks out.

'I don't think he was happy about my news.' I whisper to Beth.

'I think he's happy, but I think he wanted it to be his baby...' Beth answers. I let out a sudden laugh at Beth's comment and clamp my hand to my mouth, which makes Beth laugh; we sit there giggling and gossiping till ten, then the phone rings in my office, which startles us both.

'Hello Drake Teely's office, Lucy speaking... yeah... yeah... okay... yeah... both of us? Okay bye.'

'We have to go see Cathy in the art department.' I shrug my shoulders at Beth.
As we stroll along the hallway, Cathy's head pops out her office and she ushers us in and shuts the door.

'Whoa what's wrong?' I ask.

'Drake might be getting fired.' Cathy stares at us.

'What?' Beth and I say together.

'I heard that they're getting a new computing system in from a company in town called 'fresh-something'.

'Freshman's?' I question.

'Yeah, you know it?'

'Yeah, it's where Jack works?' I instantly wonder why Jack's company is becoming our new computing system.

'I can find out from Jack.' I answer half hoping they will agree to my suggestion. Both Beth and Cathy nod their heads at me. We head back to our floor, into my office. I dial Jack's office.

'Hi Jack Base please.' I request. Beth sits at the chair opposite my desk. I get a nervous feeling in my stomach whilst I wait to be transferred.

'Hello, Jack Base?'

'Hi babe, it's me.'

'Hey, I don't have time to talk, can it wait?' Jack says sharply.

'Oh, it was about your company coming over to mine.' I answer. Jack is silent.

'Jack?'

'I'll talk to you later, bye.' He hangs up the phone. I look at Beth, confused by this experience.

'What did he say?' Beth raises her eyebrows.

'When I asked, he went silent and said he will speak to me later.' Beth's face drops just like mine did. The rest of the day went by way too slowly for my liking. I didn't have that much work to do, so I sat there thinking all day.

# CHAPTER TEN

At midday I sit at my desk and unwrap my sandwich from the cafe, as I open my mouth to take my first bite Beth comes bursting into my office.

'Did I miss any gossip?' She asks panting and then sitting on an abandoned chair in the corner.

'I found out about Freshman's if that's what you mean?'

'Yeah, that.' She answers still catching her breath.

'It's nothing juicy, the company we're with now, their contract is up and Freshman's are taking it over.'

'Oh, I rushed here for nothing.' She complains.

'Why are you late?'

'I had to visit the doctor, it's the only day they could do.'

'Oh, okay.' I shovel some more food in my mouth.

'So, how's baby?' A smile spreads across her face.

'Hungry, I haven't stopped eating – I'm going to get really fat.'

'No, you won't, I didn't and I ate like a pig.' She admits. I stop mid-chew.

'You have a child?'

'Yeah, didn't you know?'

'Um no, how old? Girl or boy?' I ask, embarrassed I didn't know.

'Girl and she's four.'

'What about her dad?'

'We've been married for seven years.'

'Really? How did I not know any of this?'
'I don't like to share my personal information or be treated differently so I take my rings off before I come in.'

'Oh…'

'Heard anything about Drake?' She asks taking her coat off as she changes the subject.

'Nuh-uh.' I answer as I swallow my food.

'This place is boring.' She groans. I nod while downing my water.

'What you doing for Christmas?' Beth asks.

'Oh god, I try not to think about it.'

'You do know its next week, yes?'

'Yep.'

'What have you got Jack?'

'Um… nothing?'

'WHAT?' Beth shouts and makes me jump.

'What?' I frown.

'You have to get him something.'

'Like what?'

'You – but not the everyday you.' Beth pulls a magazine out of her bag.

'You carry that around with you?'

'Yes. Victoria secret is not porn, so wipe that look off your face.' I sit in silence while I trying to get a look at every page while she's flicking through.

'Like this?' she points her finger on a teddy Santa outfit.

'Really? What about Beano?'

'It's loose, so its fine, we can go after work if you want?' she looks at me with such hope.

'Okay fine.'

**************

As I push myself throw the front door with the millions of shopping bags, Jack does a double take at me from the sofa.

'I wondered where you were' he said while getting up to help with my bags.

'Yeah sorry, I went Christmas shopping.'

'Anything for me?' Jack asks looking in the bags.

'Yes.' I slap his hand.

'Hey, no hitting.' He pouts.

'I do but it's a weird present.'

'Weird? Like bondage weird?' He asks with a raised eyebrow.

'No don't be stupid, it's nothing like that.'

'Okay, show me. It can be an early present.'

'No, I'm embarrassed, I'm just going to take it back.'

'No no no no!' He contests, dragging me to the sofa.

'Okay I'll put it on now, but if you laugh...'

'My present is clothes for you?' he asks confusedly, then his face shows that it clicks.

'Yep.'

'Oh good, I'm locking the door.' As I fumble around putting the red netted teddy on, I pull my hair band out and let my hair fall. I reluctantly look in the mirror before I swing open the bedroom door.

'Wow' is all Jack can say whilst staring at me from across the room.

'I told you it's weird.'

'It's not weird, it's freaking sexy as hell.' Jack gets up and literally power walks over to me, picks me up, rests me against the wall and kisses me deeply.

\*\*\*\*\*\*\*\*\*\*\*

I untangle myself from a sleeping Jack and tip-toe to the living room, closing the bedroom door behind me, order pizza and put my feet up. As I'm flicking through the channels, I hear the bedroom door open. I look over the back of the sofa to Jack in his boxers, bed hair and yawning.

'Hey gorgeous.' He kneels in front of me and kisses me deeply again.

'Is this going to happen every time you see me in this?'

'No, the bit in the bedroom will happen every time I see or think of you in this.' He starts kissing my neck and running his hands up and down me.

'Jack calm yourself, I'm eating before any more exercise.'

'Done deal babes, what have you ordered?'

'The usual.' He kisses my lips and stands up.

'I'm putting the notebook on.'

'As long as you stay in that I'm not fussy.'

'Jack, stop being a pervert.'

'I have a meeting at nine, at your office.' He says, changing the subject.

'Oh really? Why?' I sit up really concerned.

'Just dotting the I's and crossing the T's.'

'Right okay, so nothing bad.'

'No, it's all fine.' As we snuggle together on the sofa waiting for our pizza, my phone suddenly rings, interrupting our peace.
'Hello? Sarah?... you're outside the door?' I raise my eyebrow at Jack.

'What you doing there?......do you now? I'm not dressed for company.....okay give me a minute...bye!' I turn to Jack.

'Sarah is having dinner with us.' Jack just nods, not fazed by it at all. I slip my dressing gown on over my teddy to let Sarah in.

'Babe, you took your time.' Sarah complains.

'I was wearing this.' I open my dressing gown and flash her.

'Smoking,' she giggles, 'bet Jack had the time of his life.'

'Jack did indeed.' Jack answers.

'So, when's the pizza getting here?' Just then the buzzer on the door rings.

'Hello?'

'Pizza.' I buzz them straight up.

'I only ordered mine and Jack's usual, not the trio.' I look over to Sarah.

'It's cool, so what's new?'

'Not much, I went Christmas shopping today.'

'Really?' Sarah fake-gasps.

'Yep its true.' Jack adds.

'Shush you over there.' Sarah quips.

'Shush you, pizza stealer.' He jokes back.

'Okay truce.' Sarah gets up and shakes Jacks hand and giggles.

'Girls are weird.' He comments.

'Are not.' I say in defense while slapping his arm. My phone then jumps to life again, a text from Belle's new American number.

*Hey, are you free to talk?*

Blunt but to the point I suppose, no kiss, I wonder if all English people are like that. I text her back.

*I'm at home with Jack and Sarah, what's up? X*

'Who's that? And why are you frowning?'

I look up to see Sarah staring at me, whilst Jack is paying

close attention to The Notebook again.

*Can I pop round I need your advice badly? X*

'It's Belle, she said she needs my advice badly.' I frown again.

'Oh, I wonder if it's juicy!'

'Sarah, it could be important.'

'Doubt it, what do the English have to worry about?'

'That's a strange question, even for you.'

'Ha-ha.' Sarah answers as the buzzer goes again.

'That damn buzzer will be the death of me.' Jack pipes up.

'Shut up Maureen.' Sarah barks back at Jack with a smile. As Jack and I give Sarah a confused look, Belle comes out of the lift.

'Can we go in your room?' Belle grabs my hand and runs into my bedroom.

'Sure.' As I shut the door, I turn the lock.

'What's up?'

'Dean and I had a massive argument.' She sobs.

'About what?'

'I got offered a job.' She sobs again.

'That's great, why did you argue?'

'It's in L.A.'

'Oh...'

'Yeah that's what he said, but I get an apartment paid, a company cell, and a secure visa for two years.'

'That's a really good offer, does Dean not want to move with you?'

'No.' She starts crying, then there's a knock at the door.

'You guys okay?' Comes Sarah's voice.

'You can let her in.' Belle shakes her hand at the door. I get off the bed and unlock the door for Sarah to come in.

'What's up Belle?' Sarah asks as she sits next to Belle, putting her arm around her shoulders.

'Belle got offered a job in L.A!' I look at Sarah.

'Really? That's so cool!'

'Is it?' Belle looks up at her with tear stained eyes.

'Yeah it's a great opportunity.' In the other room I hear the phone ring, and Jack mumbling. I look at Belle and Sarah who I don't think have realized.

'Why doesn't Dean want to go?' I ask.

'He doesn't want to leave you lot, which I do understand you know, I'm not a bitch, I don't want to drag him away…'

'No one said you were, can't they offer you the same job here or closer?' Sarah is still cradling Belle.

'I... don't...think...so.' Belle answers in between sobs. We all look up at the door as we hear it open. Dean walks in with his head hung, and looks like he's been crying too. I get up and give Dean a hug which he gladly takes and continues to sob like Belle.

'I... can't...handle...all...these...feelings...in....one...go.' Dean says between sobs in my neck.

'it's okay, no one said it was easy.' Jack then enters the bedroom.

'Is everyone okay?' He asks, but no one answers him.

'Dean and Belle, you can stay in here and talk. We'll be out here if you need anything, okay?' Jack decides. Dean wraps his jump over his hands and wipes away his tears and nods his head, Belle gets up off the floor and sits on the end of our bed.

'Do you want me to order you food?' I ask them both.

'Yes please Luc.' Dean answers me. I shut the bedroom door

and well up. I breath in to stop myself from actually crying, take my seat back on the sofa and stuff my face with cold pizza and flat cola. When the film finishes, I get up and slowly and quietly opened the door to my bedroom, to find Belle and Dean asleep in each other's arms.

'We're sleeping in the spare room tonight.' I whisper to Jack as I shut the door again.

'Okay.'

'You can stay on the sofa if you want Sarah? I'm going to bed.' I get to the spare bedroom and take off my dressing gown and jump in the massive bed. As I snuggle under the cover, Jack comes in and jumps on the bed next to me.

'Don't for one second think you're sleeping for the next forty-five minutes' Jack whispers in my ear.

'Oh, what a charmer…'

\*\*\*\*\*\*\*\*\*\*\*\*

I wake up with a jolt and feel disorientated, before I remember where I am.

'You alright babe?' Jack asks me sleepily.

'Yeah I just had a bad dream.'

'It sounded alright to me, you told me you loved me.' Jack says while stretching.

'I did?'

'Yeah you're so adorable,' he leans over and kisses my nose, 'I love you too.'

'Now that's more romantic.' I tease while kissing him. Then, I get up, and walk into the living room. Sarah is still fast asleep on the sofa, so I poke my head into my bedroom where Belle and Dean are still sleeping. I tip-toe to the kitchen and slide up onto the counter, flip the kettle on, stretch and yawn. Jack joins me, standing in front of me with his hands on my hips inside my dressing gown. He pulls me towards him so our pelvises are touching and he starts kissing my neck.

'Cut it out.' Comes a voice from the living room. We both look over with a smirk.

'Morning beautiful.' I call out to Sarah.

'Morning.' Sarah sleepily answers.

'How did you sleep?'

'Good, surprisingly.'

'Morning…' We all look over to my bedroom door where Belle comes out.

'Morning – does everyone want coffee?' As Jack helps me off the counter, I grab some mugs and make the drinks.

'Can we share a cab when you leave for work?' Belle asks.

'Err yeah, sure…'

'Morning Dean.' I hear Sarah say.

'I had a really good sleep.' Dean states while stretching.

'Looks like crying helps everyone sleep.' I say.

'Seems that way.' Belle agrees.

'I'm having a shower.' I look over at everyone and walk off to the bathroom. I take my time in the shower and wash off the last couple of days. I sing to myself, to take my mind off of work today.

'Ready?' I walk out my bedroom and look at everyone.

'Using your Marc Jacobs today?' Sarah asked while eyeing up my bag.

'Of course,' I smile, 'let's go get a cab.' We all make our way downstairs, where Sarah says her goodbyes. Jack, Dean, Belle and I jump in the next available cab. As we pull up outside my building, I get out, say my goodbyes to Jack, and make my way inside.

'LUCY!' I hear, and as I turn around sharply, I see Cathy running at me in six-inch heels, a hot cup of coffee in her hand.

'Cathy, you okay?!'

'Yes, I have some gossip for you and Beth!' Cathy then grabs my arm and starts running again. As we ding onto the eighteenth floor, Cathy orders Beth to get some coffees and meet in my office for talk on a new book. I lift my eyebrows, confused by the meeting about a new book when she leans a centimeter away from me and gently says:

'Drake is in his office so I can't speak loudly.'

'In that case, shouldn't we go to your office?'

'Oh god yes we should – BETH!' As we leave my office, Beth is carrying a tray with three coffees on.

'We have to go to my office, sorry babe.' Cathy explains.

'Oh, okay.' Beth answers with a very confused look on her face. We approach Cathy's office. She ushers us inside and shuts and locks the door.

'What's going on?' Beth says looking at us both.

'Have a mouthful of coffee first, my loves.' Beth and I start to drink our coffee when Cathy sit at her desk with her fingers intertwined staring at us both.

'Well, Lisa has found out about Drake...'

'Well...?' I ask.
'His dad wants to sell the company, so if Drake wants it, he has to buy it!'

'How much are they selling it for?' Beth asks like she's interested in buying it.

'Thirty million dollars.' I spit my coffee out while Beth chokes on hers. I tap her back.

'You okay?' I ask her.

'Yeah, yeah.' She answers with a small voice.

'Thirty million?' I repeat.

'Will we lose our jobs?' Beth asks.

'Oh god I didn't think of that?' I add.

'Depends who buys it.' Cathy says.

'Oh my god.' Beth gasps. Just then Cathy's office phone rings.

'Hello? Yes Drake, I have your lovely ladies… of course… bye. Drake wants you back.' Cathy replies with a smirk.

'Yes boss!' I smile at Cathy and salute her. As we take a slow walk back to our office, I start thinking what other jobs I could maybe look for just in case. I sit at my desk pull out a pad and pen out of my draw:

> *a) writer*
> *b) work for another editor*
> *c) become a cat lady*
> *d) retire and live off Jack*
> *e) become a stripper*

I wonder if I could be a stripper… I shimmy my shoulders in a mock dance. No, no, stripping is not for me. I scribble over option E. I log back into my computer to find an email from Jack.

*From: Jack Base*
*Subject: dinner?...*
*To: Lucy Winter*
*12/20/2010 11:45*

*Dear madam,*

*Would you accompany me on a date to an extremely posh hotel/restaurant tonight?*

*Love you, Jack*

*I.T manager at Freshman's LTD.*

*'Oh, you're so cute, Base…'* I think to myself as I reply.

*From: Lucy Winter*
*Subject: dinner?...*
*To: Jack Base*
*12/20/2010 12:00*

*Dear Sir,*

*I would feel honored to accompany you to an extremely posh hotel/restaurant tonight.*

*Love you back,*
*From Lucy and Beano*

### P.A. to Drake Teely at Teely's International

I now have to think of what to wear, as I mentally look through my wardrobe. I find the dress I want and match some shoes, think of my make-up and hair.

'God, I should be a stylist.' I accidently say out loud.

'Really?' Drake says, interrupting, as he walks into my office.

'Yeah, I think I'd be pretty good at it.'

'Right, of course you would.'

'What's up?' I knot my hands together and lean on my elbows on my desk as Drake takes a seat in front on my desk.

'Have you heard?' Drake answers without looking at me.

'About the company?'

'Yes.' Drake picks some non-existent fluff off of his trousers to keep his eye away from mine.

'Then yes, I heard your dad wants to sell it.'

'I just don't know what to do Lucy.' Drake looks at me with tears in his eyes, *crap I can't deal with men crying.*

'Beth and I will help you… and Cathy will.' He looks up at me again.

'You'd help?'

'Yeah, why wouldn't we?'

'I thought – no it doesn't matter what I thought, how can we make the company good again?'

'Make more book deals, make them cheaper, go to more countries, do celebrity autobiographies.'

'Oh, they're good ideas actually.' Drake answers with his trademark smile plastered on his face.

'I'm calling a meeting and we can discuss it.' I offer. Drake nods at me so much his head might fall off. He returns to his office, so I pick the phone up and called through to Cathy.

'Cathy, its Lucy, please be at the meeting room in five minutes...bye. Beth please come in here.' I put the phone down when I hear Beth walk around her desk and knock on my door.

'Hey Lucy, everything okay?'

'Yeah, yeah, please sit. I have a master plan.'

'Right…' Beth lifts one eyebrow and looks at me like I'm crazy.

'Can you carry these for me, and these' I dump two massive piles of pads, paper, pens and manuscripts in front of her and run through the adjoining door to Drake's office.

'Drake, meeting room, come on.' I ran to his desk in my heels and grabbed more manuscripts, pads and pens.

'Follow me, you two!' As we march down the corridor to the meeting room, we bump into Cathy also carrying pens and paper.

'Think we have enough pens and paper?' Beth jokes.

'Plenty with what I'm planning!' I respond.

'I think I should promote you.' Drake admits.

'You can, I would love that, but I'll be gone for a while on maternity leave soon...'

'Oh yeah, I forgot about that!' I smile sweetly at Drake as I push the meeting room door open with my butt.

'Can you take a pad and a pen and choose a seat please.'

'What's this?' Beth held up a pad.

'I don't know, what does it say?' I answer sorting through manuscripts
Beth then reads my list:

> *a) writer*
> *b) work for another editor*
> *c) become a cat lady*
> *d) retire and live off jack*
> *e) become a stripper*

I stop still and look up at Drake, Cathy and Beth all laughing at me.

'That's my list of jobs I could do if I lost this one.'

'A stripper? You serious girl?' Cathy adds with a little cackle.

'No, so let's start this meeting, shall we?'

'What's it about?' Beth asks, putting my list on the desk.

'Lucy has some really good ideas on how to get the company functioning again and she wants us to work as a team.'

'Super woman over there, course she has ideas.' Cathy smirks.

'Go,' Beth points her index finger at me, 'we're listening.'

'Right okay, we could expand the company by selling our books in different countries? We could get more publicity by publishing celebrity autobiographies.'

'Oh, I love the celebrity bit.' Beth squeals.

'Has a celebrity asked you then?' Cathy asked while scribbling something on her pad of paper.

'Not exactly, but if we could ring round and ask them, they might do it through us.' I suggest.

'We need to make a list of celebrities who we can contact and ask if they want to do a book deal with us.' Drake says.

'Okay I love Alex Jones, can we ask him?' Cathy asks.

'Okay yep who else? Beth, list people you want, because I'm not a good celebrity person.' I admit. As she does, Cathy, Drake and I start noting down people.

'Okay, we've got:
a) Alex Jones
b) Erupt (the whole band)
c) Claire Armstrong
d) Channing Tatum
e) James Lloyd'

'I've made my list' Beth announces.

'Let's have a look.' I hold my arm out reaching for the paper. Cathy leans over my shoulder and we read the list together out loud.

'I like this list' Cathy says.

'Yeah, me too. Drake?' He just nods and smiles in response.

'I'll write a letter and I'll forward it to Drake and he can send them.' Beth says while scribbling more notes on her notepad.

'Okay, that sounds fair.'

'I'm crossing that off the list then – the first part of our reinvention is planned.' I announce.

'What about the other countries, how are we going to do that?' Cathy asks, as we all look at each other.

'Um, I'm not sure if I'm honest. Maybe ring some companies in England and ask if they're interested?' I frown and look at everyone in turn, for validation.

'Right okay, let's get to work!' Drake looks at us all, before slapping his hand on the desk, and making us all jump.

'Meeting adjourned!'

'Let's go and start this thing!' We all go back to our offices, to start our master plan. As I sit at my desk, I kick my heels off and open my emails. There's a new one from Jack.

*From: Jack Base*
*Subject: dinner?...*
*To: Lucy Winter*
*12/20/2010 14:23*

*Dear madam and beano ;),*

*I'm happy to see you have accepted my request of dinner, I have made an appointment with a great sales lady at Bloomingdales called Sarah Wildon at 5:30, she will help you find a dress.*

*I will pick you up at 7pm from your place.*

*Your love, Jack*

*I.T manager at Freshman's LTD.*

I smile to myself and pick up my phone to text Sarah.

*Hi, I hear I have an appointment with you at 5:30 x*

The rest of the day is a drag, filing paper work and reading over cover letters asking stars to write an autobiography for our company. It's more stressful than I thought it would be. I check my emails, notice the time and squeal in excitement. *'It's weird how he asked me and it's a posh dinner'* I think to myself before logging off, and heading to the door.

'Night Lucy, see you tomorrow!'

'Yeah, night Beth, see you tomorrow!'

'BYE LUCY.' I hear from Drake's office.

'BYE DRAKE.' I shout back and smile at Beth.

'Are we having another meeting tomorrow?' Beth asks as I turn around to walk out.

'Only if we get good news between now and the morning.'

'Okay give me your number and if I hear anything, I'll text you.' Beth said handing me a scrap bit of paper and a pen.

'Oh okay.' I write my number down on the scrap paper and hand it back with a smile. I reach the bottom floor of the building and make my way to the main entrance, shivering from the cold air I can already feel and quickly put my coat on. I haul a cab as I'm not brave enough to walk in the cold and maybe lose my toes. I pay the cab driver when we reach

Bloomingdales and make my way inside, *ahh heating*. I don't even make it to the reception desk before Sarah recognizes me and shouts at me across the shop.

'LUCY!' I make a sharp turn and walk towards her.

'Hey Luc.' Sarah squeals while hugging me tightly.

'I can't breathe.' I manage to get out.

'Oh sorry,' and she let go, 'what kind of outfit do you want for tonight, missy?'

'Glamourous.' I smile at her.
'Like Jen Aniston? Or Angelina Jolie? Or Scarlett Johansson?'

'A bit of them all.' I look at her.

'Right this is going to be harder than I thought!' Sarah grabs my hand and pulls me down some aisles. She suddenly stops in front of me, while I wasn't paying attention, so I bump into the back of her.

'Sorry.' I mumble.

'I've found the perfect dress.' She pulls out a floor length strapless black dress with black shiny sequins all over it.

'WOW.' I stand there staring at it with an open mouth.

'Yeah, so you're wearing this, and put on your Louboutin's, Lily is doing your make-up and I'll do your hair, yeah?' All I

220

do is nod at her, still dumbstruck from the beautiful dress.

'I need this dress back by tomorrow, with nothing on it, okay?' Sarah orders, while I still stare at the dress.

**************

At six-thirty on the dot I stepped out my bedroom in my floor length strapless black sparkly dress, my black Louboutin's, my hair in a chignon and simple make-up.

'What you think?' I ask Sarah while twirling.

'Wow you scrub up good.' Sarah answers, while grabbing her camera.

'I'm going to take a picture, because you look so freaking gorgeous!' While we wait for Jack, I'm on strict orders from Sarah not to sit down because I'll crinkle the dress, but I'm allowed to take my shoes off until Jack arrives.

'So, what's this dinner for?' Sarah ask while sitting up on the sofa.

'I don't know.' I answer. *I really have no idea.*

'Well you look gorgeous and Jack will be here soon, so I'll give you your present now.' Sarah says while rummaging through a Bloomindales bag.

'Present?'

'Yes, but you can't keep it.' She smiles sweetly at me.

'Oh, it's not a present then.' I say, disappointed. Sarah then pulls out a clutch bag that looks just like the dress.

'So you don't have to carry your blue Marc Jacobs bag around!'

'Oh my god, thank you!' I launch myself at Sarah as the door buzzer goes. Sarah races to answer.

'Hello?'

'Hi, it's Jack.'

'Oh, do you want to come up or should she come down?'

'I'll come up please.' Sarah then buzzes Jack up while I put my shoes back on, put my essentials in the clutch bag and hide in my room.

'Is she ready?' I hear Jack ask.

'Yes, if you can sit there, I will bring her out.' I hear Jack pull a chair out from the table as Sarah comes bursting into my room.

'You ready, Cinderella?'

'I'm so nervous.' I admit while breathing in and out quickly.

'Cut it out.' Sarah hits me on the arm. I follow Sarah out of my bedroom door and I step out to see Jack on his phone, with his elbows on his knees.

'Ahem.' I clear my throat. As Jack looks up, he breathes *'wow'* under his breath. I smile at him nervously, and start touching my hair, when a hard slap hits my hand.

'Don't touch.' Sarah orders me.

'Um right, shall we go?' Jack finally pipes up.

'Yes, that would be great!'

\*\*\*\*\*\*\*\*\*\*\*

After having dinner and a bottle of wine, I notice Jack getting edgy and shifting in his seat.

'Are you okay?' I ask him.

'Yeah, yeah, I'm fine, I'm just going to go to the men's room.'

'Okay.' I frown as he walks off, get my phone out to check my messages and see one from Gemma and a missed call from a number I don't recognize. Well they can wait or ring back.

*Hi, I'll be at the apartment on Wednesday, what time do you finish work? G*

As I look around for Jack, I see him talking to a waiter, so I text Gemma back.

*Hey I finish at about 5pm you can either come to my office or hang out with Sarah or Jack or Dean x*

As I put my phone back in my bag, I notice Jack sitting back down again in his seat, this time with a gorgeous smile on his face.

'Is everything okay?' I ask him again. With the smile still on his face, he stands up, moves towards me and lowers himself onto one knee.

'Lucy will you marry me?'

## CHAPTER ELEVEN

'Morning Lucy.' Beth says across the foyer.

'Morning Beth.' I answer while sipping my coffee.

'Morning ladies,' Drake says popping his head out his office, 'Lucy can I borrow you for sec?'

'Sure, give me a minute.' As I make my way to my desk, I slump in my seat thinking about last night. I log on to my computer and check my emails. *Nothing.* I slowly stand up, leaving my bag and coffee behind and walk through the adjoining door to Drake's office.

'Ahh Lucy.' he says while picking up some paper work.

'Yep?'

'Oh, what's wrong?' Drake walks around his desk and puts his hands on my shoulders.

'It's nothing.'

'Is it Jack?' My eyes shoot up to his.

'Yeah.' I nod, sliding my jacket off of my shoulders just as Drake leaned in, kissing me.

'What is going on?' Comes a male voice from behind us. Drake immediately drops his hands as I turn around to see Jack standing in the doorway.

'Is this why you said no last night?' He questions, his eyes flitting between Drake and I.

'No Jack, it's not, it's not what it looks like.' I try to plead with him.

'Why else would you be kissing your boss?' He throws the papers onto the floor as Beth comes running in.

'What's going on?' She asks. Jack and Beth both look at me for an explanation.

'Can I speak to you in my office, Jack?' I grab his arm towards the adjoining doors leaving Beth and Drake in his office. As I shut the door, I hear Beth say *what the hell* and what must be her slapping Drake.

'Jack, this is not what it looks like, sit down and I'll explain.' Jack stands in the doorway not knowing whether to sit or go.

'Sit.' I order, pointing my finger at the chair. Jack sits in the chair opposite me with his puppy dog eyes that makes me want to cry. He must be heart broke. I said no to his proposal and then he's seen me kissing Drake.

'Drake called me in his office and asked me what's wrong, he guessed it was you, I slid my jacket off as he kissed me, I was as shocked as you were!' I explain.

'Then why didn't you stop him?' He is still angry.

'It happened the second before you walked in, literally.' I shifted in my chair and kicked off my shoes. Jack still stares at me.

'Jack, please say something?'

'So, you weren't leaving me for Drake?' He asks with tears in his eyes.

'No way!'

'Then why did you say no last night?'

'Jack, I have my reasons, but I don't want to upset you even more.'

'Do you not love me, Luc?' He asks as a tear runs down his face.

'Oh god, Jack, of course I do.' I kneel down in front of him.

'I said no because I don't want you to feel you have to marry me, just because I'm pregnant. I want to be sure it's your child before I marry you, so you don't leave me, I want to me su-'

Jack kisses me before I could even finish.

'Lucy, I love you and I want to marry you, I want you to be Mrs Base. I would love for Beano to be mine, and I'll love it either way, but we have the rest of our lives to make more that are mine.' Now it's me crying, sat on my knees on the floor in front of Jack.

'Jack?'

'Yeah?'

'Yes, I will marry you.'

'Oh my god, you have made me the happiest man in the world right now!' He pulls me up from my knees and wrapping his arms around me in a hug.

'I love you, Jack.'

'I love you too Lucy.' There was a tiny knock at the door.

'Come in?'

'Hi,' Drake says entering my office, 'I'm so sorry. I don't know what came over me.'

'It's okay Drake, don't worry.'

'I heard your news though; congratulations.' Drake shook Jack's hand.

'Thanks.'

'Sorry to interrupt, but I need you Lucy in the meeting room in five minutes.'

'Sure, I'll meet you there.' Drake left my office.

'Should we tell people first or update it on Facebook?' Jack smiles at me.

'I haven't been on Facebook in weeks, I don't even think I said I was in a relationship…'

'Ouch.' Jack smiles at me again.

'But I'd love to tell everyone, I'll call Mom and Dad tonight, but I want to tell Gemma in person, she will be here tomorrow.'

'Okay, we can get Dean and Belle over, with Sarah and Gemma have a party.' Jack says while putting his coat on.

'Sounds good.' I give Jack a soft kiss.

'See you tonight, Mrs Base…'

'We're not married yet.' I smile as he leaves. I quickly pick up all the paperwork from my desk, grab my bag and my phone and run to the meeting room. I open the door with my butt again and dump everything on the big table.

'Hi.' I smile at Beth, Drake and Cathy staring at me.

'Congratulations!' Beth says, getting up to hug me.

'I'm not a hugger, but congratulations.' Cathy says whilst I'm mid-hug with Beth.

'Right, let's get down to business.' Drake interrupts.

'I have some good news,' Beth squeals, 'I have had a reply from Alex, Daniel, Lewis and Tom from Erupt. They want to have a meeting with us about a book.'

'Oh my god, that's excellent!' I say, as I jump out of my chair.

'When are they coming in?' Cathy asks, a little more contained than I was.

'On the seventh of January. So, I've booked them in this room at ten on that day with Lucy and me for the book interview, then Cathy if they like the idea you will then go through front covers, pictures blah blah blah with them and Drake all you have to do is say yes.'

'Yes.' Drake replies.

'Good boy.' Beth says, stroking his arm like a dog.

'So, all engines go.' Cathy says.

'God, I'm excited, you know I won't sleep properly till then!' I squeal.

'Me neither! Beth squeals back. We start jumping on the spot together.

'If you two have quite finished,' Drake interrupts us again, 'I have some news too.'

'Oh, okay sorry.' Beth mumbles as we both sit down again.

'I have an interview booked with Carly Jacobs.' He reveals. Beth gasps so much that I thought she was going to faint.

'THE Carly Jacobs?!' She says with her hands flapping around in the air.

'Yes, THE Carly Jacobs, she has been looking to do a book and with the good things I offered she took our deal.'

'When is she coming in for an interview?' I ask while getting the office diary out.

'Twenty-ninth of December at one.' Drake says reading off of a piece of paper.

'Okay.' We all agree. After our four-hour meeting, sorting places, interviews and getting everything sorted, we end it there.

'Any plans tonight Lucy?' Beth asks as we pack up.

'Yes, we're having a party to celebrate the engagement.'

'Oh, that's nice.' Cathy smiles at me.

'Yeah, you three can come if you want?' I offer.

'Oh really? Beth claps her hands.

'I can come for a drink.' Cathy winks at me.

'I don't think that's a good idea after this morning.' Drake replies.

'It's fine Drake, it's all sorted out, it was a misunderstanding.' I say.

'Can I bring my husband? Beth asks while tapping on her phone.

'Yeah sure, what about your daughter?'

'She's at a friend's house tonight.'

'Okay. I'm just going to text Jack and let him know.'

*Hey babe, Beth, Bradley, Cathy and Drake are coming for drinks tonight xx*

As we all head off to our offices to get our stuff and turn off our computers my phone buzzes in my hand.

*Babe that's cool, see you shortly beautiful xxxx*

I check my emails when I reach my office and I have one from *my dad?!?*

*From: David Winter*
*Subject: internet*
*To: Lucy Winter*
*12/21/2010 16:45*

*Hi love me and your Mom just got the internet!*
*Love Mom and Dad*

*'This is weird...'* I think to myself.

'You ready?' Beth's head pops around my door.

'Ready?'

'Yeah, Drake is letting us leave early, with all the good work we have done today.' She smiles at me.

'Oh, great! Yeah, five minutes.' Her head disappears. I log out my emails and turn off my computer. I head downstairs, and we all grab a cab over to mine. We make our way upstairs to Sarah, Dean, Belle, Jack's friend Nick, and Jack waiting for us. I get my phone out of my bag and check it. I have a missed call from a number I don't recognize. *Hmmm.*

\*\*\*\*\*\*\*\*\*\*\*\*\*\*\*\*\*

As the night comes to an end, Beth and Bradley say their goodbyes and leave with Drake and Cathy. Dean and Belle leave so it's just me, Sarah, Nick and Jack left.

'I'm sorry but I have to go to sleep. Good night.' Sarah says, yawning.

'Night babes.' I kiss Sarah's cheek.

'You two can stay in the guest room, Gem's not back till tomorrow.' I offer Sarah and Nick.

\*\*\*\*\*\*\*\*\*\*\*\*\*\*\*\*\*\*

I wake up at six on the dot, with Jack half on top of me. I lift his arm off and I make my way into the living room. I sit in the arm chair with my legs hanging over the arm rest. I press my index fingers to my temples. *'Please don't get a headache.'* I mumble to myself.

'Talking to yourself is the first sign of madness.' Comes a voice that makes me jump.

'Oh god!' I scramble on the arm chair.

'Sorry.' Nick replies, sitting on the sofa opposite me.

'I think not drinking gives me more of a headache than drinking.' I complain. Nick belly-laughed and stood up. We head over to the kitchen together.

'Right, as you're up the fluff you need looking after.' Nick says, filling up the kettle.

'Oh, right thanks.'

'Coffee? Breakfast?' He offers.

'Yes and yes. Toast please, and something for my headache.'
I point towards the cupboard on the other side of the kitchen,
where Nick walks over and rummages around till he finds
some pain killers. I hold my hand out.

'Hold up, I need to see if it's safe for Beano.' I smile at
myself then I hear Sarah coming out of the guest room.

'Want coffee Sarah?' Nick asks her.

'Yeah please.' I follow Sarah onto the sofa.

'Want to know some really cool news?' Sarah nods.

'Teely's are publishing an autobiography for Carly Jacobs
and maybe Erupt!'

'What?' Sarah's mouth hangs open in disbelief.

'What?' I answer with a smile.

'THE Carly Jacobs?'

'Yes.'

'The. Real. Living. Human. Carly. Jacobs?' Sarah says
slowly, processing the information.

'Yes.' I laugh.

'OH MY GOD!'

'Shhh Sarah its only seven.' I stand up and put my hand over her mouth.

'I want to meet her.' She says while pulling my hand from her mouth.

'What's going on?' Jack sits in my arm chair.

'Teely's are publishing Carly Jacob's autobiography and maybe Erupt's.'

'Oh, that's cool I love Erupt.' Nick mentions.

'Oh yeah, they're all fit.' I point at Sarah.

'Yes, they are, remember when we went to see them?'

'Oh yes I do, I loved them. I always wanted to marry Alex.' I add cupping my heart and sighing.

'Which one is he?' Nick asks. Sarah and I look at each other and back at Nick.

'You don't know which one? Oh my god!' Sarah screeches.

'Alex Jones is the main singer, Dan Armstrong is the bassist, Matty Land is the drummer, one guitarist is Lewis Hardy and um… the other guitarist is um…' I answer, counting them off on my fingers.

'Oh, what's the guitarist's name?' Sarah joins in the questioning.

'Tom Richards!' I suddenly remember.

'Yeah, that's him!' Sarah smacks me on the back.

'Jesus, you two you need to calm down…' Jack mumbles. As Sarah and I are laughing my phone starts to ring. I jump up and stare at the screen.

'Who is it babe?' Sarah calls after me.

'I don't know, it's a number I don't recognize. They've rung me twice already.'

'Answer it!' Sarah orders.

'Hello… yeah I'm Lucy…oh…okay…how did you get my number? Oh, you could have left a message at the office…yeah let me get a pen and paper…'

'Who can that be?' I hear Sarah whisper as I walk into my bedroom.

'I have to be in the office early this morning.' I call out to the guys in the lounge and run to the bathroom to take a shower.

'Why?' Sarah comes running after me.

'I'll explain in a minute.' As I get in the shower a massive grin appears on my face. I just spoke to lead singer Alex Jones from Erupt on the phone and he wants to meet me in the office. I get a feeling of butterflies in my stomach. I finish washing in record time and jump out the shower. I run to my room, and get dressed. I put on my interview dress for a confidence boost, and I kick my bedroom door while blow-drying m hair to get Sarah's attention.

'You alright?' Sarah asks.

'Yeah, can you do my hair in a wave my hair please? And do my make-up?'

'Sure, now will you tell me what the phone call was about and why you're dressing yourself up.' Sarah looks at me.

'Okay but don't scream, or squeal, or screech or anything, promise?' Sarah holds her hand out to shake on the fact.

'Promise.'

'Alex Jones phoned me to ask if he could move the interview we had to Thursday and he wants to see me about it.'

'Oh my god!' Sarah mouths at me.

'Breathe Sar.' I tap Sarah's shoulder.

'Oh my god!' She mouths at me again.

'Yes, I know, so I'm dressing myself up so I look good for Alex Jones.'

'Oh my god.'

'Sarah, can you say something else?'

'Oh my god, no.'

'Well that's a little better, snap out of it so you can do my hair and make-up.' After half an hour, we left my bedroom. Nick and Jack are heading out the door.

'We're going to Betty's, so we will see you later' Jack says trying to kiss me as I was ducking around him.

'Don't kiss me on the lips, I have lip gloss on.'

'Right.'

'Or on the cheek.'

'Right, um, is the hand okay?'

'Yes' I held my hand out for him to kiss.

'I'll catch you later babe.' They left and then Sarah starts jumping around.

'Right, I have to leave, I'll call you straight after' I promise.

'You better.'


I arrive at the office knowing it was way too early for Beth to be here. A little upset we didn't do our morning ritual of greetings, I head to my office, slinging my bag on my desk as the phone starts ringing.

'Hello?'

'Well hello, Lucy Winter, this is the front desk, I have a very gorgeous, man at my reception asking for you.'

'Thanks, can you send him up please?'

'I will in five minutes, so I can stare at him some more.' I giggle to myself as I put the phone down. At least it will give me some time to check my emails and get myself together. I open my emails. I have one from Gemma and Mom and Dad.

*From: Gemma Winter*
*Subject: homecoming*
*To: Lucy Winter*
*12/22/10 07:36*

*Lucy, I have to stay an extra day but I will be at your office at about 3ish Thursday see you then xxxxxx*
*Gem*

And the one from my parents.

*From: David Winter*
*Subject: internet*
*To: Lucy Winter, Gemma Winter*
*12/22/10 08:13*

*Dear Girls,*
*Your Mom and I now have the internet, I sent you and*

*Gemma and email yesterday but neither replied so I'm guessing you didn't receive them, but I think I've worked it out and hopefully you will get this one.*
*We will be traveling to your apartment on 12/24/10 to spend Christmas with you.*
*Please reply so I know you have received it.*
*Love you lots*
*Mom and Dad*

As I finish reading the email, I hear the lift ding, I'll email them back later. I jump up from my chair and run towards my door. I poke my head out to see Alex Jones standing in the reception area, in his black skinny jeans, white Queen t-shirt and a black leather jacket. *Yummy.*

'Hi.' I say, sticking to the one syllable until my voice stops shaking.

'Oh hi.' Alex answers.

'Please come in.' I watch Alex walk across the reception to my office, while putting his phone in his jacket pocket. I feel like a teenager staring at a poster of him on my wall – blue eyes, slick black hair and gorgeous dimples – I'm sixteen again.

'Hi, sorry for calling you on your number, but the lady that called me and left a message didn't leave a contact number. But at the end of the message, she didn't put the phone down properly and I heard her read a number out that someone had just given her, so I wrote it down and called it.'

'Oh yeah that would be me.' I smile.

'So yeah, sorry for changing plans but we go on tour two days before I arranged to come in, so I needed to change it. Will tomorrow be okay for the band to come in?'

I'm still absolutely, completely star struck. All I can manage is a creepy smile and a nod.

'Yeah we're really excited about this book deal!'

'That's cool.'

'Are you okay?' Alex frowns at me.

'Yes, I'm fine, why do you ask?'

'You just seem...I don't know...weird. No offence...'

'Absolutely none taken. I'm sorry. I'm so in love with you and your band. My friend and I used to go see you at gigs, we have all your albums and posters and I used to think I would marry you, so actually meeting you is a massive slap in the face.'

'Right...' Alex raises an eyebrow, 'well it's always nice to meet a fan.'

'Thanks.' I gush.

'You're gorgeous though, I wouldn't mind marrying you.' Alex says while getting his phone out his pocket.

'Um...'

'Sorry, that was a bit up front.' He puts his hand in his perfect hair and fiddles with it.

'No worries.' I try and smile normally, but I'm still sure I look creepy.

'I've just been invited to a party would you and your friend like to come? It's James Lloyd's party.'

'Really?' *Oh my god I just got invited to a famous person's party.*

'Yeah sure, I'm getting a car there, so I can stop by your place and pick you both up?'

'That would be so freaking amazing!'

'Cool, I'll call you later.' Alex leans forward and rips some paper out of my pad. I take it from him.

'That's my number.' He winks at me.

'Oh, right thanks.' I fold it in half and put it in my bra.

'Cool!'

'Can I ask you a few questions for the book before you go?' I ask not making eye contact with him and grabbing a pen and paper.

'Shoot.' Alex points his finger at me and leans his elbows on my desk.

'Will the book be about the whole band?'

'Yes.'

'Do you want it to cover your tour?'

'Yes.'

'Do you want it to cover personal things, like place of birth, parents, siblings?'

'Erm maybe.'

'Do you want to have your own sections with your information or the book to be a big questions and answers format?'

'Own sections. Is that cheesy?'

'No not at all.' I manage.

'Can I ask you some questions?' Alex winks at me again, if he carries that on, I'm going to melt in this seat right now.

'Yeah sure.'

'What's your full name?'

'Lucy Winter'

'How old are you?'

'Twenty-three.'

'Cool, where do you live?'

'Fifth avenue.'

'Awesome, I live in Brooklyn, are you single?'

'Yes?' *NO what was I doing?*

'Even better, want to go to dinner with me tonight before the party?'

'Sure' *NO! what power does he have over me?*

'Great, I'll call you with the time and place.' Alex stands up and comes around to me on the other side of the desk. I stand up, and he stares into my eyes, grabs my hand and kisses it.

'It was an absolute pleasure meeting you Lucy, I'll see you later.' He leaves and I slump down in my chair and putting my forehead on my desk. *'What the hell?'* I whisper to myself. I picked up my phone and dial the only person who'll understand.

'Hello, Sarah Wildon.'

'Sarah, I need to talk to you urgently.'

'Okay, I don't have to be there till ten, meet me at Clive's.' I put the phone down just as it buzzes.

***It's Alex, meet me at the plaza at 6pm x***

'*Oh my god it's started.*' I whisper aloud, my wildest dreams have come true and I can't do anything about it. I run out to the reception scribble a message for Beth.

**Beth,**
**I've been in this morning and had to run out quick. Can you let Drake know please?**
**Lucy x**

I bolt for the lift and wait patiently for the lift to reach the eighteenth floor. As it dings, I go to step in, but I'm stopped by someone pushing me out I looked up to see Beth.

'Hi doll, where you going?'

'Sorry Beth, I'm in a rush. I left you a note, I'll be back in a bit.' I jump in the lift as the doors were closing. As I made my way to the front door of Clive's I see Sarah immediately.

'Babe, what's up? Is it Jack? Is it beano?' She asks, touching my tummy.

'Neither.' I look away from her.

'Diet coke!' I shout at the bar keep while tapping the bar.

'Lucy!' She says in a tone that sounds like my mother telling me off.

'Alex Jones came into the office, yeah?'

'Following so far…'

'He asked if I was single and I said yes, and he asked me to dinner and I said yes and I said we'd go to a party at James Lloyd's house with him tonight.' Sarah gripped onto the bar so tight her knuckles turned white.

'We're going to James Lloyd's party with Alex Jones? Am I awake?'

'Did you listen to the first bit?'

'Not really.' She downs her drink, giving her empty glass to the bar keep with a nod.

'Sarah, I lied to Alex, what am I going to do? He doesn't know I'm engaged or pregnant!' Sarah chokes on her drink.

'Don't tell him he might un invite us!' I raised my eyebrow at Sarah.

'Really? That's dreadful…'

'Oh my god, I'm totally getting with James…'

'Oh god, maybe you weren't the person to talk to.'

'Yes, I am. Don't worry go on the date and tell Jack it's for work. He won't mind, you're not marrying Alex, so you don't have to tell him anything.'

'I don't? I always wanted to marry him.' I scrunch my face up.

'And, he still asked you out…'

'Yeah.'

'Jesus, girl you're going to marry Alex.' Sarah then let out a witch cackle laugh.

\*\*\*\*\*\*\*\*\*\*\*\*

My stomach feels like butterflies are going to burst out of it as I stood waiting for Alex. I felt my phone vibrate in my clutch bag.

*It's Alex, I'm running 10 mins late, sit and order what you want I'll be with you shortly xx*

Okay the butterflies died a little, knowing I wasn't going to see him for another ten minutes. Time to console myself. The door man opens the door for me and gives me a smile like he knows.

'Hi, do you have a reservation?' The girl at the entrance asks.

'Um yeah, I'm meeting Alex Jones.' She looks me up and down.

'I love your dress, oh and your shoes…very sexy!'

'Um, thanks?'

'I'm Marie.' She holds her hand out for me to shake it.

'Hi, I'm Lucy.'

'Please follow me.' She grabs two menus. I follow her through the restaurant, and she points me in the direction of a corner booth, with candles.

'This is Alex's favourite seat.' Marie explains.

'Thanks.' I climb in.

'Can I get you a drink?'

'Sure, diet coke please.'

'Coming right up.' She runs off, only to return two seconds later throwing the menus at me.

'Sorry I forgot to give you these!'

'Thanks.' I pull my phone out of my pocket to text Sarah.

*Sar this place is amazing…*

As I press send, I see my diet coke being placed in front of me.

'Thanks.' I mutter. I slip my phone back in my bag, and as I reach out for my drink, I see Alex sitting opposite me with a sexy half smile on his face.

'Hi.' I whisper. Alex is wearing suit pants with a white shirt tucked in, unbuttoned at the top and a suit jacket on. *He looks fit.*

'Hi,' he answers, 'you look gorgeous.'

'Thanks.' I smile, mesmerized by him.

'Do you want to order?' He asks, picking up his menu.

'Sure, what's good here?'

'Everything. This is The Plaza. Can I ask you something?'
'Sure.' I answer, not moving the menu that covers my face.

'How is such a gorgeous girl single?' He hooks his finger over my menu and pulls it down.

'I don't know.' I say, blushing while I answer.

'Hey excuse me – are you Alex Jones from Erupt?' Alex looks up at a fat guy standing next to him, chewing very loudly on his gum, with a pen and pad in his hand.

'Yeah who are you?'

'I'm Gus, can I get an interview?'

'Are you kidding, we're having dinner?!'

'Is this your girlfriend?' Gus asks, pointing his pen at me.

'We're just friends.' I add, with a tight smile. Then Gus writes something on his pad of paper and nods.

'Hey, what are you writing?' Alex reaches up for the pad and snatches it from Gus's hands.

'Hey, give it back!' Gus shouts. Alex stands, and throws the pad of paper across the restaurant.

'Hey just because you're famous doesn't mean you can be rude!' A girl shouts at Alex, while passing Gus his pad.

'I would like to have a quiet meal with my friend, without people like you ruining it!' Alex shouts, pointing at them both.

'Alex, please calm down it's fine!' I soothe.

'Yeah, do what the dog says!' The girl shouts. *WHAT?* Now I'm mad, I march over to the girl and slap her hard in the face. Alex drags me away from the crowd of people that has formed. The crowd keep following us though, people shouting and pushing each other. I loose Alex and then I feel a punch to my stomach. I fall to my knees. *'Beano'* I whisper to myself.

'LUCY!' I hear Alex shout, when a man picks me up from the floor and carries me through a door at the back.

'I just got punched in the stomach.' I say through sobs.

'I know, I saw love, you okay?'

'No, I'm pregnant!'

'Oh shit, I'm calling an ambulance!' The bodyguard says while putting me down on a couch and pulling his cell out his jacket. I scream in pain as a scratching pain surges through me. I grip my stomach and start to cry.

'Lucy? You okay?' Alex is at my side.

'Ahh no I'm not!'

'You're bleeding…' I lift my hand and look at it.

'I'm not bleeding.' I look up at Alex as he points between my legs with a horrified expression.

'Ambulance is on its way.' The body guard tells me while stroking my hair. I find myself fighting to keep my eyelids open.

'Did you get stabbed?' I sleepily shake my head as darkness overtakes.

'She's pregnant.' Is the last thing I hear the bodyguard say.

## CHAPTER TWELVE

I refused visitors. I refused Jack, my parents, Dean and Belle, Sarah and even Alex. Thinking about it all makes me well up again. I bend my knees up and wrap my arms around them while leaning my chin on top. On my own. Since the news that I lost Beano I don't want company. I've locked myself away. I hear a tiny knock at the door, and a head pops around.

'Lucy Winter?' The doctor asks.

'Yeah?' I manage through sobs.

'You can go home today, it's Christmas day tomorrow. It might do you good to be around people.' He comes over and sits on my bed and places his hand on mine.

'I don't want to see anyone.'

'I know this is going to be hard, I can't even begin to imagine understand your pain, but your baby would have wanted you to carry on.' All I can do is nod and sob.

'Do you want some tea or coffee before a nurse comes in to help you?' I nod at him again.

'Okay Lucy. I'll sort that out for you.' He says, as he gets up from the bed.

'Doctor?'

'Yes, Lucy?'

'Instead of a nurse, can my friend Sarah help me?'

'Of course, I'll send her in.'

'Thank you.' I smile tightly at him and go back to my fetal position. I begin to cry, harder this time. I'm going home without my baby, I let go of my legs and sit up straight, catching sight of myself in the mirror.

*'Oh god…'* I whisper to myself while touching my face, not quite believing its mine.

'Hi?'

'Sarah?' I spin round to see my friend standing sheepishly next to the door. I run over and hug her with all my might.

'Hey Luc.' She hugs me back but not as hard, like I'm a china doll.

'Do you mind helping me?' I look at her.

'Of course, not' she strokes my hair. As we both sit on my bed looking through the clothes I had to wear, the Doctor returns, clasping two cups of steaming coffee.

'There you go, girls.'

'Thanks.' I mumble. It feels good to be drinking something other than ice chips.

'I'll leave you to get dressed, I'll be back in fifteen minutes.' He leaves my room.

'Are you sure you don't want to see anyone?' Sarah asks me, handing me a top.

'Not for a minute.'

'Okay. Alex has been here.' I spin my head to look at her.

'Really?'

'Yeah, I explained the situation to him.' Sarah says, looking away from me.

'Oh, what did he say?'

'Nothing really. He was more interested in how you were, he blames himself.'

'It wasn't his fault.' I say, trying to defend him.

'I know, and I tried to tell him, but he wasn't having any of it.'

'Is he here now?'

'No, he went home, so did your Mom and Dad, Gemma, Dean and Belle.'

'How is Jack?'

'Devasted, he hasn't stopped crying.' That makes me start crying again. I've been so wrapped up in how I felt, I forgot about Jack and everyone else's feelings.

'It's okay Luc.' Sarah pulls me in for another hug.

'Where is Jack?'

'He's in the waiting area, he hasn't moved since you were brought in.'

'Can you call him in?'

'Sure.' Sarah jumps off the bed and runs out of the room. Five seconds later she drags in Jack.

'Jack.' I whisper and hug him tightly.

'Are you okay?' He whispers into my hair.

'I'm holding up.' He sniffs and starts to cry again against me.

'I'm so sorry.' I kiss him.

'It's not your fault Lucy.'

'Lucy, you need to get changed and get home to see everyone.' I nod and reluctantly let go of Jack. Sarah helps me get changed while Jack sits on my bed, calming himself down.

After fifteen minutes the Doctor comes back, with some papers.

'How are we all?'

'A little better thanks.' Jack sniffs.

'We're all ready to go.' Sarah says, stroking my arm. We head home and when we reach our apartment I slowly climb out. Looking up, I see that my lights were on, so I'm guessing everyone is there waiting for me. I make my way to the door and call the elevator. Jack and Sarah join me, carrying my bags.

'Sorry.' I mumble.

'Come on, Luc.' Sarah says, while putting her arm around my waist to help me stand up. As we reach our apartment front door, Jack opens it and lest it swing open. Everyone in side stands up and stares at me. I let go of Sarah and go straight to my bedroom, jump into my bed under the covers and start crying to myself again. I hear the muffled sounds of my family talking amongst them self but can't make out what they're saying. I curl up tighter into a ball and rock myself to sleep.

\*\*\*\*\*\*\*\*\*\*

I wake up gently the next morning, reaching my arm over to Jack's side of the bed but he isn't there. I sit up and look at the clock which says it's nine. I pull the cover off and make my way to the living room. The curtains are open and the sun spills in. Mom and Dad are watching T.V. and drinking coffee, and Jack's in the kitchen making pancakes, singing and dancing to by Wham!. I can't help but smile.

'Good morning, love.' Dad says whilst walking over to me with his arms open wide. I accept his warm hug.

'Hey Dad.' I mumble into his chest. He squeezes me and lets me go, kissing the top of my head.

'Morning, dear.' Mom says, pulling me out of Dad's embrace to hug me too.

'Morning, Mom.'

'How are you feeling?' Dad asks while Mom walks me over to the sofa.

'A little better now I've had some sleep, where's Gemma?'

'Oh, she went to your office for something, they called you'.

'What was it about?'

'I don't know, love, she'll be back soon.'

'Merry Christmas Eve Lucy.' Jack says, carrying a plate of pancakes.

'Same to you.' My parents let me go, so I can go and hug Jack. Then he pulls the dining room chair out for me to sit on.

'Want some coffee?' Jack hands me a cup of coffee, knowing I won't turn it down. I hold my hand up to reach for it as the phone rings.

'Hello…yeah she's awake…hang on.'

'It's Gemma.' Dad hands me the phone.

'Gem…yeah…okay…is he okay? Yeah, sure he can.' I put the phone down.

'What's wrong?' Mom asks me with a frown.

'Alex wants to check I'm okay and wants to come over, so I said yes.'

'Oh, okay.' Jack replies for her.

'Jack, it's fine.' Mom strokes his arm.

'He's only checking I'm okay.'

'Okay.' Jack answers before shoving a whole pancake into his mouth. I look at Mom, but I can't read her facial expression.

'I'm going to have a shower and dressed.' I walk off to the bathroom and take a shower which feels excellent after not having one for two days. I take my time just standing under the water. Then I get out and stare at myself in the mirror. I look rough – I've got puffy eyes from all the crying. I walk out the bathroom to do my usual routine. I dry my hair, and then slap make-up on my dull face until I look respectable. I check myself out in the mirror and smile. But then I remember the last time I wore my interview dress was when I was telling Beano I wouldn't be wearing it for a while. The smile quickly falls from my face.

'Knock knock…' I turned around to see Gemma stood in my bedroom doorway.

'Hey Gem.' I reply, as I hug her.

'Hey Luc, how you feeling?'

'I'm feeling a bit better today.' I mumble into her hair.

'Good. Alex is here, he feels really bad.'

'Okay, I'm ready anyway. How do I look?'

'You look good.' Gemma grabs my hand and pulls me out behind her.

'Hi.' Alex whispers holding a big bunch of flowers. I walk over to him, very aware that everyone is staring at me. Including Jack.

'Hi.' I whisper back and he hands me the flowers. Gemma takes them off me straight away and pushes me towards him. I hold my arms out to hug him.

'I'm sorry.' He whispers to me.

'It's not your fault.'

'It is.'

'No, it's not. Stop torturing yourself.' He lets go of me and hangs his head.

'I best get going, I'll see you next week.' He says suddenly, and then he walks towards the door. Before he goes, he turns as if to say something, but then doesn't.

'I'm going to text Sarah.'

*Sarah want to get a drink with me? Xx*

My phone rings instantly.

'Hello?'

'You want to get a drink?' Sarah asks warily.

'Yes, I haven't had a drink in weeks and I really need one.'

'Right, okay.'

'So, you want to?'

'Yeah, sure,' she answers, 'I'll be round in ten minutes.' I hang up the phone and slump on the sofa.

'I'm going out and having a drink. I think I deserve it.'

'Really? You think that's a good idea?' Mom asks, testing the water between us.
'Yeah. I want to go out.'

'Lucy?'

'No. I need to go out, I am a grown up.'

'Okay Lucy, whatever you say.' Mom answers, whilst Jack stares daggers at me.

'Why are you so argumentative?' Jack barks at me suddenly.

'I don't want to talk about this right now.' I stand up, walk towards the door, grab my coat and bag and walk out. I press the elevator button and when it arrives, I stumble in and curl up in the corner and sob. I pick my phone out of my pocket and dial Alex's number. He answers on the second ring.

'Hello?'

'Hi, it's Lucy.' Silence.

'Lucy Winter.'

'Hi, yeah. I have your number saved.' Alex answers, with a half laugh.

'Oh right, are you free?'

'Um, sure, what's up?'

'Can I come over?' Silence.

'Yeah sure.' I hear some muffled noises in the background.

'Thanks. Text me your address and I'll get a cab.' I hang up and make my way outside. I see Sarah coming down the street, so I step back into a dark alley so she can't see me. I receive a text from Alex, and I quickly cup my phone so Sarah can't hear it. As soon as I hear the main door shut, I run out and haul the nearest cab.

'Where to?' the cab driver leans round in his chair to look at me. I show the text from Alex to him, and then he nods and starts driving. We eventually pull up outside a dark building.

'Are you sure this is right?' I ask.
'Yeah this is the address you showed me.' I look around at the dark street, and then get my phone out of my pocket to phone Alex.

'Hello?'

'Hi, I'm at the address you texted me but it's dark.'

'Oh, great. I'll come out and meet you.' I give the cab driver some notes, thank him and jump out, to be met by Alex.

'Hi.' He says sheepishly to me.

'Hi,' I answer with a huge hug, 'do you live here?'

'No, the band are practicing.' Alex laughed.

'Oh.'

'We won't be long, then we can go back to mine for a drink.' He puts his arm over my shoulder and squeezes.

'Okay.' Alex opens a small door from the building which leads to a big light room with the rest of the band laughing and joking. They all turn to look at who just walked in.

'Hi.' I wave timidly at the band.

'Hi.' They all say at the same time. Alex ran back to the boys.

'Want to hear a new song?'

'Sure.' I smile and the boys start playing their song.

'That was awesome! I say once they'd finished.

'Thanks, we've been working on it for weeks, it's going to be on our new album.' Matty says.

'Practice is over, I'm going home.' Alex says while yawning and stretching his arms up, making his t-shirt show his stomach. I quickly look away so I'm not caught checking him out.

'Are you coming to mine?' Alex asks me, while all the guys whoop. Alex holds out his hand so I grab it, we wave bye to the band and leave through the door back onto the street.

'I live like five minutes away.' Alex smiles at me. We reach his apartment door. He pulls the key out of his back pocket and unlocks the door.

'Wow this place is amazing!' I say, looking around.

'Thanks.' Alex mumbles from the fridge. His place is massive, with red brick walls, hard wood floors, brown leather sofas, a low coffee table in the middle and random colourful artwork on the walls. It was a studio, with the kitchen cut off buy a breakfast counter. His kitchen is pretty awesome too, with a big old blue fridge and black granite work tops.

'Wow and the view is too!' I walk towards the big floor-to-ceiling window that has an amazing view.

'I would kill to live here.' I confess. Alex walks towards me handing me a beer and holding his hands up in surrender.

'Please don't kill me!'

'I was joking – thanks.' I clink my bottle against his.

'So, what's up?'

'I just wanted to get out, I needed cheering up.'

'Oh, right what you want to do?' Alex says, sipping his beer.

'Don't know what you want to do?'

'We can't do what I want to do because you have a boyfriend…' Alex says not looking at me.

'Right…' I down the rest of my beer and place it on the coffee table.

'Right.'

'Give me a tour?' I smile at Alex.

'Sure.' He stands up and holds his hand out for me to take.

'This is the bathroom.'

'Wow!' The bathroom is massive, with what looks like an amazing power shower, and it was very modern.

'You get excited easily,' he smiles down at me, 'this is the bedroom, don't tell me wow.'

'Wow…' I nod, the bedroom has a hard wood floor, what looked like a queen-sized bed and the same window as the living room, floor-to-ceiling.

'You like?' I nod so hard that my head nearly comes off. I look up at Alex who sips his beer. I take the beer out of his hand and place it on a nearby table. I stand on my tip-toes and kiss him. For a moment he kisses me back then he pushes me away.

'Lucy?'

'I'm sorry.' I press my lips together.

'Screw it.' He bends down so we we're kissing again and lifts me up. He carries me over to the bed, places me gently on my knees on the bed, which makes us face to face. He slides his hands down my sides until he reaches the bottom of my dress and slowly pulls it over my head. I do the same to his t-shirt. He kisses me again, undoes his jeans and kicks them off while pushing me backwards onto the bed.

*****************

I wake up the next morning because of an annoying buzzing noise.

'What is that?' A voice behind me says which makes me jump. I sit bolt upright, forgetting where I am, and then it hits me.

'I'm not sure.' I get out of the bed and follow the noise but then it stops. *Ahh shit my phone.* I run over to my bag and check my phone *18 missed calls, crap.* Five missed calls from Jack, three missed calls from Sarah, six from Gemma, and four from my home.

'Hello?'

'Sarah?' I whisper.

'Lucy, where the hell are you?'

'Sarah, I stayed at Beth's house, I'm on my way home now.'

'Right okay, your Mom and Jack are going mental.'

'I can imagine. I didn't realize the time. I'm getting a cab, so I'll see you later.'

'Bye Luc.' I leave the other missed calls, I'll be home soon, and I walk back into Alex's bedroom to find him sat up on his elbows.

'You alright?' I nod at him and look around for my clothes, slowly finding them and piling them on my shoulder.

'You going?' Alex asks, surprised.

'Yeah, it's Christmas day. I should be with my family.'

'Oh god, yeah' he quickly jumps up out of bed and pulls some boxers on. I run to the bathroom and lock the door, quickly getting changed. I walk out the bathroom, grab my bag, make sure everything is in there and head for the door. I pass Alex sat at the breakfast counter eating cereal.

'Bye then.'

'I'm sorry. I'll call you.' I slam the door behind me and lean

266

up against it. I cover my face with my hands and slide down the door. I hear a tiny knock and Alex talking through the door.

'Are you okay? Can I open the door without you falling through it?' I move slowly from the door and agree. The door slowly opens, and Alex sits next to me putting his arm over my shoulders.

'Don't worry, I'm not offended that you thought I was a mistake.'

'The thing is I don't think you were a mistake. That's why I'm confused.'

'Oh right, well I enjoyed myself if that helps.' I couldn't help but laugh.

'It helps a little.' I admit.

'Try not to think about it and have a good Christmas. I'll see you next week and you have my number in case you need me for anything.'
'Thanks.' I turn to look at him. Face-to-face again, it was magnetic. We're kissing again. I suddenly pull away.

'I'm sorry.'

'It's fine,' Alex laughed, 'you best go home though.'

*****************

I slowly unlock my apartment door, hearing a gasp from my

mother.

'Lucy, where have you been?'

'I stayed at Beth's house. Where's Jack?'

'He's still in bed.'

'Okay, I'm going to have a shower and I'll make coffee.'
Mom nods at me while I walk to the bathroom and take a
quick shower. I walk into the bedroom still wrapped in my
towel, as Jack slowly wakes up and looks at me.

'Where have you been?' He asks sleepily.

'Beth's house, you okay?'

'Yeah' he gets out of bed and comes over to me, giving me a
hug.

'I love you, you know that.' He says.

'Yeah I love you too.'

'Please don't feel that you are on your own, I'm here for you
and please consider other people's feelings, we're all
devastated as well.'

'I know,' I sniff into his chest, 'I'm sorry.'

'I have a present for you, get dressed and meet me in the
living room?' I slip on a baggy t-shirt and some shorts and tie
my hair up in a ponytail. I feel a bit better after having a

shower.

'Coffee?' I ask around the room.

'Yes please.' Dad answers.
'Yes please.' Jack smiles at me across the room.

'When are we doing presents?' Mom asks.

'Let me make coffee and we can start.' I answer with a smile. As we sit and wait for Gemma to wake up, we have some family time. A little later Dean and Belle turn up and shortly after Sarah arrives. Mom, Sarah, Gemma and I all cook Christmas dinner while the boys and Belle watch old rubbish movies. The day goes quite quickly. I must have taken Alex's advice of not thinking of anything.

'Luc, can I have a word?'

'Yep.' I jump up from the floor and follow Sarah into my bedroom.

'Why were you with Alex last night and why did you lie to me?' She demands. I sit on the end of my bed and sigh loudly.

'I don't know, it was the first person on my contact list and I needed to get away.'

'Did something happen?'

'No nothing did, I met him and I watched his band practice.'

'Then?'

'I stayed in his bed and he stayed on the sofa.'

'Anything else you want to tell me?'

'No that's it.'

'Luc, you scare me some times.' She walks over to me and squeezes me in a bear hug.

'Sorry but since this Beano thing, I just can't think straight.'

'I know, babe, I'm sorry.'

'How did you know I was at Alex's?'

'I didn't. I just said a name that popped in my head and you agreed.'
'Oh.'

'Let's get Christmas out the way and then we can look forward to New Year!' Sarah holds my hand and gives it a reassuring squeeze as we walk back out to the living room. Dad gave out some drinks and we carry on talking, wearing all our Christmas presents. It was a family tradition that if you get clothing you have to wear every single item, *can you imagine?* I'm feeling good, that is until I see the text on my cell.

***Hope you had a great Christmas, you want to come to a party with me on New Year? Alex xxx***

*Oh god.* I'll text him back later once I've made Sarah agree to come with me. I suddenly think about phoning Beth about work, but I don't want to disturb her Christmas, so I decide to leave it until tomorrow. I set up the table for dinner and hand out glasses of wine. As everyone takes their seat, the food is put in front of us. Mom holds her glass up in the air to make a toast.

'Merry Christmas to everyone and a Happy New Year!'

# CHAPTER THIRTEEN

**From: Kris Parkinson**
**Subject: Book deal**
**To: Lucy Winter**
**12/29/10 09:36**

**Dear Lucy,**
**I just want to confirm it is still okay for the boys to come**
**for the interview on the book signing deal.**
**Kris**

*Sent from my iPhone*

I email back straight away as they're supposed to be here in
twenty minutes.

**From: Lucy Winter**
**Subject: Book deal**
**To: Kris Parkinson**
**12/29/10 09:38**

**Dear Kris,**
**Yes, the interview is still on. Are you still arriving at**
**10am?**
**Lucy**

**P.A to Drake Teely at Teely's International**

I push away the keyboard in frustration as Beth walks in my office with a cup of coffee.

'Thought you could do with this?' She places in on my desk and sits in the seat opposite my desk.

'Thanks' I sip my coffee. *Heaven.*

'So what time are the boys getting here?'

'Well, whenever they decide to turn up. Their appointment is at 10am but their manager is emailing me asking if the interview is still on so we'll probably be running late.'

'Do you think we will be finished by 1pm?'

'I'll make sure we are don't worry.'

'Okay.' Beth sips her coffee as I check my emails again.

*From: Kris Parkinson*
*Subject: Book deal*
*To: Lucy Winter*
*12/29/10 09:41*

*Dear Lucy,*
*We are on route to you as we speak, see you shortly.*
*Kris*

*Sent from my iPhone*

As I re-read the message I sit and wonder if he wrote the 'sent from my iPhone' so I would think he was actually on his iPhone. I look up at Beth.

'Beth?'

'Yep?'

'Do you know much about iPhones?'

'A little why?'

'When you email off of it does it send a message at the bottom of your email saying sent from my iPhone.'

'Yeah I think it does, you can change it to your name and everything.'

'Oh,' *damn,* 'they will be here shortly.'

'Oh,' Beth jumps up from her seat spilling coffee on the floor, 'I want to meet Alex!'

'Why?'

'I'm totally in love with him. Don't you think he's fit?'

'Yeah sure, in an obvious way' I take a swig of coffee to mentally prepare myself for this meeting.

'I've heard he's good in bed.' Beth continues, which makes me spit out my large mouthful of coffee.

'What?'

'You okay Lucy?'

'Yeah, yeah, fine.' I say, doing a little cough to pretend I just choked on my coffee.

'Oh, that's my phone!' Beth runs out of the room, as I pull some tissues out of the box I have on my desk and start wiping away the coffee all over my computer monitor. Then my phone rings.

'Hello, Luc-'

'It's Beth,' she interrupts me, 'the boys are here and they're in the meeting room, meet you there?'

'Yep.' I agree and put the phone down.

Right, keep it together, I tell myself. Breathe, just breathe. I pick all that I need for this meeting *minus the scotch* and make my way to the meeting room. As I reach it, I pull the handle down and enter the room. I sit at the head of the table, and sort through my paperwork, not lifting my head to look at everyone.

'Hi Lucy.' Matty says, breaking the tension. I look up at them all.

'Hi, how are all you doing?'

'Yeah, we're great, but we haven't been up this early in

years.' He jokes.

'Do you all know each other?' Beth asks from the corner.

'Yeah. Lucy came and watched us practice the other day and then stayed at Alex's' he responds. I instantly crumple my face up and rest my forehead on the desk.

'Shut up!' I hear Alex whisper to Matty.

'What?' Beth has frozen completely, staring at me.

'Can I have a word?' I ask her, beckoning her out the room. I shot Matty a deadly look.

'What happened?' Beth demands to know.

'Nothing. It was the day after I came out of hospital and I needed somewhere to go, so I called Alex and I watched them practice, I slept in his bed and he stayed on the couch, and I went home Christmas morning.'

'Oh my god,' she starts flapping her hands in front of her face 'what's his place like?'

'Um…'

'No, why didn't you call me or Cathy or your friends or family?' She keeps asking, poking me in the shoulder.

'I needed to get away from everything I knew, they were all so sad.'

'And so they should be, do you remember what happened last week?'

'Of course I do!' I sniff.

'Lucy, I didn't mean to make you cry, but you have Jack. You can't be staying at another man's house, even if nothing happened. Where does Jack think you were?'

'Yours.' I respond, weakly.

'Right okay, I'll keep this one to myself but if it happens again, I want you to phone me before you go to another man's house.'

'Okay.' I run my index finger under my eyes to get rid of all the extra mascara and tears and breathe in.

'Ready?' Beth asks as Cathy comes running towards us.

'Yep.'

'Guys?' Cathy says, out of breath.

'What's up?'

'I just needed to give you this.' She hands me a magazine. 'Um, thanks…'

'No worries.' Then she runs off. I put the paper under my arm and walk in behind Beth, back to the meeting we were holding. I do one last rub under my eyes as I sit down.

'Are you okay?' I looked up to see concern on Alex's face.

'Yeah I'm fine.' He half-smiles and nods at me. I put the magazine Cathy gave me on the desk, and sort out some contracts while Beth starts talking to them about the book. I don't feel ready to talk yet, so I look through the magazine. It's *US Weekly*. I pick it up and instantly regret it.

'Oh no!' I shout, standing up and frantically flicking the magazine open.

'Lucy are you okay?' Beth asks, confused at my outburst.

'I'm in *US Weekly* leaving Alex's place, with a title saying that Alex has a nice Christmas present this year!' I exclaim, throwing the magazine on the desk and turning to walk out.

'Wait!' I hear Alex shout after me, but I've already left. Alex comes running out after me.

'Lucy?'

'I'm sorry, I can't!' I sob but carry on walking. Alex still catches me.

'Wait,' he holds my hand up, 'don't worry.'

'How can I not worry?'

'It doesn't mean anything and I'm sure Jack will understand.' He still holds my hand.

'Lucy?' someone calls. I turn around to see Beth's head

hanging out the door.

'Sarah's on line one' she explains.

'Shit. Alex, go back to the meeting, I'll be there in a minute.'

'Okay' and he reluctantly let's go of my hand. I run to my
office as fast as I can and pick up the phone.
'Lucy, please don't panic —' Sarah starts.

'Sarah, I know.'

'You do? Thank God.'

'Yeah, what am I going to do?'

'All you have to say is that you had to drop a contract off to
him. Say Beth was with you, but they cut her out.'

'Really?'

'Yeah.' She confirms.

'Okay, so Jack won't be mad?'

'Oh, I don't know honey.'

'Shit.' I sniff.

'Please don't cry.' Sarah says.

'I can't help it.'

'Don't make me come down there…'

'I need a Sarah hug right now.'

'I have a break soon, if you want me to come?'

'I'll pay your cab fare?'

'Okay, I'll be over there in twenty.' She hangs up. I put the phone down and again wipe under my eyes, stand up, straighten my skirt and make my way back to the meeting room.

'Hi.' I mumble as I walk in.

'Hi.' Beth beams at me.

'Catch me up?'

'The boys have definitely decided to come with us for the book deal. They want their own sections which will include full names, parents, high school their dreams and whatever they want to add in. They want us to cover their tour and have picture pages.'

'Right.'

'And they have asked if the front cover can be a pencil drawing.'

'What?'

'I'll draw it.' Tom holds his hand up in the air which makes me smile.

'Yay, a smile.' Beth whispers to me.

'We have an album cover that we all like, so I'm going to draw it. We can have the front cover as a pencil work picture too.'

'Okay, that sounds pretty cool.'

'Thanks.' Tom says with a smile. Just then Kris' phone rings.

'Sorry, I have to take this.' He says, walking out.

'It's probably about the magazine.' Alex looks at me.

'Really?'

'Probably.'

'I have to explain it to Jack later.'

'What are you going to say?' Beth says while spinning in her chair.

'I need to talk to you about it.'

'You're going to drag me into this?' Beth smiles at me.

'Yeah I'm afraid so…' I half smile and shrug.

'Oh, okay what's the story?' Alex smiles at me.

'Beth and I came over to give you a contract but they cut her out the picture.'

'We should hire her to come up with reasons when we get papped' Tom says, laughing.

'It's not a bad idea' Alex agrees.

'We just have to say we went after the office had shut, gave him the contract and went home.'

'Okay, I'll do it!' Beth shakes my hand.

'Thanks.' I lean over and hug her. The phone on the meeting table starts ringing, so I answer it.

'Lucy, Sarah is downstairs.' I hear over the phone.

'Send her up to the meeting room.' I say. Kris then returns, with a less than happy look on his face.

'What's up?' Tom and Lewis ask at the same time.

'The label isn't happy about *US Weekly.*'

'Yeah, but they don't know the story.' I explain.

'What is the story?' Kris looks straight at me.

'Beth and I took a contract over to his house after work, but they cut her out to make it look like it was just me.' Then a tiny knock at the door makes everyone turn to look at it.

'Come in!' I shout, and Sarah comes walking through.

'Hi.' She says shyly. I pat the seat next to me for her to sit down, and she walks over quickly and sits.

'Hi' Erupt say to her all at once.

'Hi!'

'This is Alex, Tom, Dan, Lewis and Matty.' I point at them all in turn.

'I know who they are.' She winks at me.

'Sarah is a massive fan.' I explain.

'Well, we both are. We used to go to see you at gigs, had t-shirts, posters everything.' Sarah adds.

'Cool.' Dan answers.

'Sweet.' Matty follows.

'I'm Kris, by the way...'

'Oh, hi Kris.' Sarah waves at him.

'Oh, sorry Kris, Erupt's manager.' Sarah picks up *US Weekly* and flicks to the pages of Alex and I. She starts laughing to herself.

'What?' I ask.

'They're not very good with words...'

'What do you mean?' Alex looks confused.

'The picture of you two at his front door, it says, "Alex got his tree up in time for Christmas…"' Beth sniggers which then makes me laugh.

'That's awful!' Beth giggles.

'They obviously don't know me very well to think that getting my "Christmas tree" up was a problem' Alex jokes.

'Then there's the other picture of you two just looking at each other. It says, "looking at those legs, Alex has been a bad boy so Santa won't be visiting him this year…"'

'What? That doesn't even make sense!' Alex laughs.

'You have got good legs though…' Sarah looks at me, smiling.

'Wow, a bit of girl-on-girl action here' Tom jokes.

'Right, is there anything else you want to talk about or ask about the book deal? Before Tom starts an orgy?' Beth says through us all.

'Love it!' Tom laughs.

'No, I think we have everything we need,' Kris says, looking at a piece of paper, 'right boys?'

'We're good.' Dan finally speaks.

'So, if you're done, do you want to go to Betty's?' Sarah asks me.

'Yeah, I have another meeting with Carly Jacobs at one, so as long as I'm back in time.'

'We're being two-timed!' Matty jokes.

'What's Betty's?' Lewis asks.

'It's a fast-food café near where I live; we eat there all the time.'

'Oh, sounds healthy.' Tom says.

'You can all come if you want?' Sarah quickly adds. Alex looks at his bandmates awkwardly and shrugs.

'Beth? Kris?' I look at them.

'I can't. I'm sorry I have something I else I need to do.' Kris answers without looking up from his papers.

'Yeah, I'd love to, I'm up for eating fatty stuff.' Beth laughs.

'I love watching girls eat greasy food.' Dan says.

'That's a weird fetish, dude!' Alex slaps him on the back.

'Yeah, like your fetish.' Dan shoots back, which leaves Alex wide-eyed.

'What fetish?' I ask before my brain realizes what I actually just asked.

'He likes –'

'Nothing,' Alex interrupts him, 'nothing!' He gives him a warning look.

'Right, shall we go?' I ask, feeling distracted by the fetish thing. We all stand up from the table and gather our things. We all flag down cabs; I climb in the back with Beth and Sarah.

'One day I want to jump in a cab and shout "follow that cab!"' I joke.

'You're mad.' Beth laughs at me.

'I'm kind of used to it.' Sarah tuts. Our cabs arrive outside Betty's and all eight of us climb out. I push open the door to see Jack and Dean at our usual table eating and talking. Dean spots me first, and signals to Jack to look at me. Jack smiles at me, so he obviously hasn't seen the magazine. The smile changes to shock when seven people follow me in. I smile and give a small wave. The waitress comes over and points us towards a booth and pulls a table up to it so we can all fit around one table.

'Jack?' Sarah pushes through everyone, 'Dean?'

'Alright? Jack answers with a mouth full of bacon.

'You coming to sit with us?'

'No, I have to go back to the office in a minute.' Jack answers, and he gets up, walks over to me and kisses me, probably because Alex is here.

'See you later.' He winks and slaps my ass. Dean walks past after Jack and kisses me on the cheek.

'Bye Dean' I smile. As it gets to midday and everyone empties their plates.

'We should get back' Beth says.

'Yeah, we have Carly Jacobs coming in an hour.'

'Good luck with that,' Tom laughs, 'she's up her own ass!'

'Oh, I'll watch for that…' I look at Beth confusedly.

'I best get back. I've been gone for over an hour. Will you make burgers tonight?' Sarah asks while stroking my arm and giving me a one arm hug.

'Okay. I'll ring you later.' I hug her back.

'Bye boys…' Sarah winks at Matty.
'Later, I'll call you' he winks back at Sarah. Alex just sits there, not really saying much and he won't look at me.

'You okay?' Lewis whispers to Alex but loud enough for me to hear him. Alex just nod and leans his elbows on the table.

'I need to get home. I have some things I need to do.' Alex

looks at Dan.

'Doing Charlie.' Dan jokes. My eyes shoot straight to Alex looks at me. I look away, embarrassed I reacted to it.

'No, I don't see her anymore...' He mumbles. I take my phone out just to make myself not look at Alex. *Why was I jealous?* I shift nervously in my seat until Beth picks up that there's a problem and grabs my hand.

'Ready?'

'Yeah, thanks boys. I'll talk to you later.' I look at them all, except Alex, who looks up at me and smiles. Beth hauls a taxi outside Betty's.

'So, what was that between you and Alex?' She asks with folded arms.

'Something happened.' I close my eyes to stop the tears.

'I knew it,' she unfolds her arms and leans into me, 'spill'.

'It's what I said the other day. I went and watched Erupt practice and went to his. But we slept together in his bed.' Beth gasps.

'Oh my god,' she puts her hand on my leg, 'does anyone else know?'

'No just you, me, and Alex.' I rub away a tear.

'Don't worry, have you seen him since?'

'No, but I want to…'

'Oh…'

'I really want to see him again.' I wipe my nose in the least lady-like way ever. Beth screws her nose up.

'Oh babe.'
'It's so complicated.'

'I know, but we will work it out, we will get Carly Jacobs out of the way and then we will sort it okay?' I nod at her while I quietly think of Alex as I look at the city out of the cab window. When we get back to the office I run to my office and launch my stuff at my desk and run to the tiny kitchen for my cup of coffee.

'Same idea.' Beth winks at me.

'Oh definitely!' We both walk to the meeting room with our piles of paper, laughing and joking with each other. We don't realize Carly Jacobs and her manager are sat in the corner.

'Oh gosh! Hi!' I manage to say. I give her my brightest smile.

'So sorry we're late!' Beth offers.

'Oh no, we're early, sorry.' Carly half-smiles whilst her manager tuts.

'As we weren't expecting you to be early, will you bear with us for a couple of minutes whilst we get ourselves together?'

Beth asks, taking a seat.

'Sure thing,' Carly smiles, 'where can I get a coffee?'

'We have a kitchen if you want me to get you one.' I look up at her.

'Oh no, I'll go, it's something for me to do while you set up.'

'Oh, okay. There's one outside the building or there's a Starbucks a block away.'

'Okay great.' Carly and her manager get up and walk out the meeting room, as Beth raises her eyebrows at me.

'High-maintenance much?' Beth giggles.

'I think she's fine, but it's that butt-munch of a manager…'

'Ha-ha, yes, what an asshat!'

'We can sit here thinking of names all day, but we do really have to get ready.'

'Yep. Is Drake going to show for this interview? Or are we halving his wages?'

'Halving his wages!' I joke.

'I'll keep my wages thank you ladies.' Drake speaks from behind us. We blush.

'Hi Drake.' I mumble.

'Hi. Is Carly here yet?'

'Yes, but she and her manager went to get coffee while we set up.'

'You kicked her out?' Drake raises his eyebrows at me.

'No, no, she offered to go after I offered to make one.' I frown.

'I would pass on a coffee made by you, Luc.' Drake jokes. I gasp at him, pretending to be offended.

'Sorry Luc…'

'Nah, I would to.' I agree. After ten minutes Carly and her manager *John by the way after he introduced himself* make their way back in to the meeting room. He gets two big notepads out of his bag and three different colored pens. *Organized.* Drake introduces us all, and to my surprise Carly is very nice and not up her own ass as the boys told me. I instantly relax when Beth starts her presentation to win Carly and John over. I nod in the right places, as does Drake and we laugh where Beth makes unfunny jokes. Carly smiles a lot and asks questions while John sits there writing the whole time. *Rude.*

'So, what do you think?' Beth finally says.

'I like it, I'm totally excited for this!' Carly smiles.

'John?' Beth asks.

'Some ideas were good, but some I have issues with. You don't seem to have any control over the book contents. You should be telling us what we want in the book, not asking us.' John lists.

'Well the book is about, and from Carly Jacobs. We put in the book what her fans want to know, and we need to know what she wants to say, because god forbid you would protest if I put in something that you don't agree with.' Beth answers back, as the rest of us – including John – look at her with our mouths open.

'R-r-right,' John stammers his answer, 'if Carly's happy, then so am I.'

'I'm cool about this,' Carly smiles, 'where do I sign?' Beth slides a contract across the table for them both to sign.

'You can call Drake, Lucy, or myself if you have any questions or for anything else' Beth explains.

'Sure!' Carly autographs the contract while John does the tiniest scribble I've ever seen.

'Thank you! After the new year is out of the way, we will contact you for another meeting, photos, front cover design and the main interview' I explain, as Beth neatly piles her papers.

'Yeah, that's cool! Thank you so much for having me and I look forward to seeing you again.' Carly gets up and grabs her bag, and John scurries out after her with his head hung.

As soon as Beth is confident that they are out of ear-shot, Beth gives me her biggest smile and high fives me.

'That was such a rush!' Beth squeals.

'You did good, didn't she Drake?' I say.

'She did well.' He confirms. We all walk back to our offices feeling very good about our last two confirmed deals. Back in my office, I can't help but think about Alex again. I pull my phone out and text him.

*Hey are you okay? You seemed upset? L*

I sit back in my chair and stare at the ceiling waiting for his reply.

*I'm fine, you?*

So, Alex wasn't okay. I pick up my phone and dial his number. He answers on the first ring.

'Lucy?'

'Yeah, what's wrong?'
'Nothing. I said I was fine.'

'You don't seem fine, what was wrong at Betty's?' The silence makes me think he's hung up.

'Alex?'

'Nothing Lucy, okay?'

'I'm only trying to help.' Alex goes silent again.

'It's about me isn't it?' I ask. Again, silence.

'Alex, what is with you? Just answer me.'

'Yes, it is you.'

'What about me?'

'I like you Lucy.'

'Oh.' I'm shocked. I wasn't expecting that answer.

'Yeah, I got angry when Jack kissed you in Betty's because you're not mine and I can't do that to you.'

'Oh.' Now I'm not saying anything.

'Yeah.'

'Do you want to talk about it?'

'Um, what?'

'I can come over tonight if you want?'

'You can't in case of photographers.'

'Oh, meet me somewhere?'

'Where?' Alex sounds intrigued.

'Um…'

'I'll text you later where to meet me, okay?'

'Yeah, okay, bye.'

'Bye, babe' and he hangs up. I feel a little happier now I knew I was going to see Alex later on. I log onto my emails and see an email from Jack.

*From: Jack Base*
*Subject: Tonight*
*To: Lucy Winter*
*12/29/10 16:25*
*Lucy I won't be home tonight. I have to stay late and them I'm going out drinking so I'm going to crash at Mark's.*

*See you tomorrow I'll take you to dinner.*

*I.T manager at Freshman's LTD.*

I pick up my phone and text Alex.

*My place will be empty tonight, Jack's away x*

I reply back to Jack.

*From: Lucy Winter*
*Subject: Tonight*
*To: Jack Base*
*12/29/10 16:30*

*That's cool have a good time see you tomorrow night, I'd*

*love to go for dinner.*

**P.A. to Drake Teely at Teely's International**

My phone starts to ring, and Alex's name flashes on the screen.

'Hello?'

'Hi' Alex answers, clearly happier than before.

'You okay?'

'Yeah, so yours tonight, yeah?'
'Yeah, Jack is out with friends for the night.'

'Are you sure?'

'Yes, I am, so meet me there at six?'

'Yeah, okay babe, see you then.' He hangs up. I smile, but it quickly fades when I remember how I'm betraying my friends and Jack by meeting Alex at our place. The end of the day can't come sooner. I decide I deserve an early finish, so I pack up my things and turn off my computer. I walk out of my office to find Beth still on the phone. I lean on her desk with my elbows and wait for her to finish.

'Bye Margaret' Beth says as she put the phone down.

'Lucy?'

'Hi, I'm going home early and having my eyebrows and nails

done.'

'Oh, I'm coming with!' Beth grabs her stuff and we head to the elevator.

********************

After two hours of girly time, I feel well and truly pampered.

'God, I feel good!' Beth smiles at me from the cab.

'Me too, what are you doing tonight?' I ask Beth.

'Nothing, you?'

'I'm going out for dinner.' I smile.

'Oh, sounds nice.' The cab pulls up outside my apartment building. I pay my share and kiss Beth on the cheek.

'See you tomorrow!'

'Right back at ya!' She laughs and the cab leaves. I make my way up to my apartment and sigh with happiness knowing I'm home. I'll be seeing Alex soon. I ran to my room and quickly change into my sexy interview dress. I place my bag on the sofa just as the bell buzzed.

'Hello?'
'Hi.' comes Alex's voice. I buzz him straight up and I hold the door open for him when he walks out the lift. He slams my door shut and locks it, pulls me into a kiss whilst running his hands all over my body.

# CHAPTER FOURTEEN

'Morning.' Comes a male voice from next to me, then I feel kisses pressed against my neck, while I lie half-asleep in bed.

'Morning...' I mumble back with a smile.

'I best get home before we get found out.' That's when it hits me. *That's Alex, not Jake...* I sit bolt upright.

'Oh my god, I forgot you were here!'

'Oh thanks, I obviously didn't do a good job last night then...' Alex laughs.

'I have to get to work and you have to leave!'

'What time is Jack back?' Alex gets out of bed and pulls on his jeans.

'I don't know.' I jump out of bed and run to my wardrobe. I quickly get dressed, pull my hair into a messy bun and run back out to find Alex walking into the living room to find his t-shirt.

'Oh god!' I run past him to the bathroom, wipe away my panda eyes and put on some new mascara and lip gloss. As I stroll back into the living room, feeling a little calmer, I sigh in relief. I grab my phone and see a message from Jack. My stomach instantly drops, thinking the worst. I open the message to find a picture of Jack, sticking his tongue down a girl's throat.

'What the heck?' I say aloud.

'What?' Alex looks up from putting his shoes on.

'I've just received a picture from Jack, of him kissing a girl...'

'Oh, let's see?' Alex jumps over the back of the couch and snatches the phone out of my hand.

'Hey!' I snatch it back.

'What are you going to do?' Alex looks down at me.

'I don't know…' I frown.

'Text him and just say "what the heck?"'

'Shall I?'

'Yes, he's kissing another girl and you have the evidence.'

'Well, yeah, okay.' I text Jack back.

**What the heck is this?**

I put my phone in my bag and smile at Alex.

'We have to go. I need to be at the office.' Alex nods and picks up my bag. I follow him out the apartment. We make our way outside and haul a cab. Alex stands back and lets me climb in first. He climbs in after me and puts his arm over my shoulder.

'We didn't do any talking last night.' Alex whispers in my ear.

'Oh yeah, do you still want to talk?' I look up at him.

'I'm not complaining if it happens like that every time…' he smiles.

'No, we have to sort this out.' I look out the window.

'Okay' he reluctantly answers. When we pull up outside my work building, I try to give Alex the cash to pay for my half of the ride but he won't let me. He pulls me in for a big romantic kiss, before he lets me out the cab to go to work.

'See you later!' He winks and I shut the door. I walk into the lobby and make my way to the lift, just as I hear someone shout my name.

'LUCY!' I recognize the voice straight away so I don't turn around.

'LUCY!' The voice shouts again. I jab the elevator button and it opens straight away. I step in and press the button for floor eighteen. The doors start to close, but a hand stops them.

'Jack, I'm going to be late, let go of the door.'

'I need to talk to you!' He answers, out of breath.

'Let go of the door.' I stare at him with no emotion. He takes his hand out and looks at me with puppy dog eyes as the doors shut. I instantly relax, but I still have to force myself not to cry. The elevator dings and the doors open. I walk out slowly, making sure Jack hasn't run up the stairs. I hurry to my office and collapse on my chair, closing my eyes. I slowly bend over till my forehead rests on my desk.

'Lucy?'

'Ahh, Jack take the hint!' I say without moving.

'I want to explain.'

'I don't want to hear it.'

'Lucy please?'

'Jack, just go.'

'Will you be home tonight?'

'Wouldn't count on it if you're there' I say, regretting it a little.

'Lucy?'

'Please Jack.'

'Can I not just explain?' I reluctantly look at him. He has clearly been crying, still in his clothes he left for work in yesterday morning. He looks sad.

'Okay, quickly.'

'I was roofied!' Jack says. I look at him in disbelief and let out a laugh.

'Someone gave you the date rape drug?' I smirk at him.

'Yes, and I don't remember anything.'

'That's the shittiest lie I've ever heard, this isn't The Hangover.'

'It's true, I've just got out the hospital.' I frown and look up at him.

'You were in the hospital?'

'Yes, I didn't take that photo or send it to you!' He puts his hands in his pant pockets and hangs his head.

'I'll speak to you later.' I say, not making eye contact with him.

'What time will you be home?' He whispers.

'I'll see you tomorrow, I'll stay somewhere else.'

'Why?'

'Jack, please just give me space?' He nods at me and turns in the doorway, he pauses and turns back to face me.

'Lucy, I love you.' I look at my hands as my eyes water so he won't see. He walks out my office and I place my forehead back on my desk. I pull my phone out my bag and forward the message to Sarah and Dean. I sit back up and am shocked to see Beth sat in the seat opposite me.

'Whoa, how long have you been there?!'

'For about five minutes, you okay?'

'Not really, did you hear?'

'I heard what was being said but I didn't hear what happened.'

'Oh, I received this photo this morning' I hand Beth my phone.

'Oh my…'

'He says he was roofied and was in hospital.' I explain.

'Really?' She looks at me like I'm stupid.

'That's what he said.' I answer, smirking.

'And he wants you to believe that?'

'Yes, but I feel like I'm a hypocrite being angry, because of Alex?'

'Well you could look at it like that.' She nods.

'Or?'

'You're both not happy, maybe a break might be good?'

'I was thinking that, but Jack has nowhere to live.' I bite my lip.

'That's not your responsibility.' She pats my hand.

'Well it is, because of Alex.'

'Well okay I'll give you that.'

'I'm going to stay with Sarah tonight, come to work tomorrow, sort my head out and go home tomorrow evening.'

'Okay if you're sure, you know where I am if you need me.'

'Thanks...' I mumble while putting my head back on my desk. Then I pick up my phone as I receive a message from Sarah.

*What the fuck?? I'm going to fucking kick his ass!! You okay? Want to stay with me tonight xxxxxxxxxxxxxxxxxxx*

I smile to myself and text her back.

*I know. I've told him I'm not going home, I'm going to stay with Beth as we have some work to finish and I'll go speak to him tomorrow xxxxx*

I hate lying to people but I can't deal with Sarah tonight. All she would do is ask me questions when all I want to do is eat ice-cream, cry and watch Channing Tatum take his shirt off. My phone beeps back.

*Have you spoken to him? I'm sure he has a reason, call me if you want to talk Dean xxxxx*

Why did Dean have to be so nice for him? But then Beth is being nice to me, and she knows what I did. I'm so confused. I get a text from Jack.

*Babe, please come home tonight, we have to talk. I love you so much xxxxx*

I ignore all the texts and message Alex tonight.

*Can I stay with you tonight? I'll buy the pizza.*
I instantly get a text back, which makes me smile.

*Look forward to it, no pineapple xx*

Getting a reply from Alex makes me happier, and I feel what Beth said may be good advice. Maybe we should have a break? I log into my emails and see I have an email from George Teely.

*From: George Teely*
*Subject: Congratulations*
*To: Lucy Winter, Beth Ryan*
*12/30/10 11:45*

*Dear Ms Ryan and Ms Winter,*

*I have been informed by Drake that I should be thanking you two for helping Teely's International branch out. I hear that we have taken on two new contracts with Carly Jacobs and Erupt. Carly Jacobs is already interested in having a second book out, so that's three new contracts.*

*I would like to thank you personally by inviting you out for a business meeting with me, my wife Elizabeth and Drake on 2nd of January 2012.*
*Hope to hear back from you both.*

*Yours sincerely,*
*George Teely*

I'm pleasantly surprised by the email, and decide to check if Beth has seen in too.

'Did you see the email?'

'No, what email? Beth looks confused.

'From George Teely!' I smile.

'No.' She quickly flicks to her emails and reads it, a smile slowly forming on her face.

'Whoa!' She answers eventually.

'I know!'

'We might get a big fat raise…'

'Oh my god, we might.' I clap my hands.

'So, you seem happier?'

'I am after that, and I'm going to take your advice.'

'What bit?'

'The break with Jack and me.'

'Oh, are you sure?'

'Yeah, I think it will be good for us, even if it's only a week or so.'

'Okay, if you're sure.' I nod and smile at her, happy with my decision.

'Want to go to lunch?' Beth says clicking away on her mouse.

'Sure, where?'

'I'm not a massive fan of Betty's' she admits.

'Ah okay, let me get my bag.' I go back to my office, grab my stuff, and check my phone as I walk out. I have three missed calls from Jack and seven from my parents. I should probably find out what's up, so I ring my parents back.

'Hello?'

'Mom, what's wrong?'

'Oh, dear, we've just spoken to Jack are you okay?'

'Yes, I'm fine.'

'He said he was drugged?'

'Yeah, he told me.'

'That's a bit weird, what are you going to do?'

'I've told him I'll speak to him tomorrow about it.'
'Where are you going to stay?'

'I'll stay with Sarah or Beth until I'm ready.'

'Okay dear, well phone me if you need anything.'

'Thanks Mom, bye.'

'Bye, love you!'

'Love you too.' I hang up, a little happier that my Mom took my side and not Jack's. I text him to make sure he wasn't drugged again.

*Why did you ring?*

Plain and simple, to show him I'm still pissed off with him, and then I receive a text back.

*Just letting you know I'm staying with Dean, so you can go home without seeing me, see you tomorrow. Love you.*

I don't text back again. I'm still pissed off that now my apartment is now empty and I don't really have a reason to stay out of it. I block it out and walk back out my office to meet Beth.

'Ready?'

'Yep.'

\*\*\*\*\*\*\*\*\*\*

I log out my emails at the end of the day and turn off my computer. I feel the butterflies in my stomach because I'm going to Alex's. I haul a cab over to his apartment and ring the buzzer at his building. Alex's sleepy voice comes over the machine.

'Hello?'

'It's Lucy.' He buzzes me straight in, so I jump in the elevator and make my way to his apartment, where he stands with the door already open for me.

'Hi…' He says with a shy smile.

'Hi.' I copy his smile.

'Where's my pizza?' he says while shutting the door.

'I'm ordering in, I can't be bothered to wait in a shop for it.'

'Fair enough' and he throws his phone at me.

'Thanks, what do you want?'

'Anything, as long as it has no pineapple.'

'Cool.' He dumps himself on the couch and flings his long legs up on the side seat. He pulls his laptop onto his lap and starts typing away, as I order pizza.

'So, what are you doing?' I ask, sitting gently next to him.

'Just writing a letter to my brother, he's in Australia.'

'Oh, that's cool' I smile.

'Yeah, he's travelling. He's been away for just over a year' Alex explains.

'Where is he at the moment?' I ask.

'In Dee, why?'

'I've never heard of that' I frown.

'Have you ever been out of this country?' he smirks.

'No' I blush.

'That's why you haven't heard of it then' he strokes my hair, presses send and puts his laptop down. He leans in towards me. Our foreheads touch. It's an intense moment, but neither of us moves. The tension is broken by my phone ringing. I reluctantly pull away.

'Hello?'

'Where are you?'

'Why?'
'You're not at home?'

'No, I told you I was staying out.'

'But I told you the apartment was empty.'

'And? I knew you would come back and we would have to talk when I wasn't ready.'

'Oh.'

'Bye Jack. I'll be home tomorrow evening. I hang up, slowly breathing in and out with my eyes closed.

'Is he okay?' Alex whispers.

'Yeah.'

'So, what is his excuse?' Alex asks.

'He says he was roofied.'

'What? He could have come up with a better excuse' he answers.

'Yeah I know, he said he was in hospital.'

'Do you believe him?' Alex asks.

'I don't know, I'm going to say I need a break from him.'

'Oh?'

'I haven't really thought about it.'

'Okay, well enough. Let's have a good night' he smiles. The pizza arrives and Alex lets me put on a Channing Tatum movie, to put me in a better mood. While I ogle Channing Tatum's half naked body, Alex writes something the whole time, which I keep trying to read, but every time I lean over, he covers it with his hands, so I assume he must be writing a diary or something. After about half an hour Alex skips off to his room and appears a couple of minutes later with a red guitar and a massive smile on his face.

'What you doing?' I ask, eyeing him up and down.
'I'm writing a song' he smiles at me and sits on the floor

cross-legged.

'About what? How fit Channing is?' I joke.

'Nope.'

'Then what?'

'You.'

'Me?' I ask confused.

'You can listen to the song and work it out…' he teases. He strums on his guitar and tunes the strings, then pulls the piece of paper out of his back pocket, places it in front of him and starts playing the song. He looks really in to it and he won't make eye contact with me. He keeps staring at the paper as he sings beautiful lyrics about how I make him happy. He sings that my smile makes him smile — which turns out to be the title.

'Wow!'

'You like it?'

'Yeah! Did you write that whole thing just a minute ago?'

'Yep, while thinking of you' he blushes a little.

'Are you blushing?' I laugh.

'No' he puts his guitar down and walks over to me on his knees.

'You are! It was a very cute and beautiful song.'

'You think I'm cute?'

'Of course!'

'Good,' he pulls me in for a hug and he kisses the top of my head, 'it's getting late, are you staying over?'

'If it's okay?'

'Sure, where do you want to sleep? On here? Or in my bed?'
'In your very comfy bed.'

'Okay, I hope you know I'm sleeping in there too' he smiles.

'Of course.'

'I'm not sleeping on the couch for anyone.' I smile at his forward thinking. He puts the rest of the pizza in the fridge and holds out his hand for me to take. I turn the T.V. off on the remote and flip the light off on the way through to the bedroom.

***************

I walk out the elevator with a giant bounce in my step.

'Morning! Staying with Sarah agrees with you.' Beth beams at me.

'Oh yeah, it does' I smile back, thinking of the night before. I sit at my desk and turn my computer on as I look through the box of manuscripts that have been put on my desk with a note from Beth.

*I've stolen five of these Beth xx*

I smile, I would have let her have some anyway, saves me five to read. My phone beeps at me.

*Hi beautiful, last night was amazing, hope to have many more with you. See you soon, Alex xxx*

I smile to myself again, logging into my emails. *None – that's weird.* I start reading one of the manuscripts.

'Knock knock.'

'Come in' I look up towards my door. I'm sat back in my chair with my legs crossed on my desk, when I see George Teely standing in front of me.

'Oh, hello sir' I stand up as quickly as I can.

'Don't panic, sit down' he says while walking to my spare chair.

'How can I help you?'

'I didn't get a reply from you yesterday; I was just checking you received it.'

'Yes, Sir, I'm sorry I totally forgot to email you back.'

'That's no problem, you look busy,' he says whilst looking around my office, 'so can you make it?'

'Yes, of course I can, it would be a pleasure.'

'Good, please bring your fiancé.'

'How do you know I'm engaged?' I frown. He points at my engagement ring.

'Oh yeah, silly me' I laugh.

'It would be great to meet him, goodbye Ms Winter.'

'Bye Sir.' He leaves my office. I get comfortable in my chair and carry on reading the manuscript.

A little bit later Beth comes into my office.

'You coming for lunch?'

'It's lunch time?' I ask looking at my watch.

'Well, yeah, it's nearly two!'

'Jesus, I didn't even realize the time.' I stand up and grab my bag. As we we're walking to the elevator, Beth links her arm with mine and smiles at me.

'Where we going?'

'I'm not that hungry' I reply.

'So, Starbucks and a muffin?'

'Sounds perfect' I reply. When we reach the ground floor, the guy behind the main desk calls us.

'Lucy? Beth?' We both turn around to see him running towards us.

'What's up?'
'George Teely left these here for you' the guy hands us both a piece of paper.

'Thanks' I look it over as Beth squeals.

'$2,500 bonus?' I ask her, shocked.

'That's what it says' she smiles at me.

'Good shopping trip this weekend then!' I laugh, all I can do is laugh.

'Let's plan that at lunch!'

'Where shall we go?' Beth asks me.

'On a plane somewhere?' I can't take my eyes off the cheque.

'You're not going to faint, are you?' Beth asks me.

'No, why?'

'You've gone pale' she drags me into Starbucks and tells me to sit while she orders our drinks. I pull my phone out to tell some people that I'm now a millionaire… *sort of*…

*Guess how much my bonus was for just this month? Xx*

I send the same text to Sarah, Gemma and Alex, and place my phone on the table while I wait for a reply. Sarah is the first.

*How much? Taking me to Paris? Lol S*

I smile. Alex is next.

*How much babe?*

And Gemma is last.

*I'm guessing a lot by the message…what are you buying me? G xxxxx*

I reply to them all with the same message.

*$2,500 xx*

Just then Beth returns to the table with giant drinks.

'Whoa!'

'We can afford it now' Beth laughs.

'True, have you told Bradley yet?'

'No.'

'Why not?'

'I don't know.'

'Do it now!' I laugh.

'Shall I?'

'Yeah, do it' I say, tapping her phone screen. I receive replies back from Alex, Gemma and Sarah.

*WOW, where you taking me for dinner? A xx*

*WHOA, you must have done good xx*

*WHAT THE…...shopping's on you then, I might marry you J S x*

I look up at Beth, who was still typing a message.

'My friends only want me for my money' I joke.

'Do you want to deposit the cheque on the way back to the office?'

'Yes please, the quicker it's in, the quicker I can spend it!'

'It's weird being rich' Beth says, staring at her coffee.

'I'm going to buy a satchel.'

'What are you? Jesus?' Beth says while laughing and pointing at me.

'It's pink…'

'Oh, that makes it perfectly fine' she jokes.

'Sure it does.'

'We should go to L.A for the weekend!'

'VEGAS?' I shout.

'Whoa, calm down' Beth looks scared.

'Sorry, I really want to go to Vegas' I blush, with the whole café was staring at me.

'Little steps,' Beth says while stroking my arm, 'let's walk and talk before we get kicked out.'

We get back to the office after an hour and a half lunch break… *Ooopss!* I look at my phone to see I have a missed call from Jack, so I phone him back.

'Hello?'

'Jack, what's up?'

'Just checking you're coming home tonight?'

'Yes, I'll be there at half five.'

'Okay, good, I have something for you.'

'Jack, what have you done?'

'Bought you something.'

'Oh god, okay, I'll see you later, bye.'

'Bye Lucy'. I hang up just as my office phone rings.

'Hello Lucy sp–'

'Lucy its Beth, I have George on line one.'

'Oh great,' I press line one, 'hello?'

'Lucy?'

'Yes, hello sir.'

'Hi.'

'Hi, how can I help?'

'Oh, right yes, I need you to do a favour for me?'

'Okay, what's that?'

'I need you to go to Las Vegas to get another contract signed.'

'Really? Who is it for?'

'James Lloyd, he's been in contact after speaking to Alex Jones.'

'Oh right.' *Thank you, Alex!*

'So, can you go?'

'When do you need me to leave?'

'On the 2nd, so we will have to reschedule our dinner.'

'Oh okay, is Beth coming?'

'Of course, she is your business partner now.'

'Okay great.'

'I'll get your flights, petty cash, credit cards and all things sorted and I'll need you to come in tomorrow at some point to pick them up.'

'Oh course.'

'Great, see you tomorrow.'

'Bye.' I hang up with a huge smile on my face. I phone Alex.

'Hello?'

'ALEX, I'M GOING TO VEGAS ON THE 2ND!' I shout.

'Are you now?' he laughs.

'Yes! I'm so excited.'

'Okay, calm down, I also have some news for you.'

'Okay…'

'I'm also going to Vegas on the 2$^{nd}$.'

'WHAT?'

'And I'm the one introducing you to James Lloyd!'

'WHAT?'

'So, we get to spend four days in Vegas together.'

'OH MY GOD' I scream. Beth comes running into my office.

'Lucy what's wrong?'

'Alex, I'll call you back.'

'Okay' he answers.

'Beth, sit down.'

'Okay, is everything okay?'

'Yes, Teely's International are paying for me and you to go to Las Vegas from the 2$^{nd}$ to the 6$^{th}$; we get a company credit card AND we're interviewing James Lloyd!' Beth sits in stunned silence, just staring at me.

'What?' she whispers.

'What bit do you want me to repeat?'

'Can you check I'm awake?' she says.

'Um, how?'
'I don't know?' I laugh at her and walk around my desk to hug her. She slowly stands up and accepts my hug. As I put my arms around her, I pinch a small bit of skin under her arm.

'Ouch' she pushes me off.

'I was checking you're awake' I smile.

'I have to tell Bradley, what about my daughter?' she asks, frowning.

'Um, will Bradley look after her?'

'He should do, shouldn't he?'

'Yes, he should after he found out what your bonus was' I smile.

'True.'

'Also, Alex is the one that recommended us to James, and he will be with us to introduce us.'

'That's cool, do you think we deserve an early night. We have tomorrow off by the way.'

'Oh, cool then yes, let's go home.'

# CHAPTER FIFTEEN

'Owww' I suddenly wake up when an elbow jabs me in the ribs.

'Come on, they're calling us' Alex says, grabbing my bag.

'BETH?' I shout towards the shop.

'COMING!' I hear back. I make my way to the gate and take my bag off of Alex. Being a rock star and all, Alex had paid extra to travel first class, but Beth and I refused to spend our shopping money on an upgrade.

'Morning, ma'am, ticket please.' I hand over my ticket, which she reads, then she checks the screen and looks back at the ticket.

'You've been upgraded,' she smiles at me, 'please make your way to the red door in the corner.'

'How?'

'I'm sorry, I don't have that kind of information.'

'Oh.'

'Hi!' Beth stops next to me out of breath.

'Hello, ticket please?' the lady asks Beth. She does the same to Beth's ticket that she did to mine.

'You have also been upgraded, please make your way to the red door.' Beth looks at me confusedly.

'I don't know…' I shrug. Beth and I walk over to the red door and hand our tickets to the man stood there. He lets us through the door. We enter the lounge and see Alex sat in a chair with a glass of champagne and a smile.

'You upgraded us?' I point my finger at Alex.

'Guilty.'

'Thanks, Alex!' Beth says and slumps into an over-fluffed arm chair, as a neatly dressed girl hands us a glass of champagne each.

'Thanks' I mutter. I sit in a comfy chair, rest my head on the back and stare at the ceiling. I had told Jack we should go on a break and I felt a lot worse than I thought I would feel. Jack was heartbroken and moved into Dean's apartment, while Dean and Belle were in L.A. for two months for Belle's work. I had explained the situation to Alex and he was very understanding, but we had spent pretty much every day and night together since. I was happy with life, but I just felt guilty. Beth understood my problem and agreed she wouldn't judge or moan. Beth and I had also kept our bonuses, so that we can go shopping in Las Vegas, and go to the slots and casinos to try and win double our money…

'What you thinking about?' My thoughts are interrupted by Alex.

'Winning millions on the slots.' I say without moving.

'Are you still asleep?' he laughs, poking me in the arm.

'Nope, I'm in a happy place.'

'That's good. I'll leave you in there, so you're in a good mood when we land.' I smile, but I'm not sure if he sees. Alex gets up from his chair and walks off. I don't see where he went, so I sit up properly, accepting another glass of champagne and I look at Beth.

'It's quite nice in here.'

'To right' Beth agrees, downing her drink.

'Where did Alex go?'

'Not sure, babes' she gets up and follows the lady with the drinks, taking another one. I smile to myself – this should be a good weekend.

********************

'We're staying here?' I look up at the Bellagio hotel in disbelief.

'Sure, courtesy of Teely's International' Beth smiles.

'How many rooms?'

'Two, but I'm guessing you two can share' Beth smiles.

'To right,' Alex says putting his arm over my shoulders, 'I'll get the room keys' Alex says handing me his luggage. Beth and I wait in the middle of the lobby.

'God, I love George so much, and Alex obviously for getting us a free trip here!' Beth says, clapping her hands.

'Me too, this is amazing!'

'We've been upgraded' Alex says as he comes running back to us.

'Again?'

'Yes, by the manager because I'm famous' he smiles at me.

'Oh.'

'We're in the penthouse' Alex looks at us both with raised eyebrows, waiting for our reactions.

'OH MY GOD' Beth screams, and I quickly clasp my hand over her mouth and giggle.

'Let's go before we get kicked out.' Alex grabs his luggage and points towards the elevator. We ride in the lift in silence. Beth is in the corner shaking with excitement. We step out the elevator to a big – *no, it's massive* – room, with sofas and a DJ deck in the centre, a bar and floor-to-ceiling windows which are three times the height of Alex. The middle of the room is sunken and the walls have big tasteful pictures of naked women in black and white. I can't speak, let alone breathe.

'Where are the rooms?' Beth whispers to me.

'I don't know' I whisper back.

'Do you two want to see the bedrooms?' Alex asks across the big room, and he throws a door open which leads to a corridor.

'You can have this room, Beth?' Alex opens a door on his left. Beth steps in and nearly faints. The windows were as big and open as the ones in the living room, with an over-sized bed and an en-suite in the corner.

'Oh my god' Beth whispers in disbelief.

'We will leave you to unpack, babe' I say to Beth while I pat her shoulder. All she does is nod. Alex places his hand in mine and pulls me out.

'This is our room.' Alex lets me step in first.

'Wow!' I look around, the room is just as big, with a huge bed, it's awesome.

'Isn't it awesome?' Alex says like he was reading my mind.

'Awe. Some.' I repeat.

'Yes.' He takes my bags and places them on the big dressing

table, and pulls me towards the bed.

'We're going for dinner tonight' he smiles and kisses behind my ear.

'Anything you want, Mr. Rock Star who gets an upgrade to the penthouse for free.'

'Aren't you lucky you have me here?' he asks.

'Oh, very!' I say in my fanciest voice.

'Knock knock,' Beth comes in the door, 'wow, you guys, this is great but my room is better... You can see the strip from my window, imagine what it looks like in the dark with all the lights on!'

'Breathe' I smile at Beth.

'I can't!' She falls on the bed next to Alex.

'We're going for dinner tonight, I made a reservation.' Alex pokes Beth in the stomach.

'Really, where?'

'The Palm.'

'Because he's a rock star and can get into anything because he's famous...' I smile, patting Alex on the head.

'I love that you came, we get treated like rock stars too' Beth sits up.

'At least one of you is pleased I'm here,' Alex jokes, 'oh by the way the boys are coming out tomorrow night. James told his friend we were coming over and they asked us to do a gig, you don't mind, do you?' Alex looks at me.

'Everyone talks too much in Vegas' I fall backwards and cover my eyes with my forearm.

'Can we come?' Beth asks.

'Yep, you're already on the guest list' Alex confirms.

'I should have become famous ages ago,' Beth jumps up and opens my suitcase, 'I'm wearing your pink bandage dress babe.'

'Sure.' I don't move, but I know that even if I say no or try to fight her for it, I'm going to lose.

'Cheers, I'm going to shower. When are we leaving?' Beth turns on her heels in the doorway.

'At eight, is an hour and half long enough to get ready?'

'Don't ask stupid questions' Beth laughs and leaves.

'Hey' Alex poke me.

'Hhmm'

'I have a present for Beth.' I sit bolt upright.

'What is it?'

'I paid for her husband to come out.'

'WHAT?'

'Is it bad?'

'No way, that's so nice of you, when does he get here?'
Alex's phone ring in his pocket. He quickly gets it out and
answers.

'Hello...yeah...penthouse...I'll meet you at the lift...bye,' He
stands up,
'make sure she doesn't come out of her room' and he heads
towards the lift.
'Knock knock' I mimic, as Beth opens the door and pulls me
in.

'Do you need help unpacking?' I ask, not really sure how to
distract her.

'No not really, I'm just going to get in the shower, have you
seen it?' Beth grabs my forearm and pulls me towards the
bathroom.

'It's nice for a shower.'

'Totally nice' Beth pulls me in the bathroom a little more.
She had left the shower on, so the floor was a little wet.

'Look at the shampoo' I walk towards the shampoo and slip
in the water, taking out Beth as I go down.

'Girl on girl' comes a male voice from the doorway. We both look over to see Alex and Bradley stood in the doorway smirking.

'Bradley?' Beth asks.

'Yeah babe, Alex paid for me to come out' Beth gets up in record time, runs across the floor and launches herself at Bradley. Alex carefully walks over to me and pulls me up of the floor.

'Thanks' I mumble.

'She's with my mum' I hear Bradley say to Beth. I'm guessing Beth asked where her daughter was.

'Do you have enough room for Bradley at dinner' Beth reluctantly lets go of Bradley.

'Yeah I do, and his name is on the list for the gig.'

'You're good' Beth winks at him.

'Thanks,' Alex blushes again, 'we should go get ready.'

'Yep.' Alex and I walk out of their room and make our way back to ours. I run straight to the bathroom to check that ours was just as cool, and to my relief it is.

'Oh,' I whisper to myself, 'yes!' I turn the shower on, and from previous experience I walk back to the bedroom carefully.

'I'm having a shower' I tell Alex.

'I'll meet you in there.' I giggle and pick up an extra towel for Mr. Rock Star.
After one of the best showers ever, I walk over to my already open suitcase, thanks to Beth, and I search around for an outfit.

'What are you wearing?' I ask Alex, without looking away from my pile of clothes.

'Suit pants, shirt and tie, and maybe my suit jacket if you're lucky.'

'Oh, very James Bond' I smirk and look over my shoulder at Alex, still dripping wet with a towel around his waist. I finally pick a silver strapless dress that stopped mid-thigh, pick up my Louboutin's and start drying my hair. I steal a handful of Alex's hair wax and give myself a messy bed-head style. I sit at the dressing table and apply my make-up.

'Are you ready?' Beth asks, poking her head around the door.

'Nearly, let me see you' Beth walks in and stands behind me so I could see her in the mirror.

'You scrub up good!'

'Thanks' Beth is wearing my baby pink off the shoulder bandage dress; she lifts her leg to show off her shoes.

'Oh, very nice!' She is wearing my silver Jimmy Choo

strappy sandals, she has her hair down and straightened, with her usual flawless make up. I stand up and straighten my dress,

'What do you think?'

'I want to marry you' she looks at me with an open mouth.

'COME ON GIRLS' Alex shouts from the living room. We link arms and walk over, giggling to each other until we reach the men. Bradley is dressed like Alex, but his suit was a grey/blue, while Alex has a jet black one. They both looked handsome.

'Wow, what happened to Alex and Bradley?' I joke.
'I was going to say the same about you two' Bradley laughs out loud.

'Thanks!' Beth walks over to Bradley and links his arm with hers. I do the same to Alex.

'You look fucking awesome' Alex kisses my hair.

'Right back at you Mr. Rock Star.'

'You look more like a rock star in that dress than me, every man will be wearing a suit.'

'You look super sexy though' I wink up at him. We all climb into the elevator and make our way to the ground floor to get into a waiting limo.

'A limo?' I look up at Alex.

'Of course. I am a rock star…' he smirks. The limo stops outside The Palm. I try to climb out without showing my panties, but I don't think I got away with it.

'Hello sir, do you have a reservation?'

'Yes, under Alex Jones.'

'Oh, very well,' the maître d' picked up four menus, 'follow me.' Alex slides his hand down my forearm until he reaches my hand. He entwines his fingers with mine and gives a little squeeze and smiles. We all follow the maître d' through the restaurant, the deeper we go, the darker the lights get. We reach a table in the corner. Alex pulls a chair out for me to sit on.

'Thanks' I tip my head back to smile at Alex.

'You're welcome' he leans down and kisses me gently on the lips. Bradley pulls the chair out for Beth as she sits opposite me. She reaches her hands across the table and put hers on top of mine.

'Are you okay?' she mouths at me.

'Yes, this is amazing!' She nods as Bradley and Alex come back to the table. They both took their seats. Alex puts his arm over the back of my chair as the maître d' places an ice bucket with a bottle of champagne and four flutes inside.

'Sir,' the maître d' hands Alex a flute with a small amount of champagne in it. Alex sips it, nods, and hands the flute back.

The maître d' fills the rest of the flutes.

'Can I take your order?'

'Oh yeah, have you two decided?' Alex asks Beth and Bradley.

'Um' Beth answers.

'I can give you a few more minutes.' The maître d' smiles and nods and walks away.

'I'm having steak' Alex gives me a dirty smile.

'This meal is going to cost me my whole bonus' Beth jokes, looking at Bradley who looks worried.

'It's on me guys, and literally the best thing here is the steak.'

'No, we can't let you pay-' Bradley tries to reason before Alex cuts in.

'I'm paying.'

'Oh, well, thanks man!' Bradley shook Alex's hand with a smile.

'What you having babe?'

'Um, I'll have the same as you' I smile at Alex and put my menu on top of his.

'What about you two?'

'We're having the same.' Beth places both menus on top of ours.

'Is that Byron Mykels?' Bradley points across the room with his mouth open. We all turn to look. Byron Mykels is a football player, really tall and all muscle, with jet black hair and the brightest blue eyes I've ever seen. His cheekbones could cut glass.

'Probably, there are always famous people here'. We continue to stare at Byron.

'He's really fit in real life' Beth manages to get out. Alex turns in his seat, looks over towards Byron and shouts.

'Hey man!' Byron's head shot up.

'Dude!' Byron jumps up from his chair and comes over to the table. Bradley looks like he's going to have a fit.

'How are you?' Byron asks as soon as he reaches Alex.

'Good, you?'

'I'm awesome.'

'This is Beth, Bradley and Lucy.'

'Hi y'all,' Byron leans into Alex and whispers, 'the Lucy you were telling me about?' Alex just nods in response which automatically makes me worry.

'Do you want to join us' Alex asks Byron.

'Nah, I can't I'm having a meeting for some new publicity.'

'Lucy works at Teely's International, and she's looking for more people to publish autobiographies for.' Beth and I both choke on our champagne.

'Is that right?' Byron walks around Alex and crouches down between us.

'Yeah, that's correct' I smile.

'Would you be interested in having a business meeting with me?'

'Sure, when is good for you?' I ask.

'I'll ring Alex tomorrow and we can sort something out.' He winks at us, kisses us both on the cheek, stands up and heads back to his table.

'I can't believe it! I'm rolling in famous people!' I clap my hands together and bring Beth back to the present.

'Oh my god, I suddenly love my job!' Beth smiles at me. I smile back.

'Me too.'

'This totally is a high five moment' Beth lifts her hand in the air, and I slap it.

'George is going to have a heart attack when we tell him' I joke.

'Shot gun!' Beth shouts.

'Ahh man, we can both do it.'

'Now?' Beth stands up.

'Looks like it' I follow her to the bathroom.

'Even the toilets are better than my apartment' Beth says, looking around.

'Yep' I pull my phone out of my bag and hand it to Beth. She dials George's number.

'Hello?'

'Hello George, its Beth Ryan.'

'Ahh Beth, is everything okay?'

'Yes, we have some good news for you. Byron Mykels wants to have a business meeting with us tomorrow, about a book deal.'

'Good work girls!'

'Thanks, so can we go ahead?'

'Of course, the more people you get signed up, the bigger the bonuses. Let me know what happens, goodbye for now.'

'Goodbye!' I put my phone back into my bag and we head back to the table.

\*\*\*\*\*\*\*\*\*\*\*\*\*\*\*\*\*\*\*\*\*

We stand outside The Palm, waiting for the limo to turn up.

'Can we go to the cas-eee-noo' Beth asks, drawing out the word.

'If you're up for it,' Alex says, 'where do you want to go?' 'The Fountains' she laughs at Alex.

'What? How much have you drunk?'

'Don't ask stupid questions' Beth stammers, as Bradley holds her up.

'I think we should just go back and sleep this off and go out tomorrow. We're here for four days' Bradley, the voice of reason, explains to Beth.

'Yes sir' Beth stands upright and salutes Bradley, which makes me laugh.

'Is it okay if we go tomorrow?' Bradley asks Alex and I.

'Sure, I could do with sleeping to get rid of the jetlag' I answer and Alex agrees. We all climb into the limo, and Beth fumbles around with buttons until the roof opens. She stands up with her head poking out the roof.

'Oh, for the love of god' Bradley says while putting his face in his hands.

'I'M THE QUEEN OF VEGAS!' Beth shout, which again makes me laugh.

'Let me have a go!' I pull myself up on Beth's arm, squeezing through the gap.

We arrive at the hotel, and Bradley picks Beth up, carrying her back to the room.

'Do you want to go to the room or do something else' Alex asks me.

'I need to get my stuff together for the meeting with Byron Mykels, so I'll head up.'

'That's cool, I'll be up in a minute.' He kisses me on the forehead. I make my way over to the elevator. I turn around to see a girl throw herself into Alex's arms and Alex returning the hug. She's tall and slim with big Dolly Parton red hair, a silver bikini with little tassels on and knee-high silver boots. I try not to worry, especially when Alex looks around, presumably for me. I raise one eyebrow. *Shall I follow?* I turn on my heels and head back for the elevator. I make it to the room and open the door. I see Beth's shoes and bags thrown on the couch but Beth and Bradley are nowhere to be seen. I kick my shoes off and walk to mine and Alex's bedroom. I fall backwards on the bed and sigh.

'THIS IS LIKE THE QUEEN'S PALACE!' I hear Beth

shout. I get up and pull out a t-shirt out of Alex's luggage. I take my dress off, slip the t-shirt on and crawl under the cover and snuggle. Eventually Alex enters, his tie undone and his jacket in his arm.

'You awake?'

'Hmm.'

'Want a cuddle?'

'Who was that girl?'

'Which girl?'

'You know which one.'

'She is an old friend.'

'Hmm.'

'She is!'

'Hmm.'

'Lucy, come on!' Alex climbs on the bed and crawls up so he was lying next to me.

'Hmm.'

'Lucy, are you jealous?'

'Hmm.'

'Will you talk to me?'

'Fine.' I pull my arms out of the cover and lean against him and wrap my arms around his waist. He lifts my head and puts his arm under my head and pulls me into him.

'Do you get jealous a lot?' Alex whispers into my hair.

'I'm not jealous; I was just seeing if you would hide it or lie about her when I saw you.'

'So, it was a test?'

'Sort of.'

'Oh.'

'I'm going to sleep.'

'I don't think so...' Alex laughs.

*********************

I wake up before Alex, who is lying diagonally across the bed on his front, snoring. I get up gently and pull on some leggings, making my way to the living room. I see Bradley reading the paper and Beth holding herself up on the big window.

'Morning' Bradley says. Beth spins around so fast she lands on her ass.

'Morning,' I answer, 'good night?' Beth looks a lovely colour of green and Bradley looks like he hasn't slept.

'Hhmm,' Beth moans, 'I feel like shit!' She puts her head in her hands.

'Yes, well don't drink so much then' Bradley says, picking his paper back up.

'Have you two eaten?' I ask.

'Nope.'

'Shall we go to the buffet?' I smile at them.

'Yeah, I suppose we should.'

'I'll go wake up Alex.' I run back into the bedroom to find Alex on a phone call. I jump up on the bed and straddle him.

'Hi' I mouth. He gives me a big smile.

'Sorry I have to go…yeah I'll see you at five…bye.' He puts the phone down.

'We're going for breakfast, you coming?'

'And there's me thinking you came to see me!'

'I saw enough of you yesterday, now we get to stuff our faces with food…' I smile.

'Oh, I love you too' Alex laughs back. I freeze on the spot.

'What did you just say?'

'That I loved you too.'

'Yeah that's what I thought.'

'It's a figure of speech.'

'Yeah, okay' I frown to myself. Alex gets out of bed and pulls on his skinny jeans and a Ramones t-shirt and sits on the end of the bed. I slip on a light green maxi dress with some sandals.

We make our way to the buffet. Beth gets comfortable with her forehead on her forearm, occasionally sitting up to drink her coffee.

'I'm so hung over' she mumbles. Bradley returns to the table with two plates of food piled so high I thought they were going to fall off. Alex comes back over with a bit of everything, and I slowly make my way to the food, dragging Beth with me so we could choose our breakfast.

'What you fancy?'

'Oh don't!' She lets go of my hand and runs off towards the toilet. *I hope.* I pick up a plate but nothing really sticks out to me.

'Hi beautiful.' A young man is stood next to me dressed in a suit, with a plate of food.

'Um, hi' I smile and carry on looking around.

'Are you here for a wild girl's weekend?'

'Um, no but thanks for the compliment?'

'Oh, sorry I didn't mean it like that.' The guy smiles at me.

'Right.'

'I'm Craig.' He holds out his hand, I reluctantly shake it.

'Hi, I'm Lucy.
'

'Ah cute name, want to go to dinner with me tonight?'

'I can't, I'm interviewing Byron Mykels tonight.' I step away
from him.

'Excuse me?' Craig is suddenly at my side again.

'What?'

'Byron Mykels?' he asks like I just made it up.

'That's what I said Greg.' I say his name wrong on purpose to
show I'm not interested.

'It's Craig, how do you know Byron?'

'Because I'm dating his best friend' I turn around and point
towards Alex, who is staring at us.

'You're dating Alex Jones?' he asks again, like I made it up.

'Yes, are you deaf or stupid?'

'Stupid by the way he hasn't walked away yet' Beth stands on the other side of Craig.

'I think I'm still drunk' Craig says and looks at Alex again, who's relaxed a bit now Beth is with me.

'You alright babe?' I ask Beth around Craig.

'Yeah I was just sick and I feel a hundred times better!' She smiles and starts piling up the scrambled egg on her plate.

'So, can I meet Alex?' Craig asks.

'Um, you want to speak to Alex? After you just asked his girlfriend to dinner?'

'Yeah, he didn't hear me.'

'But he was watching' I point with my thumb over my shoulder. Craig looks over at Alex and quickly turns back. He begins to walk away.

'YEAH GET LOST!' Beth shouts at him.

'God, your friend is a freak' he says, while tutting at her. Beth leans her head on my shoulder.

'I'm not a freak, am I?'

'Of course not.' I smile, picking up a croissant.

'I need to sit down.' Beth walks away from me. I follow her back to the table and smirk at Alex, who didn't look happy.

'Who was that guy' he asks me, handing me a cup of coffee.

'His name was Craig.' I take a bite of my croissant.

'How do you know him?'

'I don't.'

'He asked her out.' Beth pipes up.

'Yeah, thanks Beth.'

'He did what?' Alex sounds pissed off.

'Well actually, he asked if I was here for a wild girl's weekend' I smile.

'That fucker' Alex growls.

'That's rude' Beth snorts, while shovelling egg in her mouth.

'He wanted to be my friend when I told him I couldn't go to dinner because I was interviewing Byron Mykels, and I knew him because I was dating his best friend.' I smile and kiss Alex.

'Right.'

'Calm down.' I stroke his arm.

'If he comes back, he's dead.' He kisses me on the cheek. Craig obviously has a death wish, because he comes walking over to our table, dragging another guy with him.

'Did you not get the message before?' Alex stands up.

'I came over to ask for a photo or autograph and to show my friend'.

'Well let me think about it,' Alex frowns, 'no.' He sits back down. I turn to him and whisper in his ear.

'Please calm down, remember what happened last time?' Alex leans back and stares at me while he thinks about what I said.

'Sure, you can have a picture with me.' Alex suddenly stands up again with a fake smile on his face.

'Cheers dude.' Craig pulls his phone out his pocket and hands it to his friend. Alex looks very uncomfortable while Craig does a thumbs up pose next to him. Craig and his friend switch over and do the photo thing again.

'Thanks dude' Craig slaps Alex on the back. Alex flares his nostrils and tries to do another fake smile. Craig turns around and looks at me.

'Do you want to go to dinner another night this week?' I stare at him in disbelief.

'That's it.' Alex says, pulling his arm back and punching him straight in the face.

'Whoa!' Bradley chucks his fork down and stands in-between Alex and Craig's friend, while Craig was on the floor bleeding from the nose.

'What the hell?!' Craig says while holding his nose.

'You just got punched by Alex Jones!' His friend high-fived Craig.

'True, cheers for the photos.' Craig says and walks off with his friend.

'I thought there was going to be a full-on fight' Bradley says before sitting down again.
'Alex you need to control your anger, I told you not to and you know what happened last time. You got in a fucking fight. I thought that would have been enough for you to keep your fists still, but obviously not.' I throw my fork on the table and storm off.

Beth catches up and grabs my arm, pulling me into a side room.

'Lucy?'

'I'm sorry.' I sniff.

'What was that about?'

'I didn't want him to get in trouble and I lost a baby last time he got hot-headed.'

'I know, I know…' Beth whispers while pulling me in for a hug.

'Why does he have to always punch someone? Greg meant no harm!'

'I thought it was Craig?'

'Oh yeah' I smile and sniff.

'Do you want a couple of minutes before you come back?'

'No, I'm good.' I wipe my index finger under my eye and wipe away my tears and smudged mascara. I link my arm with Beth's and rest my head on her shoulder while we walk back. I sit back down in my seat.

'I'm sorry' he says.

'You better be' I touch his tense leg under the table.

'I just don't know why I get so angry' he peers at me through the bit of hair that had fallen in front of his eye.

'We can talk about it later, let's just enjoy breakfast.'

# CHAPTER SIXTEEN

James had asked that we do the meeting in our penthouse, so we wouldn't be interrupted. He said he would arrive at seven in the evening, and now it is nearly eight. Bradley and Alex have gone to the casino to get out of our way, so all we can do is wait. Fifteen minutes later, James comes running in throwing apologies around to Beth and I.

'Girls I'm so sorry-' he starts.

'It's fine' Beth whispers while staring at him. He sits in the middle of the couch between us.

'So, where do we start?'

'You need to read this.' Beth hands him a piece of paper.

'Then what?'

'If you agree, then we need to go through how you want the book, what information etc. etc. etc.' James nods while reading. He leans his elbows on his knees.

'Do you want a drink?' I ask James.

'No, I'm good, thanks.' He answers, not taking his eyes off the paper. Beth sits on the floor, and puts all she needs around her, ready for him to finish reading. We twiddle our thumbs and make awkward smiles at each other as we wait.

'Done.' He smiles and hands the paper back to her.

'So, what do you think?' Beth smiles.

'I love it,' Beth beams at him like she was going to explode, 'so what now?'
Beth looks at me.

'We need to pick a picture for the front cover, and what information you want included.' I explain.

'Okay, shoot.'

'Your birth name?'

'Yeah.'

'Your place of birth.'

'Yeah.'

'Your birthday?'

'Yeah.'

'High schools and or college?'

'Yeah.'

'How you got your break?'

'Yeah.'

'Your friends and family?'

'Yeah.'

'Basically, is there anything you don't want us to put in?' Beth asks, tapping her pen on the paper.

'Um, you can pretty much put anything you want in, I don't have any secrets. I do want a memorial page for my Granddad please.'

'Sure, what's his name?'

'George Thomas Lloyd II. He died on 14th July 2009, but he always took me to auditions, always helped me, and always believed in me. I wouldn't be where I am if it wasn't for him.'

'Right.' I see Beth wipe a tear from her eye.

'Can I have pages with photos on?'

'Yep' she writes fast before she can forget what he was saying.

'Of friends and family and such things.'

'Course, anything else?'

'Can I do a shoot with you for the cover?'

'Of course, anything else?'

'Nope, I think that's it.'

'Cool.' Beth carries on writing stuff down.

'Do you have an idea of what kind of picture you want?' I ask. James turns his head to look at me.

'Black and white, it makes my skin look flawless.'

'Okay' I frown at him.

'Are you doing deals with anyone else?' he asks me.

'We've got Erupt, Carly Jacobs, you and we've got a meeting with Byron Mykels this week.'

'Wow, you've been busy then!'

'Indeed.'

'You're going to be rolling in money' James smirks.

'Yeah, we should be.'

'Sounds excellent, well when you girls get back to New York give me a ring and we can sort the rest out. I'll be back on the eighth.'

'Okay, thanks.' I take the business card he holds out for me.

'How are you girls getting to Erupt's gig?'

'We were going to leave after you.'

'Well, you can get in my car with me. I'm going there after this' he smiles at me.

'Oh great!' I get my phone out of my pocket to text Alex.

*James is giving Beth and I a lift to the gig, we will meet you and Brad there soon xxx*

'Are you getting changed?' Beth asks me, still writing stuff down.

'Um, I wasn't going to.'

'Oh' she frowns.

'But I will now…' I sigh, while James laughs. I get up from the couch and walk towards my room. I look through my luggage case, searching for inspiration. I have to dress like a hipster if we're going to a hipster club to listen to hipster music… I find some black skinny jeans, borrow Alex's Queen t-shirt and tie it up at my waist to show my midriff. I grab my black leather jacket, slip on my Louboutin's, give myself a bed head style again and cover my eyes in black eyeliner. I would definitely pass as a rock chick. I grab my light pink satchel and put it over my head so its across my body and walk back to the living room.

'Wow, is that you?' James says, standing up. Beth spins round on the floor to check me out.

'That's better, now you'll fit in.' Beth says while turning back to her paperwork.

'Thanks, when are we going?'

'In like five minutes,' Beth mumbles, 'I'm going to change quickly.' I sit next to James and check my phone to see I have a reply from Alex.

*Okay babe, see you soon xxx*

'I just have to text Alex and tell him how fit you look.' James is smiling and putting his phone in his shirt pocket.

'Right…' I think that is a little weird. Then I got a text. From Alex.

*I can't wait to see you now that James has filled me in on your outfit, nice Queen t-shirt btw xxx*

That makes me feel uncomfortable. James has even gone to the trouble to tell him what t-shirt I have on.

'So…' James says, placing his arm over the back of the couch.

'So, have you got a girlfriend?' I can't think of a better question.

'No, not at the moment.'

'Oh, sorry.'

'Don't worry, I'll get one, it's not hard for me.'

'Oh…' *Big headed sleaze.*

'How long you been going out with Alex?'

'I don't think we are an actual couple, but we've been seeing each other for a about a week or so.'

'Oh, so it's nothing serious' James leans in towards me.

'I'm not sure, it's probably best to ask Alex' I say while standing up.

'I'm ready' Beth announces. She's wearing some light blue jean short shorts, with her multi-colored high-top trainers, a baggy t-shirt, and a jean jacket. It looks like she stepped out of the set for The Fresh Prince of Bel Air.

'You like?' she looks at James and I.

'Beautiful,' James smiles at her, 'shall we go?'

As we head out of the room, James can't work out which one of us he wanted to stare at so took turns, thinking we don't notice. We reach the bottom floor and make our way out to the front of the building and climb into a Mercedes that was waiting for us. After an awkward drive to the gig, we don't even get checked if we're on the list as we walk in after James. We spot Bradley first, leaning against the bar, bobbing his head along to the band that are playing. Then we spot Alex leaning against the bar next to Bradley with what looks like groupies around him. Bradley is completely into the song, so I can't say for sure if he even noticed the girls are there. As the three of us slowly make our way over to the boys, the crowds start to gather around Alex and James. Beth, Bradley and I all move down the bar to give them some room.

'Want a drink?' Bradley shouts at us over the music. We both nod and Bradley asks for two beers. He passes us both our plastic cups full of warm beer. It reminds me of being nineteen and being at emo gigs with Sarah, drinking warm beer and jumping around.

'Thanks' I smile at Bradley, as Beth hit my cup with hers.

'Cheers!' Then I feel someone's arms around my waist and chin on my shoulder. Automatically thinking its Alex, I smile and put my beer down.

'Nick?' I turn around, then stare in disbelief at Nick, Jack's best friend.

'What are you doing in Vegas?' he asks, looking around.

'I'm working, what about you?'

'Having a well-deserved holiday. I'm sorry to hear about you and Jack.' I look at the floor.

'Me too,' Nick looks behind me, towards Beth and Bradley, 'oh sorry this is Beth, my partner and this is Bradley, her husband.'

'Hi!' Bradley says, shaking his hand.

'Hello!' Beth says.

'It's so weird to see you here.'

'Yeah, so who's this Alex guy?'

'He's in a band.'

'I know, I've done my research. Is he here? I want to meet him.'

'Sure,' I smile, 'hang on.' I turn around and head towards the group of people still surrounding Alex and James. I push my way through, getting very bitchy looks in my direction until I reach Alex.

'Lucy!' He picks me up and kisses me.

'Hi! Will you come meet my friend?'

'Sure thing, sorry guys I have to go' he says to the crowd. They all boo at me, but I pull him out the crowd and towards an awkward looking Nick.

'This is Nick.' I point at him.

'Hi!' Alex says, shaking his hand.

'Hi, nice to meet you.'

'How do you know Lucy?' Alex says, trying to be heard over the music.

'I'm a friend of Jack's.'

'Oh…' Alex says, and steps back.

'We've known each other for years' I add.

'Okay.' Alex replies.

'Well Lucy, I best go back to the friends I abandoned. Give me a text tomorrow and we can have dinner or something.' Nick says, reaches for another hug.

'I will,' I promise and hug him back, 'bye.'

'That wasn't awkward at all' Alex says flatly.

'Jack aside, I've known him since I was in high school.'

'Okay,' he leans down and hugs me again while kissing down my neck, 'you look super cute. You suit this kind of lifestyle.' He smiles into my hair.

'Thanks, when are you on stage?' Alex looks at his watch.

'In about ten minutes want a drink?'

'I've got some warm beer, thanks' I smile at him.

'Beer? I wouldn't have you down as a beer girl.'

'You have to drink beer at a gig, it's the law' I answer back, downing my beer.

'Don't do that again, it turns me on' he whispers in my ear and takes the empty cup out of my hand.

'Do you two need a room?' Beth pushes us into the bar.

'No, but he does look hot. I might need one soon,' I smile and poke my tongue out at her, 'hey, that guy over there looks like Paul Bevans!' I point, as Alex turns around.

'It is.'

'What? For real?'

'What?' Beth asks,

'That's Paul Bevans over there' I point across the room again.

'Who?'

'Paul Bevans?'

'I heard his name, but I don't know who that is.'

'He's the lead singer of Uncontrollable!'

'I don't know who Uncontrollable are.'

'Beth Ryan, you are dead to me!' I smile and nudge her.

'Sorry, I'm not into this kind of thing.'

'Okay I'll let you off.'

'Thank you, I don't know how I would have slept otherwise…' she smiles at me and puts her arm around my neck, pulling me in for a hug.

'Guys, I have to go on stage for a sound check, then we're on.' Alex explains.

'Good luck!' Beth and I say at the same time.

'Thanks, can I have a good luck kiss?' He leans down and kisses me, then he runs off.

'I can't wait to hear them play!' Beth says.

After about ten minutes of sound checking, Alex finally introduces the band.

'Hey guys, thanks for coming down! We're going to-' then someone from the band coughs and Alex turns around, his back to the crowd. He speaks to the band then turned back.

'Sorry guys, we had a problem but it's all good!' The band start playing their music and Alex sings along. Some songs I know the words to and others I don't, but I bob along anyway. I stare up at Alex, who I can tell is looking in my direction but I don't think he can see me. I step back and bump into someone, spilling my beer down Beth's back. I turn around quickly and find myself face-to-face with Paul Bevans.

'Hi, oh my god, I'm so sorry.'

'It's cool, don't worry.'

'Hi, I'm Lucy.'

'Paul.'

'I'm totally your biggest fan.'

'Really?'

'Yeah, and I totally know where you're from.'

'Okay, where?'

'Wales.'

'That's close enough' he laughs.

'Did you play tonight?'

'No, I'm just here to have a good time.'

'Oh, I'm here to watch my boyfriend play.'

'Yeah, who's that?'

'Alex Jones.'

'Really?'

'Yep, he's totally killing it.'

'Agreed, can I get you a beer?'

'Go for it, are the boys here?'

'Yeah, they're around.' I stand at the bar talking to Paul for a bit longer, about America, Wales, music, his band, and Erupt. I was too deep in conversation to realize that Erupt aren't playing anymore and that another band is playing.

'Hey!' Paul waves across the bar.

'Hi' Alex says, out of breath.

'You're finished?'

'Yeah, like five minutes ago' he jokes, and points towards his sweaty t-shirt.

'You did well!' Paul slaps Alex on the back.

'Thanks! I don't mean to break this party up, but we need to go.' Alex looks at me.

'It's cool. Well it was nice to meet you Lucy.'

'You too!' I shake Paul's hand and then I'm dragged off by Alex.

'Where are we going?'

'Hotel.'

'Why? Where are Beth and Bradley?'

'Because I said so. They're staying for a bit, then coming back.'

'Okay, I totally met Paul Bevans.'

'I know, I saw.'

'He was so nice.'

'Yeah I know.'

'And I love his accent.'

'Uh-huh.'

'Are you friends?'

'Yep.'

'How did you meet?'

'Don't know.'

'Are you even listening to what I'm saying?'

'Totally.'

'I have three legs.'

'Yep.'

'I'm pregnant.'

'That's cool.'

'Alex?' I stop walking, 'what is the rush?'

'I have something planned, come on, get in.' He opens the car door for me and keeps waving his hand around until I get in.

'Okay, keep your hair on.' Alex laughs and runs around the other side of the car and gets in.

The cab ride back to the hotel is silent, with Alex just staring out of the window the whole time.

'Alex, what's up?'

'Nothing.' After a while we turn up outside the Bellagio. Alex pays and pushes me towards the door while following. He holds my hand with a strong grip and pulls me to the elevator, jabbing at the button.

'They should invent something for elevator buttons, so that when you're in a rush you can get it here faster.'

'Okay...'
Once the elevator arrives, we quickly head up to the penthouse, where Alex walks me to the couch.

'Sit and stay.'

He runs off towards the bedroom, so I get up and look out of the window. The sun is starting to go down, and the strip is starting to light up. It does look beautiful for the middle of the desert. I rest my body against it, the glass is cool and helps cool me down.

'I thought I told you to stay' Alex says, reappearing from the corridor.

'Sorry…' I run back over to the couch and sit down.

'Good, now close your eyes.'

'Okay.' I reluctantly close my eyes. I can hear Alex walking over to me.

'Don't open them.'

'I won't.' I try to listen to what he is carrying, but he isn't giving anything away.

'Okay, you can open them.' I slowly open my eyes to see Alex's guitar leaning on the couch, and Alex standing behind me.

'This is for you.' He hands me a single rose.

'What's this for?'

'You know what, and I also have a song to sing for you.'

'Oh.'

'I'm sorry, its rubbish I only found out yesterday.'

'Found what out yesterday?'

'That it's your birthday today.'

'What?'

'It's your birthday.'
'Who told you that?'

'Sarah, I texted her and asked when it was, then she told me it's today.'

'Oh.'

'Are you angry at me?'

'No.'

'Why didn't you tell me?'

'I don't like to celebrate my birthday.'

'Why?'

'I don't know.' I shrug.

'Okay, well I have a song for you' he says, trying to change the subject.

'Okay.'

I sniff as he starts to play the song, and I cry the whole way through the song.

'That was beautiful.' I sob into his shoulder once he's finished.

'Why are you crying?'

'Because you're cute, and that was lovely and I'm so happy.'

'So, it's happy tears.'

'Yeah.'

'Okay, that's good then.' We sit on the couch together for what feels like forever. I slowly sit up and look at Alex, who laughs at me.

'What?'

'You look like Alice Cooper.'

'Oh god, I forgot about my make-up, it's all over your shirt!'

'Don't worry about it, Lucy. I do want to talk to you though, about us.'

'Right.'

'I know you have just gone on a break from Jack and you're fragile from the stuff that has happened, but is there something here for us?' I lean on Alex's chest.

'I would like something to happen between us.'

'You would?'

'Yeah, I like you Alex. I know this might sound heartless, bearing in mind the way we met, but I don't love Jack anymore. I know it's too early to say, but I think I'm falling in love with you.'

'You are?'

'Yeah, sorry if it's too soon.'

'I don't think so, I feel the same way.' I sit up and look Alex in the eye.

'You love me?'

'Yeah, I do Lucy.' I lean back down on his chest and start sobbing again.

'Are they good or bad tears?'

'Good,' I sniff, 'all I ever do is cry, how can you love that?'

'That I could live without, but I can't live without you. I had something planned but I think it's way too early.'

'What's that?'

'To prove how much you mean to me I brought you this.' He hands me a blue velvet box. I sit up and frown. I open the box slowly to find a ring.

'What's this for?'

'It's not a proposal unless you want it to be. B that says I want you forever.'

'So, an eternity ring?'

'Sure?'

'I love it.'

'Good.'

'You want to get married?' I remember what he said.

'Well yeah, I do at some point. I'm only twenty-five, but I want you to know that I would love to marry you. When it's the right time.'

'Okay.' I take the ring out the box and put it on my finger.

'I need to eat. Want to go out or order in?'

'Definitely order in. After what you just said, there's no way I can keep my hands off you in public.' Alex gives me the sexiest smile I've ever seen on his face, and it makes my insides melt.

\*\*\*\*\*\*\*\*\*\*\*\*\*\*\*\*\*\*

As we lie on the living room floor, having eaten and drunken too much, I'm happy relaxing in Alex's arms on the floor.

'When are Beth and Bradley coming back?'

…'t know I gave them some money and told them not to …e back till at least midnight.'

'Oh, you bought off my friends.'

'Yep.'

'So thoughtful.'

'Yep.'

'I think James is a sleaze.'

'What?'

'I don't like him.'

'He's a bit of a ladies' man.'

'You don't say,' I joke, 'he made me feel uncomfortable.'

'Well, you did have your midriff showing.'

'I thought you liked that?'

'I do, but I don't like other guys seeing your midriff.'

'Oh, jealous, are we?'

'Maybe.'

'Jealously doesn't suit you Mr. Rock Star.' Alex just smiles at me.

'Want to go win the big bucks and maybe get so drunk we end up married like on Friends?' Alex asks me.

'Why the hell not?' We both get up from the floor, put our shoes on and head out. Once we reach the casino floor, I get nervous.

'I've never been in a casino before.'

'Don't worry, I'll look after you.' Alex pulls me to the slots, pulls a handful of quarters out his pocket and puts one in the machine. He starts pressing the buttons.

'I have no idea what you're doing' I confess, staring at the screen, trying to see what he was doing.

'You don't have to know what you're doing – ahh I lost! Want a go?' Alex hands me a quarter.

'Okay, talk me through it.'

'Put the quarter in.'

'Yeah.'

'Press this.'

'Yeah.'

'Press this.'

'Yeah.'

'Don't touch anything.'

'Okay.'

'Now press that.' The machine starts playing some music really loudly.

'Oh my god, have I broken it?!' I leap up from my seat but Alex just stares at the machine with his mouth open.

'You won...' Alex whispers.

'What?'

'YOU WON!' Alex shouts.

'WHAT?'

Some woman in the silver outfit I saw the girl the other night wearing comes over with a bottle of champagne and hands me a glass, then gives Alex one.

'How much did I win?' I ask her.

'Forty thousand ma'am.'

Everything went black.

'Lucy?' I open my eyes to see Alex leaning over me, 'you okay?'

'Here's some water.' Alex looks up and takes the water from

a man. He helps me sit up.

'Are you okay?' He looks at me.

'I'm fine,' I try to stand up and pull myself onto a stall, 'I won right?'

'Yeah!' Alex laughs at me.

'Well, technically it was your quarter, so you won.'

'No, it was yours. I stole it from your wallet.'

'No, you didn't.'

'I did, so it's yours.'

'We can share it!'

'No!'

'Yeah!'

'No!'

'It can pay for our wedding then.' Alex froze.

'What?'

'I was joking.'

'It was a good idea.'

'We will talk about this later, I need to get used to being rich first.'

'Let's go get drunk.'

'Deal.'

## CHAPTER SEVENTEEN

I wake up to the sound of birds chirping and a breeze blowing on my back. I look around at my surroundings to find I'm on a sun bed by the pool, wrapped in a towel.

'Excuse me?' I look around, still half-asleep and see a guy sat on the sun bed next to me.

'Hi…' I grumble, moving round to lie on my back. I cover my eyes from the sun.

'You okay?'

'Hi, um… where am I?'

'By the pool.'

'Well yeah, which hotel?'

'The Bellagio.' He laughs.

'Oh, thank god,' I stand up and throw the towel on the sun bed, 'nice to meet you.'

'And you.' I make my way back to the lobby and find the elevator. I lean against the wall of the elevator, climbing up the height of the hotel without barfing everywhere. I search for the key in my pocket but can't find it. I lean my forehead against the door and crumble my face. I can't find my phone either so I have to just knock the door down. After ten minutes of constantly thumping on the door, Alex opens it.

'Morning.' He mumbles, half-asleep.

'Hi.' I push past him and run to the bathroom to vomit.

'Nice to see you too!' He shouts after me while shutting the door. As I wrap myself around the toilet bowl, Alex comes and sits next to me.

'Where were you?' He asks me, pulling my hair from my face.

'Asleep by the pool.'

'I lost you around one in the morning.'

'What was I doing?'

'Well, you started pole dancing in a competition with another girl, then you went to the toilet and disappeared.' He laughs.

'Oh, we didn't get married, did we?'

'Not that I know of.'

'God, I feel like shit.'

'Have a shower and get some sleep.' He strokes my hair and leaves the room.

'Sleep? At a time like this?'

'If it makes you feel better, I'll get back in bed as well!' Alex shouts from the bedroom.

'Done deal.' I get up from the floor, brush my teeth and run into the bedroom, jumping on the bed next to Alex.

'Cuddle time!' I climb under the duvets and snuggle into Alex.

'Do you remember last night?' Alex whispers.

'Yeah some bits.' I shrug.

'What about the money?'

'What money?'

'Slots.' I sit bolt upright and gasp.

'Oh my god, yes I remember!'

'You're loaded!'

'Well, sort of…'

'What do you mean "sort of?"' Alex sits up next to me.

'You're rich.'

'I didn't win that much, did I?'

'You honestly don't remember?'

'No?' I look confusedly at Alex. Why couldn't I recall how much I had won? Had I knocked my head?

'You did faint…' Alex replies, reading my mind.

'Oh really?'

'Yeah, you won forty thousand dollars!'

'Oh my god I totally remember!' I jump out of bed, and run down the corridor to Beth's room, and burst into the bedroom without knocking.

'BETH?'

'What?' she grumbles from under the duvets.

'I WON FORTY THOUSAND DOLLARS LAST NIGHT.' That gets her attention.

'What?'

'I WON FORTY THOUSAND LAST NIGHT!' I repeat.

'ARE YOU SERIOUS?' Beth screams at me, and jumps at me for a hug.

'Yes!' We jump around and laugh together.

'So, what are you going to do with it?'

'I don't know,' I slump to the floor, taking Beth with me, 'the excitement has got to me.'

'Go get ready, and we will go out. We have two days left to enjoy Vegas.' Beth says, jumping up.

'What's there to do? This is the middle of the night for Vegas!' I answer.

'Sky diving? Helicopter around the canyon?' Bradley suggests.

'I want to go in a helicopter! Let me ask Alex?' I jump up from the floor and run back to the bedroom where Alex is still lying in bed, waiting for me.

'Have you calmed down?' He says, smirking at me.

'Not even a little bit, want to come in a helicopter ride around the canyon?'

'That sounds cool, when?'

'When everyone is ready.' I smile.

'Sounds great. I should get dressed then.' Alex slips out of bed in his boxers and stretches.

'Looking good!' I tease him.

'Right back at ya…' Alex winks at me.

**************

'Right, before we get into the helicopter, you have to be weighed, so the weight is distributed evenly, then we will give you jump suits and helmets and then we'll set off, any questions?'

'What's your name?' Beth puts her hand in the air.

'My name is Andrew. I have ten years of experience, so don't panic, you're in safe hands.'

'Right, okay.' Beth answers.

'This way,' Andrew points across the room, 'stand on these.' He points at Bradley.

'Okay…'

'Off,' Andrew shouts, 'now you.' He points at Alex.

'Okay.'

'Off,' he shouts 'you!' He points at me.
'Shall I take my shoes off?'

'No, leave them on.'

'Okay, okay…'

'Off,' he then points at Beth, 'you.' Beth climbs on the scales.

'Off.'

'Right, now that's done, I can tell you where you're sitting. Bradley, Alex and Lucy are in the back and Beth is up front. When you're all changed, meet me out front and we'll be off.' Andrew walks out of the room.

'Oh my god, lets rush…' Beth says sarcastically.

'Come on, I want to see the canyon!' Alex says with his jumpsuit tied around his waist.

'Alright, give me a minute!' I joke, pulling the jumpsuit up my leg.

'COME ON LADIES WE HAVEN'T GOT ALL DAY!' Andrew shouts.

'We're not ladies?' Bradley quizzes, while pointing at Alex.

'He's joking because we're taking too long…' Beth explains, putting on her helmet.

'Oh right…' Beth walks over to me, carrying a helmet, as I zip up my jumpsuit.

'Here.' Beth passes me the helmet with a smile. Alex and Bradley stand at the door waiting for us to follow. As I strap my helmet on Beth giggles, jumping up and headbutting me with her helmet.

'Let's go!' She runs past Alex and Bradley, out the door.

************

As I admire the view of the canyon, I hear Andrew's crackling voice over the headphones.

'Right guys, we'll circle the canyon for fifteen to twenty minutes before we land, then decide what you want to do.' Everyone nods, not taking their eyes off the view. It's beautiful. The sun is shining and you can see the ant-sized people standing on the look-out point.

'We will be landing very soon.' Andrew's voice comes through the headphones again. As we circle the canyon, we get lower and lower to the floor, and the dust flies everywhere as we stop. The propellers come to a stop, and we all climb out.

'That was the worst feeling in the world' Beth comments, a nice green shade to her skin.

'Oh Beth, you drama queen.' I laugh and hug her a little too tightly as she retches and barfs all down my back.

'Oh my.... that's gross!' Alex steps back, retching.

'I'm...so...sorry' Beth sobs, wiping her mouth.

'I have sick all down my back.' I stand on the spot in disbelief.

'You are not getting back in my 'copter in that!' Andrew

points at me.

'Oh thanks, I'll walk back from here, shall I?' I answer back angrily.

'It will take you hours.' Andrew looks at me like I'm stupid.

'Yes, thank you captain obvious…' I growl back.

'Right, guys, this isn't going to help anyone,' Alex cuts in, 'take that suit off babe, Andrew, do you have a spare in there?'

'I'll look.' Andrew sheepishly walks off. I take my jumpsuit off and kick it across the floor. Beth is still crying to Bradley and Alex moves away from my sick covered outfit. When Andrew appears with another suit in his hand, he throws it at me.

'Thanks.' I mumble, and slowly put it on.

'I think we should head back' Andrew mumbles to Alex.

'Good idea.'

'You lot are the most dramatic group I've ever had.' Andrew jokes.
'Yeah, let's get going before this turns into a Jerry Springer episode.' Bradley comments.

'Can we go straight back, without all the moving?' Beth says, while retching.

'Yes, we can go straight back. You will be charged a hundred dollars if you're sick in the 'copter.'

'Oh god, hold it in Beth.' After Bradley straps Beth in her seat, I whisper into his ear.

'If she throws up, I'll pay.' I wink at him. Alex gives both of us a look, as if he's jealous of a secret.

*******************

Beth and I lay across the floor and couches of our living room, watching Crossroads and eating pizza.

'We have to meet Byron Mykels tonight.' Beth looks at me with pizza hanging out her mouth.

'Oh yeah, what time?'

'Eight, I think.'

'What time is it now?' Beth picks up her phone and clicks the button.

'Six-thirty.'

'Ages then.' I smile and shovel a slice of pizza in my mouth.

'Thanks for paying Andrew today when Bradley barfed in the helicopter.'

'No worries.' I giggle.

'When is Alex back?'

'He says he will be back at ten-ish, he's practicing.'

'Is he gigging again?' Beth kicks the pizza box away from her.

'No, just hanging out.' I smile at her.
She smiles sweetly back at me, just as Bradley comes walking into the room, feeling extremely sorry for himself.

'Girls.' He grumbles and nods as he walks past us to the kitchen. Beth and I laugh to ourselves.

'Stop laughing at me!' Bradley appears behind us again.

'We're not, we're laughing at the film.'

'Sure you are,' Bradley sips his glass of water 'where's Alex?'

'He's practicing.'

'Oh right.' Bradley nods.

'Did you have something planned?'

'No, I was just being nosy.' Bradley stands up from the arm of the couch and walks back to his room.

'Do you think we could get Byron to come up here?' I make a face at Beth.

'I can call his manager and ask him.'

'Oh yes, please, I can't be bothered to leave the room.' Beth picks up a handful of pop-corn and throws it at me.

'Ahh Beth, it's all stuck in my hair!' Beth cackles and walks across the room for her phone. She taps the screen for a couple of minutes, makes a face and puts the phone to her ear.

'Oh hello, its Beth calling from Teely's International... yes I have an appointment with Byron in about an hour... yeah... change of plan.... yes can he please come to our suite instead... yeah sure... yes I'll confirm it via email.' Beth makes another face and rolls her eyes.

'Okay thanks... bye then,' Beth puts the phone down, 'what a prick!'

'Don't! You'll make me choke!' I laugh.

'I have to confirm it via email, otherwise he can't make it.'

'Are you serious?'

'Yeah!' Beth taps away on her phone and sends the email to Byron's agent Jake. Within seconds, Beth's phone rings.

'Hello?... Byron? Yes, is that okay? Oh okay... I did think that... yeah, okay bye.'

'Was that Byron?'

'Yeah, he told me to ignore Jake, he was being stuck up and

he will be here at seven-thirty.' Beth shrugs while explaining.

'Oh well, at least he's a nice guy.'

'We best get ready…' Beth winks at me.

At seven-thirty exactly, Byron knocks on the door.

'Hi Byron!' Beth says, while opening the door to him. Byron reaches for a hug from both of us.

'Evening ladies!' He beams, distracting me for a moment. I clear my throat.

'Um, hi.'

'Do you want a drink?' Beth blushes and looks at the floor.

'I've ordered some room service actually.' Byron takes his coat off and walks past us both to the living room.

'Oh, right.'

'I've ordered champagne, and strawberries, but if you haven't eaten you can order food. I also got a jumbo beef burger.'

'What's that?' Beth asks Byron.

'Its three beef burgers the size of my hand,' Byron holds his hand out so we could see it, 'with cheese and bacon, onion rings and relish and a side order of fries.'

'Wow, sounds good!'

'I can order you both one, if you like.'

'What are you ordering?' Bradley asks with a half-asleep voice.

'How are you feeling?' Beth gets up and goes over to Bradley.

'What's wrong?' Byron whispers to me.

'Long story, but to sum it up he barfed all over the helicopter earlier...' Byron laughs.
'No way! You hungry man?' Byron asks Bradley.

'Yeah, now I've emptied my stomach I'm starving.'

'We were ordering jumbo burgers, want one?'

'Yeah please, I'd love one.' Bradley sticks his thumb up at Byron.

'I'll phone them.' Byron stands up and walks out of the room.

After a couple of hours of eating, drinking and joking around. We were all laughing so much that we couldn't breathe.

'What's going on guys?' Alex walks in with a raised eyebrow.

'Byron... is... telling... us...' I burst out laughing again before I can finish.

'Yeah, that's cool, I didn't want to hear the story anyway...'

Alex slumps off towards our bedroom.

'Ooohhhh,' Beth says in a high-pitched tone, 'touchy.' All I
can do is nod through laughing so much.

'But on a serious note, we do have to go through the deal.'
Beth suddenly reminds us.

'Oh, right yeah, let's read it!' Beth hands over a handful of
paper that Byron had to read through.

'Whoa, can you just give me highlights?' Byron looks at the
paper like it's written in another language.

'Sure.' Beth moves around to sit next to Byron.
'Let's go make more drinks.' I hold my hand out for Bradley
to take, pull him off the floor and walk to the kitchen.

'Do you want to see if Alex wants to join us?'

'Oh yeah, I should.' I skip through the living room towards
my bedroom. When I reach the door of our bedroom, I open it
slowly to find Alex on the phone.

'No you looked great... you couldn't even see it was a wig...
beautiful, you always look beautiful...'

I open the door catching Alex's attention.

'Yeah, I best go, Lucy is here... um sure?' Alex hands me his
phone.

'Hi?' I ask, and a girl starts talking to me, telling me how great I am, how amazing I am for Alex and she wants me to meet her family.

'Can I ask who this is?... Emily who?... Oh Alex's sister!' I immediately blush and Alex makes a face at me, mouthing "sorry".

'Yeah it was great to speak to you... yeah bye.' I throw the phone back at Alex.

'Ouch!'

'You could have warned me!'

'I thought you would have guessed.'

'I didn't even know you had a sister.'

'Oh.'

'Yes, awkward.'

'Did you want something?' Alex stands up and pulls me into a hug.

'I wanted to know if you wanted to come drink with us?' I lay my head on his shoulder.

'Sure.'

'Can you tell me about your family?'

'Yeah, what do you want to know?' Alex sits on the end of

the bed and pulls my arm to follow him.

'Who your parents are? Are they married? Brothers and sisters? Where they live?'

'My parents are Judy and Peter, yes they are married and happily for forty-three years, I have two brothers Eric, Justin, and a sister, Emily. She has leukemia, and they live in Boston.'

'Is that why she has a wig?'

'Yeah, you wouldn't know it was a wig though, I buy her the best made ones.'

'You buy her them, that's nice.'

'Yeah, it's the least I can do when I have the money. I brought Eric his wife's engagement ring, Justin a car and helped my mom and dad with their mortgages. I have to go home next weekend, want to come with me?'

'Yes, I would like that. Now, come have some drinks with us.' I hold Alex's hand pull him towards the living room.

'Ahh, you came back! Thought we had lost you!' Beth shouts towards us.

'Sorry, what did we miss?'

'Byron signed and we need to get drunk, because we leave tomorrow.'

'That's a good reason if I ever heard one!' Alex says while taking a drink from Beth and sitting on the floor.

'Do you want to play sevens? Byron asks, while searching for a pack of cards.

'What's that?' Bradley asks.

'Right,' Byron hands out the cards, 'who has the seven of diamonds?'

'Me!' Beth flaps it in the air.

'Okay put it down, now everyone has a go in turn. You put down the other cards, and if you have another seven you put it down. Understand?'

'A little.'

'Right, you will learn more if we play it.'

'Game on.'

*****************

'Thank you for staying at the Bellagio!' The receptionist says to me.

'Thanks!'

'Come back soon!' She calls after me. I make my way out to the front of the hotel to find our limo parked up, with Alex loading our bags in to the trunk.

'Ready to go?' Beth asks me.

'Yep, think so.'

'Let's go back to New York.' We all climb into the back seat. As the limo pulls off, I squish my face against the window and watch Vegas go past as we drive down the strip.

'Bye Vegas!' I whisper to myself.

'We'll be back, babes.' Alex strokes my back.

'I hope so, I really enjoyed myself.'

'We all did, even the helicopter part…' Beth laughs.

'Yeah looked it…' I smile at her, just as my phone flashes with a call.

'Hello?... Hi... Yes, Byron signed... we're on our way to the airport... we won't be back in New York until seven tonight... oh right... I'll ask them, two seconds.' I put the phone against my chest and turn in my seat to face everyone.

'We've been invited to Elton John's New Year's party, are you up for going?'
Beth breathes so hard in excitement, I think she might pass out. She can't get her words out. Bradley and Alex nod with enthusiasm.
'George?... Yes, we can make it, what time?... Okay, see you then... bye!'

'Lucy, I'm so glad you joined Teely's International. You have totally reformed the company and my life!' Beth beams at me.

'I think we need to get outfits before we get to New York?'

'As long as you're paying, I totally agree.' Alex smiles. I lean forward and knock on the little glass partition.

'Excuse me can you stop at the nearest clothes shop?' The driver nods and turns left.

'Here.' the driver says.

'"Encore", ' Beth raises an eyebrow, 'looks expensive…'

'We don't have to worry about money Beth, seriously.'

'Oh, right, I'm not used to this treatment.' I hold the door open for Beth.

'Good afternoon.' Beth and I are greeted by a sales assistant. He has mousey hair in a side parting, comb-over style, the biggest blue eyes I've ever seen and the sharpest cheek bones known to man.

'Hi, I'm Charlie, can I help you today?'

'Hi… um…' Beth stammers.

'Hey…' I twist my hair around my index finger.

'Have you got men's clothes in here?' Alex asks from behind

us.

'Yes sir, we do, how can I help?' Charlie answers.

'I'm looking for black skinny jeans and some new trainers.' Alex lists.

'Follow me.' Charlie points to the other side of the shop.

As Beth and I get out of the trance we're in, I started to blush with embarrassment.

'Hello ma'am, can I help?' I turn around and see yet another perfect looking person in front of me. This time it was a woman, with jet black hair in bun, big brown eyes and red lips.

'Are you okay? Would you like some water?' she speaks again.

'Oh, yes please!' She wanders off, and returns a couple of minutes later with two cups of water.

'Thanks.'

'Is there anything I can get you today?' She asks again.

'Hmm,' I nod with a mouthful of water, 'I would like some nice clothes?'

'Of course, what do you have in mind?'

'Dresses? Jeans? Nice tops?'

'Of course, follow me.' She walks off towards a corner of the shop. Beth and I follow like lost children.

'Oh my god.' I stop in my tracks in front of an orange sparkly dress with my mouth open.

'Wow!' Beth says as she sees the dress.

'This is new in today.' The sales woman smiles at me.

'How much?'

'It's twenty-two hundred.'

'I'll take it.' The saleswoman's eyes brighten and she nods at another girl behind the desk.

'I'm after some skinny jeans as well please, and maybe a nice cream top to match. Oh, and some wedge boots?'

'Wow, woman on a mission!' Beth jokes.

'Alright babe?' I look up to see Alex in a new outfit.

'You look sexy, almost like someone in a band?' I tease. 'Funny that?' Alex is wearing tight black skinny jeans, with pale blue high tops, his Beatles t-shirt, his hair combed over his face in an old-fashioned emo style and black reflective aviators.

'What you got?' he asks.

'I got a dress for Elton John's party, which will be a surprise for you...'

'Meany!' Alex pokes his tongue out at me. After Annabelle, the sales woman, helps me find some more clothes, and I had to pay a lot of money, we head to the airport.

## CHAPTER EIGHTEEN

'Hey Mom!' I answer my mobile.

'Hi dear, how was Vegas?'

'Good, we got another deal and I won some money!'

'Oh, how much?'

'Forty thousand,' the line went silent, 'Mom? Mom? Hello?'

'I'm still here.'

'Are you okay?'

'You won forty thousand?'

'Yeah Mom, how great is that?!'

'David? Lucy won forty thousand in Vegas...yeah...'

'I'm going to come see you soon, Mom.'

'What about Jack?'

'Mom, Jack cheated on me…'

'Yes, I know, dear, but do you not have feelings for him?'

'Not after what he did, and I'm with Alex now.'

'I do like Alex, your Dad said he likes Alex too.'

'I like Alex too, it's funny that…' I say sarcastically.

'I can see.'

'I've got to go, speak to you later?'

'Bye love.'

'Bye.' I sit back in my office chair, close my eyes and let out a sigh.

'Wow, that bad, huh?' I open one eye and peek at Jack stood in my doorway.

'Hi.' I close my eye again.

'How you doing?'

'I just need five minutes.'

'Want to talk?' He asks.

'Not really.'

'Lucy, I am sorry for what happened, but I don't remember it. I'm sorry I hurt you.'

'Yeah, I know, Jack.'

'Can't we just be civil?'

'We're going to have to be, because of family events and such things.'

'Yep.' Jack puts his hands in his pockets and rocks back and forth from toe to heel.

'Hmm…' I open my eyes and lean on the desk, resting my chin on my elbows.

'Well I best get back, see you later?'

'Bye Jack.' As he leaves, Beth walks in.

'You okay?'

'Yes,' I put my head in my hands, 'he looked really fit.'

'I was going to say that, but didn't want to seem heartless towards you…' Beth shrugs.

'No, its fine.'

'Want to go for drinks later? I'll phone Sarah?'

'Yes please, you're such a babe.'

'I know.' Beth beams at me, and walks out as my phone vibrates.

*Hey babe, want to go for dinner tonight? A x*

*I'm going for drinks with Beth and Sarah tonight, but I'll need a snuggle later xxxxxxx*

I slump in my chair. *Why can't I kick this mood?* I load up my emails to find nothing, not even from Gemma, then my phone vibrates again.

*I'm going out of town for two days A xx*

'He's going out of town?' I complain out loud.

'Who is?' Beth startles me.

'Oh god, you scared me! Alex is.'

'Oh, and he didn't tell you?'

'No just now, he asked me if I wanted to go for dinner but I said I was going out for drinks with you and Sarah...'

'It's fine, go see Alex.'

'No, no, it's only two days.'

'Sure?'

'Yeah, I'll text him now, is Sarah coming out tonight?'

'She is,' Beth smiles, 'can I get you a coffee?'

'Oh yes please.'

***Okay we can go for dinner when you get back, just make sure you come past for a kiss before you leave... Where are you going anyway? Xxxxx***

'Knock knock.'

'Come in.'
'Hi Lucy.' Drake waves at me while shutting the door.

'Hey, long time!'

'Indeed, I can't seem to catch you.'

'Yeah, sorry about that.'

'No, don't be sorry. You're doing a great job.'

'Oh, thanks.' I blush.

'My dad is very happy with you…and Byron has got us three more deals.'

'Oh wow, really?'

'Yes, and one of them is Huli Polly the model.'

'Oh, I love her!'

'Yes, so my dad and her management are deciding whether she comes here or we go there.'

'Can't say complain I'd about free trip to Hawaii.'

'Always a bonus!' Drake points his index finger and thumb in a gun motion and makes a clicking noise, winks and walks out. Then my intercom buzzes.

'Hello?'

'Alex on line one.' I pick up the phone.

'Hello?'

'Babe, what's up?'

'Nothing, why?'

'Are you okay about me going away?'

'Yeah, sure.'

'I'm going to L.A. to meet the label to sign some contract for another album.'
'That sounds cool.'

'Yep, I'll come by your office at three, on my way to the airport.'

'Okay, see you soon.'

'I love you very much.'

'I know. I love you too.'

'Great, see you soon, sexy.'

'Bye!' I giggle.

'You sound like you're in a better mood?' Beth placea a cup of coffee in front of me.

'Good timing. Are we eating tonight? I really want Indian food.'

'Yeah dude, let's do it. I'll get Sarah to meet us here.'

'Sounds like a deal.'

'Later honeypie!' Beth answers in an Elvis Presley voice. I feel happier and have a smile on my face from speaking to Alex. Plus, he told me that he loves me, which of course made me feel better, even though I had to see Jack. I pull a pad of paper out of my desk draw and grab a pen.

## Things to do
· **see Gemma**
· **visit Dean and Belle**
· **visit Mom and Dad**
· **buy Alex a present**

My office phone rings.

'Hello?'

'Is this Lucy Winter?'

'Yes.'

'Hi, my name is Karen Read.'
'How can I help you?'

'I'm Jack's girlfriend.'

'Okay…' I know I should be shocked, but I'm honestly just confused.

'Yep.'

'Why are you telling me this?'

'So you know.'

'Know what?' I ask, but she hangs up. *What the hell?!?* Well that's my mood ruined again. I wipe my note pad and pen into my draw using my forearm and push myself up off of my desk. I grab my bag and coat and head out of my office.

'Beth, I'm going out, I'll be back later.'

'Um, okay…' I walk into the elevator and jab at the ground floor button. Beth gives me a shy smile and a tiny wave as the doors shut. My eyes prick with tears. As the elevator reaches the ground floor I slowly walk out and wander out onto the street, look up and down and make my way to the nearest Starbucks. Once I have a coffee and a muffin, I turn my phone to silent and lay it on the table. I look around the coffee shop and people-watch. I put my earphones in, and start to daydream as I eat and drink. After two hours, I turn my pone back on and see a text from Jack.

*I'm sorry, I didn't know Karen was going to phone you! She isn't my girlfriend!! It's the girl from the other night, I'm not with her, I don't know how she got your number please don't be mad xxxxxxx*

Two from Drake.

*I have some manuscripts for you to read.*

*I need more paper for my printer.......oh secretary?*

Five texts and two missed calls from Alex.

*I'll come by at two? Xxxxxx*

*Beth said you were upset, you okay? Love you xxxx*
*Babe, where are you? Xx*

*I'm now getting worried...babe what has happened? X*

*Can you answer your phone!! Are you alive?*

Finally, two texts from Beth with two missed calls from the office.

*Where are you? Are you okay? B xxxxx*

*I need youuuuu xxxxx*

I text Alex and Beth the same text.

*Whats up? X*

I turn my phone off silent so I can hear when I get a reply from either of them.

*Are you ok? B x*

*Where are you? A xx*

Once again, I text Beth and Alex the same reply.

*I'm in Starbucks, I'm okay xx*

I pick up my trash and make my way onto the street. I literally bump into Alex. As I bounce off his chest, he grabs me by the waist so I don't hit the floor.

'Whoa!'

'Oh my god!'

'Why have you been ignoring everyone?' Alex puts one hand on each side of my face and holds my head still, staring into my eyes.

'I've been in a shit mood and I needed to get away.'

'Have you been listening to the Lost Prophets again?' I nod my head in response, without looking away from Alex. He pulls me into a hug and holds me close. As I breathe in his cologne, I start to relax.

'Who phoned you at the office before you stormed out?'
'A girl who said she was Jack's girlfriend!'

'Right…'

'I need to go back to the office, Beth said she needs me.'

'Yeah they don't know where you keep the paper for the printer.' All I can do is laugh.

'Let's go.' Alex releases his grip and kisses me before grabbing my hand and we walk towards Teely's International. When we reach my office, Beth jumps up from her desk.

'Lucy? What the hell?'

'I'm sorry the paper is —'

'I know where the paper is! Your office now. Alex, stay.' Beth glares at me while she points Alex over to the chair near the elevator.

'Lucy? Why are you getting upset about who Jack's girlfriend is? You're with Alex now!'

'I was already upset, and that pissed me off. I just needed to let off steam.'

'Why are you bothered? What is up with you?'

'I don't know.'

'You have to snap out of it,' I take a step back, I've never seen Beth like this before, 'now smile.' I smile at her.

'Good.' Beth nods her head and walks out my office.

'Have you been told off by the head teacher?' Alex's head appears around the doorframe.

'Afraid so. When are you leaving me?'

'In about thirty minutes, sorry babe.' Alex hugs me.

'Is everything okay with the label? Didn't you meet them in Vegas.'

'Yeah, they heard us play some of our new songs, and now we're signing a contract. I won't be long.'

'It's fine, I think I can survive.'

'You will order take away every night, I guarantee it.'

'You clearly know me too well.'

'Of course I do. Don't do anything I wouldn't do…'

'Doesn't leave much does it?' I giggle at Alex, who doesn't look impressed by my comment.

'Yeah, well…'

'I have work to do, and I haven't spoken to Gemma in a couple of days.'

'Crack on, I'll just sit and watch you.'

'Perv.' I tease him. Alex smiles, so I know I'm off the hook. I walk around behind my desk and tap my computer. Gemma has read my mind and emailed me.

*From: Gemma Winter*
*Subject: Are you alive?*
*To: Lucy Winter*
*01/12/11 14:26*
*Luc, it's been like four days so I'm checking you're alive? I hope you are!*
*Has Alex been to Mom and Dad's? X*

'Why would you go to my Mom and Dad's?' I muse out loud. Alex's head shoots up and he stares at me.

'Who said I was going to your Mom's?'

'Gemma asked if you had been yet?'

'Oh, your dad has some vinyl's I can have, so I'm going to pick them up.'

'Oh?'

'I was going to pick them up when you went to see them.'

'Oh.' Alex's behaviour is a little odd, but I have nothing to go on, so I leave it. I get back to Gemma's email.

*From: Lucy Winter*

*Subject: RE: Are you alive?*
*To: Gemma Winter*
*01/12/11 15:45*
*Gem,*
*Of course I'm alive, you would certainly hear if I wasn't!*
*Alex said he's only picking up vinyl's so he's going in the*
*next couple of weeks xx*

I see Alex pull his cell out of his pocket and start typing so fast he might break his hand. Or his phone.

'Easy!'

'What?' He stops like a deer in headlights.

'You're typing so fast, you're going to burn the screen out!' Alex lets out an awkward laugh and a tight smile. I leave it. He might be worried about the contract or flying.

'Hello... no, I'm with Lucy... I can't speak,' Alex looks at me, 'no I'm leaving for the airport in fifteen... yeah nearly... bye.' Alex huffs, and forcefully pushes his phone back in his jean pocket.

'Everything okay?'

'Yeah, it's all good, come here and give me a kiss?' I stand up from my desk and walk over to him. I wrap my arms around his waist and lean my face against his chest. Alex rests his head on mine, then he bends his head round and he snuggles into my neck.

'I love you.' He whispers.

'I know.' I lift my head so we're face-to-face.

'Good, never forget it.'

'I won't. I love you too.'
'Good.' Alex starts kissing down my neck and his hands flatten on my back. He runs them slowly down my body until they stop on my hips. He finds my lips. The connection between us is so passionate, like he is trying to tell me something. Because he's going away for two days, I let this moment happen and wrap my arms around his neck. He suddenly pulls away.

'I'm sorry.' He whispers out of breath.

'Don't be.'

'I think I will miss you more than I realized.' He let's go of me and slumps back in the chair.

'What's wrong?' I'm a little worried. It sounds like he's leaving me all together. Alex straightens his leg out and pulls out his vibrating cell phone.

'Hello... where? Okay give me two minutes...bye buddy.' Alex stands up and pulls me close again. He bends his legs, wraps both his arms around my hips and lifts me up, kissing me again, before he lets me slide back down his body until I'm back on my feet.

'Bye babe, see you Friday evening.'

'Bye…' I whisper as he walks out my office. I walk around to my chair and buzz the intercom.

'Beth come here?' I lean my forehead against the window to see if I could see Alex but I can't.

'Yo!' Beth breezes in.

'Alex has worried me.'

'How?'

'First Gemma said he was going to my Mom's which is weird, then he was acting strange and texting someone and got angry, then he started kissing me like he was never seeing me again.'

'I'm sure he is just going to miss you, you over-think things so much.'

'You think it's just me?'

'Err yeah!' Beth raises her eyebrows.

'Okay.'

'Have you spoken to Gemma? She thinks you're dead?'

'Why is everyone's first question to me "are you alive"?'

'Because you've been distant the last couple of days, when I phoned Sarah and asked her to come out with us, I had to explain who you were!' Beth smiles.

'Really?!'

'Of course not,' she smiles and shakes her head, 'you need a break away from work.'

'Maybe…'

'Do you want to stay in tonight, order in and drink?'

'Sounds good.'

'Always best when you're feeling down.'

'Yeah, I'm going to get like two hundred dollars' worth of alcohol.'

'You do remember it's the middle of a work week?'

'Yeah, we can tell Drake we're going to a meeting tomorrow, so we won't be in.'

'And still get paid for it.' Beth giggles.

'Yeah, I'll leave him an email.'

*From: Lucy Winter*
*Subject: Tomorrow*
*To: Drake Teely*
*01/13/2013 15:30*

**Drake,**
**Beth and I are doing inventory tomorrow on upcoming**

*books we have arranged, so we won't be in the office*
*tomorrow. If you need anything like printer paper, please*
*ask now or phone us on our cells tomorrow.*

*Yours sincerely,*
*Lucy*
*P.A. to Drake Teely at Teely's International*

'Done.'

'So, we're getting drunk tonight?'

'Yep!' I smile.

'Well, at least you're happy again…'

'Are we going to mine?'

'Yep.'

'I'm going to phone Sarah.'

'Okay.' Beth walks out my office. I dial Sarah's number and
wait for her to answer.

'Hello?'

'Hi Sarah, it's Lucy.'

'How are you?'

'Good, you?'

'Yeah, I'm good, so I hear we're going out tonight?'

'Well…'

'Change of plan again?' Sarah sounds annoyed.

'A bit…'

'Go on.'

'I'm going to buy a load of alcohol, we are ordering in loads of food and were going to talk and laugh and watch films and dance and whatever else you want to do.'

'Okay, that doesn't sound that bad, but it does sound expensive…'

'Don't worry about that… I won forty thousand dollars in Vegas.'

'Oh yeah, so you can afford it!' Sarah laughs.

'Yep, so come to mine whenever.'

'Will do, I've just got one more client and then I'm a free bird.'

'See you soon, love you.'

'Love you too.' I hang up. I feel a massive improvement in my mood already just with the promise of booze and food, and a night in with my girls. I head out of my office for the night.

'Lucy?'

'Hi Drake.'

'Hope you get lots of things done tomorrow during your inventory.'

'We will, don't worry, it will all be colour coded by the time Friday comes around.'

'Good, and I don't have any questions by the way.'

'Well then, see you Friday morning.'

'Bye girls!' Drake walks down the hall.

'Ready?' I smile at Beth.

'Been ready all day.' Beth grabs her coat and bag and we make our way downstairs. When we reach the ground floor, we head straight to Babycakes, and then the liquor store a block away. By the time we get to mine, with bags full of booze and a box of cakes, we're in a very cheery mood. We put the stuff on the kitchen counter and Beth runs towards my bedroom. She comes back out with my duvet, dumping onto the couch. She does the same with the duvet from the spare room.

'A perfect girly night in.'

'Have you put the Ben and Jerry's away, I will be depressed if it melts?'

'Oh yeah.' I put the ice cream in the freezer and then line the alcohol up on the counter. I pour three glasses of wine, get some menus out of the drawers and sit on the couch, awaiting Sarah's arrival. As soon as my butt hits the seat, the buzzer goes, so I open the apartment door and buzz her up.

'Hi!'

'Hi, it's meeeeee!' Sarah sounds like she's in a good mood as well. She runs in with a massive grin on her face.

'It's so cold outside!'

'That's why you're smiling like the Cheshire cat?' I raise my eyebrows.

'No, my last client gave me a massive bonus, that's why I'm smiling like the Cheshire cat.' She giggles.

'Oh well, congratulations then!'

'I know, I know…' She flicks her hair over her shoulder and sits on the couch next to Beth, who is under my duvet with a glass of wine.

'What films have you got, babes?' Sarah asks quickly, before downing her whole glass of wine.

'I've got Buried with Ryan Reynolds in it, or all my old ones?'

'I fancy staring at half-naked men…' Sarah replies.

'Let's watch Twilight?' Beth suggests.

'I've never seen it.' I confess.

'SHUT UP?!' Sarah shouts at me.

'So, you haven't seen Taylor Lautner half-naked?' Beth quizzes me.

'Um, no…'

'I'm team Edward.' Sarah looks at Beth.

'I'm team Jacob.'

'I'm team not Twilight.' I add.

'Oh no, you have to watch them, just to say you have!' Beth whines.

'I don't have it anyway.'

'God, how are you even allowed to be a girl?' Sarah mutters into her empty wine glass. Beth laughs so much she nearly falls off the couch.

'Can we order, I'm hungry?'

'Edward Cullen is also hungry…' Sarah looks at me.

'Huh?'

'Nothing, what menus have you got?'

'Pizza, Indian or Chinese.'

'What does everyone want?' Beth stands up.

'I want Indian.' I answer.

'I want Chinese.' Sarah pouts.

'Well, I want pizza...' Beth giggles.

'We can just order all three, we're all rolling in money at the moment!'

'True.'

'Shotgun not phoning up!' I say, jumping on Sarah and Beth.

'Did you get Ben and Jerry's? You need to earn some girl points right about now...' Sarah askes me.

'I did get Ben and Jerry's, aaand I bought some cookie dough.'

'Oh, good, you haven't disappointed on food then.' Sarah half-smiles.
'I'm going to get changed in your room.' Beth stands up and walks into my bedroom.

'Yeah, sure.'

'I need to get changed too, so you're going to have to order.'

Sarah says.

'Oh…' I complain. Sarah smiles at me and runs towards my bedroom. After about fifteen minutes, I had ordered the food but Beth and Sarah hadn't come out of my room, so I knew they were up to something. I open the door and see them sat on the floor, with a cardboard box in-between them.

'What's that?'

'I was looking for deodorant in your wardrobe and found this.' Beth says, without looking away.

'What is it?'

'A box full of stuff.'

'Yes, I can see that, who's is it?'

'I'm guessing Alex's, if it's definitely not yours.'

'It's not mine, so you shouldn't be looking through there.' I bend down.

'This is his ex-girlfriend.' Sarah hands me a photo.

'Wow, she's beautiful…'

'Yeah, she's a model.' Sarah states.

'There's pictures of him and maybe brothers and sisters.' Beth hands me a photo. She keeps rummaging and pulls out a blue velvet box.

'that's my eternity ring from Alex.' I explain.

'Can I look?' Beth and Sarah stare at me.

'Yep.' Beth opens the box, and we all gasp.

'That's not my eternity ring.' I say.
'OH MY GOD!' Sarah exclaims.

'That's a ring from Tiffanies, I've seen it in the store. It's worth like eight thousand dollars!' Beth says, getting a closer look.

'That looks like an engagement ring...'

## CHAPTER NINETEEN

'Alex is going to propose to you!' Sarah whispers.

'He's been acting weird, maybe he's proposing to someone else.' I answer.

'Don't be silly, he was all over you.' Beth rationalizes.

'I guess…'

'Wait... hang on…' Beth puts her hands out in front of her.

'What?'

'Gemma said he was going to your Mom's and he said he'd be away for two days.'

'Yeah.'

'Don't you think those two are linked?' Beth stares at me.

'Definitely' Sarah answers for me. We all jump as my cell starts to ring. I look at the screen.

'It's Alex.' I look at them both.

'Answer it but act normal.' Beth says.

'Hello?' I answer the phone.

'Hi babe, you okay?' Alex asks.

'Yeah, I'm good, you?'

'Yeah, just waiting for my flight. You sound weird, what's up?'

'Oh no, nothing. Beth and Sarah are here, we're having a girl's night.'

'Well I'll leave you to it. Oh, don't plan anything for Friday, I want to take you out for dinner.'

'Yeah okay, I won't plan anything for Friday night then.' I repeat what Alex said so Sarah and Beth can hear what is happening.
'I need to unpack from Vegas as well.'

'Oh, do you? I haven't seen your case.'

'Nah, I put it away so it wasn't in your way.'

'Oh, okay.'

'Well babe, enjoy your night, love you.'

'Love you too, bye.' I double check I've hung up before relaying what just happened.

'He wasn't acting weird, but there was Johnny Cash playing in the background.' I explain.

'Really?' Sarah asks, picking up her ringing phone. She puts it to her ear.

'Hello Mrs Winter... yeah we're good, I just have a question.' Sarah puts her phone on loud speaker.

'Okay, dear.' My Mom answers.

'If we bought cookie dough, how do we make cookies with it?' Sarah asks, playing dumb. While Mom explains how to make cookies with cookie dough, I listen to what is happening in the background.

'Oh great, it's that easy, thanks Mrs Winter, speak soon, bye.'

'Bye de-' Sarah hangs up before Mom can finish.

'That was the same music.' I explain.

'So he's defintely at your Mom's.' Beth says.

'Oh my god...'

'Are you alright?' Sarah moves next to me, and puts her arm around my shoulder.

'This is a shock.' I explain.

'Do you love him?' Beth asks.
'Yes.'

'Do you see yourself with him when you're fifty-odd?'

'Yeah.'

'Well then, be happy! He's gorgeous, and he wants you, and he will never treat you like Jack did.' Beth states with a serious face.

'Yeah.'

'Do you want to talk about it?' Sarah strokes my arm.

'I don't think there's much to talk about until it happens.' Then the buzzer rings.

'I'll get it.' Sarah jumps up and runs out, clearly hungry for food.

'Come on you,' Beth stands up and holds her hand out for me. She pulls me off the floor, 'let's go eat, and drink, and watch half-naked men. We can think about this on Friday, okay.'

'Okay.' I mutter. Beth and I walk out into the living room and grab our food from Sarah. I grab some bottles of wine, and we sit under our duvets watching films.

***************

I wake up to my phone ringing.

'Hello?' I croak.

'Morning beautiful…'

'Alex?'

'Yeah, who else would it be?'

'What time is it?'

'Eleven.'

'No, it's not…'
'Yes, it is, and I'm coming back early so I'll be back in the York at four-ish.'

'What?!' I sit bolt upright.

'Oh, you don't sound happy.'

'No, I am, it's just a shock. I was expecting you back tomorrow.' I make a face.

'Okay, well see you when you finish work.'

'I'm not in work today.'

'Oh.'

'So I'll be home all day.'

'Right, okay.'

'Yeah.'

'Okay, see ya, bye.' Alex hangs up on me. I look at the time on my cell and he wasn't lying – it is 11am. I look over at Sarah and Beth, still asleep on each other. Sarah's phone starts to ring, which wakes her up.

'Hello? Oh... um, what time is it? Yes... yes... okay, bye.'

'Who was that?' I ask.

'Work, I'm late.' Sarah whispers as she goes back asleep. I reach over and slowly pull her cell out her hand. I check her received calls and find that it was Alex who just phoned her. *Probably to get me out the house.* I wander over to the kitchen and find an empty pizza box. How on earth had Beth eaten a whole large pizza by herself? I also find loads of empty wine bottles, but I'm not in any mood to tidy up, so I just turn the kettle on.

'Morning.' I hear Beth say, and see she's come over to the breakfast bar.

'Morning, you want coffee?'

'Oh, yes please.' She groans.

'Alex phoned Sarah this morning.' I tell her. Her head shoots up.

'What?'

'He phoned me and said he was coming home today and he would meet me after work, so I told him I was home all day. He sort of freaked out and hung up, a minute later Sarah received a call she said it was work but I checked and it was Alex, probably asking her to get me out the house.'

'Ohhhh this is getting exciting…' Beth half-smiles. I make three cups of coffee while Beth puts the duvets back on my bed, after fighting Sarah for one of them for about five minutes. I carry the coffees over and we sit, looking at each other.

'So…' Beth begins.

'Yep…' I follow.

'Are you acting weird because Alex phoned me?' Sarah exclaims.

'Yes.' I answer flatly.

'He asked me to get you out the house from three until five.'

'Okay.'

'But he didn't say anything else, I promise.'

'Okay.'

'I promise.'

'Okay, I believe you!'

'Right, now that's out.' Beth jokes, while sipping her coffee.

'So, where shall we go?' I ask Sarah.

'You can come to mine, if you want, or go to the office?' Beth offers.

'Or go shopping?' Sarah cuts in.

'I don't need anything.'

'Well think of something, because I want to go.' Sarah

retorts.

'Okay.' I slurp my coffee.

'If you want, we can actually do the inventory at mine?' Beth says.

'Yeah, we do need to do it.'

'Okay, we're going round yours then.' Sarah says with a smile.

'Sorted.'

'Make sure you put away Alex's box.'

'Oh god, yeah!' Beth jumps up and runs into my room.

'When are we going then? I'm bored already...'

'Oh Sarah!' I laugh.

'Can we go for breakfast at Betty's, I bet you miss it, you haven't been in there for over a week.'

'Oh yeah, I could murder some Betty's pancakes.'

'Me too.' Beth says, while walking back in the living room.

\* \* \* \* \* \* \* \* \* \* \* \* \* \* \* \* \*

We finish our huge breakfast, *I could really do with unbuttoning my trousers right about now,* I think to myself, just as my phone starts ringing.

'Hello? Alex? Yeah, I'm at Betty's and then I'm going to Beth's to finish our work,' I roll my eyes with a half-smile, 'yeah, see you at five, bye.'

'Where's he taking you?' Sarah smiles at me.

'Jean George's.' I answer, with a worried face.

'Why do you look so anxious?' Beth asks.

'I'm scared.'

'Of what?'

'Food, the place, what Alex wants…' I list.

'It's French, you will love it.' Beth pats my hand.

'You already know what Alex wants, so you're not scared, you're nervous.'

'Yes.' I crinkle my brow, and nod.

'What are you going to wear?' Beth raises her eyebrows and stares at me.

'Oh god, I don't know.'

'Now that's what you should be worrying about!' Sarah jokes, stuffing half a pancake in her mouth.

'Can you help me?' I look at Sarah. She stops mid-chew,

opens her mouth and spits the pancake onto her plate.

'You have offended me.'

'Eurgh, did you have to do that?' I look away, retching.

'That was so gross.' Beth covers her eyes.

'Well, don't offend me and I won't spit food out!' Sarah laughs.

'I might barf my breakfast up.' I breath out heavily.

'Don't be such a drama queen, come by my work at three?'

'Yeah, we will be there.' Beth smiles.

'What about my hair and make-up?'

'I'll get the girls at work to do it, I'll tell them it's for a shoot downstairs.'

'Cheeky.' Beth giggles.

**************

Beth and I lay on her living room floor on our backs, staring at the ceiling.

'We've been doing this for about two hours now.' Beth whispers.
'Yep, I'm not ready to move yet.'

'I'm sorry but I have to. It's nearly two, when are you leaving for Sarah's?'

'I'll get a cab at quarter to three.'

'Risking it a bit?'

'It's fine, I'm not meeting Alex until five.'

'Where are you meeting him?'

'At the restaurant.'

'Oh, so how are you getting there?'

'Cab.'

'No way, hire a nice car!'

'With only a few hours' notice?'

'Yeah, where's your phone?' We start googling, but then we hear a high-pitched scream. We both look at the front door. The screaming is coming from the corridor, so we make our way out there. When we reach the corridor, we see Carly Jacobs fanning a girl who is sat on the floor.

'Um, hi?' Beth says. Carly and her manager both look at us.

'A glass of water, please?' Carly's manager, Simon orders with attitude.

'Alright.' Beth runs back in, while I sit next to the girl on the floor.

'You alright?' I ask. She doesn't respond, so I look at Carly.

'She fainted when she saw me.' Carly explains.

'Ahh, I see.' I grab the pile of paper from Simon's hands, and start waving it to create a breeze.

'Don't drop those, they're important!' He warns me, but I just roll my eyes in exasperation. Beth returns, and hands him the glass of water. He takes it and throws the water in the girl's face.
'Simon!' We all exclaim in shock.

'It woke her up, didn't it?' He protests, while handing the glass back.

'Oh my god.' The girl whispers.

'Please breathe!' Carly says with a smile.

'I'll try.' The girl answers.

'Can I ask why you're here?' Beth interrupts.

'We received an email from Drake saying I had to sign the last contract, but you weren't in the office today, so we thought we'd come and see you.'

'Oh.'

'Yes, and this is what happens when you bring stars like

Carly into buildings like this…' Simon wags his index finger between Beth, the girl and me. Carly rolls her eyes.

'How are you feeling now?' She asks the girl.

'I think I'm okay,' the girl answers, 'I'm Chantelle.'

'Hi!' Carly smiles.

'Can I have an autograph?' Chantelle asks.

'Of course, how about a picture as well?'

'Oh my god, yes please!'

'Okay, can you stand up?' We help Chantelle to her feet.

'You okay?' I ask, before letting go. Chantelle nods at me.

'Do you all want to come inside?' Beth asks.

'Yes please.' Carly answers, and we all pile into the living room.

'Want a drink, Chantelle?'

'Oh no, its fine.'

Simon walks over to where Carly and Chantelle sit on the sofa, and hands Carly a pen and some paper.

'Thanks.' She mutters.

'How's it going between you and Mr. Jones?' Carly asks me.

'It's going good, thanks.'

'He's taking her to a meal tonight, and he's been 'away' for two days.' Beth winks at Carly.

'You think Alex is going to propose?'

'Hang on a minute, you're dating Alex Jones? From Erupt?' Chantelle asks.

'Yep, and I'm not sure Carly, I don't want to get ahead of myself.'

'Well, I want to know all the juicy gossip once you find out…'

'Me too!' Beth adds.

'Beth, do you know any more famous people?' Chantelle asks.

'Yep, loads.'

'Like who?'

'Erupt, Carly, Byron Mykels…'

'I can't believe I live next door and I didn't know this, what's your job?'

'Lucy and I work at Teely's International.'

'That is so cool!'

'Thanks.' We both smile at her.

'Can we sign this contract? We have places to be, and its already quarter to three.' Simon complains.

'What?'

'Quarter to three.' He taps his watch.

'Oh god, I'm going to be late.'

'Where?' Carly asks.

'Meeting Sarah for tonight.'

'Where are you going?'

'Bloomingdales.'

'We can drop you there.'

'Can we?' Simon questions.

'Yes, we can, it's my car and my friend.' Carly answers. *That shut him up.*

Carly signs contract, takes a picture with Chantelle and then hugs her. Then we head downstairs to the car.

\*\*\*\*\*\*\*\*\*\*\*\*\*\*

'You're late.' Sarah taps her wrist as I walk in the entrance.

'Sorry, drama happened.'

'What?'

'Carly Jacobs turned up at Beth's place, a young girl saw her and fainted blah blah blah…'

'Oh drama drama drama!' Sarah giggles.

'Yep, so get me ready!'

'Drama seems to follow you.'

'Tell me about it, I dream of a drama free life.'

'No, you don't, you would miss it.'
'Yeah I would,' I smile at Sarah, 'have you got anything in mind?'

'I always have stuff in mind.'

'So…'

'Oh, right yeah, I'm thinking a pale pink, floor-length, sparkly gown.'

'Like in The Little Mermaid?'

'Huh?'

'When she's turned into a human at the end, she has a pink sparkly dress on!'

'Right, sure,' Sarah nods, *she clearly doesn't have a clue,* 'with either silver Jimmy Choo's or you can wear your Louboutin's?' Sarah looks at me.

'I would feel more comfortable if my feet were covered up.'

'Okay.' Sarah pats me on the shoulder indicating I should sit down and she walks off. She returns with the dress held up against her.

'Oh my god, that is beautiful.'

'I know right. We need to see the girls upstairs about hair and make-up.'

'Now?'

'Yes.' Sarah answers like I'm stupid. We head upstairs, and Sarah calls out.

'Chloe?'

'Yeah?' Comes a faint reply, then a girl runs around a corner.

'Ahh, Chloe, this is Lucy.'

'Hi Lucy!'

'She needs her hair and make-up done, as soon as possible, when are you free?' Sarah explains.

'I'm free now?' She smiles.

'Great!'

Chloe gets to work on my face, and after about half an hour, she steps back, looking pleased with herself.

'Wow!' Sarah says, as she steps around the corner.

'Do I look good?' I laugh.

'Um, yeah, no joke.'

'Glad you like it!' Chloe smiles and walks off.

'Right, hair.' Sarah holds her hand out to me and we walk to another section of the store.

'John?'

'Beautiful Sarah, and who's this beautiful friend of yours?' John asks.

'This is Lucy, she has a very important date tonight and we need you to make her look outstanding.'

'She already is outstanding!' John half-smiles at me, making me cringe.

'Well, we need her to look breathtaking.' Sarah senses my awkwardness and steps in.

'Well of course, please take a seat here.' He points at a big black chair. I sit down and get comfortable. Sarah pats me on the shoulder and winks at me in the mirror.

****************

'Wow,' Sarah slaps her hands to her mouth, as John sprays one more layer of hairspray for good measure, 'I love it, you look great. If Alex doesn't propose, I will.'

'Well, good luck tonight!' John says.

'Thank you!'

'Come on…' Sarah pulls me away. We head back to the dressing rooms in Sarah's department, where I slip into my dress and put on my jewelry without ruining my hair or make-up.

'Are you excited?' Sarah asks.

'I'm so nervous. What if he doesn't want to propose? What if he breaks up with me?' I look at Sarah. She just stares back.

'Sarah?'

'He won't.' She answers, looking at the floor, avoiding eye contact with me.

'You're starting to worry me now…' I frown at her.

'Your cab is here, take your purse and phone, call me later okay? Have a good time, bye.' She hurries me downstairs and into the cab, without explaining her behaviour.

When I arrive the restaurant, my car door is opened for me and a hand appears, offering to help me out. I exit the cab, and find myself in front of Alex, dressed in a tuxedo. He looked amazing.

'You look good!' Alex says, while gawping at me.

'Same to you!' I can't help but smile at him.

'Shall we go in?' He looks so handsome I can't find any words to answer him, so I just nod. Alex smiles at me.

'Good evening, can I get you some drinks?' The waiter offers as we sit down at our table.

'Can we have some champagne please?'

'Of course, sir.' The waiter walks off.

'You look beautiful.' Alex smiles at me again.

'You've already said,' I blush, 'you look so sexy...' I flirt.

'You might be wondering why I asked you here...' Alex stutters.

'yeah'
'Well, I have some news.'

'Okay?'

'We've been asked to tour England.'

'Wow, that's great!'

'For six months.'

'Oh.'

'But I want you to come with us.'

'Oh?'

'Will you?'

'What about my apartment? My job? My friends?'

'Rent your apartment out, I'm sure you can take six months out, and they can come visit us in England?' Alex smiles at me.

'It's a lot to take in at once.'

'I know, we're not going until March.'

'March?'

'Yeah, so you have three months to decide.'

'Oh, okay.'

*I don't want to go to England. What will I do without my friends? I'd have to live on a tour bus.* I knot my fingers together and stare down at them frowning, wondering what I should do.

'Babe, will you say something?'

'I'll think about it.' I manage a false smile.

'Thank you, it means a lot. I also have another question.'

'Sir your champagne.' The waiter interrupts, handing us both a glass.

'Thank you.' I smile at the waiter.

'Are you ready to order, or would you like a couple more minutes?'

'Couple more minutes please.' The waiter walks away.

'What was your question?' I look at Alex, who is smiling.

'I don't want to embarrass you, but,' Alex stands up and takes my hand, 'Lucy?'

'Yes?' Alex bends down onto one knee.

'I told you when I first set my eyes on you that I wanted to marry you. I have never lost that feeling and I'm very much in love with you. Lucy, you are the love of my life, will you marry me?'

I stare at him in disbelief, with tears dropping down my face. I try and hide my ugly crying face, so that I still look elegant.

'Oh Alex,' I manage, 'of course I will marry you!' Alex jumps up from the floor and grabs me by the waist, spinning me around, while all the other diners clap and cheer for us. Alex puts me back on my feet and leans his forehead on mine.

'You're crying?' I sob, while wiping his tears away.

'I'm so happy!' He sniffs.

'You never cry!' I laugh and kiss him,

\*\*\*\*\*\*\*\*\*\*\*\*\*\*\*\*

'Your cheque, sir.' The waiter hands Alex a leather book.

'Thank you.' Alex hands over his card.

'Thank you for tonight, I bet I look like Alice Cooper right now…'

'You look beautiful, you always do.' Alex smiles at me.

'Your card and receipt, sir.

'Thank you, can you please call us a cab?'

'Of course, sir, congratulations on the engagement.' The waiter smiles and walks off.

'I can't believe you just proposed to me!'

'You weren't expecting it?'

'No, I was talking to Sarah about it, then I thought you were going to breakup with me.'

'Really? How stupid do you think I am?' Alex smiles. He chuckles to himself while putting his jacket on and walks over to me to help me up.

'After you, Mrs Jones.'

## CHAPTER TWENTY

As we stand in the elevator to my apartment, I feel like a teenager again, because I can't take my hands off of Alex.

'Easy girl, at least wait until we're inside...' Alex kisses behind my ear, which, of course, sends shivers down my spine.

'Oh, if you want me to stop, I wouldn't do that.' I close my eyes.

'What this?' Alex kisses behind my ear again and starts kissing along my jaw line, then down my neck.

'Yeah, that.' I cling to his neck.

'Come on' he grabs my hand and pulls me out the elevator, unlocking my apartment door. The door opens, revealing a crowd of people in my living room. I drop my purse in surprise when they all shout.

'CONGRATULATIONS!'

'Oh my god!' A huge crowd of people gathers around me, hugging and congratulating me. I'm frozen where I stand. *My whole family knew I was getting engaged? What if I had said no?*

'What if I said no?' I whisper out loud.

'What was that, love?'

'What if I had said no?' I frown at my Mom.

'Would you have said no?'

'No.'

'Then why worry?' Mom pats me on the arm and kisses my cheek.

'I don't know. Where's Alex?'

'With your father and Dean.'

'Is Jack here?'

'He was invited, but he didn't want to come.'

'Oh.'

'Enjoy yourself!' Sarah hugs me and hands me a glass of champagne.

'Thanks, you kept this secret very secret.'

'I know, I'm good…'

'Yes, you are.' I feel some hands around my waist.

'Hey Mrs. Jones.' Alex whispers in my ear.

'Hey.' I lean my head back onto Alex's shoulder with my eyes closed.

'My family are coming over tomorrow.'

'Oh, I get to finally meet them?' I turn around so I'm facing Alex.

'Looks that way'. He smiles.

'I'm so excited!'

'Really?' Alex raises one eyebrow.

'Yeah, I haven't met them yet and if I'm marrying you, I have to meet my in-laws.'

'They will be at mine at one-ish tomorrow.'

'I'll come over after work then.' I smile.

'Let's celebrate!' Alex smiles at me.

'PICTURE TIME!' Sarah shouts. Everyone gathers around us as my Dad pulls out a sign that reads *CONGRATULATIONS LUCY AND ALEX.* Sarah puts the camera on the T.V. unit and quickly runs over to the crowd.

'Say cheese…' Sarah giggles, and everyone answers in chorus.

'Cheeeeese!' *Snap.*

********************

I'm surrounded by darkness, so much so that I can't see my hand in front of my face. Then, bright lights suddenly turn on, temporarily blinding me.

'Owwww!' I wince, covering my eyes.

'You're such a waste of space…' A booming voice echoes.

'You're always drunk…' Comes another voice.

'Mom?' I ask. Suddenly I'm falling down a dark hole, just like in Alice in Wonderland. I scream for help, and then a hand appears, so I grab it.

'I've got you.' A voice says, as I climb over the edge. It's Alex.

'Where are we?' I ask him, but he just stares at me with a smile on his face, like he's posing for a picture.

'Alex?' I lean forward to touch his face but he disappears.

'What the hell is going on?' I ask. Four big flood lights flick on in turn. As I look around, people wearing black floor-length hooded gowns start walking out from the darkness, towards me.

'Hello? Where am I?' They all ignore me.

'Hello?!' I ask, panicking a little more now.

'You are to be banished.' A man's voice booms overhead.

'Me? Why?'

'Death by water.' He keeps talking.

'Water?' One of the people dressed in a cloak runs over so quickly I can't move away, and throws a glass of water in my face.

'Hey!' I say, while wiping my face. Then another does the same.

'Stop it,' I groan, 'stop it!' I wipe my face again. I open my eyes to find myself laying in the bath tub upside down in my bathroom, with my face under the faucet. As I work my way out and sit up, I look over at the toilet and see Sarah, with her face against the seat.

'What a weird dream,' I clutch my head 'ouch!'

'Hmmm?' Sarah replies. As I climb out the bath tub, carefully stepping over my best friend, I walk into the living room. I hear people talking as I look around into the kitchen to find my Mom, Dad and Alex chatting over coffee.

'Where were you?' Alex looks concerned and walks over.

'Asleep in the bath tub.' I frown and rub my temples.

'Oh, that was you?' Alex hugs me.

'Yeah Sarah is in there being sick, and my head is killing me.'

'Here you go, dear, have some Advil.' Mom hands me two capsules and a glass of water.

'Thanks.'

'Maybe you should set a late New Year's resolution?' Mom eyes me up and down. I frown at my Mom. *Surely she knows I've just woken up and don't understand hints.*

'I think she means cut back on drinking, love?' Dad mutters while washing up.

'Might be a good idea,' Alex nods, 'not all together though.' He holds his hands up in defense.

'I'll cut back and stop getting wasted, I just had the weirdest dream.' I sleepily agree.

'About?'

'Nothing. It's was too freaky to relive' I pat Alex's arm, 'I'm going to get ready for work.'

'Okay babe.' I make my way back to the bathroom and kneel down next to Sarah.

'I need to get ready for work, can I have a shower while you puke?'

'Uh-huh.' She says without moving. As I climb back over my friend to get back in the bath tub to shower, I start thinking about my dream. I wonder what it was all about…

'Are you going to work?' Sarah grumbles at me.

'Yeah, I'm going to get dressed in a minute.'

'Okay, can you help me up when you leave?'

'Sure.' I smile to myself, as I rinse out the suds from my hair. I turn off the shower and turn back around to climb out, when I suddenly slip. I grab onto the shower curtain for guidance and end up taking it with me as I fall.

'Oh my god, are you okay?!' Sarah taps me with her toe.

'Shit, my back!'

'Is everything okay in there?' Alex knocks gently on the door.

'I'm on the floor, wrapped in the shower curtain.' I answer back, but it was silent on the other side of the door.

'Alex, are you laughing?'

'No babe!'

'Alex, don't laugh, I really hurt my back!' Still silence.

'Fine, I'll get myself up. Still want a hand, Sar?'

'No, I'm good.' She replies, balancing her cheek on the toilet seat.

'Sarah, that's dirty.' As I swing the bathroom door open, I find Alex on his knees, red in the face.

'Such a great help…' I climb over him.

'Sorr...ry..ba..be…' He says through laughter.

*****************

The elevator reaches the eighteenth floor, and I hobble out like an elderly woman.

'What on earth…?' Beth stares at me.

'I fell out the shower.' Beth squeezes her lips together, containing her laughter.

'Alex laughed too.' I smile begrudgingly, and hobble to my

office. I sit in my desk chair, and breathe out a sigh of relief.

'Oh, by the way?' Beth comes in.

'Oh?' My eyes shoot open.

'Sorry, I forgot, we have a meeting today with James.'

'What time?' I huff.

'In ten minutes.' We head down to the lobby to meet him.

'Ahh girls, good timing!' James says as he walks through the door, holding his hand out to shake.

'Oh, hi, James.' I shake his hand, then Beth does. Then an almighty flash appears, as cameras start taking pictures. The paparazzi have followed him into the building.

'Whoa!' I cover my eyes.

'Security!' Beth shouts. Our security guards start ushering them back out the doors. The chaos is all too much.

'I don't feel –' I start, before I barf all over the lobby floor.

'Jesus Christ' Beth is at my side in seconds, pulling my hair off of my face.

'I feel like I'm going to faint.'

'Don't you dare' Beth warns.

'Here.' James passes me a paper cup of water.

'Thanks.' I mutter.

'Want a chair?' James offers. I slowly shake my head at him.

'Are you feeling better? Can we go upstairs?' Beth looks at me with raised eyebrows. The elevator finally arrives, so we called clamber in. The elevator door dings when we reach our floor, where we see Drake with a massive smile on his face.

'Ahh, James, hello!' Drake holds out his hand.

'Hi.' James shakes his hand.

'So glad you could make it, today we're doing a little interview for your book release for T.V. commercials and a photo shoot.'

'Ohh, okay.' James smiles and nods.

'Is that okay?' Drake frowns.

'Yeah sure, can I request something?' James asks.

'Sure.'

'Can I get some pizza delivered?'

'Oh, um, yeah sure, please use the phone in my office.' Beth and I grin at each other, as James follows Drake into his office.

'Ready ladies?' Drake pokes his head round my office door.

'Yeah!' We make our way to the meeting room. James walks in and holds the door open for us, as Beth giggles.

'Thank you.' I mumble. Drake picks up the phone on the table.

'Hi Greta, its Drake, when a pizza is delivered for James, let me know on this phone and send them up, thanks.'

\*\*\*\*\*\*\*\*\*\*\*\*\*\*\*\*\*\*\*\*\*

When I finally make it through the door to my apartment, I see Alex asleep on the couch. I look around at my messy home.

'Looks like a bomb went off in here...'
'Hmm?' Alex mumbles and rolls over. I dump my bag on the dinner table with my phone and a big pile of papers. Alex's phone rings, scaring me as it disturbs the quiet.

'Hello?' I answer.

'Hi!' I hear a girl giggle.

'Who's this?' I ask with a frown.

'Charlotte, who's this?'

'Alex's fiancée.'

'Shit, she answered!' I hear her talk to someone in the

462

background and then she hangs up. I flick to his caller list to redial but they phoned from an unknown number. *Shit.*

'Who was that?' Alex croaks from the couch as he leans up on his elbow.

'Charlotte.'

'Who?' He frowns.

'I don't know, that's all she said, amongst some giggling.'

'Why didn't you ring her back?' He slowly sits up.

'Unknown number.'

'Oh, never mind,' he shrugs, leans over and grabs a can of beer from the coffee table, 'eurgh, that was warm.' As I start to clear the kitchen, I bash a plate against another.

'Easy Luc,' Alex stands and walks over to me, 'it was probably just a fan.'

'How would she have got your number?' I can't help the hurt that's apparent in my voice.

'I don't know, desperate fans find ways.'

'Okay.' I mutter. My eyes start to water.

'Are you alright?' Alex rushes over to me, and walks me out of the kitchen.

'Sit here,' he pulls a chair out for me to sit on, 'what's wrong?' He crouches in front of me and places his hands on my knees.

'Why are you crying?' He looks up at me.

'I don't know.' I whisper.

'That's helpful…' He smirks, which makes me laugh.

'I'm sorry.' I sob.

'What for? Do you want to go out tonight? Maybe take your mind off things?' He puts his index finger under my chin and lifts it up so I'm looking at him.

'No, I want to stay in and eat ice cream until I'm sick.' I half-smile.

'That I can do.' Alex stands up and bows in front of me, which of course makes me giggle like a school girl.

'I love your laugh.' He bends down and kisses me.

'Just that?' I pout.

'No, I love your mouth,' he kisses the corner of my mouth, 'I love your nose, your eyes, your cute little ears.' He kisses them all in turn and leaves a small kiss behind my ear.

'You know what that does to me…' I squirm.

'And what's that, soon-to-be-Mrs. Jones?' He smirks and

does it again.

'It makes me want you.' He kisses me once more behind the ear, brings his head back and rests his forehead on mine.

'Just that?' He smirks.

'Of course not…'

'I love your mouth.' I kiss the corners of his mouth.

'That's cheating, you can't steal what I said!' He stands up, crosses his arms and pouts.

'Why not?' I look up at him.

'Thought you wanted ice-cream anyway.' His mood suddenly changes.

'What's wrong?'

'Nothing.'

'Are you hungry?' I look at him, not really sure what to say.

'Sure.' Suddenly his phone starts ringing.

'Hello? No, I'm with Luc... Ha-ha, very funny... We were going to order food, why? I don't think tonight will be good' I look up at him.

'Who is it?'

'It's the guys, they want to practice tonight.'

'Oh right, go if you want?' I offer, hoping it will put him in a better mood.

'No no, its fine.' He answers me, as he puts his phone back to his ear. I go over, and swipe his cell straight out of his hand.

'Hey, it's Lucy.'

'Hey Luc!'

'Alex will be right with you, I can handle being on my own tonight.'

'Aww Luc, you legend!'

'He will see you shortly.'

'Alright, bye.'

'Bye.' I hand Alex his phone.

'You sure –' he looks at me confused, '– it's not a test.'

'Oh, shut up, you were a band before I came into the picture, go!' I smile and point towards the door.

'I love you Lucy Winter.' He snakes his hands around my waist.

'When have I ever stopped you doing anything?' I rest my head on his chest.

'Never, but my ex would always stop me.'

'Well, as I'm sure I'm not her, you can stop thinking that…' I wrap my hands around his neck.

'Sorry.' Alex bows his head and rests it on my shoulder.

'You're going to be late.' I whisper.

'Yeah, I'll be back later.'

'I hope so!' I laugh. Alex smiles at me and kisses me very gently on my lips.

'I love you so much.' He whispers against my lips.

'I love you too, Alex.' I wave at him as he leaves, and make my way to the couch.

'Ahh silence…' I say aloud, reaching for my cell. I call Tom, Alex's bandmate and friend.

'Hello?' He answers.

'Hi, its Lucy.'

'Oh, hey Lucy, you alright?'

'Yeah, Alex has just left, but I just wanted to ask you something before he got to you.'

'Okay, ask away.'

'Is he alright?'

'What do you mean?' Tom laughs.

'I mean in himself. Since we got engaged, he seems really distracted and sad.'
'To be honest Lucy, the only thing I can think of is that you won't give him an answer about England. I think he thinks you're going to say no, and then you will leave him. He loves you very much, he doesn't hide that fact...um... and I don't think he's handling it very well, he's getting himself ready for you to say no.'

'Oh.'

'Were you not expecting that answer?'

'No, I thought it would be something else, like he was cheating.'

'God! You don't think very highly of him then!' Tom laughs.

'No, it's not that, I love him very much, but living in England for what, six months, away from my job, friends and family. It's very difficult for me.'

'I totally understand, but he's just found the love of his life and had proposed to her, now he thinks he's losing her.'

'Right okay, and the only way to fix this is to come to England?'

'Um... yeah?'

'Would you guys not mind?' I ask. Tom laughs.

'Course not!'

'Really?'

'We like you Lucy, and we like you more because you make our best friend happy.' I smile.

'Aww, that's cute, I kinda like you guys too!'

'Good, Alex will be here soon and I don't want him thinking I'm trying to steal his girl.'

'Oh god yeah, thanks Tom, have a good practice and I'll see you all soon.'

'Bye Lucy.'

'BYE LUCY!' Comes a chorus in the background from the other guys. I giggle.

'Bye!' I hang up the phone, with an idea of how to make Alex a happier person. *Could I actually live in England, on a bus? I don't see my parents that much, I could still phone them and Gemma.* I pick up my cell and phone Sarah.

'Hi, what's up?'

'Nothing, what are you doing?'

'Not much.'

'Can you come over?'

'Sure, what's wrong?'

'I need to speak to you urgently.'

'Right, say no more, I'll be there in ten.' Sarah hangs up. I jump up and run to the kitchen, putting a bottle of wine in the fridge, so it can have a head start at being chilled. Exactly ten minutes after the phone call ended, Sarah is buzzing at my door. I let her straight up.

'Girl, I hope you realize how much I rushed and how unfit I actually am!'

'Did you run here?' I ask, confused by her breathlessness.

'No, cab.'

'How are you out of breath if you got a cab and used the elevator?' I smirk.

'Shut your mouth, I'm here aren't I?' She smiles and drops herself onto the couch.

'Drink?' I hand her a glass of wine.

'Please.' She takes the glass and downs its contents. I look at her in surprise.

'What? You know what I'm like by now, surely.'

'Sure…' I answer into my glass.

'So, what's up?'
'Alex asked me to go on tour with him.'

'Oh my god, that's so cool!' Sarah answers before I've finished talking.

'In England.' I continue.

'What?'

'For six months.' I ignore her question.

'Six months? England?'

'Yep.'

'Are you going?'

'I don't know. I need some advice. I spoke to Tom.'

'Who's Tom?' Sarah raises an eyebrow at me.

'From Erupt.'

'Oh, right, yeah, Tom, and?'

'Well Alex has been acting all strange and sad around me, so I asked Tom what was wrong with him and he said it's because he thinks I will say no and walk away.'

'But you said yes to marrying him…' Sarah double checks with me.

'Yes, so I thought that was enough for him to think I'm sticking around, but… England? I'm not sure if I can go.'

'Why not?'

'What do I do about work? You? Gemma? Mom and Dad?'

'You don't see Gemma or your parents much anyway, and they do have phones in England, you know?'

'Yeah, but work? A whole six months?'

'Can't you claim it as… um… I don't know, say you're going with the band to do research for their book.'

'Research?' I repeat, while thinking about what Sarah said.

'Yeah.' Sarah replies before she downs her second glass of wine.

'What about you? And Beth?'

'Hell, I will come to England. I've always wanted to go.'

'Really?'

'Course. I want to be a groupie for the best band in the world!' Sarah smiles.

'It doesn't sound too bad, when you say it like that…'

'You can always come back for a week or so, you will still have this place.'

'True.'

'It was a good thing I came round, wasn't it?'

'Yeah, you always make me see sense.'

'So… you're going to England?' Sarah asks, while moving to the edge of her seat.

'It looks that way!' I look at my engagement ring.

'Yes, I get a holiday to England!' Sarah stands up. I sniff.

'I best talk to Drake tomorrow.'

'Have you eaten?' I look over at Sarah, scanning my cupboards.

'No, are you hungry?'

'Yeah, starving, and I know from previous experience that I can't drink wine if I'm not eating, and Lucy, you have no food.'

'Yeah, I know!' I laugh.

## CHAPTER TWENTY-ONE

You want to take six months off work?' Drake repeats like a parrot.

'Yes Drake.'

'Geez, Lucy.'

'I know its short notice, but I can really get everything done for the tour for their book, and I can meet up with publishing houses who want to pair with us.'

'I suppose it does make sense, but six months?'

'Yeah, that's how long their tour is.'

'Right, okay.'

'Shall I give you a minute?'

'No, its fine, I will give you this. As long as you actually do the work and email it to me every week, pictures, interviews anything you have, so I can show Dad, so he believes you.'

'Oh my god, thank you Drake, I promise.'

'There's one problem.' Drake stares at me.

'What's that?'

'Do you have a laptop?'

'Yeah.'

'Oh well, then there is no problem.' I look confusedly at him, but ignore it.

'Thanks Drake, you will not regret it.'

'I better not Lucy, it will be both our jobs on the line if you screw this up.'

'Yeah, I understand.'

'Good I will tell Dad today, and I will make sure you still get paid etc.'
'Thanks Drake, best boss ever!' I smile and hurry round his desk to hug him.

'Okay, that's enough, get back to work.' Drake smirks at me. As I make my way out of his door, I walk into Beth, who's waiting for me on the other side.

'Well?' She asks.

'He said yes.'

'OH MY GOD!' Beth screeches and jumps up and down on the spot.

'Shhh…' I giggle.

'When are you telling Alex?'

'I can't wait long, I might get him to come here.'

'Do it, do it.' Beth says, still jumping up and down.

'Okay.' I pull my cell out my pocket, takes a deep breath and dial Alex's number.

'Hello?' He answers, half-asleep.

'You're still in bed?'

'Huh? What?' He sounds even less awake now.

'Alex?'

'Yep?'

'Are you alright?'

'Yeah, hang on,' I hear shuffling around, 'oh it's you.'

'Yeah, who did you think it was?'

'I didn't know who it was, I just woke up on Tom's couch. I was a bit confused.'

'Right…' I make a face at Beth.

'What?' She whispers. I shake my head at her

'What are you doing today?' I ask Alex.

'Nothing, babe, what's up?'

'Can you come to my office soon as?'

'Course, is there a problem?' He sounds panicked.

'No don't panic, there's no rush.'

'Yeah, there is!' Beth shouts in the background.

'What's up? Tell me.' He sounds nervous now.

'Seriously don't panic, just get here when you get here.'

'Okay, be there shortly.'

'Okay, love you.'

'Love you.'

'What was the face for?' Beth asks me from behind her desk.

'He sounded really confused…'

'Because you just woke the poor guy up!'

'Yeah, I did.' I laugh.

'So, he's coming?'

'Yep, I'll be in my office.'

'Okay.' As I trot off to my office, I power up my computer and check my emails. *It feels like I haven't spoken to Gemma in a while.* So, I email my parents and Gemma.

*From: Lucy Winter*
*Subject: I'm alive*
*To: Gemma Winter; David Winter*
*01/18/2011 09:45*

*Dear people who find my life interesting,*

*In March (not sure what date) I'm going to England for six months on a researching visit, to write a book on behalf of Erupt.*

*Love you lots.*

*Lucy*
*P.A. to Drake Teely at Teely's International*

As I press send, I regret the title. *Oh well, I've sent it now.* Almost immediately, it got a reply from Gemma.

*From: Gemma Winter*
*Subject: Oh dear god*
*To: Lucy Winter; David Winter*
*01/18/2011 09:50*

*Dear sister,*
*I don't normally find your life very interesting UNTIL I*
*read this email, and all I can think to say back is...*

*LLLUUUUCCCCKKKKKKKYYYYYY!!*

Gemma's reply makes me laugh, as I set to write back, I get another email, from Dad.

*From: David Winter*
*Subject: What??*
*To: Lucy Winter; Gemma Winter*
*01/18/2011 09:53*

*Lucy – that is great news, well done, will you be paid for this time away? What will you do about your apartment? Where are you staying in England? Hotel or bus? (By the way, this is your mother asking questions.)*

*Gemma – Mom said don't use God's name like that, or be mean to Lucy.*

*Love you lots,*
*Mom and Dad*

'Wow that's a lot of questions.' I mutter out loud.

*From: Lucy winter*
*Subject: Interrogation??*
*To: Gemma Winter; David Winter*
*01/18/2011 09:57*

*Mom – I will call you later and fill you in.*

*Dad – thanks.*

*Gemma – yeah, don't be mean to me ;)*

*Lucy Winter*
*P.A. to Darke Teely at Teely's International*

*From: Gemma Winter*
*Subject: Gang up on Gemma*
*To: Lucy Winter; David Winter*
*01/18/2011 10:02*

*I wasn't being mean?*

*I'm genuinely excited for her.*

*From: Lucy Winter*
*Subject: I'll phone you*
*To: Gemma Winter; David Winter*
*01/18/2011 10:06*

*I'll phone you both later xxxxx*

*Lucy Winter*
*P.A. to Drake Teely at Teely's International*

I get no more replies from that eventful conversation. Then Alex rushes into my office.

'Hey.' I look concerned.

'Hi.' He mutters.

480

'What's wrong?' I ask.

'Oh nothing, I feel sick, what did you want anyway?'

'Right, I'll get straight to the point, shall I?'

'Yeah.'

'What's up with you at the moment?' I can't help but ask.

'Nothing Lucy.' He won't make eye contact with me, but he pulls out the box that held my engagement ring out of his pocket and fiddles with it.

'Is this because you think I'm going to leave you?' Alex's head suddenly shoots up and makes eye contact with me. The bags under his eyes make him look tired.

'Um…'

'Well anyway,' I cut in before he can finish, 'I'm not okay.'

'Okay.' A hint of a smile comes to his lips.

'Why did you bring the box?'

'So, when you said you were leaving you could keep the ring safe in its box.'
'Oh, Alex, for heaven's sake, have I given you any signal to say I'm leaving you?'

'Yeah.'

'Well then...what?' I suddenly realize what he said.

'You won't come to London, so it means we will break up.' He looks like a sulky teenager.

'I haven't said I won't come to London, I said I needed to think about it.'

'Okay.'

'But I do have some important news for us both.'

'Oh god, are you pregnant?' I have his attention once again.

'Erm, no.'

'Okay.' I get up from my desk and walk over to him. Alex shifts in his chair so he's sat upright, not hanging off it. I kneel between his legs.

'Give me your hand.' I hold mine out palm up, waiting for him to give me his hand.

'This sounds very much like the end.' He mutters.

'You don't have much faith in me, do you?'

'I have trust issues.'

'Yeah, I can see that,' I add flatly, 'anyway I was speaking to Drake this morning, and we have come to an arrangement.'

'Okay…' Alex looks at me with an interested look.

'I'm doing some research for a book, with a very famous band, and they have requested that the book we are publishing covers their tour.' Alex frowns at me.

'Yeah…?'

'So, I'm going to London for six months with Erupt, and I'm being paid to take pictures, write articles, and interview them all for this book.'

'What?'

'Yeah I kinda have to as well, because I'm totally in love with the lead singer, oh and we're engaged.' I move my hand up so I can flash my ring.

'Are you serious?' Alex sits bolt upright in his chair, gripping my hand.

'Yes!' I smile up at him.

'Are you serious? You're coming to England with us?' He stands up, dragging me with him.

'Yes, I am serious.' I add while laughing.

'So, you're not leaving me?'

'No.'

'Oh my god,' he wraps his arms around me and pulls me in

for a tight hug, 'I can't believe this.' He hugs me again.

'Why did you think I was going to run?'

'Well to be honest Luc, all my other girlfriends have either run when I've mentioned a tour or come with me and then cheated on me, and I didn't want you to do either.'

'I'm not going to, I'm going on tour with you as your fiancée, and I will be your fiancée until we're married. I'm not running or leaving you, I love you.'

'I love you Lucy, but you will have to bear with me until I can learn to trust again.'

'I know, I'll wait for you.' I smile up at him.

'I know you spoke to Tom as well.' I feel him smile into my hair.

'You do?'

'Yeah he told me you were worried about me.'
'Oh.'

'I love that you worry about me, it shows me you care.'

'You were so closed off, I panicked.'

'It's all sorted now, and no one in this world can wipe the smile off of my face!'

'I'm glad.'

\*\*\*\*\*\*\*\*\*\*\*\*\*\*\*\*\*\*\*\*\*\*\*\*

'Hi Mom!' I pick up my office phone.

'Dear, when are you leaving for England?'

'March.'

'Oh, so in two and a half months?'

'Yeah, I'm not packing up and leaving tomorrow!'

'Okay, I was just checking, what are you doing with your apartment?'

'Well, I'm getting paid for this work, so I was just going to carry on like normal, it's there for Gemma if she needs it, or you and Dad?'

'Oh okay, and what's Sarah doing?'

'She is going to come visit me.'

'Oh, that would be nice, maybe we can come visit you as well.'

'I would love that Mom.'

'Us too, sweetheart.'

'I don't know where we're staying at the moment, not sure if it will be hotels or a tour bus.'

'Do you know when you're going to be in London?'

'I think Alex said it would be July time, we're starting at the top of the country and working our way down.'

'Okay, if you find out the dates, I will book us to stay in a hotel.'

'Okay Mom, I will let you know.'

'Okay, bye, love.'

'Bye, Mom.' I check out the time on my computer, where did the day go?! It's five, so I turn off my computer and start collecting up my stuff. I stand up and get a bit dizzy. *Oh, head rush.* I sit back down. Beth comes into my office to check I'm still alive as she's ready to leave too.

'Are you okay? You're so pale?'

Yeah, just got a head rush.'

'Oh, I hate those. I'm so bloated at the moment, stupid monthly.'

'You're on?'

'Yeah, why?' Beth asks, with a weird look on her face.

'We normally go on the same time.'

'I'm nearly finished.'

'What?' I look up at her.

'Oh my god!' She slowly smiles.

'Not again…' I groan.

'Oh, shall we get you a test?' I slowly nod while pouting.

\*\*\*\*\*\*\*\*\*\*\*\*\*\*\*\*\*\*\*\*

I make it through my apartment door, to find Alex cooking.

'Whoa.'

'Hey babe!'
'What are you doing?'

'I'm cooking dinner, I'm making tacos.'

'Okay, I need to talk to you.'

'Okay, talk away.'

'I'm late.'

'Late for what?' *Oh, the classic male brain, not putting two and two together when a woman says that.*

'My period.' Alex stills over the cooker and turns to me.

'You're not…?'

'I don't know,' I wave the box around in the air, 'I haven't done it yet.'

'Shall we do it now?' He turns the cooker off and walks over to me.

'If you want to.'

'I want to know,' he holds his hand out and pulls me to the bathroom, 'go!' He points.

'Okay.'

'I will wait out here until you have finished peeing, then I'm coming in to wait.'

'Bossy.' I smile and shut the door.

After I've kind of successfully peed on a stick, I call Alex into the bathroom.

'How long do we have to wait?'

'Three minutes.'

'Okay.' Alex holds my hand and sits on the edge of the bath while I sit on the toilet, lid down. We seem to be waiting a life time.

'Okay, three minutes is up.' Alex announces, looking at his watch.
'I'm scared.' I slowly pick the stick up from the edge of the sink and gaze at it.

'Well?' He asks.

'It's got two lines.'

'What?' He snatches it from my hand and double-checks.

'Looks like we're going to be parents.' Alex stands up next to me.

'Looks that way, doesn't it!'

'Are you happy?' Alex asks. I shrug.

'Are you?' I ask him.

'I wouldn't mind a mini-me running around, as long as we get married first?'

'You don't mind?' I look up at him.

'Of course not, I've got my girl right here, we're engaged and now I've just found out she's pregnant with my child, how can I not be happy?' Alex smiles, reassuringly.

'Can I tell the guys?' He looks like a kid in a candy store.

'Sure.' Alex legs it out the bathroom, returning with his cell.

'Hey, it's me, I'm going to put you on speaker.' Alex explains.

'Hi, what's up?' I recognize Lewis's voice.

'Are the guys with you?'

'Yeah.' They all say hi.

'I have some good and bad news.'

'Okay?' Lewis sounds curious.

'Firstly, Lucy is coming to London with us, that's one bit of good news.'

'Oh, excellent!'
'The bad news is that we will have to end tour a month or so early.'

'Why?'

'Because Lucy is pregnant.'

'WHAT?!' Come four surprised voices.

'Yeah dude, so she will be due around the end of tour. We haven't seen a doctor yet, but babies take nine months to cook, so you know.'

'Oh my god, I'm so pleased for you man.'

'Thanks guys. I'm cooking dinner you can come around if you want, I'm making tacos.'

'Count us in, we'll be there in half an hour.'

'Bye.'

'Bye.'

\*\*\*\*\*\*\*\*\*\*\*\*\*\*\*

I arrive outside Teely's International the next morning to be welcomed by Claire from reception.

'Hi, Lucy, right?'

'Yep.' I smile.

'This came for you.' She bends behind her desk and emerges with a big bunch of flowers.

'Wow!' My eyes widen as I reach over for them.

'You have an admirer.' She smiles at me.

'Yeah!' I laugh and start walking towards the lift. I can't walk and read the note at the same time, so I wait until I'm upstairs to find out who sent them. *Bet it was Alex, he's so romantic.* The lift dings at the eighteenth floor, where Beth gasps at me from across the lobby.

'Who are they for?' Her mouth hangs open.

'Me.' I smile and walk straight into my office, followed by Beth. I place them on my desk, dump my bag and search for the card.

*Lucy,*

*I very much regret what happened, but I know there is no real reason for it. I love you very much and that won't leave me. But I have to let you go. I hear you're happy with Alex and you're now engaged, so I wish you all the happiness in the world with your new life.*

*Jack xx*

'Jack,' bath repeats in horror, 'I thought he had already left you alone!'

'Me too.' I frown while reading the card over and over again.

'Is this a goodbye message? Like forever?'

'I don't know, shall I talk to him?'

'No,' she replies quickly, 'maybe. Yeah you should call him.'

'I should?'

'Yeah, just check he's okay.' She shrugs.

'Okay.' I sit in my chair and dial his work number.

'Hello, Jack Base.'

'Hi, its Lucy.'

'Lucy?' He asks, sounding a little confused.

'Winter?'

'Oh Lucy, sorry.'

'I just got your flowers.'

'Did you? Okay.'
'What does your message mean?'

'It means what it says.'

'Yeah, I get that, is it a final farewell? Or a friendship?'

'Well I hope we can be friends, but it's more of a peace offering.'

'Oh, right.'

'Do you like them?' He asks in a whisper.

'Yeah, I do thank you.'

'Good.'

'Right well, I must go.'

'Okay, thank you for phoning.'

'No worries, bye Jack.'

'Bye.' I can hear him just breathing and waiting, so I slowly put the phone down. I see have a text message from Alex.

**What does Jack want?**

*How does he know?!* I reply back straight away.

**Just about flowers xx**

Alex text me back immediately

**Flowers?**

I feel like it's an interrogation, so I wait a few minutes before texting back. An email arrives.

**From: Beth Ryan
Subject: Alex
To: Lucy Winter
01/19/2011 09:34**

**Lucy, Alex just phoned through, but I didn't know it was him and let it slip you were speaking to Jack.**

**SSOORRRRRYYYYY**

**Beth Ryan**

**Teely's International**

*A bit late Beth!*

**From: Lucy Winter
Subject: Alex
To: Beth Ryan
01/19/2011 09:36**

**I know, I just got a text from him, don't worry x**

**Lucy Winter**

**P.A. to Drake Teely at Teely's International**

I pick up my phone to text Alex back as it starts ringing.

'Hi.'

'Hi, why haven't you texted me back? Alex sounds pissed off.

'I was emailing an important document.'

'After you spoke to Jack?' He presses.

'It was marked urgent.'

'Right, what did Jack want?'

'I called him to ask why he sent me flowers.'
'He sent you flowers?' He is getting more and more worked up.

'Yeah.'

'Was there a note with them?'

'Yeah.'

'What did it say?' I read him the note card.

'And what did he have to say?'

'He said he meant it as a peace offering.'

'Right.'

'So…?'

'I'll see you later.' He hangs up. *Jesus!* I just can't keep up with Alex's sudden moodiness. Maybe he's tense, because his parents are here, which reminds me that I haven't met them yet, so I call Alex back.

'What?'

'Oh hiya, what a nice greeting from my fiancé.'

'Babe what's up?'

'When am I meeting your parents?'

'Tomorrow, we can go to a restaurant okay?' He sounds like he's trying to get rid of me.

'Okay, is everything okay?'

'Yeah, yeah its fine, got to go, love you.' Alex hangs up.

## CHAPTER TWENTY-TWO

'Hi Lucy, I've been waiting so long to meet you!' Alex's mom gushes.

'Oh, thank you…' I blush at her compliment.

'I'm Judy!' She says with a smile before pulling me in for a hug.

'Hi!'

'Mom!' Alex tries to pull us apart, as I'm stuck with my arms by my side and Judy clinging onto me for dear life.

'Sorry.' She sniffs.

'Hi, I'm Peter.' Alex's Dad holds his hand out to me and frowns.

'Hi, I'm Lucy.'

'I've heard a lot about you.' He smiles and puts his arm around Judy.

'Come on.' Alex ushers us all inside the restaurant. Once we're seated, Alex orders a bottle of champagne. I make a face at him.

'Oh, and some lemonade please.'

'Sure thing, sir.' The waiter walks away.

'It's so nice to see you.' Judy smiles at Alex.

'Mom, we have some news.'

'I know.'

'You do?'

'Yes, I'm a woman, I can tell.'

'Oh.' Alex seems gob-smacked.

'The only thing I have a problem with is that you're not married…' I snigger and try to hide my smile.

'Well Mom, we're also are engaged.'

'Oh,' Judy looks surprised and starts to cry, 'I'm sorry, I just never thought this day would come!'

'Mom, what's wrong with you?'

'Alex!' I scold.

'What?' He shrugs.

'Your drinks, sir.' The waiter interrupts us.

'Oh, thank you!' Alex smile, and starts pouring drinks. Peter raises his glass.

'To Alex and Lucy, to the wedding and child!' He toasts. Judy starts sobbing again.

'Cheers!' We all tap our glasses together.

'When is baby due?' Judy asks.

'We haven't been to the doctor yet, but our tour is being cut early so that we're in America for the birth.' Alex answers.

*********************

'Dr Chris will see you now.' The receptionist says to me across the lobby. Alex jumps to his feet and tries to pull me up.

'Come on!' He says like an excited child.

'I feel sick…' I reply. *I feel more than sick. Nervous even.*

'Ah, you must be Lucy!' Dr. Chris stands up as we walk into her office.

'Yeah, hi, this is Alex, my fiancé.'

'Hi Alex, nice to meet you.' Dr. Chris shakes Alex's hand.

'Hi, likewise.' Alex smiles.
'So, I believe you're pregnant?' Dr. Chris looks at her computer monitor.

'Yes, I took a test a day or so ago, and it said positive.'

'Right okay, have you had any bad symptoms?' She pulls a pad out of her draw with a pen and stares at me. Alex looks at me too.

'Not that I recall, I've not been feeling myself recently, but I never in a million years put it down to being pregnant.'

'Is this your first pregnancy?'

'Um, no?'

'Oh?' Dr. Chris looks surprised.

'She had a miscarriage.' Alex adds.

'Oh,' Dr. Chris quickly writes that down, 'do you mind if I ask how? Was it naturally?'

'Um no, I was punched in the stomach.'

'Oh, I'm sorry.' Dr. Chris looks awkwardly away from me at her computer monitor.

'That's okay, I was only twelve weeks. But I had morning sickness with that, that's why I was confused that I didn't pick up the signs for this one.'

'Right okay,' Dr. Chris finishes writing all the information down, and Alex squeezes my hand, 'shall we get you on the table?'

'Okay.' I unbutton my pants and lay on the table with my legs spread. Dr. Chris opens the curtain and pulls over the machine.

'I'm just going to put some cold gel on your tummy, and then we can see how old baby is.'

'Okay.' I grab Alex's hand, while he stands frozen to the

spot, staring at the screen.

'Here we go!' Dr. Chris starts running the device across my stomach, spreading the gel around. Suddenly a heartbeat can be heard in the room. We stare at the small shape on the screen.

'Wow…' Alex whispers.

'That's your baby,' Dr. Chris smiles at us, 'and it looks to be roughly eight weeks, so if you give me a couple of minutes, I'll work out your due date.'

'Okay.'

'I've got a rough date of August 24th.' Dr. Chris points at the screen.

'Okay, so we will have to come back in time for the birth.' Alex says, not taking his eyes of the screen.

'Are you going away?' Dr. Chris asks.

'Yeah my band is going on tour, and Lucy is coming with us.'

'Right, I don't recommend flying past twenty-seven weeks. If you're still over there near your due date, I would say you will have your baby born where you are.'

'Oh,' Alex looks at me, 'we will have to cancel the tour then.'

'No, you can't do that.'

'I want our baby born in America, and that means you can't come on tour with us. I want to be with you during the pregnancy.'

'I'll give you a minute.' Dr. Chris leaves.

'This is my job as well, I will just have to have the baby in England, I don't want you to cancel your tour.'

'Let's ask everyone their opinion and then decide.' I frown at Alex not understanding what the problem is with having a baby in another country. At least it would be safe and we would have insurance. It's not like England are going to keep it and send Alex, the band and me back to America without it.

'It will be fine, don't panic.'

'But I do panic!' Alex frowns back at me.

'Yeah, I know, but I can't let you cancel a tour while there are hospitals all over England.'

'Okay, can we talk about this later though? This place makes me feel uneasy.'

After about ten minutes Dr. Chris pokes her head around the door.

'Is it okay to come in?'

'Yeah, sure.' I answer.

'I will print out your scan picture for you and I will need you

502

to come back in to see me before you go away.'

'Okay, thank you.'

'You're most welcome.'

'Here are some pamphlets for you to read through, but if you have any questions or concerns then please give me a call or book an appointment.' Dr. Chris smiles at us and hands me the picture of the baby. The doctor pulls the curtain around me and instructs me to get dressed again.

'When can we find out the sex?' I hear Alex ask.

'When Lucy is seventeen to twenty weeks.'

'Okay, I have some names already.'

'Whoa, calm down!' I interrupt their conversation through the curtain.

'Someone's happy to be a father,' Dr. Chris laughs, 'don't get many of them at your age!'

'I'm really excited.' Alex replies.

'That's so lovely to hear.'

'Well thanks again, doctor!' I add, while emerging from around the curtain.

'No worries, Lucy, just remember what I said.' I smile and walk out of her office. I turn around to speak to Alex but he is too busy staring at the picture of our baby. He struggles to get his phone out of his pocket, but when he does, he takes a picture of the scan.

'What you doing?' I ask, as we walk out the doctor's.

'Setting my background on my phone,' he answers, 'and sending it to my parents.'

'Oh, I should tell mine actually!' I suddenly think. Alex looks up from his phone.

'I've just sent them a picture.'

'What?'

'I knew you wouldn't, so I emailed them a picture along with my parents.'

'We best move before we're photographed and spread around the magazines before our family find out?' Alex grips my hand and pulls me towards the door.

'Too late!' I say, noticing a man standing behind a tree with a camera.

'Ahh shit, get in!' Alex quickly opens his car door and pushes me in, slamming the door and running around to his side.

'Easy, I'm pregnant.'

'Sorry babe!' He leans over and lightly kisses my lips. I pick up my cell while Alex drives us home.

*Hey, I have some news, I'm pregnant xxxxx*

I run through my contacts and pick the few people I wanted to tell. Sarah, Beth, gemmal, Dean, Belle, my Mom, even though she never charges her cell and Alex has already emailed her. I press send, just as my Mom phones me.

'Hey Mom.'

'Hello, your Dad just received a picture in an email from Alex of a sonogram?'

'Yep, I'm pregnant.'

'Oh, David, it is hers!' Mom shouts.

'Yeah Alex sent it to you and his parents.'

'He's so thoughtful…' Mom gushes.

'He is.' I smile.

'How far gone are you?'

'Eight weeks.'

'Eight weeks?'

'Yeah.'

'So, you're due while you're in England?'

'Yeah.'

'You can't fly past a certain month, how are you going to get back for the birth?'

'I'll have to have it in England, Mom.'

'But then it won't be a American citizen?'

'Yes, it will, all its family are American, they won't ship it back…?'

'I suppose. When are you coming to see us?'

'Soon, it will be on a weekend. I have to go Mom, love you!'

'Love you too!' I hang up my cell and drop it back in my bag.

******************

'Hi Emily!' I pick up my cell.

'I can't believe you're getting married and having a baby!' Emily shouts down the phone.

'You better believe it Emily. How do you feel about being god-mother?' I pull my cell away from my ear as she screams.

'Are you okay?'

'I'd love to be a god-mother, but I don't think I'd be very good…' She sniffs.

'You will be great. You're gonna be the best god-mother!' I try to reassure her.

'You think so?' She asks.

'If you're as awesome as your brother, then you will be great.' I smile.

'Can I come and visit you?' I let out a little laugh.

'Of course you can.'

'You don't mind?'

'No! I would love for you to come and stay with us. I love your brother but I need some girl time too.' Emily immediately cheers up.

'Yay! Can I come this weekend?' I look over to Alex who obviously didn't know what Emily is saying.

'Um, Alex, are we doing anything this weekend? I ask as he walks over to me and sits on the coffee table in front of me.

'I don't know, I've got a gig. Not sure about you, you don't pay me enough to be your personal assistant.' Alex jokes, while stuffing as many chips in his mouth that he can humanly fit.

'I don't think I'm busy, so yeah sure, come over.'

'Oh my god, I'm so excited!'

'Just let me know when you will get here, so I can make sure I'm home.'

'Okay, I'll call you on Thursday.' Emily says, laughing.

'Okay, bye.'

'Byeeeeeee!'

I hang up, and see Alex opening the door to Bell and Dean.

'Congratulations guys,' Belle says, 'can I use your loo?'

'Loo?' I ask.

'The toilet' Dean translates.

'Right,' I roll my eyes, 'do I need to learn a new language if I'm going to England for six months.'

'Probably,' Belle answers for me, while putting the kettle on 'want a cuppa?'

'Huh?'

'Cup-of-tea.' She says slowly, as if I'm stupid.

'Um, no thanks. I'm confused, can you give me a crash course on how to speak British?'

'Sure, a couch is a settee but most people will know what you mean by couch.'

'Right…'

'A cell is a mobile.' Belle ticks off her fingers.

'Okay, shall I write this down?' I lift an eyebrow.

'I'm not going to give you an exam.' She smirks.

'Okay.' I look at Alex. Belle points at Alex's bag of chips.

'These are called crisps, oh and you should try pickled onion Monster Munch and salt and vinegar crisps.'

'Oh okay, anything else?'

'Loads but I can't think of anything at the moment.'

'I'm scared now, what if someone talks to me, and I don't understand what they say?'

'Just say you're American. I'd stay away from Cockneys though.' Belle laughs, as she sat down with her cuppa.

'Oh, I've heard of them.' I make a face.

'They're not zoo animals.' Belle answers.

'No, like when I watched Austin Powers: Gold member.'

'Right…' Belle eyes me and sips her tea.

'Can we change the subject?' Dean asks before I ask another

question about England. We all sit in silence for a moment before Dean lean forward again.

'Do you want a boy or a girl?' Alex jumps to answer.

'I want a boy, they're awesome. Girls are hard work,' he looks at me, and I glare back, 'I mean I don't mind!' Alex changes his answer.

'What about you, Lucy?' Dean tries to hide his smirk.

'I don't mind.' I say, while thinking about it. I totally want a girl so we could team up and out vote Alex. I smile to myself.

'What?' Alex looks at me.

'Nothing.'

'Hmm…' Alex narrows his eyes at me.

'When will you go to England?' Belle asks.

'We arrive in Edinburgh first actually, in March and then we'll work our way down the country.' Alex answers.

'So are you going to all the major cities?' Belle asks again.

'Yeah, I have a list of the cities, I'll grab it!' Alex jumps up and finds his laptop.

'Glasgow, Edinburgh, Newcastle, Belfast, Leeds, Manchester, Sheffield, Liverpool, Nottingham, Leicester, Birmingham, London, Reading, Bristol, Cardiff, Bournemouth and

Portsmouth.' Alex reads without as much as taking a breath.

'Whoa!' Belle blinks.
'There will be different venues in each area.'

'Of course.' Belle answers.

'We were asked to play at an Isle-of-Wight festival but we just don't have time.' Alex replies.

'Oh.'

'And now it's been cut short because of the baby, so it's only just over four months long now.'

'Oh yeah, of course.'

'Did I go to the Isle-of-Wight?' Dean asks Belle.

'No, you were too scared after my Dad told you that the people who live there have three arms and five eyes.' Belle laughs.

'Oh, that place...' Dean makes a face and sits back on the couch.

'They don't, just to clarify...' Belle holds her hands out in front of her.

'Good to know.' Alex shakes his head while smirking at Dean.

***************

'Morning Lucy!' Beth sings as I step out the elevator.

'Morning!' I smile back.

'What's on today?' Beth jumps off of her chair and follows me like a lost puppy into my office.

'Um not much, I don't think.' I shrug at Beth.

'Oh.'

'I think I have a box of manuscripts to be sorted through and read.'

'Oh, any I can read?' Beth eyes brighten up.

'always' i smiled back
'Great, gimme!' Beth walks over to my desk and makes for the box.

'I need to go shopping.' I pout.

'Want to or need to?' Beth asks, not taking her eyes off the box of manuscripts.

'Need to,' I giggle, 'I still have some money left over from Vegas.'

'Just some…' she frowns at me, 'you spent it *all*?'

'Oh no, I still have a lot of it left.'

'I was going to say!' Beth answers, with some kind of relief in her voice.

'I'm going to go to Bloomingdales, I think.' Beth sighs.

'Oh, what it's like to have money…'

'You have money?'

'Hmm…' She makes a noise while flicking through the box still.

'Are you having troubles?'

'Oh no, no, no, no.'

'So, I'll take that as a yes?' I raise an eyebrow at her.

'No, no, no.'

'Beth?'

'Okay yes, Bradley is having trouble at work and my bonus and paycheck just about covered us this month.'

'Why didn't you mention it?'

'Because its embarrassing?' Beth stops looking through the box.

'Beth, I'm your friend, you can ask or tell me anything.' I stand up and open my arms for Beth to walk into them if she wants. Beth thinks for a second and walks over and hugs me.

Tightly.

'Do you want to borrow some money?' I say into her ear and getting a mouthful of her hair.

'No, I'll be fine.' She sniffs.

'If you need anything, just ask okay?'

'Yeah.'

'You have my number, ring me, text me, turn up on my doorstep, I don't care.' I smile at her.

*****************

'She liked everything I picked out, bought it, then sent it all back saying it wasn't right for her, like what the hell is that about? I got a bit mad and if I had seen her, I would have told her what I thought about it, so I've lost my commission on her buys!'

'Sar?'

'Yes?'

'Breathe and calm down.' I laugh at Sarah trying to explain her story, eat and drink at the same time.

'I got to keep some of my commission because she was here for like 4 hours, running me like a bitch! So, have you planned England at all?' Sarah asks me.

'Belle was teaching me what slang they use.'

'Are you going to have to eat scones and drink tea all the time?' Beth asks.

'I'm sure they have other food?' I joke.

'So, do you know what cities you're visiting?' Sarah questions.

'Yeah, there's loads, I have no idea what they are…' I put my hand in the air to get the waitress's attention to order more fries.

'Are you going to come back talking like the Queen?'

'I doubt it, I'll be with Alex and the guys, so I won't pick it up that easily, and you lot will come visit, so I'll be surrounded by Americans the whole time really.'

'true true' sarah smiled at the waitress for dropping two plates of fries on our table, she bent over and blew on them
'eww don't spit on the fries man' beth waved sarahs face away
'easy you two' i laughed 'no fighting in here'

\*\*\*\*\*\*\*\*\*\*\*\*\*\*\*\*\*\*\*\*

I fall in the front door with bags full of clothes, shoes and everything else I could fit in them.

'Thought you were at work?' Alex looks confused. He's sat crossed legged on the floor playing his guitar, with bits of paper everywhere.

'Um, I was but Beth got upset, so we went shopping.' I dump the bags on the floor.

'Why was Beth upset?'

'Bradley is struggling at work and they don't have that much money.'

'Huh? They have no money but yet you went shopping?' Alex frowns.

'Well yeah and no! I went shopping and brought some things for Beth.' I smile as sweetly as I can.

'Oh, with your riches from Vegas?'

'Are you jealous?'

'Um, no.' *Which means he was.*

'I bought you something too.' A smile spread across Alex's face

'Really?'

'Yeah, but if you don't agree with spending me my riches, I'll take it back.'

'Um, I totally agree with you spending your riches…' He stands on the couch cushions and jumps over the back of the sofa so he's standing in front of me. He puts his hands on my

hips, leans down and starts kissing my neck.
'Well as you seem so happy that I brought you a present, I
have some good news.'

'Hmm.' Alex mumbles.

'I got you two.'

'Where are these presents?' I turn around and pull a
box wrapped in silver paper out of one of my massive bags
and hand it to Alex. He shakes it, then opens it, pulling out
the black converse with a Batman symbol on the sides.

'You have to pick the second one up tomorrow.' I hand him a
business card out of my pocket. It's for the guitar shop just
around the corner.

'Serious?' He keeps looking between the card and me.

'This is your "congratulations on going on tour" present.'

## CHAPTER TWENTY-THREE

'Ahh, Lucy!' Mom opens the door and pulls me in for a huge, overdue hug.

'Hi Mom!'

'Hi Alex.' Dad holds out his hand to shake Alex's.

'Hello.' Alex returns the shake. Mom and I move out of the doorway so Alex can come in and put the suitcases down.

'I'll help you carry them upstairs.' I hold my hand out to grab
a suitcase, but Alex slaps my hand away and narrows his eyes
at me.

'Erm, no you won't.'

'Oh no dear, come and have a drink.' Mom grabs my wrist
and pulls me towards the kitchen and points at the table, I
presume for me to sit.

'What do you want to drink?'

'Wine?' I joke.

'Lucy!' Mom says in her warning voice.

'I was joking, Mom.' I roll my eyes.

'You can have tea, water, orange juice?'

'Orange juice please.

'Are you making coffee?' Dad walks in with a hand-drill in
his hand.

'If you want one, then yes.'

'Thank you.' He bravely walks over and kisses her on the
cheek, which makes her smile. *Aww.*

'Alex?' Mom looks at the door frame.

A response follows Alex running down the stairs so fast

everyone thinks he's fallen.

'You alright lad?' Dad asks looking around the door frame.

'Yeah, yeah, I'm good.' Alex walks into the kitchen out of breath. I frown at him but he smiles and sits down next to me.

'Oh,' Mom drops the kettle and runs out the room, 'Mrs. Walley!'

'Who?' I mouth at Dad. Dad rolls his eyes.

'The next-door neighbor.'

'Oh.' I get up from my seat and finish making coffee for Alex and Dad. Then Mom returns, carrying a bunch of lilies.

'Do come in Eileen.' Mom ushers, followed by who I'm guessing is Eileen Walley.

'How do you do?' She greets us.

'Hi, I'm Alex.'

'Oh Alex? The man who makes music?' Alex looks up.

'Um yes, that would be me.'

'Oh, I've never met anyone like you before.' Eileen took my seat and holds Alex's hand. *Was she flirting with my boyfriend in front of me?*

'Well, count today as your lucky day.' Alex answers, still

smiling.

'It can't be a good job to be doing if you have a baby coming?' Eileen says, and the smile drops off of Alex's face.

'Well, my band is quite well known and we make a lot of money, so it's not a worry.' Alex adds, flatly.

'And you're dragging her to England, away from her family when she needs them the most...' Eileen raises an eyebrow at him.

'He's not dragging me, it's my job to go along. I have my family, they are coming to visit me and I'm sure there are hospitals and medical staff to help me if I need it.'

'Oh I, um...' Eileen tries to backtrack.

'Think it might be best if you pop back tomorrow?' Dad suggests, sipping his coffee.

'Yes of course.' Eileen stands up quickly and scuffs the chair against the floor before she ran out. I look over at Alex. He slumps in his chair, crosses his arms and pouting, like he was a fourteen-year-old being told off by his parents.

'Don't take it personally.' Dad says before I could.

'Alex?'

'What?' He answers me.

'Don't.'

'Don't what? She's only saying what everyone is thinking, including me.' He walks out the kitchen and runs up the stairs.

'Alex?' I go to follow when Dad grabs my arm.

'Just leave him.' Dad closes his eyes and nods at me. I frown at the stairs, not really knowing how to handle this.

'Dad? What do you think?'

'Well love, I can't say much, as it's both your choices to make but as long as you have stable money coming in. How long will Alex's band be successful?'
Oh my god, why hadn't it crossed my mind before now? I hadn't planned for the future of our baby. My eyes start to well up.

'Oh no you don't,' Dad hugs me, 'it will all be fine, you have us, and Alex's parents if you need anything.' He strokes my hair while I sob into his shoulder.

'Oh, what's wrong?' Mom appears in the doorway

'Eileen upset Alex.' Dad explains for me.

'Where is Alex?' Mom asks.

'He ran upstairs, we're just giving him time to calm down.' Dad squeezes me a bit tighter and begins stroking my hair again.
'Oh, dear.'

'I didn't think she would be that much trouble.' Mom sounds shocked.

'That comment was a bit uncalled for.' Dad says exactly what I'm thinking.

'Yes, yes, I agree.' Mom puts her arms around Dad and I for a huge family hug.
'Go and speak to him, love.' Mom wipes away my tears. I sniff and nod, making my way to the stairs.


When I reach the room Alex and I are staying in, I stand looking at the door for a second to steady my breathing and my unattractive dry sobs. I enter and find Alex lying on his back on the bed, with his arms folded under his head, staring at the ceiling with a death look on his face.

'Hi…'

'Hi.' He mutters back, not moving.

'Are you okay?'

'Having my exact worries said out loud by a complete stranger, yeah I'm good, excellent in fact.' He says sarcastically.

'I wasn't worried.' I add, not really sure how to comment on the situation.

'Well, you should be.'

'Why? Has something happened to the tour? The band?' Alex finally moves, sitting up.

'No, nothing.'

'Then why do we need to worry, we have my parents, your parents...' I slowly walk over to the bed and sit on the opposite end to him.

'Lucy, it's just,' he scratches his head, 'I'm the man of the family, it's my job to make sure we have money coming in, we have a stable life, where you and Alex junior feel safe...'

'I already do feel safe, I have a good job, you have the best job in the world.' I smile and reach across to touch his hand.

'Yeah at the moment, but what if you leave work to have more kids or look after Alex junior, and one day I'll be a has-been with no income.'

'Alex, stop putting yourself down.' I move up the bed a bit more, until I'm sat next to him. He looks at me, still with hurt in his eyes.

'I worry.' Then he hangs his head. I have never seen Alex like this before.

'I know you worry, but that's so far in the future, Alex junior will be at least twenty-five when that happens, you'll all want to become family men.' Alex sniffs.

'You have so much faith in me.' Alex mutters against my

lips.

'Of course I do, I love you.' I smile and look into his eyes.

'Oh Lucy I love you too, and baby.' He rubs my belly. I wrap my arms around his neck and hug him tightly, as he wraps his arms around my waist and returns the squeeze.

'We'll be alright, won't we?' He asks in my ear.

'More than okay.' I giggle.

'I'm cooking a homemade meal tonight, because, well, frankly I don't think you two do much cooking at home...' Mom points her finger at us like we we're being told off.

'Sounds good.' Dad answers for us.

'Good.' Mom smiles and walks out.

***************

'Mom, I really can't eat any more,' I rub my stomach, 'I ate so much I think I'm going to have a food baby, as well as a human one.'

'You have only had one portion!' Mom says.

'It was very nice, but I'm full.' I smile and slowly breathe out. Alex shovels it in his mouth like he's never going to see food again.
'At least Alex is enjoying it.' Mom pats Alex's hand.

'Hmm.' Alex makes a noise at her.

'It was lovely, dear' Dad says, while pushing his plate away, 'but I know what you mean by a food baby.'

'Well,' she stands up and carries her plate to the sink, 'I bought cake.'

'Cake, really?' I quickly spin in my chair

'I thought you were full.'

'I can squeeze cake in!' I joke.

'I taught you well.' Dad laughs.

'Hmmm…' Alex agrees, nodding his head, while chewing a mouthful of spaghetti.

***************

'Hello?' I answer my cell without even looking who it is.

'Babe, I don't know how I'm going to handle you not being here for six months if I can't even handle you being away for two days.' Sarah laughs down the phone.

'We will have to just call each other all the time.'

'Agreed, when are you back?'

'We're leaving this evening. Did you want to go out?'

'Oh no, I have a date.' Sarah mutters.

'You have a date, good for you!'

'Who has a date?' Alex mumbles next to me.

'Sarah has a date.' I cover the end of my cell.

'I can still hear you…' Sarah laughs.
'Sorry, Alex is being noisy.' I giggle.

'He's such a gossip.'

'I can hear you,' Alex says before rolling over, 'I'm no gossip.'

'Anyway, Lucy?' Sarah asks.

'Yep.'

'Can I break into your apartment and steal some clothes?'

'Um… can you not use a key?'

'Well yeah, but I'm really just asking permission to enter more than anything.'

'Oh yeah, you can enter.'

'Good, because I'm already in your closet.'

'Oh.'

'At least I asked before I told you where I was…'

'True, who's your date with?'

'He's in a band.'

'Which one?'

'You don't know them.'

'Sarah.' I warn.

'Okay, don't tell Alex' she says, then she whispers, 'it's Daniel.'

'What?' I ask, happy for her, yet surprised.

'Yeah, we've been talking a lot lately.'

'Really?'

'Yeah is that bad?'
'No way, that's excellent, we can be groupies together.'

'Shhh, Alex will guess who it is.'

'Oh yeah.'

'Okay, who is it?' Alex sits up and stares at me.

'Shit, Lucy!' Sarah chastises.

'Sorry…'

'She's going on a date with Dan.' I say to Alex.

'Really?' Alex sounds as surprised as I did.

'So what outfits are you stealing?' I try to change the subject.

'Your pink dress, I think, and your Louboutin's. Oh, and your silver clutch.'

'Okay, well enjoy, call me later.'

'Oh, I fully intend to.'

'Bye!' I place my phone back on the bedside table and snuggle next to Alex.

'You're too warm.' I immediately move back.

'You're nice and cold and refreshing…' He turns over.

'God, Alex.' I mutter while he wraps himself around my whole body.

'Hmm…' He smiles and kisses down my neck.

'Don't do that…' I giggle, and start slapping his arm.

'Why?' He carries on.

'We're in my parent's house…' I can't help but giggle at him. He starts kissing along my chin until he reaches my mouth. He stops, opens his eyes and looks at me. He leans in and kisses each side of my mouth.

'I love to hear you giggle.'
'Are you two awake?' A knock and voice come through the door.

'Yeah.' I answer.

'Good,' then Mom walks into the room, 'do you want to come to the mall with us?'

'Oh yeah, I do.' Alex lets go of me and sits up.

'Good, we're leaving in half an hour, right Lucy?'

'Uh, sure.' I answer, not moving to get up.

'Good, be down stairs in half an hour.' Mom turns on her heels and struts out.
Alex jumps out of bed and pulls on his skinny jeans, his converse and a t-shirt from his suitcase. I slowly sit up, as Mom returns.

'Here,' she hands me a biscuit, 'a ginger biscuit, they say it keeps morning sickness away, eat it.' She walks back out. I walk down the stairs and make my way into the kitchen for a drink.

'Morning, dear,' Dad says with a smile, 'we have a present for you.'

'Oh?' *I love presents.*

'Here.' Mom hands me a bag. Alex stands next to me. I dip my hand into the bag and pull out something wrapped in tissue paper. I rip the tissue paper off, and there is a baby-grow with "I heart my Mom and Dad" printed on the front.

'Turn it over.' Mom says, smiling. I turn it over, and see it reads "I inherited my good looks from my Grandparents". I smile while tearing up. Then, I pull out a small box, with a small silver bracelet inside.

'Oh, thank you!' I sniff.

'I know it's really early, but as you're going away, we thought we should give them to you now.' Mom smiles.

'I love them!' I hug my parents.

'It's tiny,' Alex sizes up the baby-grow, 'what if I break it?'

'You won't.' Mom hugs Alex who can't take his eyes off the baby-grow in his hands.

'I thought that before we had you and your sister.' Dad pats Alex on the back but looks at me.

'I want to get married.' Alex whispers.

'What?' I ask.

'I want to get married.' He says a little louder.

'You're already engaged love.' Mom points out the obvious.

'Yeah, but I want to be married to you before we go on tour.'

'Oh...'

'What do you think?' Alex stands in front of me and holds my hand.

'I want to be married to you as well.' I smile up at him.

'Oh my god, a last-minute wedding!' Mom is panicking.

'We can have something small, then have the proper thing when we get back?'

'That sounds easy.' Dad says.

'What do you think?' Alex asks me again.

'Sounds like a plan.'

***************

We don't quite make it to the mall, we don't even leave the house. Mom and Dad start packing to drive back with us. Alex calls his parents and I call Beth, Sarah and Gemma. The house is a mad rush. Mom phones the registry office back home to see if they have any spaces and the only one is in two days time. It's a little sooner than we even expected, otherwise we'd have to wait another six months or longer, and I would have a baby by then too. I sit and watch the chaos unfold in front of me but it makes me smile. I'm pregnant with the love of my life's baby and, of course, I'm engaged to marry him. My life could not be any better at this moment in time.

********************

'The car is late, my dress is ripped and god knows what the "church" is going to look like? Alex is probably thinking I've got cold feet and oh my god!' I inhale and exhale deeply.

'Calm down, it's not good for the baby!' Sarah slaps my arm.

'We can wait or we can get in a cab. I've told your Dad and he's going to pass the message onto Alex so he stays put. Your dress is fine you can't see it.' Mom tries to reassure me. I just nod.

'The car is here!' Beth runs into the apartment.

'Come on.' Mom and Sarah both hook an arm under mine, and pull me to my feet. Sarah holds the door open for me when I climb into the back seat of the car.

'Is my make-up okay?' I ask.

'Yes.'

'My hair?'

'Yes.'

'My dress?'

'Yes.'

'Okay.' I lean my head against the back of the seat and watch New York as we drive through it. We finally arrive, and climb out. I straiten my dress and take a big breath.

'Ready?' Sarah looks at me.

'I think so.'

'Okay.'

'I'll go tell them you're here.' Beth runs through the double doors. Sarah, Mom and I all follow behind. Then, the doors open and I hear the music start. I slowly step around the corner to be met by Alex's parents, Emily and his brother, the band, Beth her husband and daughter, Dean, Belle, my Dad and Gemma. They all turn and smile at me. I walk up the aisle arm in arm with my Mom and Sarah behind us. When we reach the altar, Mom kisses me on the cheek and walks off to sit down with Sarah. I turn to face Alex who smiles at me. I smile back, all my worries melting away.

# EPILOGUE

'The baby is looking good and healthy so far.' Dr. Chris smiles up at me.

'Great!' I beam back at her.

'I'll print out a new picture for you.'

************

When I leave the doctor's office, I head straight to the subway, answering my phone call.

'Hello?'

'Hi babe, have you left already?' Alex asks, out of breath.

'Yeah, I've just left.;

'Oh, I finished early and I thought I would make it in time.'

'Oh, I'm sorry, I was just getting on the subway to show you the new picture.'

'You're getting on the subway?' Alex asks in disbelief.

'Um, yeah?'

'Can't you get a cab?'

'I'm not made of money, Alex…' *I still have money left from Vegas, so I was really…*

'Yes, but it's safer.'

'Where are you?'

'Near the doctor's office, where are you?'

'Outside the doctor's office.'

'Oh, wait there.' I crouch down and put my bag on the floor to search for the scan picture, but where was it?
'Hey,' Alex stops in front of me, 'let's see then?' He holds his hand out.

'I'm trying to find it.' I reply with attitude.

'It's in your pocket.' He reaches forward and pulls it out.

'Oh yeah!'

'So, this is Alex junior?' He smiles with pride.

'Yes, but we're not calling them that.' I link Alex's arm with mine as we walk.

'What's wrong with the name Alex?'

'Nothing, but I can't deal with two of you being called Alex.'

'That's Alex-ist.' He puts his arm around my shoulders and pulls me in towards him, kissing my forehead.

'That's not even a thing.' I giggle.

'Are you hungry?'

'Um...' I screw up my face.

'Let me rephrase that... I'm hungry, you need to eat, and so does baby.'

'I can't really argue with that, can I?'

'Good, Sarah and Beth are there.'

'Really?'

'Yeah.' He looks at me.

'Cool!'

'Sarah kept phoning me and asking me questions but I didn't

know the answers…' He shrugs and smiles.

'Ahh, Sarah never changes…'

*****************

As I step in the door to Betty's, Sarah and Beth screech and everyone in the cafe covers their ears for protection.

'Lucy!' Sarah calls, waving her hands around. I slowly walk over with Alex behind me, gripping my hand.

'Hi!' I smile sweetly at them, sitting down in the booth and pulling Alex with me.

'Let's see then?' Beth beams at me. I hand over the scan picture.

'Awww, so cute!' Sarah stares at the photo.

'What can I get you?' The waitress asks.

'Hi, I'll have coffee and pancakes.' Alex requests.

'Orange juice and toast please.'

'Sure.'

'Ermm, I'll have coffee and pancakes too.' Sarah says.

'I'll do the same,' Beth orders, 'thank you.' The waitress nods, and walks off.

'Tell me about your plans for England?' Sarah asks, while handing me back my picture of the baby.

'We will be in London in June, so feel free to come over then.' I smile at Sarah.

'We'll be in hotels because of Miss Pregnant here.' Alex points his thumb at me and rolls his eyes.

'You're leaving next week...' Beth says, sadly.

'It's gone so quickly.' Sarah agrees.

'I will miss you at work. I'll have to come over and see you.' Beth smiles.

'Yeah sure, Dean and Belle are coming over in July because we will be closer to her parents then, and Mom and Dad are coming over while we're in London.'

'You won't feel home sick with everyone from home around you!' Sarah laughs.

'Well yeah.' I nod, accepting my glass of orange juice from the waitress.

'Has Belle taught you more English slang?' Beth asks, before sipping her coffee.

'Pants to them are panties...' I pull a face.

'Well, good luck with that...'

'I think we will be okay, I've been there loads of times and I'm still welcome.' Alex adds.

'Yes, but we're talking about Lucy here!' Sarah raises an eyebrow.

'Good point.' Alex nods.

'Hey, I'm not that bad!' I try to defend myself.

'We will just have to see about that…' Sarah, Beth, and Alex all laugh at my expense.

Printed in Great Britain
by Amazon